TOMES OF THE DEAD

S

Inside the southw... ...st,
sweat and flaring c... ...ts
bawled at their crews ...ere
made as magazines were spent and new ones fitted onto
the sliders, as winches were worked to ratchet the catgut
bowstrings back into position. With repeated, ear-dulling
bangs, each new missile was unleashed as soon as it
could be placed. There was no attempt to aim. Because
of the angle of vent in the tower wall, the projectiles
were always shot cleanly onto the bridge. And again they
wrought horrible carnage, slicing figures in half, gutting
them where they stood. One bolt hurtled across in a black
blur, pinioning a Welshman through the midriff, carrying
him with it, pinioning another, carrying him, and even
pinioning a third – three men like fish flopping on a spear
– before it plunged into the midst of their countrymen
on the far side. The archery machines sewed the ground
on both sides of the bridge with arrows. Countless more
Welsh were caught in this relentless fusillade, many of
them hit multiple times – through the arms, through the
body, through the legs – and yet still, though reduced to
limping, seesawing wrecks, they proceeded across.

"This is not possible," Gurt shouted. "There should
be a carpet of corpses by now. I don't see a single bloody
one!"

WWW.ABADDONBOOKS.COM

An Abaddon Books™ Publication
www.abaddonbooks.com
abaddon@rebellion.co.uk

First published in 2010 by Abaddon Books™, Rebellion Intellectual
Property Limited, Riverside House, Osney Mead, Oxford, OX2 0ES, UK.

10 9 8 7 6 5 4 3 2 1

Editors: Jonathan Oliver & Jenni Hill
Cover: Nick Percival
Design: Simon Parr & Luke Preece
Marketing and PR: Keith Richardson
Creative Director and CEO: Jason Kingsley
Chief Technical Officer: Chris Kingsley

Tomes of The Dead™, Abaddon Books and Abaddon Books logo
are trademarks owned or used exclusively by Rebellion Intellectual
Property Limited. The trademarks have been registered or protection
sought in all member states of the European Union and other countries
around the world. All right reserved.

ISBN: 978-1-907519-10-9

Printed in the US

TOMES OF THE DEAD

STRONGHOLD

PAUL FINCH

Abaddon Books

WWW.ABADDONBOOKS.COM

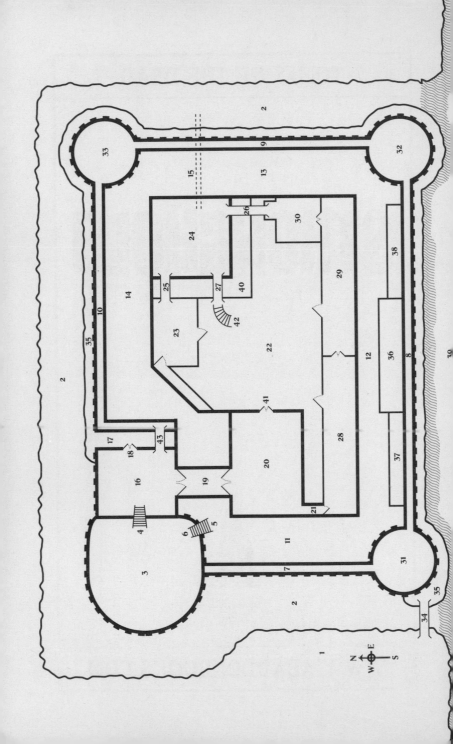

GROGEN CASTLE KEY:

1. Western bluff
2. Outer moat (dry, 30 ft deep)
3. Barbican (60ft high)
4. Stair (between Barbican and Gatehouse)
5. Stair (between Barbican and Bailey)
6. Postern gate
7. West curtain-wall (50 ft high)
8. South curtain-wall (50 ft high)
9. East curtain-wall (50 ft high)
10. North curtain-wall (50 ft high)
11. West bailey (outer courtyard)
12. South bailey (outer courtyard)
13. East bailey (outer courtyard)
14. North bailey (outer courtyard)
15. Keep sewer (subterranean)
16. Gatehouse (multi-levelled interior, 70 ft high)
17. Entry passage
18. Main gate
19. Causeway (20 ft above bailey)
20. Constable's Tower (multi-levelled interior, 100 ft high)
21. Inner Fort wall (80 ft high)
22. Central courtyard (also called 'inner ward', contains numerous sheds, shacks and outbuildings, serving as stables, servant quarters, hospital shelters, etc)
23. North Hall (non-fortified, multi-levelled interior)
24. Keep (multi-levelled interior, 150 ft high)
25. Gantry drawbridge (connecting North Hall to Keep, 90ft high)
26. Gantry drawbridge (connecting baronial state rooms to Keep, 90 ft high)
27. Keep drawbridge (20 ft above courtyard)
28. Barrack house (non-fortified, multi-levelled interior)
29. Great Hall (non fortified, multi-levelled interior)
30. Baronial state rooms (non-fortified, multi-levelled interior)
31. Southwest tower (multi-levelled interior, 100 ft high)
32. Southeast tower (multi-levelled interior, 100 ft high)
33. Northeast tower (multi-levelled interior, 100 ft high)
34. Southwest bridge
35. Berm path
36. Old stable block
37. Support scaffolding
38. Support scaffolding
39. River Tefeidiad
40. Keep moat (dry, 30 ft deep)
41. Ramp (down from Constable's Tower into courtyard)
42. Keep outer stair
43. Gantry drawbridge (connecting Gatehouse to north curtain-wall, 30 ft above entry passage)

Note: The castle kitchens and refectory are located on the ground floor, running beneath the barrack house and the Great Hall. The castle chapel is a cellar, located beneath the kitchens. None of these are visible from this perspective.

CHAPTER ONE

1295 AD

IT WAS EARLY March, but spring still hadn't arrived. The woods to either side of the River Ogryn were not yet in flower. They were black and tangled, laced with grey mist. Within a month the river would be foaming and thundering, swollen with melt-water from the heights of Plynlimon, but for now it was an icy trickle, meandering down the shallow valley, zigzagging between tumbled rocks and fallen branches covered with frost.

At the head of the valley lay a mound of weapons. For the most part they were swords, axes and spears, though there were also improvised farm tools – scythes, flails, reaping hooks. The majority were tarnished and chipped, their hafts or hilts bound with fleece and homespun linen. If they'd been honed to sharpness, it had been done inexpertly; many of the blades had a keen edge but had been thinned to the point where they were brittle. Others had already cracked and broken.

Even so, it was agonising for the Welshmen to surrender them. They passed the mound in their ones and twos, grudgingly discarding their implements, throwing surly glances at the group of mounted figures watching from close by. The foremost of these was a woman sitting on a roan mare. She was of early middle age and extraordinarily handsome, green eyed and feline in her beauty. A hooded coat of white fox fur shielded her from the chill winds, and her long red tresses were bound with a copper circlet. She was Countess Madalyn of Lyr, a noblewoman of high standing in this region. When Powys had been a kingdom in its own right, her family had held its eastern populace in thrall, but, with fair governance and courageous leadership, had stirred loyalty rather than resentment. Now that Powys was a dominion of the English Crown, she was viewed with less affection. Her passion for her people was not doubted, and some regarded her fondly as a living embodiment of happier days, but many either mistrusted her as a collaborator or saw her as a pawn in a greater political game over which she had no control.

Countess Madalyn's daughter, Gwendolyn, was mounted alongside her on a milk-white pony. She also was clad in luxurious furs, and though fairer even than her mother, more slender of build and with an elfin prettiness, in truth she was little more than hogannod; an inconsequential girl, who would some day inherit the countess's title and lands but probably none of her spirit. The passing Welshmen paid her no heed, though when it came to the third mounted figure they either glared at him with open hatred or spat at his horse's feet.

He was Corotocus la Hors, marcher baron of the English realm and Earl of Clun. He was a trim, broad-shouldered man in his late thirties, handsome with close-cropped brown hair, a trimmed beard and moustache, and piercing blue eyes. Fully girt for war, he wore a crimson tabard emblazoned with his heraldic black eagle belted over his suit of black mail, a cross-hilted longsword at his hip, and a thick bearskin cloak at his shoulders. His horse, Incitatus, was a black stallion, sleek and powerful, maybe sixteen hands to the withers. Like its master, it had been born and bred in a crucible of war. As the Welsh trudged past, it tossed its mane at them, snorting and pawing the rutted ground.

"These fellows of yours don't know when they're beaten," Earl Corotocus observed. "I'll give them credit for that."

"They weren't beaten, my lord," Countess Madalyn said. "They surrendered voluntarily."

Neither spoke English as their first language, but, despite their lilting accents, it was the easiest way for the Anglo-Norman lord and his Welsh counterpart to converse.

"Then they aren't stupid either," he replied. "Though they could mind their manners."

"You surely don't expect them to welcome English dominance in their land?"

"If I'm honest, my lady, I have no expectations. I'm here purely to exercise my duty. If I were to falter in that, King Edward's mighty hand would crush me as surely as it would crush you and all this peasant race you claim kinship with."

Countess Madalyn glanced round to where Kye, her personal bodyguard, stood watching her back. An immense, bear-like fellow with a dense black beard and brooding countenance, he had been instructed from the outset not to rise to English provocation. He nodded his understanding of this order.

"Feeling the way you do, my lord, I'm grateful, but surprised, that you accepted the truce," the countess said.

Corotocus shrugged. "Peace terms must always be taken seriously when the alternative is laying siege to a bastion like Grogen Castle. Something tells me these fellows would not have fled it as quickly as the Breton sot assigned to hold it against them."

Grogen Castle, only twenty miles from here, had been abandoned by its royal castellan without a blow struck in resistance to the Welsh army who'd encircled it. Its puny garrison of Breton mercenaries had spent more time drinking and whoring than preparing for war and, when the time had finally come, had discovered that they'd lost all appetite for the hardships of battle. This was in stark contrast to the Welshmen now trailing down the valley. Despite having some mail shirts between them, they were mainly clad as foresters – in hose, felt boots and hooded woollen jerkins. Yet they were a rough, hardy sort, dark eyed and sullen of brow. They were all shapes and sizes; some were young, some old, but they had a vigour and robustness that the average English peasant lacked. Corotocus knew why. The main industry in this part of the kingdom was sheep rearing rather than rood-work. This was physically demanding work carried out on a mountainous landscape of coarse pasture and tumbling, boulder-strewn valleys. The simple act of moving from place to place built up great reserves of strength and stamina in the natives. On top of that, their barbarous tribal customs had toughened them in other ways, and they'd had no option but to grow used to the cold, wet gales howling in from the Irish Sea.

"I'm glad you understand," Countess Madalyn said. "It's very important to these men that you realise they didn't give up the castle because they are frightened of a fight. After Prince Madog's defeat at Maes Moydog, I was able to persuade them that the cause is futile. That it would have meant another prolonged war of annihilation and that, even if they were victorious in the end, the result would be burnt homes, ravaged farmland, famine and pestilence."

Corotocus nodded. "You did right. You are a good mother to your people."

His household champion trotted up from behind, a swarthy Aquitainian knight, whose brutish face was bisected down the middle by an ugly cleft. The relic of a deep scimitar wound incurred many years earlier, this had now left him with features that were weirdly asymmetrical, one eye slightly higher than the other, his mouth slanted, his nose, what remained of it, horribly crooked.

"That's the last of them, my lord," he said.

"You're certain, Navarre?"

"Four hundred men in total have surrendered their arms and are returning to their homes."

This appeared to be true. No more Welshmen now appeared. The last handful was already fifty yards down the valley.

"Good," Corotocus said. "Du Guesculin!"

Hugh du Guesculin, his chief herald and banneret, rode forward. Like Navarre, he wore mail and the earl's household livery. He also carried the earl's gonfalon – a long pole from the top of which the black eagle billowed on a crimson weave. But he seemed less of a warrior. He was portly, with a clipped moustache and dainty manner.

"My lord?" he enquired.

"Begin the punishment."

Countess Madalyn glanced at the earl, puzzled. He smiled coldly. Du Guesculin summoned a page, who put a hunting horn to his lips and blew a single, clear blast.

"Kye!" Countess Madalyn said.

The gigantic bodyguard hurried forward, his mail coat clinking under his leather corselet. He had a spear in one hand, a kite-shaped shield in the other, and a sharp scramsax tucked into his belt. But he didn't get a chance to use any of these. Navarre, who had quietly dismounted, stepped up from behind him and stuck a dagger into the side of his neck. The giant sank to his knees, eyes goggling. He clutched at the jutting hilt, blood bubbling through his fingers. Gwendolyn screamed in horror. Countess Madalyn didn't at first see this. She was distracted by a wild shouting, and now stood in her stirrups to peer down the valley.

Why were feathered shafts whistling back and forth through the frigid air? Why were Welshmen dropping where they stood?

Then she saw the English archers. Having donned leather over their mail as camouflage, they emerged in packs from the trees on either side. The graceful curve of their longbows, as they were strung and drawn with professional speed and precision, was as distinctive as it was terrifying.

"Earl Corotocus!" she cried. "What is this?"

"War cannot just be extinguished, my lady, like a candle you snuff, or an ember you put your foot upon." Corotocus mused. "Though putting one's foot down is an apt phrase at this moment."

The Welshmen in the valley ran in all directions, but arrows flew with unerring accuracy. Like fleeting streaks of light, their steel heads buried themselves in flesh, muscle and bone. Very soon, the valley bottom was dotted with the wounded and dying. Some of those still standing attempted to forge to the valley sides, where they could grapple with their tormentors. But the crossfire was so thick that they were riddled with shafts and dropped like human pincushions, or, if they managed to make it, received a knife in the ribs or the crushing blow of a warhammer to the top of their skull.

Countess Madalyn watched through tear-blurred eyes.

"You traitorous pig!" she wept. "You gave us your word."

"One does not give one's word to country oafs and expect to be taken seriously, countess. These men are outlaws. They lived as such, and will die as such."

Some Welshmen struggled back towards the valley head, as though to retrieve their weapons. But Navarre and others of the earl's personal mesnie greeted them with laughter and double-handed sword strokes, lopping their legs from under them, sundering their necks at the shoulder. More knights, these mounted, appeared at the lowest end of the valley, where the open, tussocky sward made it safe for their horses. Most wore the earl's red and black livery, but there were others, tenant knights from his wider demesnes, who sported personal devices on their surcoats and shields. It made for a colourful scene as they cantered back and forth, lowering their lances to skewer the Welsh as they ran, or hacking them down with longswords and mattocks. Some fell to their knees and begged for mercy – but were simply ridden over, their bodies torn and trampled by smashing, iron-shod hooves. One stout fellow attempted to grab the lance of a knight decked with blue and white chevrons. The knight released his weapon, but circled around, drew his battle-axe and clove the fellow's cranium.

Even those lying injured were not spared; hunting spears were flung at them as riders galloped past. One older Welshman, his jaw hanging shattered and left eye dangling from a crushed socket, crawled to the river's edge, only to have his face pressed under by a hoof until he drowned. Owen Anwyl, the disinherited Welsh noble who had first seized Grogen Castle, was spared the butchering blade, but buffeted again and again by horses and struck with the hafts of axes and the pommels of swords, his visage streaked with gore from his lacerated scalp. Eventually a halter was looped around his neck and tightened, and he was hauled around the valley on his back.

Countess Madalyn shrieked as rude hands were now laid on her.

It was Navarre, his lopsided face written with goblin glee. He dragged her from the saddle and threw her to the ground. She struggled, but could not stop him plucking the pearls from her throat or the rings from her fingers. When she spat and clawed at him, he punched her – not hard enough to knock her unconscious, though his fist was like a bone mallet inside its rawhide glove. She was left stunned by the blow, only vaguely aware that her daughter was also pulled screaming from the saddle and divested of her jewels.

After that, the two women were violated.

Countess Madalyn's fustian gown and the fine silk under-tunic were torn wide open, and her breasts exposed. She winced as Navarre kneaded them like two lumps of dough, sobbed aloud as he feasted on them, suckling, biting, chewing until her blood flowed.

Earl Corotocus and Hugh du Guesculin sat through it all, unmoved. As Corotocus surveyed his triumph, he summoned his page and accepted a chicken drumstick and a goblet of mulled wine.

In time, the carnage drew to a close. Spiked maces, caked with brains and bone fragments, still crashed onto heads and shoulders. Flailing hands were still severed at the wrist, but few Welshmen were left on their feet. Tiring of the sport, Corotocus's knights took those few surviving and hanged them from the surrounding trees. One by one, their gibbering pleas were lost in gargled chokes.

At the sight of this, Countess Madalyn wailed like a baby, but she was struck dumb when she saw her daughter, every scrap of clothing now stripped from her body, trussed with rope and thrown over the front of her horse like a deer. Holding her rent garments together with one hand, the countess tried to intervene, only to be knocked to the ground by Navarre. Laughing, he jumped up behind the captive girl and slapped her naked buttocks.

"Your daughter will be held as surety for your good behaviour," Earl Corotocus said. "At some point in the future, if this land remains at peace, it may please me to marry her to a henchman of my choice – someone I can rely on to treat her in the manner to which she will soon become accustomed."

"You whoreson!" the countess hissed, kneeling upright, her emerald eyes burning with outrage. "You goat's whelp!"

"Insult me all you wish, my lady, but understand one thing. There is more at stake here than the pride of your piffling people. I am lord of the Clun March, but I am more than just a name. In France, I was charged with defending the king's Gascon possessions. We were overwhelmed by sheer numbers, but the king heard about the destruction I wrought on his foes, how my men and I slew hundreds, thousands. He was grateful, and I was rewarded with lifelong investment not just in this – the most difficult corner of his realm – but with lordships all across Wales. Be under no illusion, I intend to hold my possessions and, in due course, to expand them. But these constant revolts are becoming tiresome. I cannot have the king suspecting that his trust was misplaced. Du Guesculin!"

"My lord?" the banneret said.

"Du Guesculin, by my reckoning, there are twenty villages between here and Grogen Castle. Lay waste to them. Torch the houses, scatter the women and children, hang the men and boys. And make a good show of that, du Guesculin – I want gibbets on every hill and every crossroads, each one laden to breaking point."

"Of course, my lord."

"Earl Corotocus, you will pay for this!" the countess snarled.

"Countess Madalyn, we all pay in the end."

Before he left, he made a special example of Owen Anwyl, having his hands bound behind his back, his legs broken with a pollaxe, and then suspending him by the feet from a tree-limb at the highest point of the valley.

CHAPTER TWO

THE CASTLES THAT King Edward built in Wales after his first war of conquest, some twenty years earlier, had formed a stone collar intended to choke the spirit of native resistance. Designed by the master military architect, James of St. George, they were each one a towering, impregnable bastion, a glowering fastness that came to dominate and oppress the land for miles in every direction. Their very names had now become a byword for invincibility: Conway, Ruddlin, Flint, Harlech.

Grogen Castle was no exception.

It stood on the north shore of the River Tefeidiad, right on the water's edge, and was approachable only from the west due to hilly moorland and thickly wooded terrain in the north and east. It consisted of an outer curtain-wall, some fifty feet high, a fortified Gatehouse, a Barbican, a Constable's Tower, and an Inner Fort, the walls of which stood eighty feet. Inside the Inner Fort were the main buildings – the halls, kitchen, barrack-house and the final defensive structure, the Keep. When Corotocus's men first came in sight of Grogen, there were mutters of awe – due as much to its appearance as to its size. In England it had become the fashion for wealthy nobles who owned privately licensed castles to paint them in glowing colours – white, blue or red – so that they shone from the leafy landscape like objects in fairy tales. But King Edward's Welsh castles were different animals. They were military strongholds so bereft of adornment or luxury that the Welsh poet Euan the Rhymer had described them as 'spikes of Hell thrust out through Cymru's fair hide.'

Grogen fulfilled that vision perfectly. It was comprised entirely of grey granite cemented in huge blocks. Its colossal walls and towers were sheer and bleak, and fitted with projecting upper gantries, which were massively crenelated and equipped with swinging timber panels from behind which an avalanche of stones, darts and boiling oil could be launched. Its only windows were narrow slits through which arrows could be shot and javelins thrown.

However, much more of a shock to Corotocus and his men was not the pitiless nature of this fastness, but the many figures manning its awesome defences.

"What the hell is this?" the earl swore, reining his horse at the front of the column. He slammed his visor open. "Du Guesculin, what in Satan's name is this?"

The banneret lifted his wide-brimmed helmet and, shielding his eyes against the early-morning sun, focussed on the figures dotting the top of the curtain-wall and the parapet of the Barbican. At this distance it was impossible to discern who they were, but there were plenty of them and their blades and helmets glinted.

Others of the earl's men now rode up, among them William d'Abbetot, his chief engineer, Captain Garbofasse of his mercenary battalion, and Craon Culai, who commanded a company of the king's infantry attached to the earl's retinue for the duration of the war. They were equally surprised and, having been assured that the castle was theirs for the taking, not a little alarmed.

"Someone tell me what's happening here!" Corotocus bellowed.

He rarely allowed himself to get angry in front of underlings, but now he'd lost face. His cheeks reddened, there was froth on his lips. "Did some of Anwyl's dogs stay behind? How could the bloody place have been reoccupied when he only abandoned it yesterday? Someone explain this to me!"

"Why do none of them move?" Culai wondered. A tall, thin man with pinched features, he seemed spooked by what he was seeing, and it was indeed an eerie sight – the figures on the wall were silent and motionless. Too motionless, some might say, to be living men.

"Are they dead?" Garbofasse asked.

"Neither dead nor living," came another voice. Ulbert FitzOsbern, an older knight wearing a red and blue harlequin mantel over his mail, cantered to the front of the column. "My lord, most likely they're scarecrows."

"Scarecrows?" Corotocus said.

Ulbert nodded. "I saw this done often during de Montfort's rebellion. Castles expecting siege but held by only a handful of troops, would create scarecrows – dummies stuffed with straw – and prop them on the battlements. Given an iron cap and a spear each, it looked to all the world as if the place was strongly garrisoned."

Corotocus laughed loudly, partly to conceal his relief. "Of course. That Breton wastrel de Brione only had a few men. When he heard the Welsh were coming, he'd have panicked. Once again Ulbert, we're grateful for your wisdom and insight." He regarded his other lieutenants sternly. "It comes to something when a homeless knight, an errant wanderer who is only with us to pay off his family's debts, provides a solution while the rest of you stand around like frightened children."

They hung their heads, abashed.

There was still, of course, the possibility that this could be a trap. The earl's force might approach the castle's main entrance thinking it safe, only to be struck by a deluge of missiles. So lots were drawn and ten men selected to go forward. The rest of the army, six hundred in total, arrayed itself on the western bluff to watch.

While to the south Grogen Castle was bordered by the deep, broad flow of the Tefeidiad, it was surrounded on its three other sides by a moat, which had been hacked from the living rock on which the fastness was built. This moat was about ten yards across and thirty feet deep. During the spring thaw, mountain streams emptied into it from the north, but at present it was dry and filled with rubble. The only way to cross over it was via an arched stone bridge at the castle's southwest corner. Having managed this, an enemy force would be required to follow the 'berm' path, a narrow footing running between the base of the south-facing curtain-wall and the inner edge of the moat. This turned at the castle's southeast corner, passed alongside the east-facing wall and the north-facing wall, until finally reaching the main entrance, which was set between the Gatehouse and the north-facing wall in the castle's northwest corner. By this time, of course, the enemy would have been subjected to prolonged attack from overhead as it was forced to circle the entire stronghold.

As the ten chosen men readied themselves, donning not just their helms and shields, but additional plating on their elbows, shoulders and knees, the rest of the army waited. Among them were Ulbert FitzOsbern and his twenty-two year old son, Ranulf.

One of the duties the father and son had been given was to guard Countess Madalyn's daughter. Partly of their own volition, but also at the instigation of Father Benan, the earl's chaplain, who thought it unseemly that Gwendolyn should be naked among so many men, they'd loosened her bonds and given her a cloak to wrap herself in. Though streaked with dirt and tears, she sat upright on her pony, taut with anger but determined to maintain her dignity. When Ranulf offered her a drink from his water bottle, she didn't lower herself to reply.

"It's your choice," he said, turning back to the castle.

The FitzOsberns were tall, well-built men. Age had wizened Ulbert's neck and thickened his paunch, but, thanks to countless clashes in battle and tournament, his son was flat bellied, barrel-chested and stout of limb. He had grey eyes and a lean, square jaw. When he pulled back his mail coif, he shook out a mop of sweaty, straw-yellow hair; sure proof that his family – though they'd intermarried many times with Norman stock, hence their surname – had its origins in Saxon England.

Navarre galloped up to them, his horse chopping turf as it slid to a halt.

"The girl rides with the vanguard," he said.

"Why?" Ranulf asked.

"Isn't it obvious? To lessen the chance of attack."

"I thought the idea was to draw an attack... if there's to be one."

"Earl Corotocus wishes to lose as few men as possible, FitzOsbern. But he needs to know what we're facing. With the girl as a human shield, we'll likely draw a non-fatal response."

Ranulf glanced unhappily at his father, who shrugged.

"Ranulf FitzOsbern," Navarre said in a sneering tone. "I wouldn't like to think you were about to disobey Earl Corotocus."

Ranulf handed over the reins. Navarre rode away, leading Gwendolyn's pony behind him at a fast trot. The girl sat stiffly, but now looked frightened. She glanced back at Ranulf and his father as if suddenly thinking them a better option than whatever lay ahead.

"Earl bloody Corotocus," Ranulf said. "Corotocus? Where did he get that name? Doesn't it sound like a demon to you?"

"It sounds more Gaelic," Ulbert replied.

"The Gael people would be insulted... those that haven't been slaughtered." Ranulf's voice tightened with disgust. "I've never seen such savagery as in the last few days."

"He treats his English subjects the same way."

"His English subjects can appeal to the king."

"And would the king listen? You know the law of the March. Men like Corotocus thrive here because the king needs brutes to control the border."

"That doesn't excuse him.

"Agreed. By any standards, his atrocities are perhaps... over elaborate."

"Atrocities to which we're a part, father."

"We're excused, Ranulf. We're here through fealty."

"Fealty?" Ranulf shook his head. "We agreed to pay our debts by fighting for him."

"Which we have done, many times."

"Yes, and which I'll gladly do again. Show me armed opposition and I'll fight it now. But I'm tired of terrorising the weak and helpless."

"You should watch what you're saying, boy," another knight said as he walked by, leading his horse. He was Walter Margas, one of Corotocus's tenants. By all accounts he'd done well in the earl's service, but he was now an old, embittered fellow with watery eyes and a grizzled grey beard. His wore a distinctive surcoat of blue and white chevrons but, with his potbelly and bandy legs, he didn't cut a striking figure. "Rogue knights like you are ten-a-penny. The earl could dispense with you tomorrow, and he wouldn't lose a wink of sleep."

"And as for cowards like him," Ranulf said when he'd gone, "do we really want to fight alongside them?"

Ulbert chuckled. "Would you expect to find Margas alongside you if there was real fighting to be done?"

"Father, this isn't a joke."

"Then you must make it one!" Ulbert snapped, turning impatient.

Despite his mild manner, Ulbert was in his mid-fifties and a battle-scarred veteran. He'd served more lords than he could remember, several of whose reasons for waging war were less than worthy and whose methods of prosecuting it were, in truth, appalling. But he'd learned through long experience that taking a moral view was a waste of energy and emotion – all it would do in the end was prevent you sleeping at night, and in wartime you needed your sleep. Thus far on this expedition he'd tolerated Ranulf's distaste for the earl's techniques, but now he feared that it might bring trouble for them.

"We're in Earl Corotocus's service for a term of seven more years – on oath," he reminded his son. "With luck we'll spend the remainder of those years in this castle, doing nothing more than waiting and watching from our guard-posts."

"Seven years... holed up in there!"

"Some men would be glad. The whole army of Hell couldn't get at us in there." For some reason, Ulbert shuddered at that thought.

Below them, meanwhile, the small vanguard of ten men and one woman proceeded down the grassy slope to the bridge, the earl's gonfalon fluttering above them. Still, the figures on the battlements were motionless. The rest of the earl's host lapsed into silence as they watched. Nervously, the vanguard crossed the bridge, rode around the castle's southwest tower, which was cut with numerous, slanted vents so that missiles could be poured onto the bridge from close range, and advanced along the riverside berm. No attempt was made to interfere with them, and gradually the other troops began to relax.

"So far so good," Ranulf said.

Ulbert didn't reply.

The vanguard reached the far end and, when it turned at the castle's southeast corner, vanished altogether. Long minutes followed, which became half an hour, and then an hour – before a rider returned to view, galloping pell-mell across the bridge and up the hillside.

"It's open, my lord!" he cried. "The main entrance is open! Grogen Castle is ours!"

"And the garrison?" Corotocus shouted back.

"As you said, sir... straw men. Effigies."

"So now it was Earl Corotocus who said that," Ranulf observed.

"Of course," Ulbert replied.

The earl marshalled his host, and, with a beneficent air, led it downhill.

His household retainers rode directly behind him. After these came the royal contingents: detachments on loan from King Edward's own Familiaris Regis – the men-at-arms under Craon Culai, the crossbows under Bryon Musard, and the longbows under Davy Gou. After these marched a Welsh sub-chief called Morgaynt Carew – he and his small group of discontented warriors didn't like the English, but had worse grievances against Madog ap Llywelyn, the architect of the uprising. The tenant knights from the earl's estates followed and then came the men on oath, the likes of Ulbert and Ranulf. At the very rear came Garbofasse and his mercenaries, a motley band of cutthroats and outcasts. They wore few colours, but were heavily mailed and carried a vast assortment of weapons, everything from falchions to mauls and morningstars, from halberds to broadswords and scimitars. Garbofasse himself was a brutish giant, with long black hair and famously disgusting breath. In the twenty villages Corotocus had sacked, it was these men who'd partaken most – burning cottages, raping women, revelling in the bloodshed as if bred to it from birth.

"I'd be happier without these scoundrels at my back," Ranulf grumbled as he steered his horse downhill.

"Better they're on our side than against us," his father replied.

The berm path was an unnerving experience. All the way along it, they were acutely aware of the projecting walk fifty feet overhead, and its many 'murder holes' through which all types of objects could be dropped upon them. The curtain-wall rose like a sheer cliff to their left, its skirted base narrowing the path until only two horses could move along it abreast. With a shallow slope into the river on the right, this wasn't unduly perilous, but when they turned the southeast corner and found themselves alongside the moat, it was a different matter. The column hugged the curtain-wall as it processed. Those on the outside, man or beast, only needed to stumble or slip once and they'd plunge thirty feet onto jumbled rocks.

When they finally reached the castle's main entrance, it was an immense gateway recessed to one side at the end of a deep entry passage. Proceeding down towards it, one could still be attacked from overhead via the Gatehouse battlements or via the curtain-wall, which bounded it on the left. However, the gate itself, a massive oaken structure, faced with iron, was open, and the portcullis behind it had been raised. They rode through, their hooves clattering in the long, vaulted tunnel, and then out and along a timber causeway, which passed twenty feet above the bailey, a yard hemming in the Inner Fort. At the south end of the causeway stood the Constable's Tower. This was a miniature castle in its own right. In shape if not size, it reminded Ranulf of the great Tower erected on the north bank of the Thames, but again its gate was open and its portcullis raised. They rode through, passing along another vaulted tunnel and out into the precincts of the Inner Fort, descending a ramp into the central courtyard where, among many thatch and wattle out-buildings, an entire stable block was located.

With their squires and grooms scampering ahead to provide berths for their animals, the knights and men-at-arms shouted and jostled as they dismounted, the sounds of which echoed to the high ramparts. Only slowly and with much good-natured disorder, did they fall into their separate companies.

Last into the courtyard, moving at a leisurely pace as always, rode Doctor Zacharius. With him came the covered wagon filled with salves and herbs and medicines, driven by his assistant, Henri.

Zacharius, a prized surgeon, was a youngish, clean-shaven man, with long dark hair, green eyes and a wolfish countenance. Even now in the midst of campaign, dressing well was important to him. He wore a blue serge gamache, a brown felt hood with scalloped shoulder-pieces, bright yellow hose and blue, long-toed boots. By contrast, Henri was a pallid, tremulous youth wrapped in a dark, woollen cloak spattered with roadside mud. The general feeling, though no-one knew this for sure, was that Henri was one of the doctor's numerous illegitimate offspring, though in this particular case, given that he was being taught the surgeon's skill assiduously and thus preparing for a career of his own, he was probably the outcome of a liaison with a high-born lady.

"Place is completely empty – no serving wenches, not even a scullery maid," Navarre said, approaching the doctor on foot. He chuckled. "Could be a barren spell for you, Zacharius."

Zacharius smiled as he dismounted. "But at least it will end when I leave this place. When will yours end, Navarre?"

Navarre's cockeyed smile faded. "My lord says you have the pick of these buildings for your personal quarters and your infirmary. If anyone disputes your decision, you have his authority."

Zacharius nodded as if he'd expect nothing less.

Navarre scowled as he turned, leading his horse by its bridle.

"Reached the limits of your power, Navarre?" Ranulf wondered, having just emerged from the stable and overheard. "Again?"

"No man is fireproof, FitzOsbern," Navarre retorted. "Anything can happen to any one of us at any time. You'd do well to remember that."

He led his horse away, Ranulf gazing after him, thinking that their incarceration in this place was likely to be even more onerous than he'd first thought.

CHAPTER THREE

EARL COROTOCUS OPTED to put his headquarters in the Constable's Tower, for this controlled both the main entrance and access to the Inner Fort, and therefore the entire stronghold. Above its entry tunnel, there were various rooms. All were functional – made from cold, bare stone and bereft of wall hangings or furniture, though they had hearths where fires could be kindled, and bales of straw and piles of fleeces to provide bedding. Word soon came that the storehouses in the central courtyard were filled with grain and barrels of fruit and salted pork. There were also kegs of wine and cider, and a deep well in the kitchen, from which a pail of fresh water had already been drawn.

One by one, the earl's lieutenants were allocated their positions. Garbofasse and his mercenaries were to take the Gatehouse, and the earl's household knights the Constable's Tower. The royal contingents would be spread through the castle, the crossbows in the southwest tower, the men-at-arms along the curtain-wall, the longbows to any vantage point of their choice. Carew and

his Welsh malcontents, deemed less trustworthy, were assigned
to the Barbican, a low but heavily fortified tower just west of
the Gatehouse, where they could man the castle's main piece
of artillery, a huge stone-throwing trebuchet, but where, more
importantly, the earl could watch them. Lastly, the earl's tenant
knights would reinforce the defenders on the curtain-wall.

"That leaves us, my lord," Ulbert said, speaking not just for
himself and his son, but for three other indebted knights – Tomas
d'Altard, Ramon la Roux and Gurt Louvain.

"Take the curtain-wall on the south side, overlooking the river,"
Corotocus told them dismissively. He was seated at a long table
in the Constable's Tower's main chamber. A map of the castle
and its surrounding environs had been found in a chest, and lay
unscrolled in front of him. "Bed in the barrack house in the Inner
Fort. Rotate your sleeping arrangements with the others. I never
want less than half the garrison on watch."

Ulbert bowed and retreated.

"And the girl, my lord?" Ranulf asked. "Do we house her in
the barracks too? I'm sure there'll be a side-hall or ante-chamber
where she can have some privacy."

"She can have her privacy in the Keep."

"The Keep?" Ranulf said.

As the final refuge, the Keep, a gargantuan square edifice, was
perhaps the grimmest part of the castle. It stood in the northeast
corner of the Inner Fort, taking up almost a quarter of the central
courtyard. It had its own moat, which could only be crossed at
ground level by a drawbridge, or ninety feet in the air by two
gantry drawbridges connecting to it from the North Hall and the
State Rooms. It had few windows; its precipitous walls, which
were much thicker than any others in the castle, rose unbroken
for an incredible one hundred and fifty feet. It was unimaginable
that anyone should try to storm such a structure. But it was
equally unimaginable that anyone, save the lowest felon or most
dangerous rebel, should be imprisoned inside it. There'd be little
light in there, even less clean air, and probably no sanitation.
The girl would be completely alone, for none of the men would
be stationed there unless the castle's outer defences fell.

A few seconds passed, before Earl Corotocus glanced up from his map. "Ranulf, is that disapproval I hear?"

"How could I disapprove, my lord, of such a fair and Christian-minded judgement?"

All around the chamber, where a number of the earl's men were still loitering, breaths were sucked through gritted teeth. Father Benan, who had been kneeling in prayer before a corner table with a crucifix etched on the wall above it, looked around and gaped. Ulbert stepped forward, thrusting Ranulf out of the way.

"Apologies my lord. My son is a fool who often speaks out of turn."

Corotocus pushed his chair back. He regarded them both coolly. "You're right, Ulbert. Your son is a fool... but at least he tells me the truth. I'd rather have men around me who are honest in their feelings than toadies who simper and scrape." He stood up. "Ranulf, walk with me."

Ranulf glanced at his father, who averted his eyes.

The earl took a spiral stair, which led out onto the Constable's Tower's roof. Some of his household were already up there, using bellows to pump life into a brazier. Others hugged themselves in their cloaks. At this height, the wind gusting from the peaks of the northern mountains was edged with ice. Ranulf found himself gazing over a rolling, densely wooded landscape, much of it still shrouded with mist.

"You understand, Ranulf," Corotocus said, walking to the western parapet, "how empires are built?"

Ranulf followed him warily. "We're building an empire, my lord?"

"You find my methods abhorrent." Corotocus posed it as a statement rather than a question. "So do I. That may surprise you, Ranulf. I don't like what we're doing here any more than you, but unfortunately we can't choose the necessities we face in life. Only two things can control a recalcitrant race – strength and more strength. Not just the strength to defeat them on the battlefield, but the strength to do what you must to suppress them afterwards. Never underestimate a people's self-pitying spirit, Ranulf – it can be a great motivator. Likewise, don't be fooled by these claims the Welsh make that they are different from us, that they're a separate nation who have earned the right to self-rule and an indigenous culture. The native English thought the same when first they were conquered, but it wasn't long before their world was consumed whole and, in the long run, made better for it. In any case, how have these Welsh earned the right to self-rule? They were as tyrannised by their own lords as they ever have been by ours. They've staged revolts against their princes, they've waged civil wars, their mythology is filled with blood and treachery."

"With all respect, my lord..." Ranulf was cautious about voicing too much concern. He knew Earl Corotocus's reputation for meeting dissent with an iron fist – he'd seen it for himself, he'd been part of that iron fist. But, for now, the earl was calm, almost genial. And why shouldn't he be? He'd captured his main objective without losing a single man. "With respect my lord, that doesn't make what we do here right."

"'Right'?" The earl seemed amused. "What is 'right'?"

"The code tells us..."

"The code is a fantasy, Ranulf. Invented by frustrated French wives who dream of replacing their ancient, worm-riddled husbands with handsome young lovers. You are a fully girded knight. Tender in years, but you earned your spurs in battle. You've already seen enough to know that wars are not won by fair play or courtly gestures."

He put a fatherly hand on Ranulf's shoulder.

"Ranulf, Edward Longshanks is a king who would be Caesar. Once this war is won, he will march against the Scots. He intends to rule the whole island of Britain, from the toe of Cornwall to the Wood of Caledon, from Wight to Northumbria. But right now he is watching the Welsh March. This is a troublesome region for him. If we who are appointed to guard it can curb this menace once and for all, he will be more than grateful. There may be better rewards here than simple relief from the debts we owe." He moved away along the battlements, only to stop and glance back. "But Ranulf... I will not dangle this carrot indefinitely."

Suddenly there was steel in his voice.

"They tell me you and your father played no part at the River Ogryn." His expression hardened. His blue eyes became spear-points. "They say you spared lives in the villages we razed on the road here. Very gallant of you, Ranulf. But that may have been a mistake. As things are, I am your lord. I'd prefer to be your lord and your friend, but I can just as easily be your lord and your enemy. Listen very carefully... if I will not sacrifice my fortune and glory for these vermin that call themselves Welsh, I certainly won't sacrifice it for an upstart boy."

Ranulf said nothing.

"Do we understand each other, sirrah?"

"Yes."

"I didn't hear you."

"Yes, my lord."

Half an hour later, Ranulf locked Gwendolyn in the Keep. He found the largest, airiest room for her that he could, but it was still damp and filthy, filled with decayed straw and rat-droppings. He turned deaf ears to her tearful pleas. As he walked away along the cell passage, he refused to look back at her white hands clawing through the tiny hatch in the nail-studded door.

When he ascended to his post on the south-facing curtain-wall, his father was already there, sharing the warmth from a brazier with Gurt Louvain, a rugged looking northern knight draped in a green, weather-worn cloak. Two of the scarecrows had been flung to one side. They were hideous, soulless objects – sackcloth suits stuffed with rags and bound to stick frames. Their faces had been made up with streaks of what looked like dung or mucus. Weirdly – probably because the Breton troops had been bored – some of these faces were smiling exaggeratedly, almost dementedly – like caricatures from Greek or Roman drama. It gave them a sinister air, as if they knew something the English didn't and were delighted by it.

"How long must we rot in this hellhole?" Ranulf asked of no-one in particular.

Ulbert shrugged. "Until the king deems the rebellion quelled. And the longer that takes, the happier I'll be." He indicated the land beyond the river, its dense conifer wood receding into the blanket of mist. Nothing moved over there, neither man nor beast. "Look at that. Isn't that beautiful?"

"Beautiful? I see emptiness."

"Exactly." Ulbert shoved another log into the brazier. "No-one for us to kill, and more importantly, no-one to kill us."

"That's because there's no-one left."

"Don't fool yourself, Ranulf," Gurt Louvain said. He was a doughty man, but his bearded face was icy pale. Anguished by the slaughter they'd wreaked over the last few days, he'd developed a nervous twitch. He glanced at the silent trees beyond the river, and the shadows between them. "There's always someone left."

CHAPTER FOUR

ALMOST TWO FULL days passed before Countess Madalyn reached the secret hafn, and by then she was a wreck.

Famished, frozen and faint with pain and weariness, she tottered down a path winding steeply between groves of silent alder. Below her, the hafn – or 'hollow' – was filled with mist. Its trees were twisted stanchions, the spaces between them strewn with rocks and stones. Footsore and filthy, still clad in her ragged, bloodstained garb, she stumbled forward until, at the north end of the hollow, she came to a sheer cliff face. It was hung with rank vegetation, but had split down the centre. At the base, the fissure had widened into a triangular cavity just large enough to accommodate the body of a small man.

The countess regarded it warily. Her eyes were sore with weeping. Unbound, her hair hung in a flame-red tangle, giving her an appearance of madness, but she wasn't so mad as to go blundering into a place like this without hesitation. After several agonised moments, she cursed her lack of options, dropped to her knees and crawled into the aperture. On the other side, a passage that was little more than a rabbit-hole led through the rock. It was a cleft rather than a bore; its sides ribbed and jagged, its narrow floor deep in razor-edged shingle. She scrabbled along regardless of scrapes to her hands and knees, unconcerned that her torn clothes snagged and tore again. At length the passage opened into a cavern filled with greenish light, the source of which she couldn't identify.

She descended a flight of crudely cut steps. The walls in here were inscribed with ancient carvings – spirals and labyrinths, the shapes of men and beasts cavorting together. Reaching level ground, the steps became a paved path weaving between steaming pools. Overhead, water dripped from the needle tips of innumerable stalactites. Ahead, three figures stood on a raised dais. Countess Madalyn walked with a straighter posture; she groomed her hair with grubby fingers – anything she could do to regain a semblance of dignity.

The figures wore hooded white robes, girded at the waist with belts of ivy. The central one held a knotted staff, yet he wasn't old. His face was broad, pale and clean-shaved apart from a black goat-beard, which fell from his chin to his belly. His eyes were onyx beads: unblinking, inscrutable.

"The Countess of Lyr honours us with her presence," he said, his deep tone echoing in the vaulted chamber.

For all her dirt and blood, Countess Madalyn stood proud before him. "I haven't walked half naked for ten miles just to be flattered, Gwyddon."

"Has your god finally abandoned you?" he asked.

"Nor did I come here to discuss religion."

"Then what? Politics?" Gwyddon gave a sickle-shaped smile. "At which you are clearly a novice to be so easily outmanoeuvred by a marcher baron, when the rest of the world knows the marcher barons are nothing but brute-butchers, the blunt edge of Edward's anger."

"Don't lecture me, druid!" Her voice was a strained croak. "I've been trying to broker a peace for our people while you and your pagan rats hide in holes in the ground!"

Gwyddon's smile faded. To either side of him, his fellow priests, older men with white beards and wizened faces, frowned at her blasphemy. There was a chorus of whispers, and the countess realised that others were close by – men and women, children too – all acolytes of the ancient religion, huddled in the shadows beyond the misty pools.

"Bring the countess some food," Gwyddon said loudly. "Bring her a cloak as well. And a chair."

"I want none of these things," she retorted.

"Nevertheless, you will have them. We may be pagans, but we are still respectful of rank."

Three figures scurried up, recognisable as slaves by their shaved heads and the brand marks on their brows – though whether male or female it was difficult to tell. One laid a cloak of ram's fleece over the countess's shoulders. The second produced a wooden chair, onto which she lowered herself painfully. The third brought a table, and placed on it a bowl of steaming rabbit broth and a flagon of mulled wine. Up until now the countess had ignored her gnawing hunger, but the mingled aromas of sweet carrots, boiled cabbage and succulent braised rabbit-flesh almost overpowered her. She struggled not to fall on it with gusto, though she didn't actually stop eating until she'd scraped the bowl clean, at which point she drained the flagon in a single draught. The wine was rich, spiced with orange and ginger. And it was hot – a heady warmth passed through her cold, battered body.

Gwyddon watched without comment.

"You've heard what happened?" she finally asked.

"Of course."

"Ill tidings travel quickly in Wales."

"In Wales is there any other kind of tiding?"

"What King Edward is doing makes no sense." She shook her head, as bewildered as she was still horror-stricken. "Does he expect to win people over when he appoints someone like Corotocus and gives him a free hand? How does he think he'll gain his subjects' love?"

"You are mistaken in thinking that he wants their love,"

Gwyddon said. "In these far reaches of Britain, he is content to have their fear."

"You don't seem disturbed by that."

"Why should I be? As you say, we are rats living in holes. And who drove us here? Not the English, not the Normans – the Welsh."

"Pah! In other countries you'd have been exterminated."

"We'd have been exterminated here had Christian monks had their way. Only the sympathies of certain noble families ensure our survival. Your family for instance, countess."

She stood up abruptly. "Don't mistake me for someone I'm not, Gwyddon. I don't sympathise with heathens."

"So why tolerate us in your domain?"

His voice was deep, melodious. He peered down at her, his eyes glinting. The emerald vapour writhed around his tall, enrobed form like a brood of ethereal vipers.

"I... I..." Countess Madalyn was briefly entranced by the vision. "I... don't believe in slaughter."

"You didn't believe in slaughter once," he corrected her. "Why else are you here now?"

"They've taken my daughter."

"I know."

The countess was even more bewildered. How could he know about that? How could he even know about Corotocus's deception? Word of the disaster would travel, but she had come straight here, walking stiff and lame like one dead, but tarrying neither to talk with folk nor to look back over her shoulder. She'd taken short routes through dark woods and hidden valleys that were known only to a chosen few. As her anger ebbed, the countess was increasingly aware of the mystery in this strange, subterranean realm. Its ceiling was speckled with a million tiny lights, like stars in a miniature cosmos. The images on the walls appeared to have moved or changed since she had first seen them. The air was heavy with intoxicating fragrance.

"M-my daughter is all that matters to me," she stammered. "I won't stand by and allow her to be abducted."

"And yet there's nothing you can do. Most of your own warriors went to serve Madog or Anwyl... and now lie slain."

"Can you help me?"

"Ahhh, so we get to the crux of it."

"Don't play games with me, Gwyddon! You know why I'm here."

"It will cost you."

"Cost me?"

"We have no country, Countess Madalyn. No sense of people. Your plight is unfortunate, but of no great concern to us. If your nation was driven en masse to the chopping block and beheaded one by one, my chief regret would be the waste of so much sacrificial blood."

"And how much will it cost me?" She appraised the gold moon-crescent pendant on his breast, the gem-encrusted rings on his fingers, the silver dragon-head pin clasping his robe. "I'd imagine the greater the supplicant, the higher the price?"

"How much do you offer, countess?"

"If you can guarantee the safe return of my daughter..." She faltered briefly, but steeled herself. "If you can guarantee the safe return of my daughter, and the destruction of Earl Corotocus... I will give you half my wealth, half my lands. And protection for you and your sect for as long as there's breath in my body."

He smiled thinly. "Not enough."

At first Countess Madalyn thought she'd misheard. Only in fables and folklore had such a reward been offered.

"Not nearly enough," he added.

"You ask me to beggar myself?"

"I ask nothing of the kind. You can keep your earthly goods, if they mean so much to you."

"In God's name, what do you want?"

He pursed his lips, which, now that she was close to him, looked redder than blood. "No more, countess, and no less than an equal share in the power your victory will bring."

"Power? I seek only the return of my daughter."

"And the destruction of an English marcher lord."

"I only ask that because I know I'll have no choice."

"Countess Madalyn, you will have no choice come what may. If Earl Corotocus dies they'll send someone else, and you'll need to destroy him as well. And the one after that. And the one after that."

"What are you asking... that I start a full-scale war?"

"How many more of your villages must they burn? How many people must they hang? Full-scale war is already upon you."

"The uprising has been crushed with horrendous loss of life. If I were to start another now, it would mean an apocalypse for Wales and its people."

"Your people need only a leader – a proper leader. Someone fearless and respected. You could fill that role, countess. Just as Boudicca did twelve centuries ago. The difference is that, unlike Boudicca, you will have me – and I will ensure that the apocalypse falls on England."

"How?" she asked.

"Allow me to show you."

CHAPTER FIVE

DOCTOR ZACHARIUS WAS born the younger son of a wealthy merchant in Bristol.

Initially, he did not promise much, though this only lasted a short time. Despite an indolent youth and an alarming lack of interest in the family shipwright business, he soon showed an aptitude for learning. In response to this, his father sent him to a monastery, so that he could train for the priesthood. But, in various ways, Zacharius blotted his copybook with the holy fathers, and, after much soul-searching, his father took him out of the Lord's care and paid for him to attend the medical school of St. Gridewilde's at Oxford University.

The beneficiary of a generous stipend, Zacharius here became a renowned frequenter of taverns and brothels, but at the same time embarked, at last, on a serious course of study. He was fortunate in that his personal tutor, a Franciscan friar, who had once been a devoted student of Canon Grosseteste, taught medicine without mysticism and introduced Zacharius to a Latin translation of the

Kitab al-Tasrif, an Islamic treatise dedicated to the science of surgery, an in-depth analysis of which, though he didn't realise it at the time, would raise the young medical student far above the level of the common garden barber-surgeons, whose butcher-shop clumsiness had given the surgical arts so bad a name for so many decades. Zacharius was so inspired by this venerable tome that, on completion of his studies, he paid from his own pocket to have a personal copy made.

His first position after graduation was with the Premonstratensian abbey-hospital at Titchfield, in Hampshire, where, though he was regarded as an all-round skilled practitioner, he particularly excelled with the surgeon's knife. When a novice at the abbey – a nephew of the abbot no less – was brought in from the fields with a severely broken leg, Zacharius, taking his cue from the Kitab al-Tasrif, performed a delicate invasive operation, opening the damaged limb cleanly, repairing the shattered bone, then sewing the wound up and applying splints, and all while the casualty was insensible through a herbal-induced anaesthesia. Within a few months, the novice had completely recovered, with almost no ill effects.

The abbot was so impressed that he spread the word, until it reached the ear of his cousin, Earl Corotocus of Clun, who was in search of a medical expert of his own. When Earl Corotocus offered him a post, Zacharius at first resisted. His cell at Titchfield Abbey was different from those of the monks, who were given to asceticism – he had a carpet, a divan, a roaring fire, tapestries on his walls, shelves lined with books. Compared with this luxury, life in a military environment was not so attractive. But, of course, there were still certain things that Zacharius could not have at Titchfield, which Earl Corotocus could provide in abundance, primarily wine, women and song.

For these reasons alone, and no others, he finally joined the earl's household. Of course, not everybody approved.

"Why are you preparing your infirmary in the open air?" Father Benan wondered.

On Zacharius's instruction, servants had now helped Henri move barrels of water and sacks of grain from several outhouses in the central courtyard in order to make space for beds, though these outhouses were little more than straw-thatched shelters with neither walls nor doors to keep out drafts.

Zacharius glanced up from where he'd laid out a central table and was in the process of arraying his instruments. "My dear Benan, the rooms in this fortress are noisome and stuffy..."

"It's Father Benan," the priest interrupted.

Zacharius smiled to himself. "If any patients are admitted to my infirmary while we're here, Father Benan, the best thing they can have is fresh air."

"But it's only March. And it's cold."

"In which case we bed them with warm blankets and place braziers filled with hot coals alongside them."

Benan chewed his lip uncertainly. He was a youngish man, but plump, with a pink face and, despite his shaved cranial tonsure, long, white-blonde hair cut square across the fringe. Though he mistrusted scientists in general, and Zacharius in particular, he secretly shared the doctor's penchant for foppery and good living. Even now, in the midst of a war, he wore white silk gloves adorned with his rings of office, and a white silk tabard over his hooded black robe.

"You don't intend to open a hospital for local sick people?" he asked.

Zacharius laughed. He well knew Benan's 'High Church' views on this sort of thing – namely that it was important to alleviate suffering wherever possible, but that pestilence was God's punishment for sinfulness, and that to combat it could be seen as a form of heresy. On previous campaigns, in an effort to win the hearts and minds of a local populace, Earl Corotocus had thrown Zacharius's service open to local peasants and villagers, at his own expense – much to Father Benan's chagrin.

"My question was a genuine one," the priest said.

"So was my response," the doctor replied. "You think after what we've done in this land, anyone would come here? Even if their bowels were riddled with worms, their limbs rotted with leprosy?"

Benan chewed his lip. There was no riposte to so valid a point. He eyed Zacharius's surgical instruments. Apparently the doctor had commissioned their manufacture himself, again paying out of his own private funds. They included forceps, a scalpel, a bone-saw, a curette, a retractor, and a curved needle. To Benan's eye, they looked less like instruments of medicine and more like implements of torture. Of course, in his heart of hearts, he knew that Zacharius meant well, despite his lecherous proclivities, and that these menacing items had no more to do with the Devil and heresy than the swords and spears wielded by the earl and his soldiers, but these were confusing times to be a priest.

"I hope you have cause to treat no-one while we are posted in this castle," he finally said.

Zacharius shrugged. "So do I. But for different reasons than you, I think."

Benan was affronted. "My concern for the welfare of men's souls is more important than your concern for the welfare of their bodies."

"That is a higher philosophy, Father Benan, that many of your fellow clerics no longer share." Zacharius fixed him with a frank stare. "First of all, the Church itself educated me in these arts. The Franciscans at Oxford encouraged me all the way. At Titchfield it was the same. But even among those few who objected, it's amazing how quickly a man's principles can be put aside when he himself comes down with a sickness."

As always, Father Benan left Zacharius's company frustrated rather than irked, nervous rather than righteous. He returned to the castle chapel, which was located beneath the kitchen, and sandwiched between the barrack house and the Great Hall. As befitted a functional military outpost, it was little more than a subterranean chamber, built from bare, grey stone and austere in that typical Norman style. The altar table itself was a slab of granite. The pews were stiff, wooden things, embellished neither with carving nor cushion. There was no presbytery here, not even a sleeping compartment containing bedding. He'd seen no altar cloths, no silver candlesticks, no precious vessels of any sort; no doubt, if there had been some they were now in the grasp of the Bretons or the Welsh.

The contrast between this place and his sumptuous residence at the earl's great castle on the River Severn near Shrewsbury could not have been more marked. There, he had had a huge four-poster bed with blankets of feather down, servants at his beck and call, good food, good wine, silver plates to dine off if he wished. The chapel there was lined with white plaster and inlaid with frescoes telling tales from the Bible. There were statues on pedestals, holy inscriptions in the footways. The thuribles and chalices were of white gold; the altar was bathed daily in the reflection of a huge stained glass window, which depicted the Saviour ascending to a deep blue heaven, his noble brow crowned with roses.

What did Benan have for a window here?

A cruciform slit high in the east wall, through which sunlight might occasionally find its way, though only via a series of connecting shafts. Even during daytime it provided almost no illumination.

The dour environment matched the priest's mood. Yet again, he knelt at the altar and prayed for guidance, though he was increasingly worried that this was a vain hope. Earl Corotocus, though a valued member of the royal court and a steadfast defender of the faith, was a cruel and violent man. He kept a great house and ran orderly estates, he undertook the most dangerous missions in the name of his king, but there was nothing Christian in the way he conducted his campaigns – they lacked both chivalry and magnanimity; he was rarely generous to those he defeated. Not only that, he employed a man like Zacharius, whose sins were deemed tolerable because of his uses, and yet whose uses were also of questionable virtue. And, of course, Benan himself was no saint, no martyr. He hung his head in shame as he prayed. He never spoke out against the earl's excesses. He rarely questioned Zacharius any more for fear that the doctor's glib tongue would tie him in intellectual knots.

The earl's army was in a poor moral state right now, Benan reflected. They had crushed the Welsh easily, without losing a single man, without incurring so much as a minor flesh wound. That had seemed very unlikely given the initial circumstances of this uprising. A number of English-held castles had been besieged or, in the cases of Hawarden, Ruthin, Denbigh and

Grogen, captured. The town of Caerphilly had been burnt to the ground. To have then entered the fray and triumphed so easily, it was tempting to say that God was on the side of Earl Corotocus. But deep down inside, Benan had a nagging fear – based as much on common sense as on clerical instinct – that the exact opposite was true. And that God would very soon prove this.

CHAPTER SIX

"Countess Madalyn, what do you know of the Thirteen Treasures of Britain?"

At first the countess was too distracted to respond. They had emerged onto a barren hillside. After the green fog of the cave, she was disoriented by the glaring daylight. There was also a stiff, raw breeze. It wasn't as bitingly cold as it had been earlier, but her body ached with fatigue and she hunched under her fleece.

"Thirteen Treasures?" she said. "Artefacts... artefacts from myth?"

"Not myth, my lady... history." Gwyddon strode on. "Wondrous weapons of war gathered by the founder of my order, Myrlyn, as protection for Britain after Rome's legions were withdrawn. Yet, one by one, in the darkness and chaos of those strife-torn ages, all of them were lost. All except one. This one."

He came to a halt. Countess Madalyn halted alongside him.

In front of them, a large circular vat made from something like beaten copper was sitting on a pile of burning logs. Two younger priests used poles to stir the concoction bubbling inside it. There was a noxious smell – it was sickening, reminiscent of burning dung. Foul, brackish smoke rose from the vat in a turgid column. When the countess came closer, she saw a brown, soup-like liquid, all manner of vile things swimming around inside it. At this proximity, its hot, rank fumes were almost overpowering.

"This effluent?" she said. "This filth...?"

"Not the filth," Gwyddon replied. "The thing that contains it."

"A cauldron?"

"Not just any cauldron. You've heard of Cymedai?"

She looked sharply round at him.

He smiled. "I see that you have."

"This is the Cauldron of Regeneration? But that is only a legend."

"Certain details concerning its origins are legend. Not all."

She appraised the cauldron again. There were no eldritch carvings around its rim, as she might have expected, no images or inscriptions on its tarnished sides. It looked ordinary, in fact less than that. It might have been something she'd find covered in cobwebs in a cellar or the cluttered corner of an apothecary's shop.

"It was never the property of two ogres living in a bottomless lake," Gwyddon said. "Its creators were never roasted alive in an iron building that was actually a giant oven. But there is some truth in the story. It was brought here from Ireland to keep it from the Irish king Matholwch, who sought it for his own. Once in Britain, it was given to the care of Bendigeidfran, who was slain resisting the Irish invaders. It was, as the bards tell us, broken in that fight, but it was later repaired and hidden again. For centuries its whereabouts remained a mystery, until Myrlyn located it. Since then, it has passed from one generation of our order to the next, always in safekeeping."

He spoke fondly, and with his usual eloquence. But Countess Madalyn was fast becoming weary.

"I come to you with a genuine grievance, Gwyddon. I offer you a fabulous reward. And you mock me with this!"

"Mock you, countess?"

"Both you and I know that this is some harmless cooking pot."

"Indeed?"

He clapped his hands, and a young slave stepped forward. It was one of those who had served Countess Madalyn earlier. In full daylight, she identified him as a boy, though, by his cadaverous face, emaciated frame and the brand-mark on his forehead, which looked to have festered before it finally healed, servitude had been cruel to him. The mere sight of the wretched creature touched her motherly nature. Christendom forbade human slavery, and now she understood why.

Gwyddon, of course, had no such scruples. Reaching under his robe, he drew out a bright, curved blade and plunged it into the slave's breast, driving it to the hilt, and twisting it so that ribs cracked. Blood spurted from the slave's mouth. He sagged backward on his heels, but only when the blade was yanked free did he drop to the ground.

For a long moment Countess Madalyn was too aghast to speak.

"Have I... ?" she eventually asked, her voice thick with disgust. "Have I quit the company of one devil only to be wooed by another?"

"Everything I do has a purpose, countess."

"Everything Earl Corotocus does has purpose..."

"Wait and you will see."

Gwyddon signalled and one of the acolytes from the cauldron came forth with a ladle. Gwyddon took it, knelt, and carefully drizzled brown fluid over the slave's twisted features. When the ladle was empty, he handed it back, rose and retreated a few steps, all the time making some strange utterance under his breath.

Nothing happened.

"Master druid," the countess said. "As a Christian woman, I cannot..."

He hissed at her to be silent, pointing at the fresh-made corpse.

To her disbelief, she saw a flicker of movement.

Though the blood still pulsing from its chest wound darkened and thickened as the beat of its heart faltered and slowed, the body itself was beginning to stir. There was no rise and fall of breast as the lungs re-inflated; the eyes remained sightless orbs

– unblinking, devoid of lustre. But there was no denying it; the slave was struggling back into a ghastly parody of life.

First it sat upright, very stiffly and awkwardly. Then it climbed to its feet with jolting, jerking motions, more like a marionette than a human being. The undernourished creature had been stick-thin and ash-pale before, but its complexion had now faded to an even ghostlier hue. Its mouth, still slathered with gore, hung slackly open.

Gwyddon's acolytes muttered together in awe. The chief druid himself seemed shaken. He licked his ruby lips. Sweat gleamed on his brow.

The corpse stood there unassisted, as if awaiting some diabolic command.

At length, Gwyddon came out of this daze and snapped his fingers. An acolyte rushed forward with a towel so that he could wipe his crimson spattered hands.

"This... this is not possible," Countess Madalyn stuttered, circling the grotesque figure. "How can he have survived such a wound?"

"He didn't," Gwyddon said. "He's as dead as the iron that slew him."

She waved a hand in front of the slave's eyes – they didn't so much as blink. Gingerly, she prodded him with a finger. Even through his blood-drenched tunic, she could tell that his flesh was cooling. She prodded again, harder – the slave rocked but remained upright, staring fixedly ahead.

"This is hellish madness," she breathed.

"This is the Cauldron of Regeneration," Gwyddon said. "As the Mabinogion states, it makes warriors of the slain."

"Warriors? This vegetable! This mindless thing!"

"Could he be more perfect for the task? He'll follow any order, no matter how fearful. He'll feel no pain, no matter how agonising. He'll commit any deed, no matter how atrocious."

"And he can't be killed?"

"Countess, what is already dead cannot die a second time."

"I don't believe you. This is druid trickery."

Gwyddon regarded her icily, and then re-drew his curved blade and spun back to face the slave. With a single overhand blow he hacked into the fellow's neck, not just once, but twice, thrice, in fact over and over, cleaving through the sinew. The countess stumbled backward, a hand to her gagging mouth. But Gwyddon hacked harder and harder, blood and meat sprinkling his robes, blow after butchering blow shearing through tissue and artery and, at last, with a crunch, through the spinal column itself.

With a thud, the head fell to the ground.

The slave remained standing. From his feet, his own face peered upwards, locked in the grimace of death, yet somehow with a semblance of life.

Even after everything she'd been exposed to, Countess Madalyn was nauseated, faint with horror. Only amazement at the seeming miracle and the importance of retaining her aristocratic bearing kept her from running shrieking. Again, she circled the mangled figure, though it took her some time to gather coherent thoughts. Enormous but terrible possibilities were presenting themselves to her.

"If he's a warrior, why didn't he try to resist you?" she asked.

Gwyddon found a clean corner of the towel, and dabbed it at the blood dotting his face. "I raised him, and therefore I am his master. He will not attack me. He cannot attack me."

"If this is true, why have you waited so long to bring this weapon to our notice?"

He shook his head at such a foolish question. "Whose side should I have rewarded with it? The Norman-English, who covet Welsh land and seek to make serfs of its people? Or the Welsh and Irish, whose Celtic Christianity is a harder, more barbarous brand than anything found east of Offa's Dyke."

She turned to face him. "So why give it to us now?"

"I don't give it to you."

"Why do you offer it?"

"As I say... now the Welsh have a figurehead. Someone who isn't driven merely by lust for plunder, like Gruffud. Or by personal ambition, like Madog."

"And, of course, someone who is sympathetic to the old ways?"

"Of course. After what you've witnessed today, how can you fail to be?"

Countess Madalyn looked again at the mutilated slave. She knew she was viewing something that couldn't be, yet her eyes did not deceive her. Even truncated, with his head at his feet, he stood rigid to attention. She prodded his chest, his back, his shoulder. He remained standing. She circled him again to ensure there wasn't a pole at his back.

"You've resurrected a murdered slave, Gwyddon," she finally said. "An impressive feat of magic. But can this thing on its own – this ruined, headless cadaver – prevail against Corotocus's knights? Can it resist his slings and catapults?"

"It won't be on its own."

"And how long will it take to raise an army of these horrors, with one cauldron, and one potion? This thing will have rotted to its bones before you're finished. In God's name, we'll all have rotted to our bones."

"Normally perhaps," Gwyddon said. "But I think we're all about to benefit from a change of season. There's a hint of spring in the air, wouldn't you say?"

Two more of Gwyddon's acolytes now approached the cauldron with sticks and stirred its contents vigorously. Thicker, even more noxious fumes swam into the air. Gwyddon tracked their upwards path. The sky was pregnant with grey cloud, much of it already tainted by the smoke that had risen steadily since the brew was first heated. The countess recalled her earlier thoughts that the wintry chill had lessened, that the frost was melting – and now the first drops of rain began to fall. Polluted rain, as was clear from the brown smears it left on the druids' white robes. Rain which, when she cupped it in the palm of her hand, looked and smelled like ditch water.

A bolt of lightning suddenly split the sky over Plynlimon; thunder throbbed like a thousand battle-drums. The rainfall intensified until it was teeming, a waterfall pouring from Heaven. Gwyddon's acolytes fled to find shelter, but not Gwyddon himself. He was lost in a reverie of prayer, his arms crossed over his breast, a clenched fist at either shoulder. His eyes were closed, his broad, bearded face written with ecstasy as the water streamed from it.

*　　*　　*

The rain didn't just fall over Powys; it fell all over north and central Wales, thrashing on mountain, forest and valley.

The narrows tracks linking the region's hamlets had already been churned to quagmires by the passing of Earl Corotocus's army, but now became rivers of slurry. The charred shells of the cottages and crofts shuddered and sank in the deluge. Those Welsh who'd survived the earl's passing hid, weeping and gibbering, under any cover they could find. And those who hadn't survived, those whose ragged forms adorned the gibbets and gallows on every road and ridge to the English border, started twisting and jerking in their bonds. To the north, on the tragic field of Maes Moydog, the mountain of Welsh corpses, cut and riven and steeped in blood and ordure, was also washed by the rain – and slowly and surely began to twitch and judder. In the chapel graveyards – even those graveyards that were long abandoned and overgrown – the topsoil broke and shifted as the rain seeped through it and the green, rotted forms crammed underneath slowly clawed their way out.

CHAPTER SEVEN

THE SKIES OVER Grogen Castle were black with swollen clouds. Torrents of rain poured, drenching the mighty walls, flooding the walks and gutters. Even indoors there was no respite. Cold, wet wind gusted through the rooms and tunnels, groaning in the chimneys, extinguishing candles, whipping the flames in the guardroom hearths. Rainwater dripped from every fault and fissure.

In the Keep it was too dark almost to find one's way. Ranulf ascended from one level to the next, with a loaf, a bundle of blankets and a water-skin under his right arm. In his left hand he carried a flaring candelabra; an oil-lamp hung from his belt. He added a little fuel to each wall-sconce he passed and put a candle flame to it, creating a lighted passage, though all this really did was expose the cockroaches scurrying across the damp flagstones and the bats hanging from the arched ceilings like clusters of furry fruit.

When he unlocked the door to the cell it was so heavy that he had to heave it open. Gwendolyn was sitting in a far corner, knees clasped to her chest, her back rigid. The only window was a high slot, too narrow for a human to pass through, and deeply recessed – it must have been ten feet from the start of its embrasure to the finish. Even in bright sunshine, it admitted minimal light.

"I've brought you this," he said, placing the lantern at the foot of the steps, and lighting it with a candle. "I'll replenish the oil every so often."

Gwendolyn didn't reply. She looked pale, her pretty features smudged with dirt and tears. Her hair, once like spun copper, hung in grimy rat-tails.

"I've also bought you these." He laid the blankets down, walked over and offered her the loaf and the water-skin. She still said nothing, gazing directly ahead as if seeing neither him nor his gifts.

"You need to eat, my lady."

"My lady?" She seemed surprised, before giving a cackling laugh. "I see your bachelry still deceives itself with Arthurian pretension?"

"You need to eat."

Reluctantly, she took the bread and water. At first she only nibbled, but soon capitulated to her hunger, tearing the loaf apart with her teeth and fingers. Ranulf glanced around the cell. The filthy straw gave it the stench of a stable. Water ran down its black brickwork. Having seen the quarters allocated to the men in the barrack house, there were few facilities at Grogen that were much of an improvement on this. Though of course the men hadn't been violently abducted, stripped naked, beaten and sexually assaulted.

"I don't suppose..." he said. "I don't suppose it would do any good to apologise?"

She looked up at him, again surprised. "On behalf of whom – yourself, or the bloodstained madman you serve?"

Ranulf wasn't sure how to respond.

"Let me spare you the trauma of trying to answer," she said. "You're right, it won't do any good."

"I'm not happy about what's happened here."

Ranulf wasn't quite sure why he'd admitted that. Before coming up into the Keep, his father had reminded him that the girl was nothing more to them than a prisoner, the spoils of war, a pawn in a greater game. It was unfortunate for her, but there were always winners and losers in the politics of strife. Ulbert had concluded by strongly advising that whatever was going to happen to Lady Gwendolyn would happen, and that their first duty was to themselves and their family name. They mustn't allow "futile sentiment" to endanger their cause.

Yet, if the prisoner was aware that Ranulf had taken a risk expressing sympathy to her, she was unimpressed.

"I'm sure your unhappiness will be great consolation to those who've died," she said. "Or who've been maimed, or left destitute."

"I understand your anger. Earl Corotocus is a pitiless man."

"And those who willingly serve him? What are they?"

"We don't all serve him willingly."

She smiled, almost maliciously. "Spare me your conscience, sir knight. If it's torturing you, I'm glad. You'll find no absolution here."

"To make things easier, I can only suggest that you comply with the earl's wishes." He retreated towards the door. "No matter how distasteful you find them."

"Comply with the earl's wishes? I think you mistake me for someone else. I will do no such thing, not least because in a very short time the earl and you murderers he calls his retainers will all be dead." Ranulf waited by the door as she laughed at him. "You think this fortress will protect you, Englishman? Welsh vengeance is about to fall on you people with a force you can't imagine."

"Your spirit does you credit, my lady. But don't hang your hopes on how easily the previous garrison here was overwhelmed. To call them 'foolish sots' would be an insult to both fools and sots. Earl Corotocus is of a different mettle; a monster yes, but a soldier through and through. His mesnie has been hardened by battle over many years. In addition, they're nearly all English-born. From birth, they've been raised to view the Welsh as the foe over the mountain, as an enemy existing purely to be crushed."

"Foe over the mountain?" Like many who obsess that they are oppressed, Gwendolyn found it difficult to grasp the concept that her oppressors might feel they acted from a just cause. "What have my people ever done to you? *You* are the aggressors! You always have been!"

"When I was a child, miss, I lived on the shore of the River Wye." Ranulf mused. "I grew up hearing stories of how Prince Gruffud burned Hereford, the capital city of that region, and slew its entire population."

"That was nearly two-hundred years ago."

"King Edward has learned from the mistakes his forebears made. He won't tolerate hostile states on his borders."

"We're not hostile to you."

"Even neutral states must be viewed as hostile. Better to have a wasteland at your door than a tribe of barbarians whose loyalty your enemies can buy for a few cattle." He shrugged. "At least, that's the king's view."

"By the sound of it, it's a view you share."

"I understand the reasoning, even if I disapprove of the methods."

"Well in that you've set me a good example." She smiled coldly. "When my kinsmen get hold of you, forgive me if I understand their anger and merely disapprove when they tear you apart between their horses."

There was a sudden echo of voices from the passage. Ranulf withdrew from the cell, closing the door and locking it. At the next corner, he met Navarre carrying a flaming torch, and one of Garbofasse's mercenaries.

"Where did you put the Welsh slut?" Navarre asked.

"Who needs to know?" Ranulf said.

"Murlock needs to know, if he's to look after her."

Ranulf looked at the mercenary properly. Murlock was a brutal, bearded hulk, several inches taller than most men, his massive, ape-like frame crammed inside a steel-studded leather hauberk.

When he grinned, fang-like teeth showed through a mass of dirty, crumb-filled whiskers.

"You're no longer the official jailer here, FitzOsbern," Navarre explained. "I thought you'd be pleased – one less onerous duty for you."

"And this whoreson is taking over?"

"The earl asked Captain Garbofasse for a man whose special skills fitted the task. Garbofasse nominated Murlock."

In the Welsh villages Corotocus had attacked en route from the Ogryn Valley, Garbofasse's mercenaries had taken a lead role in terrorising the populace; setting fire to cottage roofs, slaughtering animals in their pens and raping women and girls. Murlock, for one, had barely been able to keep his breeches laced. But he hadn't just raped them, he'd sodomised them, he'd beaten and kicked them, and made them watch as he'd personally tied the halters around the necks of their husbands, brothers, fathers and sons, and hoisted them up until they swung and kicked in the smoke-filled air.

Ranulf fixed Navarre with a disbelieving stare. "Are you out of your mind?"

"Are you out of yours, FitzOsbern? I wouldn't like to report that you've objected to yet another of the earl's orders."

"This boor... this animal, will *hurt* her."

Navarre shook his head soberly. "No. He's under orders to be gentle."

Murlock gave a snorting, pig-like chuckle, and Ranulf launched himself forward, grabbing the fellow by the Adam's apple and slamming him back against the wall.

In the same second, the tip of Navarre's dagger was at Ranulf's throat.

"Yield now!" Navarre snarled. "Right now, or I'll slice you open like a pear."

Ranulf didn't yield; not at first. He leaned on Murlock harder, mailed hands clenched on his windpipe, squeezing. Murlock's breath was caught in his throat. He couldn't breathe, yet he was grinning. His teeth showed like rotten pegs; his piggy eyes had narrowed to murderous little slits.

"You think I won't?" Navarre said. "I warn you, FitzOsbern... you know the earl likes nothing better than to make an example of one of his own. Nothing has made him more feared."

Ranulf finally stepped back, glistening with sweat, breathing hard. Gasping, Murlock sank to his haunches.

"You're swimming against a tide that will overwhelm you, boy," Navarre said, withdrawing his blade.

Ranulf turned and stalked down the fire-lit passage.

"FitzOsbern!" Navarre called after him.

Ranulf was ten yards away when he glanced back.

"The key, FitzOsbern! A cell door is no use without its key."

Ranulf took a long, heavy key from his pouch and dangled it from his fingers. "Come and get it."

Murlock lurched along the passage. He reached for the key and Ranulf dropped it into his palm, but then grabbed his wrist, yanked him forward and met him on the point of the chin with a club-like fist. Murlock was hurled sideways, caromed from the wall and collapsed to the floor, where Ranulf kicked him in the guts, dropped onto him with his knees and pounded his head and face, knocking out his teeth and smashing his nose like an over-ripe plum.

"That was nothing personal," Ranulf hissed into Murlock's ear. "Just a lesson I learned at the abbey school in Leominster. Prior Barnabus taught it us each morning with a willow switch – in case we transgressed during the day and he wasn't around to witness it. So be warned, you harm a single hair on that girl's head and this isn't even a hint of what awaits you."

Ranulf straightened up, kicked the fallen mercenary once more, for good measure, and glanced around. Navarre was watching intently, his mouth frozen in a half-snarl.

"Don't look so outraged, Navarre. I gave him the key, didn't I?"

CHAPTER EIGHT

EARL COROTOCUS'S MILITARY might was the envy of his fellow magnates.

As controller of a troubled corner of the kingdom, he already had rights to maintain armed forces that went far beyond his normal feudal obligations. In addition to this, as one of the foremost barons of the realm, descended in direct line from Roland la Hors, one of the original Norman warlords who'd descended on England like a pack of rapacious wolves in 1066, he had greater influence than most and even greater wealth. His estate comprised innumerable fiefs, castles, honours and titles, every one of which could be used to generate additional soldiery and military funding. Very quickly and perfectly legally, he could put a private army into the field that was almost of a size to challenge the king himself. The warriors he had at Grogen were only its spear-tip.

He was also a student of the most modern methods. Where Earl Corotocus was concerned, battle could no longer be left to the wild chance of heroic charge over level field, nor a single combat between picked champions. Though both the Church and the knightly code frowned on him for it, he had an avowed belief in the usefulness of irregular forces, in hit and run raids, in assassinations and ambushes. His personal household was supplemented with warriors drawn from far beyond his demesnes. Not trusting exclusively to such fanciful, out of date devices as homage and fealty, the earl would willingly take scutage from those less able of his vassals, and use it to obtain quality swords and lances from much further a-field. Hence the presence in his mesnie of paid war-dogs like Navarre, originally from the Aquitaine, and the employment of free-companies like Garbofasse's band who came from all parts of the country and were largely felons and cutthroats.

Yet the most feared section of the earl's military power was provided neither by knights nor mercenaries, but by machines. He'd long studied Greek, Roman and Saracen documents brought back from the East. He'd read detailed books written by the master siege-breaker Geoffrey Plantagenet, and now regarded machines not just as the key to destroying enemy citadels and strongholds, but as the ideal means to inflict vast casualties on enemy forces. Even before his campaign in Gascony, where the fighting was so bitter that all rules of gallantry were dispensed with, Corotocus had been collecting these monstrous contraptions – sling-throwers, ballistae, arbalests – either capturing them, purchasing them or having them custom-built. He now possessed three mangonels that any king or emperor would have been pleased to have in his arsenal, and which he'd christened *War Wolf*, *God's Maul* and *Giant's Fist*. These were gigantic counterweight catapults, which could hurl immense grenades fashioned from rock, lead or iron over huge distances. He'd also acquired a scoop-thrower, similarly designed to the mangonels, but with a broad bucket for discharging masses of smaller projectiles such as fire-pots or heaps of chain and rubble.

All of these siege engines, and many others like them, were now en route to Grogen Castle, disassembled and packaged in over a hundred wagons, travelling west along the Tefeidiad

Valley. The earl had initially summoned them because he'd expected that he'd need heavy weapons to strike the castle walls. In the event, they were no longer a necessity, but it had seemed sensible that the equipment should still be brought. Of course this hadn't allowed for the weather.

It was now late at night and the rain had ceased, only to be replaced by a cold, wraithlike mist. The forest tracks had turned to quagmires and, with loaded wagons sinking to their axels and horses to their fetlocks, progress was torturously slow. The infantry guarding the artillery train were also having trouble. Each man carried his personal supply pack in addition to being well armed and wearing a thick mail hauberk. Thus heavily burdened, they'd been marching three days, were already footsore and exhausted, and now had liquid mud to contend with. While it was misty between the trees, the sky had cleared so it was also ice-cold. Men and horses' breath smoked as they trudged along. Every piece of clothing was wringing wet. Every boot or shoe squelched. The black mud coated everything.

Two men were perched on the driving bench of the foremost wagon: Hugo d'Avranches, a portly old knight, who served as quartermaster at Linley Castle – one of the earl's smaller bastions, but the place where the bulk of his artillery was usually stored – and Brother Ignatius, a young Benedictine, who served as Hugo's clerk. Another of the earl's knights, Reynald Guiscard, famous for his quick temper and mane of fiery-red hair, but prized for his self-taught skills as an engineer, came cantering up from the rear.

"God's blood, d'Avranches!" he bawled. "How could you bring us along a road like this? The wagons are tailing back for miles."

These weren't the first angry words they'd exchanged in the last few hours. Brother Ignatius sighed, anticipating yet another loud, futile argument.

"Do you think there are any proper roads through this wretched country?" d'Avranches growled.

"You should have found something better than this! The earl gave you maps!"

"I can't read a bloody map in the bloody dark and the bloody pouring rain!"

"No, and you're too old and bloody blind to read one in the bloody daylight as well, aren't you! But you're too worried about keeping your precious position to let anyone bloody know about it!"

"Name of a name!" d'Avranches swore. "I'll not be spoken to like that! Come near me, my lad, and you'll feel my gauntlet!"

Both men were among the highest ranking in the earl's circle of tenant knights, each sporting the prized black eagle crest on his crimson livery, but they rarely saw eye-to-eye. Guiscard leaned forward from his saddle, deliberately putting himself in swatting range.

"If you'd given as much effort to watching what you were doing, Hugo, as you do to talking out of your backside, we wouldn't be in this predicament!"

"I'll not be blamed for the weather!" d'Avranches howled. "You blasted tyke!"

"My lords, please," Brother Ignatius said as patiently as he could. "Please. We can't be more than five or six miles from the castle."

"Except that we're on the wrong side of the river," Guiscard retorted. "Because this dolt insisted on fording it back at Nucklas."

D'Avranches swore and brandished his whip. "The earl's first message said that it was best to travel south of the Tefeidiad because the bulk of the rebel forces were north of it!"

"And his second message detailed the Earl of Warwick's victory at Maes Moydog," Guiscard replied, "and his own victory at Ogryn Valley. They're beaten, for Christ's sake!"

D'Avranches grunted, unable to deny this.

As the earl's official quartermaster, his priority was always to protect the heavy weapons. Corotocus had once said: "If men's lives are forfeit, it's a sacrifice I must live with. Men can be replaced. My mangonels cannot!" But on this occasion d'Avranches knew that he'd been over-cautious. Now on the south side of the Tefeidiad, the next point at which they could ford the river again was a good five miles west of Grogen Castle. Which meant they weren't five miles from their destination, as Brother Ignatius had suggested, but more like fifteen. In addition, there was still the possibility that, after the afternoon's rainstorm, the river level would have risen and the ford might not be useable for some considerable time.

"Maybe we should camp here?" Ignatius said.

Guiscard glanced around. He'd been thinking the same, but wasn't happy at the prospect. The wagon train snaked far back through the darkness, making the erection of even a temporary stockade impossible. They were in a forest, but ironically there wasn't much cover. High ground rose to the south and sloped away to the north, but it was thinly treed.

"Up to our knees in sludge and dung," d'Avranches complained. "It'll hardly make for a comfortable night."

"If the Welsh are beaten, there's nothing to stop us lighting fires," Ignatius said.

Guiscard was undecided. He wheeled his horse about. They were still relatively close to the English border, but there was something about this place he didn't like. The woods were eerily silent even for March. There wasn't a hint of wind, so the mist hung in motionless cauls between the black pillars of the trees.

"Is there a delay, my lord?" came a gruff but tired voice. It was Master-Serjeant Gam, who'd plodded up from the rear.

"Aye," Guiscard said. "Send the word. We bivouac here."

"Here, my lord?" The seasoned old soldier sounded surprised.

"I doubt we'll find anywhere better on this road. Tell the men to pitch their tents among the trees, but in circles, with thorn switches for cover. Draw lots – one in every ten to stand on guard duty. Four-hour shifts. Make sure you find decent picket points, Gam. We don't know that the enemy's *completely* defeated yet."

The serjeant nodded and stumped away, only for Ignatius to suddenly point and shout. "Ho!"

They glanced south, to where the silver disc of the moon hung beyond the ridge. Two twisted tree trunks were framed against it.

"I thought I saw something," Ignatius said. "*Someone.*"

"Someone?" Guiscard asked.

"He was against the moon. Coming over the rise."

"Probably a stag," d'Avranches said.

"It was a man. Look... *another!*"

This time they all saw the figure. It was tall, rail-thin, and it came quickly over the rise and descended through the darkness towards them. Another followed it, moving jerkily. This one too vanished into the murk. The crackling of wet undergrowth could be heard as the figures drew closer.

"Beggars?" d'Avranches said.

"In the middle of a war?" Guiscard replied. His gloved hand stole to the hilt of his longsword.

"Refugees?"

"And they'd approach an English baggage-train?"

"We should have sent outriders," Ignatius said in a small voice.

"When we give alms to the poor, you can tend to *our* business," d'Avranches advised him. "We'd have lost all contact with outriders in that storm."

"No, he's right," Guiscard said. His voice rose as he spied another two or three figures ascend over the rise. "We should have sent outriders. *Alarum! Alarum! Master-Serjeant, your trumpeter if you pleee...*"

His words ended in a hoarse shout, as he was dragged from his saddle.

D'Avranches and Ignatius were at first too startled to respond. Guiscard shouted incoherently as he wrestled with someone in the muddy ditch on the north side of the road – which, it occurred to them, meant that danger was not just threatening from one side, but from *both*.

Ignatius now spied flurries of movement ahead of them. The point-footman, who'd been carrying a lantern on a pole as he marched at the front of the column, had been knocked from his feet. The pole stood upright in the mud, its lamp swinging wildly, only partly revealing two ragged shapes that were setting about the footman like wolves on a carcass.

"Good God!" d'Avranches said, focussing on dozens of forms suddenly streaming through the misty woods towards them.

Cries began sounding along the road behind. A carrion stench pervaded the entire column. Ignatius stood up and peered back. It was difficult to tell what was happening, but figures seemed to be wrestling between the wagons and carts. Horses whinnied.

Someone gave a gargled shriek. Ignatius looked towards the moon – more and more shapes were coming over the rise: tattered and thin but moving with strength and purpose.

Alongside the wagon, Guiscard got back to his feet. He hadn't had time to free his longsword from its scabbard and his shield was still strapped to his back, but he'd managed to draw his dagger and plunge it into his opponent's breast before rolling the body away. However, there was no respite. Another twisted shape lurched at him through the gloom. Guiscard drew his sword and pulled up his coif. In the brief half-second before this new foe attacked, it passed through a ray of moonlight, and he glimpsed its face – its mouth yawning open and glutted with black slime, its eyes hanging from its sockets on stalks. What looked like a rope noose, its tether-end chewed through, was tight around its neck.

Guiscard struck first, swinging his sword in an overhand arc, splitting the abomination from cranium to chin. It still grabbed hold of his tabard, and he had to strike it again, this time hewing through its left shoulder before it overbalanced and fell. He raised his sword a third time, intent on chopping it to pieces, only to be halted by a searing pain in his right calf. Gazing down, he saw his first assailant, the one he'd thought stabbed in the heart, biting through his tough leather leggings. Thrusting his sword down, Guiscard transfixed it via the midriff and leaned on the pommel heavily. With a wet *crunch*, he sheared through its spine and pinned it to the mud, whereupon, rather than dying, it commenced a wild, frenzied thrashing.

Guiscard staggered backward, stunned. There were shouts and screams all around him, along with a weird, inhuman moaning. The stench had become intolerable – thick, putrescent, redolent of burst bowels, stagnant waste. He was leaped onto again, this time from behind. He flipped his body forward and threw his assailant over his head. But more of them ghosted in from the front and side. He unslung his shield and slammed it edge-on into mouth of the nearest one, but the thing only tottered. Guiscard's coif was then ripped backward; cold, mud-covered fingers rent at his hair. He tried to spin round, but hands were also on his throat. He was dragged back down to the mud, where he was unable to use his sword. He unsheathed his dagger again, but it was wrested from his grasp. He hammered at them with his gloved fists, but it made no difference. Fleetingly, a face peered into his that was little more than raddled parchment; its nose was a fleshless cavity, its eyes shrunken orbs rolling in bone sockets.

On the wagon meanwhile, both Hugo d'Avranches and Brother Ignatius were rooted to their bench. They pivoted around, helpless to move or say anything.

"They can't die!" a man-at-arms screamed as he went haring past. He made it several yards into the trees before he was bludgeoned with a knobbly branch. He sank to his knees, only to be overwhelmed by more dark, stumbling figures.

Ignatius shook his head dumbly. He didn't know what he was going to do. He didn't know what he *could* do. But then a weight fell on him from behind. A ragged shape had scaled onto the back of the wagon and scrambled over its canvas-covered cargo. The sheer weight of it bore him from the bench and into the mire.

As a rule, Ignatius didn't like to fight. He felt it incompatible with his vocation. But as scribe and accountant to a professional soldier, it was impossible to avoid the occasional confrontation. He'd prefer not to be wearing mail over his black burel; he'd prefer not to be carrying the cudgel, the round-headed iron club by which clergymen were permitted to wage war. But he was glad of both now. The thing that had him down was cloaked by darkness, though a sickening reek poured off it. It ripped at his throat with bare hands that were slimy and flabby. He kicked at it, making good contact, though of course this was with a sandaled foot rather than a boot or sabaton, and the assailant would not be deterred. Ignatius grabbed the cudgel from his belt and smashed it across his foe's skull, which flew sideways at an angle that surely betokened a broken neck. The thing's grasp was weakened and Ignatius was able to push it off and scramble up.

It was still too dark to see what was happening. Strangely, there was no clangour of blade on blade or blade on shield, but the woods were filled with gruff shouts and agonised shrieks, and always that eerie dirge of moans and mewls.

Stammering the Act of Contrition, Ignatius tried to climb back onto the cart, only for a hand to catch his mail collar and yank him backward. He fell again into the mire. He couldn't see his attackers properly, though they were ragged and wet and stank to high Heaven. The skirts of his robe had flown up and, though he always wore under-garb in winter, this was made of thin linen and was easily torn aside. The next thing he knew, a hand that was hard like wood but as strong as an eagle's talon had gripped his genitals. Ignatius screamed in outrage, but another of them fell on top of him, smothering him with a torso that was like sticks under rotted leather.

Teeth snapped closed on his manhood like the jaws of a steel trap.

Ignatius's shrill squeal, as his maleness was torn from its root, pierced the night. Such pain and horror briefly gave him new strength, and he was able to throw off the figure smothering him, only to see that yet another was standing astride him, silhouetted by the moon. With skeletal arms it raised a heavy stone above its wizened head, and slammed it down onto his face. Blow after mighty blow crushed the monk's youthful features, flattening his tonsured skull until a hideous porridge of blood and brains oozed from his eyes, ears and nostrils.

On the other side of the wagon, Guiscard, caked in mud and filth, was being rent slowly apart. His mail had protected him to some extent, but now they lay on him in a heap, gnawing at his scalp, numerous pairs of claws trying to throttle him. Only with Herculean efforts, did he throw a couple of them off, and kick himself around in a circle to try and scramble back to his feet – but that was when the wagon began to move. On the driving bench, d'Avranches, white-faced with shock, was snapping the reins like a madman. Unnerved by the pandemonium, the horses ploughed forward, the wagon's heavy wheel passing over Guiscard's right leg. Bones exploded as the limb was crushed. Guiscard's ululation was deafening, but d'Avranches didn't hear it. He kept on snapping the reins.

All Guiscard's other cuts and sprains sank to insignificance as he rolled in the treacle of blood, mud and brains. He barely responded as his assailants swarmed back over him, fleshless fingers pinching his tongue, trying to rend it from his mouth, a stinking maw clamping on the side of his face and, with a vicious jerk, gouging out his left eye.

D'Avranches himself didn't get far. The wagon rolled perhaps ten yards before running into deep ruts. For all his whipping and cursing the animals, and for all their strenuous efforts, they made no further progress. Drawing his sword, the aged knight jumped down, but immediately turned an ankle and fell on his blade, snapping it in two. He clambered back to his feet, managing to draw his mattock and bury it in the skull of a figure lurching towards him. It tottered away, taking the mattock with it. D'Avranches's ankle-joint was on fire, but the urge to survive numbed it just enough for him to stumble off along the road. The pole-lantern was still planted a few yards ahead. The point-soldier who'd been felled lay next to it, his crimson innards scattered around him. Those responsible had moved on to attack the wagon train, but of course there were others – many others. D'Avranches hadn't reached the light before he sensed their contorted shadows skulking from the undergrowth to either side, tottering onto the road ahead.

Sweat-soaked and gasping for breath, he halted beside the light. He stared around, but from every direction they were pressing towards him.

He puffed out his chest and thrust back his shoulders. He might have run a few paces when panic overtook him, he might have left his comrades to die, but now he was about to die himself, and he would meet the challenge resolutely – as he'd always been determined to. He drew his final weapon, a small crossbow. Cranking the string back and fitting a dart onto the stock, he took aim. Though aged and corpulent, with legs bandied beneath his immense gut, Hugo d'Avranches was still a knight in the service of Earl Corotocus of Clun and King Edward of England, and he would make sure these rapscallions knew that.

But when they came into the light, it was a different story.

When he saw their cloven skulls, their smashed jaws and eyeless sockets, the clotted brains that caked their blue-green faces, the ribs showing through their worm-eaten rags – his courage failed him.

They were inches away from falling upon him when d'Avranches placed the crossbow at his left temple, and shot its lethal dart deep into his own head.

CHAPTER NINE

RANULF WAS IN the castle kitchen, with a hunk of bread under one arm and a bowl in his hands, when Hugh du Guesculin caught up with him. After the events of the last few days, Ranulf wasn't particularly hungry, but he now had a full night's watch duty ahead and knew that he had to get something into his belly. In addition, the game broth, which Otto, the earl's corpulent Brabancon cook, now ladled into his bowl from a huge, steaming pot, smelled delicious.

"I've been looking for you," du Guesculin said.

Ranulf didn't at first respond, even though, with nobody else in the kitchen, du Guesculin could hardly have been addressing anyone else.

"FitzOsbern, I said..."

"I hear you," Ranulf said, picking up a spoon.

Du Guesculin smiled in that usual self-satisfied way of his. Stripped of his mail, he now wore comfortable clothes: green hose and a hooded green tunic, with long, unbuttoned sleeves. He had donned a dagger at his belt in place of his sword. He'd even brushed his bobbed black hair and clipped his short moustache; all the more remarkable given that he was sharing the earl's spartan accommodation in the Constable's Tower.

"I hear you've formed quite an attachment to our prisoner?" he said.

Ranulf shrugged. "Then you hear wrongly."

"Ahhh... so you object to being replaced as her personal jailer because you deemed that an easier tour of duty than standing sentry on these walls?"

"At least I'd be out of the weather." Ranulf made to move through the archway into the refectory, but du Guesculin stepped into his path.

"Except that I don't believe a word of it, FitzOsbern."

Ranulf feigned shock. "You don't?"

"I believe that you feel sorry for the girl, or guilty about the way she's been treated, and are now concerned for her welfare."

"What you believe or don't believe is of no importance to me."

Ranulf pushed his way past and sauntered down a flight of four steps into the refectory, a low, vaulted chamber, lined with benches and long tables, but currently empty due to the lateness of the hour. He sat, tore his bread into pieces and, one by one, began to dunk them in the broth. He tried not to show irritation when du Guesculin sat down across the table from him.

"You really dislike me, don't you, FitzOsbern?"

"I don't have any feelings about you at all."

"Do I disgust you?"

Ranulf smiled. "You don't really want me to answer that question, do you?"

Du Guesculin pursed his lips. "You consider that you're not part of this tragic affair, is that right?"

"I wish I wasn't."

"How noble of you. But let's not conveniently forget the past, FitzOsbern. You are only in the earl's service because you yourself are a murderer."

Ranulf eyed him coldly, but continued to eat.

"Don't be embarrassed about it," du Guesculin added. "There are few men who reach your age in the order of merit without making... shall we say 'errors of judgement'. Even fewer reach Earl Corotocus's age. Tell me, what did you think of his wife, Countess Isabel?"

"I never met her," Ranulf said, wondering where this was leading.

"She died a considerable time ago, of course. Now that I think about it, well before you joined the earl's mesnie." The banneret hooked his thumbs under his straining belt in an effort to get more comfortable. "Contrary to popular legend, it was not the earl's dark moods that drove Countess Isabel to her early grave. In fact, he was very devoted to her. When they married, she had few prospects. She was the daughter of a landless troubadour, who came to England during the reign of Henry III. She brought no title, no dowry. It was a love-match, you see. Earl Corotocus hoped to raise a family with her – to have many children. Unfortunately, it didn't work out that way. Four times she failed to deliver a living child. The final occasion was the death of her. Earl Corotocus was devastated. He never tried to marry again, and his entire personality changed. He became a colder, harder man..."

"What are you trying to say, du Guesculin? That having failed to build an empire of the heart, Earl Corotocus sought to build an empire of land?"

"Something like that."

"And why are you telling me all this?"

"I thought I should give you some insight into his character."

Ranulf laughed as he dunked more bread and crammed it into his mouth.

Du Guesculin watched him carefully. "And into mine."

"I don't need insights into your character, du Guesculin. I know it perfectly well already. You're the earl's device, a mechanism, a thing of cogs and wheels rather than flesh and blood."

"How eloquently you speak... for a rogue knight without a penny to his name."

"You can thank my mother for that. At her insistence, I was taught much more than the skills to bear arms. Many lessons

I learned at her knee, du Guesculin. I loved her deeply. When she died, I too was devastated. But I didn't become a tyrannical savage."

"Again, how noble of you. You're too perfect, FitzOsbern. It's almost a pity to sully your angelic thoughts with harsh practicalities, but I shall do it anyway, as we all will benefit. You're aware that the Welsh girl we hold is lawful heiress to most of Powys, the largest province in Wales?"

"Of course. And?"

Du Guesculin chuckled. "You may be a fierce warrior and a learned speaker, but you clearly lack a political grasp. Think about this. Earl Corotocus already holds the March, and a number of disparate lordships on both sides of the Welsh border, but they are dotted here, there and everywhere. Were he to be made undisputed lord and master over all of Powys, he would control the entire middle section of Wales, its absolute heartland. Think of the potential of this. There would be no more scope for rebellion running the length and breadth of the country. In fact, there would be no scope for rebellion at all. The border wars would end."

"And would the people of Powys serve the earl willingly after the things he's done here?"

"What matter? They would still serve him – willingly or unwillingly – because they would have no choice. Oh certainly, there would be hostility. But you know the truth about Wales – their own princes have been as cruel or incompetent, or both, as any Anglo-Norman lord imposed by the Crown. In time they would acquiesce, and the earl could relax his stranglehold. Life would become easier for everyone."

"They might not acquiesce so quickly if they perceive that he has wrested the province by force from their rightful liege, Countess Madalyn."

Du Guesculin smiled. "This is the clever part, FitzOsbern. Perhaps there is no need for him to wrest it by force... if he can acquire it by marriage."

Ranulf shook his head with slow disbelief. "You mean to Lady Gwendolyn?"

"No, of course not – to her invisible twin sister! Who else do you think I mean?"

"The king would never agree to that."

"Of course he would. The king is in the process of fully incorporating Wales into the realm. And he'll use any method available to him. If that means investing one of his most loyal vassals with a significant portion of it, why should he even hesitate?"

"Countess Madalyn would never agree."

"What does that matter?"

"Lady Gwendolyn would never agree."

"Ah!" Du Guesculin raised a finger. "That is where you play *your* part, FitzOsbern. If you have genuine feelings for the girl, perhaps it would suit all of us if you were to, shall we say, 'advise her where her best interests might lie'?"

"I see. And where do you play *your* part?"

Du Guesculin puffed his cheeks at the burdensome task that he himself faced. "I need to convince Earl Corotocus. He has no patience with these Welsh. He sees them as outsiders, barbarous brutes. He'd want to spend as little time here as possible."

"In which case he would appoint a seneschal to rule his Welsh lands for him, no?"

Du Guesculin made a vague gesture. "Quite possibly."

"And that, du Guesculin, is where you *really* play your part?"

"I have served his lordship faithfully for twenty years. Is it not time I was rewarded?"

Ranulf gave a wry smile. "If I'm not mistaken, you have extensive lands around Whitchurch, with matching estates at Oswestry?"

"You are not mistaken, FitzOsbern. But Wales is new territory, and much wilder. I think there will be a greater degree of autonomy."

Ranulf laughed. "You mean you can rule like a great nobleman? Maybe even take a title? Count of Lyr? What about Earl of Powys... how does that sound?"

Du Guesculin stiffened at the mocking tone. "What I propose is perfectly reasonable."

"Why don't you just go the whole hog, du Guesculin? Travel to Rome, make up some scandalous lies about your own wife's lack of fidelity, get an annulment, then return and woo the Welsh girl yourself?"

"I've explained the situation," du Guesculin said, standing up. "From this point it's up to you. As things stand, the Lady Gwendolyn is our enemy and our hostage. Becoming her friend would not be the wisest course. The earl already has half an eye on you as someone he doesn't fully trust. On the other hand, were you to make your relationship with the girl profitable to us, things could be very different."

"Different for whom?"

"You and your father have nothing, boy. When you are released from the earl's service, assuming you survive that long, you will still have nothing. I, however, may have important posts to fill here in Wales. Why not think about that?"

He strode from the table.

"Du Guesculin!" Ranulf called after him.

Du Guesculin turned on the steps.

"Du Guesculin, what do you not understand about the meaning of the word 'atrocity'? These people hate us with a passion that you apparently can't conceive."

Du Guesculin shrugged. "Hatred is one emotion that can be bought and sold, FitzOsbern. Some day, I will prove that to you."

CHAPTER TEN

THERE WAS NO cockcrow to announce the dawn.

Ranulf first became aware of it when a finger of light crept along the eastern horizon. He and Gurt Louvain had held the night watch together and were on the south curtain-wall, gloved, hooded, wrapped in their cloaks and crouched against a brazier, which was now virtually dead. They'd barely spoken during the long, slow hours. Similar small groups were dotted at regular intervals around the entire circumference of the castle. They too were muted; as silent as the effigies the company had found on arriving here. Some of the weird mannequins still lay on the wall walk, though most, having unnerved the men with their mocking expressions, had been torn to pieces or hurled down into the bailey.

Gurt muttered something about the morning coming at last. Ranulf grunted an acknowledgement. He laid his sword against the embrasure and lifted the timber panel to peer out. The only sound was the soft ripple of the river as it slid by in a glassy sheet. The woods on its far shore were still in darkness.

"I don't know about you, but I'm ready to sleep," Gurt said. He was pale, sallow faced, and clearly younger than Ranulf had first thought. His unshaved whiskers and the dust and dirt of the campaign had for a time masked his youthfulness. His tall, solid physique and strong Northumbrian accent had also made him seem older.

"How did you end up in the earl's debt, Gurt?" Ranulf asked.

"Well," Gurt replied, "it wasn't easy."

He chuckled. Ranulf chuckled too. It alleviated things a little.

"I was squired to John de Warenne."

"The Earl of Surrey?" Ranulf said, surprised.

"Yes."

"Quite a character."

"And a great tourneyor." Gurt became thoughtful. "He taught me a lot. When I was knighted, he attached me to the household of his senior tenant, Walter Bigod."

"Another legend."

"And another great tourneyor. We fought at all the major events – London, Northampton, Dunstable. I did well personally. Or so I thought. In truth I didn't really understand the value of money. My sister was married to a landed knight in Yorkshire. He died not long after they exchanged vows. Hugh of Cressingham, the king's grasping treasurer, was my sister's overlord. He sought to claim the escheat and turn her out. I stepped in and offered to buy the fief as a smallholding, using my personal fortune. Those were the actual words I used, 'my personal fortune'."

He smiled bitterly.

"I was naïve. There was little land attached to that fee – a few roods, a couple of plough-teams, a fishpond. Barely enough to keep the cottars alive, let alone we two and the families we both hoped to have when we found spouses. Eventually I offered to sell it back to Cressingham. In fact, I offered it to him as a gift if he would provide for us in some capacity. But he wasn't interested. The estate had acquired debts. That was when Earl Corotocus stepped in, proposing to settle what we owed and take charge of the property. He had lands close by, and saw our estate as a tactical purchase. If I'd known that, maybe I could have struck a harder bargain. As it was, I was grateful to have the financial millstone taken off me. In return for that favour, my sister became his ward and I was bound to seven years military service."

"Seven years?" Ranulf said. "I didn't see you in Gascony."

"I only began paying my dues last January. Already I'm regretting it. Does it get any easier campaigning with Earl Corotocus?"

Ranulf snorted.

"How about you?" Gurt asked. "What do you owe him?"

"What don't we owe him?" Ranulf shook his head. "My family lost everything in the blood feud between Bohun of Hereford and Clare of Gloucester. That was quite an unpleasant affair. Hereford and Gloucester had never been easy neighbours. In fact, they fought over just about everything. But the real conflict broke out between them over the castle of Morlais. It was a bitter squabble, which turned repeatedly into open violence. Raid followed raid. There were brawls in taverns, brawls on the highway, kidnappings. My father was Hereford's vassal, so he played a full part. The king eventually had them all arrested – that was in 1292, and the charge was waging private war. The two earls were fined heavily and had land confiscated by the Crown. My father and selected other knights, who'd declared for their overlords, were disinherited. Overnight, we went from landed gentry to destitution. My mother was ill at the time and unable to stand the shock."

"I'm sorry," Gurt said.

"It happens. She had the sweating sickness and might've died anyway. The main thing is, with mother dead, my father became errant again. He took me out of squiredom and knighted me himself. Like you, we fought in the tournaments, but as privateers. We did moderately well – made enough to live. But later that year, at Clarendon, father's destrier was wounded in the thigh and lamed. Not only did we take nothing from the tournament, our earning potential was halved. Desperate, we travelled to Wayland Fair, where we put every penny we had into buying father a new horse. It was a fine specimen, and even at that hefty price we thought it was a bargain. Then, three days later, we were accosted in a tavern by one Philip de Courcy, nephew to the Bishop of Norwich. He said he recognised the horse. Claimed it was one he'd had stolen not three months earlier, and accused us of theft. Father was outraged, but also worried. We were landless knights, nobodies without protectors – and this was a capital offence. So we demanded trial by battle. We two, father said, would fight de Courcy and any three of his knights, either in pairs or all at the same time. We would prove our innocence before God. Perhaps realising that, with our lives at stake, we were very serious about this matter, de Courcy took the latter option. Even so, it was a one-sided affair. Up to that time, I imagine de Courcy had bullocked his way through life on the strength of his uncle's name. Two of his men were wounded and withdrew from the fight early, and then de Courcy was killed. It was my blow that struck him. With this very sword."

Ranulf lifted his longsword from the embrasure. Like most battle swords, it was functional rather than handsome. Its two-edged blade had been honed many times, but was still chipped and scarred. Its great cross-hilt was bound with leather.

"I cut through his aventail and severed his windpipe." Ranulf re-enacted the fatal swipe. "*My* blow, but father said that if there was any blame, *he* would take it." He relapsed into brooding silence.

"There was blame attached?" Gurt eventually asked.

"Of course, even though we had many witnesses. The contest was fought on an open meadow outside the town, with the reeve's full permission. But the bishop, who also happened to be sheriff of that county, was enraged by the outcome. He had us arrested and imposed a massive wergild. There was no possibility we could pay it. It looked like death for us. But word of the incident had now reached the ears of Earl Corotocus, who was en route to Yarmouth with his army to take ship to Gascony. Always on the lookout for 'special soldiers', as he called them, he was happy to pay the fine for us."

"And how long have you been returning that favour?"

"To date it's been three years. We have seven remaining."

Gurt looked puzzled. "You might have lost the war in Gascony, but surely you took booty? Couldn't you have bought your way out by now?"

"Father has never wanted to."

"Your father would rather serve? He seems a mild man."

Ranulf stood up, stretching the cramp from his chilled limbs. Again, he lifted the panel. Milky daylight was flooding across the Welsh landscape. White vapour hung in its fathomless woods.

"In his old age, father's become introspective. 'Forget the tournament', he says. 'Earl Corotocus fights *real* wars. That's where the plunder is. When we've served our term, we'll be wealthy. Our lives will be restored'."

"And I thought he wanted to while away this war in the safety of Grogen Castle?"

Ranulf shrugged. His father had become a conundrum to him. Even though only a few years had passed, it was difficult to compare the pale, withdrawn figure that Ulbert FitzOsbern now was with the laughing, brawling, golden-haired seigneur who'd once welcomed all guests – whether bidden or unbidden – to his stockaded manor house at Byford, who'd always ridden in his overlord's vanguard roaring like a demon, twirling his battle-axe around his head. Regret, guilt, a sense of failure – they could do strange things to even the toughest man.

"It's hardship, misery... penance for the loss of our home," Ranulf finally said. "To father, this service is something we deserve. Something we must work off through blood and toil, though under Earl Corotocus it's usually someone else's blood."

"And that doesn't worry your father?"

"Not as much as it once did. Once, he was a moral man, a strict adherent to the code. Now he is focussed purely on 'cleaning his slate', as he calls it."

Gurt was about to reply when they heard a curious noise. At first they weren't sure what it was or where it came from – it echoed over the river and into the forest on the south shore. They glanced around, puzzled. Slowly, it became clear that what they were hearing was a voice calling out – but a fearsome, pealing voice, eerily high pitched.

"Eaaarl Corotocus!" it seemed to be saying, though the distance and the acoustics of the castle's outer rampart distorted it. "Eaaarl Corotocus!"

Gurt leaned through the embrasure. All along the curtain-wall, the other sentries were doing the same. As one, they looked unnerved.

"It's coming from somewhere to the west," Ranulf said.

From their position, they could just make out the south edge of the western bluff. The Inner Fort and the towering edifice of the Constable's Tower masked the rest of it.

"Eaaarl Corotocus!" the voice called again. It sounded female, though there was nothing sweet or gentle in it.

"What the devil's happening?" Gurt wondered.

Ranulf offered to go and see, suggesting that Gurt stay at his post. Gurt nodded, buckling on his sword-belt.

The quickest access down into the bailey from the curtain-wall was afforded by a mass of support scaffolding, which had various ladders zigzagging through it. Ranulf scaled down one of these, and followed the bailey around the outskirts of the Inner Fort until he'd reached the castle's northwest corner, at which point he climbed a steep flight of steps and passed through a barred postern onto the Barbican. From here, he entered the Gatehouse and traipsed back along the Causeway to the Constable's Tower. In total it was a ten-minute walk, and he still had to ascend to the roof of the Constable's Tower, by which time Earl Corotocus had been wakened from his slumber.

The earl, clad only in boots and leather breaches, with a bearskin cloak swathed around his muscular torso, was by the western battlements. He looked uncharacteristically tousled, though marginally less so than Hugh du Guesculin, who had also thrown on a cloak but still looked ridiculous in a full-length woollen nightgown. Navarre, more predictably, was already harnessed for war in his mail and leather. This applied to several other of the earl's household knights, who had been posted here and had shared the night watch between them. Of Corotocus's lieutenants, only Davy Gou, captain of the royal archers, and Morgaynt Carew, the Welsh malcontent, were present. At the north end of the Causeway, Garbofasse and his mercenaries watched from the top of the Gatehouse.

"Eaaarl Corotocus!" the voice came again, just as Ranulf emerged onto the roof. "Earl Corotocus, I know you are in there!"

"Good God," the earl said with slow disbelief.

Ranulf joined him by the battlements. On the western bluff, several figures were ranged a few yards apart. One was on horseback and positioned further down the slope from the others. By her shape, she was a woman. She wore flowing white robes, and had long, flame-red hair.

"Is that the Countess of Lyr?" du Guesculin asked, astonished.

Ranulf leaned forward, but there was no mistaking her. The early morning murk had cleared, to leave the sky cloudless and pebble-blue. The other figures were men. They also wore white, but their hoods were drawn up, showing only their beards

"Eaaarl Corotocus!" the countess cried again, her strident tone echoing. "You are a liar, a thief and a murderer! And I am here to tell you that your tyranny will not be endured. Neither in this land, nor on our border."

Ranulf glanced at the earl. Corotocus was stony-faced but listening intently.

"Earl Corotocus, you and your garrison will vacate Caergrogwyn! After that you will vacate the march. But before you do any of these things, you will surrender your arms and armour, and any plunder you have taken from my people. You will also return my daughter, Gwendolyn. Be warned, if she has been harmed in any way, the price for you and your men is death."

"Feisty bitch," Carew muttered.

"She's got spirit, I'll give her that," Corotocus said. He turned to one of Gou's archers. "You, fellow? Can you strike her from here?"

The archer took off his broad-brimmed helmet and shielded his eyes. "She may be out of range, my lord."

"Try anyway." Corotocus turned not just to the other royal archers present, but to bowmen from his own company. "All of you. A purse of gold for the first man to hit her."

The bowmen set about their task, flexing and stringing their longbows, and letting fly. But it was impossible. First, they had to clear the bailey yard, then the outer curtain-wall, then the moat, and after all that the countess was still high on the bluff, from which she watched their efforts with studied silence. One by one, the goose shafts whistled harmlessly into the abyss.

"We have ballistae in the southwest tower," du Guesculin said. "Any of those will knock her from her insolent perch, my lord. I only need have them brought up here."

Corotocus shook his head. "It's not worth the trouble."

"My men have the trebuchet on the Barbican," Carew said.

"Why waste a valuable missile?"

"We should send someone out there," Navarre snarled. "She's insulted you in front of your men. She must face the consequence."

"Insults don't trouble me, Navarre. The men will stop listening after a while. Let her rot out there."

The earl made to go below, but the countess called again.

"Eaaarl Corotocus! Your silence does you no credit. You are a coward who hides behind his king's walls rather than faces his enemy in the field."

"Away, woman!" he shouted back. His face had reddened slightly. "Be thankful your daughter hasn't become my soldiers' plaything."

"That would be very like you, Earl Corotocus," she replied. "To vent your wrath on a helpless child. Just as you vented it on Anwyl's men after first tricking them into disarming themselves. Do you ever stand and fight, lord of the realm? Have you ever won a battle with bravery alone?"

Corotocus was aware of his soldiers listening along the castle's western walls. They knew he was a fierce warrior and skilled commander, but they also knew that he paid no heed to the customs of chivalry. Maybe, for the first time, some of them were wondering about the apparent non-courageousness of this policy.

"Let me go out there." Navarre begged. "I'll silence the hag."

"It might be an idea after all," Corotocus said. "Too many rabble-rousers go unpunished these days."

"Who are those people with her?" Ranulf wondered.

"Whoever they are," Navarre said, "they'll share her fate."

Ranulf turned to the earl. "My lord, before we attack, might I speak to her?"

Corotocus raised an eyebrow. "You think you can do better than I?"

"With respect, you deceived her once. She might find it difficult to trust you."

Navarre spat. "We don't need her to trust us! She should be hanged and quartered, as Prince Dafydd was."

Ranulf ignored him. "My lord, pacification should follow conquest. Isn't that always King Edward's will?"

Corotocus shrugged. "Try if you wish."

Ranulf turned and shouted: "Countess Madalyn!"

"Who speaks?" she called back.

"An English knight."

"Once you'd have been proud to wear that title."

"Whore," Navarre muttered.

"The war is over," Ranulf shouted. "It makes no sense to start it again."

"This war will never be over until Earl Corotocus and his like have ceased to threaten my people."

"You seek further destruction, madam? Madog's rebel army has been vanquished."

"You may break our bodies, English knight, but you will never break our spirit."

"Countess Madalyn... there will be more deaths."

There was a brief silence, before she replied: "Only yours."

"That's what you get for reasoning with ignoramuses," Navarre stated. He turned to the earl, pulling on his gauntlets. "I'll bring you her breasts, my lord, so that you can play *jeux de paume* with them."

Corotocus nodded.

"I wouldn't be too hasty, Navarre," Ranulf said. "Look."

Additional figures had begun to appear on the bluff, not just from the wooded area above the countess, but all along the western ridge. Within a few moments there were several hundred of them, but more continued to swell their ranks.

"Dear God," du Guesculin breathed. "Who are they?"

Navarre's angry self-assurance had faded a little, but he still sneered. "They don't look much like soldiers."

It was difficult to tell for certain. Over this distance, the gathering force was comprised of diminutive figures, none of whom could be seen clearly. There was the occasional glint of mail or war-harness, though most seemed to be wearing peasant garb, and tattered peasant garb at that. One or two – and at first Ranulf thought he was hallucinating – seemed to be naked. This sent a greater prickle of unease down his spine than their overall numbers did. There was now perhaps a thousand of them, but still more were appearing.

"From the north too, my lord," someone shouted.

Everyone looked, and saw processions of figures crossing the high moors to the north of the castle. They were thinly spread, moving in small groups or ones and twos, and, in many cases, limping or stumbling as though starved or crippled. They resembled refugees rather than soldiers, but all together there must have been several thousand of them. By the time they joined the countess on the western bluff, they'd be a prodigious host. Although the English held this bastion and were armed to the teeth, they were suddenly outnumbered to a worrying degree.

"Still think you can buy and sell the Welsh people, du Guesculin?" Ranulf muttered.

Du Guesculin couldn't answer; he had blanched.

"They're still only peasants," Navarre scoffed.

"If so, they're armed," Ranulf observed.

"What are scythes and reaping hooks to us?"

"I see real weapons," Carew said.

Most of the ragged shapes were carrying implements, and though many of these looked to be little more than clubs or broken farm tools, others were clearly swords, axes, poll-arms.

"Where the devil did they get their hands on those?" du Guesculin said.

"Our artillery train maybe?" Ranulf glanced at Crotocus. "Wasn't it expected to arrive last night?"

The earl didn't reply, but regarded the gathering horde with growing wariness.

"My lord, this is some riff-raff," Navarre protested. "They won't assault this castle. How could they possibly expect to take it?"

"What is that ungodly stink?" someone asked.

A noxious smell, like spoiled meat, was drifting on the breeze.

"Pig farmers, ditch diggers," Navarre said. "Which is all they are."

"That, my lords, is the smell of war," the earl said abruptly. "Muster your men, if you please. Prepare for battle!"

CHAPTER ELEVEN

BELLS RANG THROUGHOUT the castle for most of that morning. Clarions sounded in every section. But Countess Madalyn waited in silence on the western bluff, as did her army, its disordered ranks eerily still. By eleven o'clock, the walls of Grogen Castle were bristling with swords, spears and arrows knocked on strings; every defender was fully mailed. Even the grooms and pages had been called up and given blades. And yet still nothing happened.

Ranulf, on the south curtain-wall, with Gurt to his right and Ulbert to his left, wondered if this delay owed to some previously unseen notion of Welsh chivalry, but he soon dismissed the idea. More likely the countess was waging a mental attack before the physical one. She was letting it be known that she had no concern about whether the English were prepared to receive her or not; that she was undeterred by their readiness, their armour, their weaponry. The battle would only commence when she decided, for it was she, not Earl Corotocus, who was dictating this day's strategy.

Of course, Earl Corotocus was never one to waste an opportunity. While the countess dallied, he'd prepared his defences to their utmost. Though his personal artillery wagons might not have arrived, the castle had several engines of its own, and these were quickly marshalled. On the Barbican, Carew and his men, under the direction of William d'Abbetot, prepared the trebuchet, swivelling it round on its colossal timber turntable so that it faced the western bluff, then stockpiling rocks and lead weights, some as heavy as four hundred pounds. It took three of them to load just one such missile into the sling, and half the company to pour sweat as they lined a dozen more in the trough. They also set aside a pile of 'devil's sachets' – linen sacks, loosely tied with lace, each one containing ten smaller boulders, a payload that would spread mid-flight and cut a gory swath through massed infantry. At the entrance to the Gatehouse, meanwhile, the gate was locked and chained, the portcullis drawn down. Behind this, a fire-raiser was brought into position. This was a fiendish device: a massive steel tube mounted on two wheeled carts. At one end, a gigantic pair of bellows allowed its crew to expel wind through it at great force. At the other, which flared like a trumpet and, with a deliberate sense of irony, had been carved to resemble the gaping mouth of a Welsh dragon, a cauldron was suspended and filled with lighted coals, sulphur and pitch. When working at full capacity, great billowing clouds of flame could be expelled by it, engulfing anyone who managed to tear down the outer gate and attack the portcullis.

In the southwest tower, there were four levels of ballistae. The lower two comprised polybolas, immense crossbows designed to project large single bolts and fitted with windlasses and magazines so that they could discharge repeatedly and quickly. The upper two levels contained lighter weapons, archery machines constructed with cradles from which sixteen clothyard arrows – fitted either with barbed or swallow-tailed heads – could be shot at the same time. All these frightful devices were built into the actual fabric of the tower, in specially designed rooms containing masses of scaffolding, and angled at a downward slant so to discharge through horizontal ports cut into the outer wall. On the normal parapets on the top of the other towers and turrets, and on the curtain-wall, every archer and crossbowman had ample time to accumulate bushels of arrows. The rest of the men provided themselves with other, less sophisticated missiles – stones, spears, javelins, grenades made from interwoven nails and spikes, and barrels of naptha – a highly flammable mixture of oil and resin, which they could pour on the heads of their assailants.

Father Benan was visibly unnerved by these preparations. He'd seen war before of course, but had previously stayed clear of the actual battlefield.

"I shall return to the chapel and sing a mass for the preservation of our souls," he said, crossing himself at the sight of so many axes, mattocks and cleavers.

"Sing one for the Welsh first," Corotocus advised him. "I'll soon be sending a hundred-score of them to God's hall of judgement.

But if the Welsh were daunted by the sight of the rearmed stronghold, there was no sign. In fact, Ranulf didn't think he'd ever seen as quiet or composed an enemy. Only as the noise of the English activity – the clanking of mail-clad feet on steps and walkways, the clinking of hammers, the rattling of chains, the shouting and the banging and bolting of iron doors – faded, did he realise that no sound at all issued from the vast army outside, except perhaps for a distant low moaning, which more likely was the wind hissing on the wild Welsh moors. There was no beating of drums, no blasting of horns, no guttural roars as the various companies psyched themselves up for combat. Yet neither did he think he'd ever seen so drab a band. He didn't expect glorious heraldry, but few banners or standards flew. The predominant colours were greys and browns; many of the enemy sported nothing more than filthy rags. And, of course, there was that foul fetor, which had got steadily thicker until it now seemed to have settled over the castle in a malodorous shroud.

"How many of them, would you say?" Gurt wondered. "Ten thousand?"

"Even ten thousand wouldn't normally be enough to assail a fortress like this," Ranulf replied. "But..."

"But?"

Ranulf couldn't explain.

"Don't worry, I know," Gurt said. "Sometimes emotion alone will win the day. You can only tyrannise a population so much before it turns on you like a tiger."

"Are you a student of treason as well, Master Louvain?" Walter Margas wondered, walking past them towards the nearest ladder. Despite his age and world-weariness, he was still an efficient eavesdropper. "You two are made for each other. You should get a room in a tavern sometime where you can whimper your sedition together."

"Are you leaving us, Walter?" Ranulf asked. "Surely not? Not when the battle's just about to start?"

Margas's wizened cheeks coloured. "Perhaps you'd rather I defecated up here on the parapet?"

"I'd rather you got back to your post. You can drop your guts with everyone else, when the fighting's over."

"Are you calling my courage into question, sirrah?"

"You were very active on the River Ogryn, as I recall. Riding against unarmed footmen. These odds are less to your fancy, I take it?"

Margas's lips tightened with rage. "When this is over, FitzOsbern, I'll report you both to the earl. You'll find he takes a dim view of those who spread defeatism."

"If you're hiding in the privy, how will you know when it's over?" Gurt asked.

Margas was visibly furious. Spittle leaked into his unkempt beard – but there was nothing else he could do. Aware that others were listening and watching, he trudged back along the wall to his post.

"Useless sack of puke," Gurt said under his breath.

"He likes his cowardly butchers, does Earl Corotocus," Ranulf added.

"If you gentlemen would concentrate on the day," Ulbert interrupted them, "I'd be obliged. There's movement afoot."

To the west, large numbers of the Welsh host were suddenly shambling – *shambling* was the only word Ranulf could think of –

down the bluff towards the southwest bridge. There was nothing military about it. They descended in a mob, stumbling, jostling each other. In appearance they were lambs to the slaughter, for they marched neither behind shields nor beneath a protective barrage of missiles.

On the Constable's Tower, Navarre laughed.

"This is going to be too easy, my lord."

Corotocus said nothing, but watched carefully.

The southwest bridge was extremely narrow, and had neither barriers nor fences on either side of it. It had been constructed this way deliberately so that visitors to the castle – whether welcome or unwelcome – could only file across it two at a time, and all the way would be in danger of falling off. The southwest tower, which directly overlooked it, didn't just contain the ballistae, but had been allocated to the crossbowmen, and these were the first to strike. Their bolts began slanting down. The rest of the defenders watched expectantly for the Welsh to start dropping, and for a resulting pile-up of bodies as those behind tripped over them. But this didn't happen. The Welsh crammed onto the bridge regardless of the deadly rain.

"They call themselves 'royal archers'?" Gurt said. "They haven't hit a damn thing!"

Ranulf was equally confused. The king's crossbowmen were supposedly elite troops, highly disciplined and skilled.

"Village bumpkins couldn't miss from that range," Ulbert said.

The downward slope of the bluff was log-jammed with figures, all pushing mindlessly forward. They were hardly difficult to hit. The crossbows in the southwest tower were now joined by longbows stationed further along the curtain-wall, these too in the hands of expert marksmen from the royal house. Sleek shafts glittered through the noon sunlight as they sped from on high, though no obvious carnage resulted. However, it was soon clear that they actually *were* striking their targets, as indeed were the crossbow bolts – but the targets kept on coming. The first few had reached the other side of the bridge and were on the berm, at the very foot of the southwest tower. Those defenders at that part of the castle marvelled that there seemed to be women among them. Not only that, but a lot of the Welsh were already bloodied, in some cases heavily as though from severe wounds. Bewilderment and fear spread among the English. Several of the Welsh visibly bore the broken shafts of arrows. One half-naked fellow appeared to have been transfixed through the chest, yet still he hobbled over the bridge.

On the Constable's Tower they could do little more than shout encouragement to their bowmen, but they too were baffled by what they were seeing.

"They must be better armoured than they appeared to be," Navarre said.

Corotocus didn't respond. His heavier weapons now spoke for him, the polybolas projecting their terrible four-foot missiles, the archery machines unleashing showers of arrows, the shafts of which rattled onto the stonework of the bridge, riddling those figures caught in their path.

The effects were satisfyingly ghastly. With their bodkin points and wide, fin-like blades, the ballista bolts drove clean across the bridge into the massed throng on the other side, ploughing bloody alleyways. There were roars of delight from the castle walls. For a brief second the bridge was no longer crowded – ten or twenty figures had pitched over the side into the moat, falling thirty feet onto the rocks below. Some remained on the bridge, but had been felled where they stood. Yet it wasn't long before this latter group got back to their feet, despite their horrendous wounds. One's head had hinged backward, hanging by threads of sinew. Another had been sheared through the left thigh – incredibly, almost comically, he recommenced his advance by hopping. The laughter slowly died on the castle walls. Even the archery seemed to falter in intensity. Ranulf's hair prickled as he sighted one fellow coming off the bridge who looked to have been pierced by an arrow clean through his skull.

Inside the southwest tower, it was a chaos of dust, sweat and flaring candle-light as the ballista serjeants bawled at their crews to work harder. Frantic efforts were made as magazines were spent and new ones fitted onto the sliders, as winches were worked to ratchet the catgut bowstrings back into position. With repeated, ear-dulling bangs, each new missile was unleashed as soon as it could be placed. There was no attempt to aim. Because of the angle of vent in the tower wall, the projectiles were always shot cleanly onto the bridge. And again they wrought horrible carnage, slicing figures in half, gutting them where they stood. One bolt hurtled across in a black blur, pinioning a Welshman through the midriff, carrying him with it, pinioning another, carrying him, and even pinioning a third – three men like fish flopping on a spear – before it plunged into the midst of their countrymen on the far side. The archery machines sewed the ground on both sides of the bridge with arrows. Countless more Welsh were caught in this relentless fusillade, many of them hit multiple times – through the arms, through the body, through the legs – and yet still, though reduced to limping, seesawing wrecks, they proceeded across.

"This is not possible," Gurt shouted. "There should be a carpet of corpses by now. I don't see a single bloody one!"

On the Constable's Tower, Earl Corotocus summoned a nervous squire.

"Take a message to Captain Musard in the southwest tower, boy. Tell him that, Familiaris Regis or not, if he and his men don't start *killing* these brainless oafs, I'll send them outside with sticks and stones to see if they can do a better job that way."

When the message was delivered, the bombardment on the bridge intensified. The air whistled with goose-feathers. The Welsh crossing over were struck again and again. Dozens more were knocked into the moat, hurtling to its rocky floor, and yet, like those who'd fallen before them, always scrambling back to their feet no matter how broken or mutilated their bodies. They even tried to climb back out, and with some degree of success. A feat that seemed inhuman given that the moat walls were mostly sheer rock.

Ranulf glanced sidelong at his father. Ulbert had lifted the visor on his helmet; always stoic in the face of battle, it was disconcerting to see that he wore a haunted expression.

Many Welsh were now progressing eastwards along the berm, intent on circling the castle and approaching the main entrance at its northwest corner. This meant that the defenders on the curtain-wall were also able to assault them.

Lifting the hatches in the wall walk, they had a bird's eye view of the enemy trailing past below, and so dropped boulders or flung grenades and javelins. It had negligible effect, even though numerous missiles appeared to hit cleanly. The sheer force of impact hurled some Welsh into the river and the current carried them away, though even then they writhed and struggled – albeit with broken torsos, sundered skulls, eye-sockets punctured by arrows. Ranulf saw one Welshman clamber back out from the water, only to be struck by an anvil with shattering effect, blood and brains spattering from a skull that simply folded on itself – and yet he got back to his feet and continued to march. Gurt saw another struck by a thrown mallet; the mallet's iron head lodged in the upper part of the fellow's nose, its handle jutting crazily forward like a rhino's horn – and yet the Welshman, who already looked as if his lower jaw was missing and whose upper body was caked with dried gore, trudged onward.

No agonised screeches or froth-filled gargles greeted the defenders' efforts. There was a sound of sorts – that low moaning, which initially the English had mistaken for the wind. Now that the Welsh were so close, it was clear they themselves were the source of it. But it wasn't just a moaning – it was a keening, a mindless mewling; utterly soulless and inhuman.

At the southwest bridge, more and more Welsh fighters poured over to the other side. Inside the southwest tower, the ballista serjeants yelled at their men until they were hoarse. Bowstrings snapped under the strain and were urgently replaced; the cranks and gears of the war-machines heated and heated until they couldn't be touched. Captain Musard came down again from the tower roof, now frantic. He threw himself to the vents to look out. The enemy should have been lying in heaps on both sides of the bridge. They should have been cluttering the bridge itself. The moat should have been running red with their blood, stacked with their mangled corpses. But it wasn't. Each new salvo darkened the sky. The impacts of missiles slamming into bone and tearing through flesh were deafening. Yet always the Welsh came on. Musard watched, goggle-eyed, as a trio of limping Welshmen crossed the bridge in single file, skewered together on the same length of shaft. He ordered them cut down, butchered. He vowed death for any bowman who failed to strike them. One after another, darts and arrows found their mark, embedding themselves deeply but not even slowing the demonic threesome.

By now, the foremost of the Welsh attackers had reached the point of the curtain-wall where Ranulf, Ulbert and Gurt were stationed.

Ranulf saw one who had lost his left arm, left shoulder and much of the left side of his torso. It had presumably been torn away by a ballista bolt – jagged bones, bloodied and dangling with tissue, jutted out – yet the creature still marched. More to the point, he wasn't even bleeding. The air around him should have been sprayed crimson. Ranulf was so entranced by this unreal vision that when his father clamped a mailed hand onto his shoulder, he jumped with fright.

"Fire!" Ulbert said. "Ranulf, wake up for Christ's sake! We must use fire!"

The call went along the battlements, but only slowly. Barrels of naptha were wrestled forward, but many defenders were in such a daze that they might have tossed them over as they were. Ulbert had to shout to prevent the precious mixture being wasted.

"Timber!" he cried, pushing his way along the walk. "We need timber too, down on the berm. We must form a barricade and ignite it. Bottle them up along the path and we can burn them all as one."

Only a handful of men responded. The others gazed with disbelief at the torn, battered figures below, some disembowelled, their entrails dangling at their feet, others dragging partly severed limbs. Many were human porcupines they were so filled with arrows. Yet they moved on in a steady column.

"Timber!" Ulbert bellowed, having to cuff the men to bring them to their senses.

The only timber available was a derelict stable block in the bailey. Three burly men-at-arms clambered down ladders and broke it up with hammers and axes. Soon, bundles of smashed wood were being hauled up the wall by rope.

"Down there!" Ulbert shouted, indicating a spot about thirty yards ahead of the Welsh force, which at last was being hindered by the avalanche of stones and spears.

The wood was cast down until a mountainous pile had been formed, blocking the berm. Several barrels of naptha were poured onto it, but firebrands were only dropped when the first Welsh reached it. The resulting explosion was bright as a starburst. The rush of heat staggered even the defenders, who were fifty feet above.

Despite this, and to Ranulf's incredulity, the first few Welsh actually attempted to clamber *through* the raging inferno. A couple even made it to the other side, though they were blazing from head to foot and, finally it seemed, had met their match. First their ragged clothing burned away, followed by their flesh and musculature. One by one, they sagged to the ground. Equally incredible to Ranulf was that none of them tried to dunk themselves in the river, the way he'd seen the French do in their camp on the Adour when the earl had catapulted clay pots filled with flaming naptha right into their sleeping-tents.

Behind this burning vanguard, more Welsh fighters were advancing. Some attempted to circle the conflagration, but again they stumbled into the river and were swept away. Others, at long last, began to display a notion of self-preservation. They halted rather than blundered headlong into the flames and, as Ulbert had predicted, were bottled up along the berm, cramming together for hundreds of yards. Naptha was sluiced onto them all along the line and lit torches were applied, creating multiple downpours of liquid fire. There was nowhere for the Welsh to run to, even if they'd been minded to. Many of them – too many to be feasible – stood blazing together in grotesque clusters, melting into each other like human-shaped candles. The stench was intolerable, the odour of decay mingling not just with the reek of ruptured guts and splintered bones, but with charring flesh and bubbling human fat. Yet only slowly did they succumb, without panic or hysteria, collapsing one by one. Thick smoke now engulfed the battlements, though it was more grease and soot than vapour. The defenders' gorge rose; cloaks were drawn across faces. Walter Margas, his blue and white chevrons stained yellow with vomit, staggered around like a dying man.

When the smog cleared – and it seemed to take an age – all that remained on the path below was a mass of black, sticky carcasses, twisted and coagulated together, yet, unbelievably, bodies still twitched, still attempted to get back to their feet. Unable to see this latter detail, those on the Constable's Tower cheered. They were watching the bluff, where the remainder of the Welsh host was finally holding back from the bridge, perhaps having realised that further attempts to circumnavigate the castle via the berm were futile.

On the curtain-wall there was less euphoria.

"Two hundred," a man-at-arms stammered. "We must have accounted for two-hundred there!"

"And if you times that by how *often* we killed them, the number should be closer to two thousand," Ranulf replied.

"This is the work of devils," Gurt said, leaning exhaustedly. Dirty sweat dripped from his face. Ulbert too was pale and sweaty, his red and blue tabard blackened with cinders.

"Just be warned," he said. "This isn't over."

"But if that's the best they can do," Gurt insisted, "try to march around the outside of the castle – which must be over a mile – we can attack them with fire all the way. We'll incinerate the lot of them."

"*Is* that the best they can do?" Ranulf asked. "Or were they just probing? Testing our defences?"

"The latter," Ulbert said. "Now they know that to reach the main entrance, they must first smash the curtain-wall."

"And how will they do that, sir knight?" Craon Culai wondered. He was a tall, lean fellow with a pinched, sneering visage. Captain of the royal men-at-arms, but originally low born, he'd long resented the air of authority assumed by the equestrian class. He lifted off his helmet, yanked back his coif and mopped the sweat from his hair. "Do they command thunderbolts as well?"

He was answered by a deafening concussion on the exact point of the battlements where he stood. Three full crenels and a huge chunk of the upper wall exploded with the force, shards flying in all directions, slashing the faces of everyone nearby. Culai and the three men-at-arms standing with him were thrown down into the bailey, cart-wheeling through the scaffolding, hitting every joist, so that they were torn and broken long before they struck the ground.

It was a dizzying moment.

Ulbert wafted his way through the dust to the parapet and peered across the Tefeidiad. On its far shore, three colossal siege-engines had been assembled, each one placed about thirty yards from the next. Diminutive figures milled around them.

"God-Christ," he said under his breath. "God-Christ in Heaven! The earl's mangonels!"

Ranulf and Gurt joined him, wiping the dust and blood from their eyes. There was no mistaking the great mechanical hammers by which their overlord had shattered so many of his enemies' gates and ramparts. The central one of the three, *War Wolf*, had already ejected its first missile. The other two, *God's Maul* and *Giant's Fist*, were in the process.

Their mighty arms swung up simultaneously, driven by immense torsional pressure; the instant they struck their padded crossbeams, massive objects, which looked like cemented sections of stonework, were flung forth. All of the defenders saw them coming, but the projectiles barrelled through the air with such velocity that it was difficult to react in time.

Ulbert was the first. *"EVERYBODY DOWN!"*

On the roof of the Constable's Tower, Corotocus and his men moved en masse to the south-facing parapet, drawn by that thunderous first collision. They were just in time to see the next two payloads tear through upper portions of the curtain-wall, fountains of rubble and timber erupting from each impact, a dozen shattered corpses spinning fifty feet down into the bailey. One missile had been driven with such force that it continued across the bailey until it struck the wall encircling the Inner Fort. Huge fissures branched away from its point of contact.

The earl's expression paled, but as much with anger as fear. Blood trickled from the corner of his mouth as his teeth sank through his bottom lip.

"Good... good Lord," du Guesculin said. "They've raided the artillery train. Taken possession of our catapults."

"And how are they operating them, this peasant rabble?" the earl retorted. "Have they engineers? Can they read Latin, Greek... none of my diagrams and manuals are written in Cymraeg, as far as I'm aware."

Had he been on the river's south shore, Earl Corotocus would have had his answer. Already, the three great machines were being primed again. The hard labour – the cranking on the windlass, the retraction of the throwing-arm – was provided by mindless automatons, some in shrouds, others naked, many in rags coated with gore and grave-dirt. They moved jerkily, yet with precision, speed, and unnatural strength. But when there was skilled work to be done – the measuring of distance, the weighing of missiles in the bucket – it fell to three figures in particular.

They too were ravaged husks; heads lolling on twisted necks, gouged holes where eyes had been, organs rent from their eviscerated bodies. Yet Corotocus would have recognised them: Hugo d'Avranches, Reynald Guiscard and, notable in his black Benedictine habit – which now was blacker still being streaked with every type of filth and ordure – the walking corpse of Brother Ignatius.

CHAPTER TWELVE

FOR THE REST of that first day, the Welsh army stood in silence on the western bluff while the three mangonels did their terrible work. Projectile after projectile was launched across the Tefeidiad. One by one, they struck the upper portion of the curtain-wall or its battlements. The only breaks in this pattern came when delays were caused by the contraptions having to be partly disassembled so that they could be moved on their axes to take aim at different sections.

Wholesale damage was caused. Tons of rubble cascaded into the bailey and onto the berm, burying the dead and maimed of both sides. By late afternoon, the English had lost close to forty men, their shattered bodies flung like so much butcher's meat down through the scaffolding. There was no danger of a major breach being caused – the wall itself was nearly twenty feet thick, its outer face shod with granite, its core packed tight with brick rubble, but the position on top of it was becoming untenable.

A message was soon sent to the roof of the Constable's Tower, requesting permission for the south wall's defenders to withdraw to the Inner Fort. It was rebuffed. As the earl's decision was relayed back, another three thunderbolts struck. One passed clean through a gap already blasted in the battlements, ripping the legs off an archer who was attempting to cross the damaged zone via loose planking. Men scattered in front of the other two, but impacts like claps of doom threw out blizzards of splinters and shards, in which twelve more men were slain and twice that many wounded. One lay on the smashed parapet with his belly burst, his exposed guts hanging down the wall like a mass of ropy tentacles.

"Go and talk to the earl," Ulbert shouted to Ranulf as they crouched together. "I'd go myself, but with Culai dead I'm the only one left here with any seniority. Reason with him, plead with him. At this rate, every man on the south wall will be dead by nightfall."

Ranulf had taken his helmet off earlier because it was so dented by repeated impacts. He tried to put it back on, but it would no longer fit. Cursing, he tossed it away, sheathed his sword, slung his shield onto his back and clambered down the scaffolding.

"Ranulf?" his father called after him.

Ranulf looked up.

Under his raised visor, Ulbert's face was smeared with dirt and blood. He wore a graver expression than his son had ever seen. "Politeness costs nothing. Insolence may cost us a lot."

Ranulf nodded and continued down.

In the bailey, it was difficult to work out just how many men lay dead amid the piles of broken masonry. Several of them had been dashed to pieces, their constituent parts mingled in a macabre puzzle of butchered bone and bloody tissue. Father Benan was present. He wore his purple stole and stood with hands joined in the midst of this gruesome tableau. When he heard Ranulf's footsteps, his eyes snapped open. They were wide, rabbit-like; his cheeks were wan with shock, his brow dirty and moist.

"I'd move out of this place," Ranulf said. "There's more where this came from."

"When... when we first arrived," Benan stuttered, "I offered to hear all the men's confessions. But the earl said it wasn't necessary. That we wouldn't be attacked."

"The earl is not always right. It's a pity it's taken us so long to realise that."

"Dear God!" Benan's eyes were suddenly brimming. "To serve Earl Corotocus and die unshriven? That's not a fate I'd wish on anyone."

Ranulf didn't like to dwell on such things. He couldn't remember the last time he himself had taken confession. "I'm for the Constable's Tower, Father. You should come with me. You're in danger here."

There was a colossal boom as another missile struck the wall behind them. An entire tier of scaffolding fell spectacularly. With a shriek, a man-at-arms fell with it. Benan flinched, but shook his head.

"I must offer a requiem."

"For these scraps of meat?"

"Their souls may yet be saved."

"Father, there are other souls in this castle who could use your prayers. And they still live."

"Go to them. I will join you anon."

Ranulf turned and jogged away up the bailey, though in his full mail it was hot, hard work. He again had to make his way through the Barbican and the Gatehouse, from the tops of which, respectively, Carew's Welsh malcontents and Garbofasse's mercenaries were watching the massed force on the western bluff with a mixture of fear and awe. These two groups in particular faced a dire consequence if taken alive, and the prospect of either that or death suddenly seemed significantly closer than it had done a couple of hours ago.

Ranulf hurried back along the Causeway. By the time he'd climbed to the top of the Constable's Tower, he was streaming sweat and blowing hard. Fresh blood trickled from a slash on his brow. Earl Corotocus was at the south battlements, with various of his lieutenants around him. The rest of his household stood further back, their shields hefted, their weapons brandished. All eyes were fixed on the river's distant shore, and the great war-machines at work there.

"My lord!" Ranulf said, shouldering through.

Corotocus barely glanced at him.

"My lord, you've denied us permission to withdraw from the south wall?"

"That is correct." Corotocus said. He seemed less uneasy than those around him, but there was a tension in his brow. His eyes were keen, blue slivers.

"My lord, you've seen that we're under a very heavy barrage?"

"No-one ever said that fighting the Welsh would be easy, Ranulf."

"Fighting the *Welsh*?" Ranulf struggled to hide his exasperation. "It's come to your attention, has it not, that we're facing more here than just the Welsh?"

"Ahhh... more talk of witchery. It's all over the castle at present. And yet it's so powerful, this witchery, that they've resorted to using catapults – our own catapults, no less – to force entry."

"Either way, my lord, they will soon succeed."

Corotocus turned and looked at him. "Especially if those men I appoint to defend my stronghold have no stomach for it."

"My lord, we are only asking to withdraw to the Inner Fort. It's a more defensible position."

"Return to your post, sir knight."

"My lord, we have nothing to strike back at the mangonels with. In due course they will pound the south wall to rubble. Must all the men there die to prove a point?"

"It would take a decade to pound that wall to rubble, FitzOsbern, as you know. Even with a dozen mangonels."

"My lord, the men on that wall face certain death."

"Death!" Corotocus roared, spittle suddenly flying from his lips. "So be it! If they must die to preserve this bastion, they must die. I won't surrender the outer rampart and allow these devils to walk into our precincts unmolested!"

"So you admit they're devils?" Ranulf said quietly. "A rare moment of honesty from you..."

"You impertinent..."

The earl went for the hilt of his sword, but before he could unsheathe the steel, William d'Abbetot appeared, quite breathless. Close to seventy, bald and white-bearded, he was exhausted simply by his journey from the Barbican. Having removed his mail earlier, he now wore only hose and a linen shirt, both of which were clingy with sweat.

"You summoned me, my lord?" he asked.

Corotocus continued to glare at Ranulf, who glared boldly back.

"God's blood, FitzOsbern!" the earl hissed. "If you weren't born of a she-wolf in a pit of marl! How is it you're the only man alive who doesn't fear me?"

"Should I fear you more, my lord, than what waits for us outside?"

"I need only snap my fingers and you'll be thrown to them first."

"And would that serve your purpose?"

"It may be your just desert."

"We're all going to get our just deserts, my lord. Every one of us."

The earl jabbed a mailed finger into Ranulf's chest. "You stay here, FitzOsbern. *Right here!* D'Abbetot?" He turned to the elderly engineer and pointed south, just as two more projectiles made deafening impacts, dust and rubble exploding into the air. "You see our problem?"

D'Abbetot dabbed his damp pate with a handkerchief. "I do, my lord. Once they've broken the battlements on the south wall, they'll do the same on the east and north. It's only a matter of moving the engines. Of course they'll have full control of the berm path long before then."

"Unless we stop them first," Corotocus said. "How serviceable is the trebuchet?"

"It hasn't been used much in recent times, but it's in working condition. A little oil here and there, some replacement hemp..."

"Can you target the bridge with it?"

"The bridge?"

"There is only one bridge, d'Abbetot. In the southwest corner, for Christ's sake!"

"But my lord, if we smash the bridge won't we be trapped in the castle?"

"We'll also be out of reach. The Welsh can't regain the berm if the bridge no longer exists. They aren't ants, are they? They can't fill up the moat with their dead and just walk over the top."

"Especially as they don't appear to be dying," Ranulf put in.

"Well, d'Abbetot?" the earl growled.

"I'll see to it, my lord. Straight away."

D'Abbetot hobbled off.

"Have the bridge down by nightfall and I'll reward you with estates on every honour I hold," the earl called after him. He turned back to Ranulf, still having to restrain his anger. "You're quite a speaker, sir, for a rogue knight. You must have a high opinion of yourself to voice so many viewpoints in such august company."

"Wasn't it you, my lord, who said you'd rather have men who told the truth?"

"Yes, Ranulf, it was. But that doesn't mean I won't kill them for their impudence."

Ranulf pursed his lips. Perhaps it was time to hold his prattling tongue.

"You may hate my cruelty, Ranulf. You may resent my power. You may revile my ambition. But do you know what hurts the most – your mistrust of my abilities."

Ranulf could not refute the charge. His temper had got the better of him, for there was no doubt that breaking the bridge was a clever plan. No matter what demonic powers protected them, the Welsh could assail the castle with missiles for day after day, but if the bridge was destroyed they could make no further gain. They could never physically wrest the stronghold from its defenders. Of course, a prolonged bombardment would still inflict horrendous casualties.

"My lord, if they continue to pound us..."

"It will achieve little," Corotocus said. "Apart from wasting their time. King Edward plans to enter this country through the north, but he won't sit on his arse there forever. Even if he doesn't receive a plea for help from us, he'll come down here at length to consolidate his gains. Let's see how they fare then, against a host of fifty thousand. In any case, once the bridge is broken, I can withdraw all my troops from the south wall. We won't need the outer rampart any more."

Ranulf nodded. Earl Corotocus might be a brute but he'd always been a capable tactician.

"Which brings me back to *you*," the earl said. His lieutenants hovered behind him, uncertainly. Only Navarre looked pleased by this turn of events. "I can't tolerate your constant rebellions, Ranulf, or your petty treasons. So your sentence is death."

Some of the knights hung their heads. Navarre broke into a delighted grin.

"Do you hear me?" the earl said.

"I hear you, my lord."

"You think I can endure this indefinitely, boy? You think I can be defied with venom in the midst of battle, when other men of mine – better men, and more loyal than you – are dying all around? Do you think I *should* endure it?"

Ranulf said nothing.

"Be assured, if I didn't need every man in my command right now, I'd hang you from the highest gibbet in Wales. But don't be comforted, Ranulf. When this war is over, the sentence will be confirmed. And of course you must challenge it. You must claim trial by combat, as is your right. I'll be more than happy to oblige..."

Before he could say more, a shadow fell over them. They glanced up.

A dark but glittering cloud was arcing from the top of the western bluff towards the castle's northwest corner. At first it was like a flock of birds, sunlight glinting on their black, metallic feathers. But then they realised that it was debris – or 'iron hail', to use catapult crew parlance – maybe a ton of it, spreading out as it descended on the Barbican.

Its impact was deafening and prolonged. It covered almost the entirety of the Barbican roof and spilled partly onto the Gatehouse alongside it. Even from as far away as the Constable's Tower, a hundred yards to the south, the clangour of impacts, the chorus of shouts and screams was ear-splitting.

Earl Corotocus moved to the north battlements, the others joining him. Though located on elevated ground, the Barbican wasn't as tall as the Constable's Tower. Subsequently, they had a perfect view of the damage the iron hail had inflicted. The trebuchet appeared to be intact. A good number of Carew's Welsh were milling around it, though many others lay prone as though felled by hammer-blows.

"The scoop-thrower!" du Guesculin shouted. "Dear Lord in Heaven, they've got the scoop-thrower as well!"

"Of course they've got the scoop-thrower," Corotocus replied. "It's the deadliest machine in my arsenal. Would they leave that behind?"

"Why is it trained on the Barbican?" Navarre wondered.

"It's trained on the *trebuchet*, you idiot! If they break the trebuchet, we've no way to demolish the bridge and they can continue the infantry assault."

"Can't we disassemble the trebuchet and move it?" du Guesculin said.

Corotocus snarled his frustration. "There's nowhere to set it up where it'll be out of reach of the scoop-thrower unless we move it to the east rampart, where it will be useless anyway."

"What in God's name do we do, my lord?" Du Guesculin had gone white. Of them all, he had looked most hopeful at the suggestion the southwest bridge might be made unusable and the Welsh held in abeyance. "In the good Lord's name, what do...?"

"Arm the trebuchet!" Corotocus bellowed. "Smash that bridge now, before it's too damn late!"

"D'Abbetot will need Carew and his damn malcontents to help," Navarre said. "But look at the state of them."

Even after one deluge of iron hail, the priority on the Barbican had changed from mutual defence to self-preservation. There was still much shouting and consternation, but something like a retreat was in progress. Numerous wounded were being assisted up the steps to the Gatehouse.

Corotocus bared his teeth.

"Get over there, Navarre," he snarled. "Remind Captain Carew that if this castle falls he and his Welsh malingerers will be singled out for even less merciful treatment than we English. Remind them they are to assist William d'Abbetot, my senior engineer, in any way that he requests, and that this means holding their position until ordered to do otherwise. If any object, put them to the sword immediately."

He turned to another of his tenant knights, a wiry, leathery-skinned fellow in a black and orange striped mantle, called Robert of Tancarville.

"You as well, Robert. And *you*!" Corotocus pointed at Ranulf. "A chance to redeem yourself early."

Ranulf didn't suppose the Barbican could be any worse a posting at this moment than the south curtain-wall. He nodded curtly and followed the other two.

"Let's hope d'Abbetot hadn't already got up there," he said, joining them on the downward stair. "If he's dead, the trebuchet's no use to us anyway."

"Always you expect the worst," Navarre jeered.

"No, I expect the iron hail," Ranulf said. "The worst may be yet to come."

CHAPTER THIRTEEN

THE BARBICAN WAS another supposedly impregnable feature of Grogen Castle.

Standing just to the west of the Gatehouse, it was a bastion in its own right: a squat, hexagonal tower, filled with rubble so that it was basically a gigantic earthwork clad with stone and fitted around its rim with huge crenels. Its roof was broad enough not just to accommodate the trebuchet, but over a hundred men-at-arms and archers, who could assail, in more or less complete safety, any force attempting to attack the castle's main entrance. The trebuchet itself was powerful enough to shoot clean down to the river, or, thanks to its turntable base, far up onto the western bluff. It was a strong and defensible position for any company of men, but it had never been foreseen that it might be attacked from overhead. When Navarre and Tancarville arrived up there, it was a scene of carnage. The corpses of Carew's malcontents dotted the Barbican roof, while many of those still living clutched bloody wounds as they flowed up the Gatehouse stair to mingle with Garbofasse's mercenaries.

In general terms, Carew's band were poorly armed, clad in hose, leather jerkins and boots. One or two were in mail, and some wore pointed or broad-brimmed helmets, but most lacked shields to shelter beneath, and so the iron hail had taken a massive toll of them. Carew, who had also retreated to the Gatehouse, was better equipped than most. His helmet was fitted with nose and cheek pieces. He also wore a hauberk of padded felt studded with iron balls, but he'd been cut deeply across the neck. Blood gushed from the wound as he sought to bind it.

"Carew, where the devil are your dogs running to?" Navarre shouted, as he and Robert of Tancarville approached with swords drawn.

Carew spun to face him. "Hell's rain has just fallen on our heads! Didn't you see?"

"Hell is where you're headed if you don't get these wretches back to their posts!"

Ranulf now arrived, with William d'Abbetot alongside him. They'd overtaken the elderly engineer on their way here. Ranulf had held back to assist him as he puffed his way up the steep Gatehouse stair.

"You expect us to stand under the iron hail?" Carew shouted.

"The earl expects you to stand until the last man, if necessary!" Navarre retorted.

"And will you set the example for us, Aquitaine?"

"Do as you're commanded. *Now!*"

"You first, you crooked-faced ape."

Navarre raised his sword, but Ranulf stepped between them. "Fighting among ourselves is the last thing we need," he said. "Captain Carew, where do you and your men think you're retreating to?"

"We can still protect the castle entrance if we man the Gatehouse."

"The Gatehouse is also in the scoop-thrower's range."

As if in proof there was a wild shout and another nebulous shadow fell over them. Instinctively, Navarre and Tancarville lifted their shields. Ranulf did the same, but dragged d'Abbetot, who of course was not armoured, beneath his. Carew fell to a crouch, arms wrapped around his helmet. No-one else reacted before the second hail struck.

Every type of missile smashed down: bolts, nails, screws, stones, bits of chain, hunks of jagged metal. Ranulf had a sturdy shield. It was fashioned from planks and linen strips glued together, bound with iron and overlaid with painted leather. It felt as if a giant with a sledgehammer was beating on it and it was all he could do to keep the thing horizontal. When the deluge was over, the shield was buckled out of shape, though it had served its purpose – both Ranulf and William d'Abbetot were shaken but unhurt. Others hadn't been so lucky.

Garbofasse's mercenaries were better armoured than Carew's Welsh, but several of them had been struck. Ranulf saw split scalps, lacerated faces, broken limbs. All around, there were groans and gasps as dazed men helped fallen comrades to their feet. The Welsh, caught for a second time in the hail, had fared even worse. Those climbing the steps from the Barbican had been hit simultaneously by a timber beam, which had shattered three skulls in a row. The Barbican roof was under inches of debris; several dozen lay half-buried in it. Others still on their feet wandered groggily, their helms battered into fantastical shapes. Carew gazed bemusedly at his hands, which were badly mangled, the flesh torn away from several bent and broken fingers.

"God help us," d'Abbetot stammered. "We can't post anyone on the Barbican or Gatehouse under conditions like these. They'll be massacred."

"We need to demolish the bridge," Ranulf said. "That's one thing we *must* do before yielding these posts." He took d'Abbetot by the elbow and forced him down the stair, both struggling not to trip over corpses or slip on treads slick with gore. "How long before the scoop-thrower's ready to discharge again?"

"Several minutes. But that won't be long enough for us." Panic grew in d'Abbetot's voice. "I have to find the range, and that could take four or five shots. And if I can't turn the damn thing around, we can't even aim." They'd now reached the trebuchet, but every

Welshman in the vicinity seemed to be dead or critically injured. "For God's sake, FitzOsbern, get someone else down here... we can't turn the damn thing round on our own!"

Ranulf called back to the Gatehouse. In response, Navarre tottered down the steps, with Tancarville close behind. Navarre's shield had splintered and he was bloodied around the face. As they came, they rounded up several of the walking wounded.

"Christ help us!" d'Abbetot moaned. "Look at this!"

Even to Ranulf's untrained eye, it was clear that the first two volleys of hail had done severe damage to the trebuchet. The sling ropes had been severed, the padding on the crossbeam ripped asunder.

"How long to repair it?" Ranulf asked.

"Damn it, I don't know. Have we even got replacement materials?"

"Mind your heads!" someone shrieked.

Yet another shadow fell over them. Again, Ranulf grasped the engineer and dragged him beneath his shield. Tancarville raised his own shield and squatted. Navarre now had no shield. Maybe eight or nine of Garbofasse's mercenaries had joined the remaining ten Welsh still alive on the Barbican roof. Only a couple of these were quick enough to take evasive action. When the next deluge struck, it was mainly stones – of all sizes, from cobblestones, to pebbles, to pellets – banging on iron, cracking on brickwork, ripping through flesh and wood and hide. There were more screams, more gasps and grunts. Ranulf didn't know how many hundredweight of minerals were impacting on his shield as he tried to hold it aloft. His forearm ached abominably, but long before the storm ceased an even more frightening problem arose – for three human bodies also landed on the Barbican.

One came down on the top of its skull, which imploded so completely that there was nothing left of it. The others bounced across the roof like sacks of broken crockery, finally rolling to a standstill. Ranulf had heard about this before, though he'd never witnessed it – the catapulting of diseased or decayed corpses into fortifications. Normally it was an aspect of prolonged sieges, signifying that the besiegers were becoming desperate and would use any means, no matter how ghoulish, to force a capitulation. It rarely happened as early in the conflict as this.

That was when the three bodies began to twitch.

Slowly, Ranulf lowered what remained of his shield. He'd seen much here already that defied description, but what he now beheld set his senses reeling.

A trio of twisted forms rose clumsily to their feet.

They were better armed than the majority of the enemy he'd so far seen. Two were in leather jerkins and leather breeches. One had bare feet but wore gauntlets, while the other was shod with metal sabatons but barehanded; one of those hands had been severed at the wrist. The third figure, the headless one, was naked except for a mail hauberk, which hung down as far as its knees and looked something like a shroud. It soon dawned on Ranulf how appropriate this analogy was – the hauberk was indeed a shroud, for it had been put on the figure after death. They'd all of them been dressed like this after death, for evidently they *were* dead.

Ranulf now understood this fully.

These creatures were dead and yet somehow they were also alive.

The rest of the men on the roof were too preoccupied to have noticed the figures stumbling towards them. D'Abbetot was seated groggily on the trebuchet turntable. He'd been struck in the face by a stone, which had slashed his brow and spit his nose. All of Carew's malcontents had now been floored. Only one clambered back to his feet. Navarre removed his battered helmet and shook out fragments of metal, blood dripping from his brow. Tancarville was on his knees, stunned. Five of Garbofasse's men were still upright, but all were visibly injured.

"The enemy's with us!" Ranulf shouted, unsheathing his sword. Only slivers remained of his shield, so he threw it down. "In God's name, the enemy's here!"

Still the others didn't react. He swung back to face the demonic threesome, now only a matter of yards away. The headless figure was armed with a spiked mace. The one in the gauntlets had landed with a spear, though this had shattered on impact, so it had scooped up a falchion with a curved blade. The third carried a pollaxe which, though it would normally require two hands to wield it effectively, was being brandished in one hand with no difficulty.

They were true visions of horror, these walking dead men. Broken bones ground together as they advanced, white shards protruding through their pulverised flesh. Of their two remaining faces, one had been crushed to the point where a vile sewage of blood and brains flowed from its nasal cavity. The other had been pierced through the mouth by an arrow, the barbed head of which projected beneath its chin, digging into its throat. One of its eyes had been eaten away; the other was a maleficent orb glinting from a cradle of splintered bone.

"Off your arses!" Ranulf shouted, though it was more of a howl. The tough young warrior, who'd known almost nothing but war and strife since he'd first been knighted, literally *howled*. "To arms, I say!"

The three figures approached like marionettes jerking on invisible strings. But gradually they seemed to focus their energy. They became stronger, faster; they walked with a heavier, more determined tread. Even Ranulf, who'd seen them coming first, was mesmerised. He only just raised his sword in time to parry a downward blow from the spiked mace, before retaliating with a huge crosscut, which caught the headless horror across the chest. He failed to cleave the mail, but sent the creature tottering backward, and now at last the other troops realised that the Barbican had been infiltrated.

D'Abbetot's eyes goggled, even though blood was streaming into them. Navarre went for the one-handed monstrosity, thrusting and hacking with all his strength, though it fended him off with unnatural skill, catching him across the chin with the point of its pollaxe, laying open his disfigured face once again. Two mercenaries went for the one in gauntlets. One of them swung a morningstar, only for the chain to wrap around its forearm. It yanked him forward and drove the falchion into his belly, his entrails flopping out in glistening coils. The other mercenary thrust a poniard into its skull, ramming it through the bone into the tissue beneath, but it swept him aside and, snatching the morningstar, looped it around his throat and threw him over its shoulder, snapping his neck. The surviving Welshman came for it with a spear. A massive, two-handed blow took the monster in the midriff, impaling it clean through. Again it showed no pain, no weakness. Neither blood nor mucus spilled from its jammed open mouth. It grappled with the Welshman and, raising its falchion, sundered his battered helm and the cranium beneath. A third mercenary hurled a javelin, which buried itself in the corpse's gaping socket. Now there were two implements protruding from its head. Instead of succumbing, it broke the javelin's haft, grabbed the shrieking mercenary by the throat and thrust the haft's dagger-like shard into his groin. The mercenary's scream became a shrill screech of emasculation.

A few yards away, Navarre clove his opponent through the right shoulder and, with a mighty backstroke, lopped off its head. But it still came on. Only when he severed its left leg just above the knee did it topple over. Ranulf made equal gains, using massive, swinging strokes to fend his opponent to the battlements, where he was able to chop the mace from its grasp, and kick it backward through an embrasure.

Yet, they'd no sooner destroyed the assault party than a fourth avalanche of rubble struck them. On this occasion, nobody was prepared for it. One second Ranulf was standing, blade dripping, the next he was beset from above by rocks, stones and lumps of metal. His scalp and face were ripped open and he took an agonising blow on his collar bone before he was able to pull up his coif and hunker down, his arms crossed over his head. Others followed suite, though not all. Robert Tancarville flailed uselessly at the sky with his sword, and was hit in the face by a coping stone. William d'Abbetot shrieked incoherently as he was hammered to the floor, one missile after another bouncing off him, smashing his hands as he tried to protect his head.

And again there were corpses. This time a couple of them missed the Barbican altogether, crashing down its wall into the moat. But at least eight landed cleanly, and were very quickly upright. They were equally rent and mutilated, but again were clad in mail and leather and armed with every type of weapon.

Ranulf had to push himself back to his feet on the tip of his sword as the horrible spectres lumbered forward, groaning and mewling. He met the first with a two-handed blow that severed its trunk at the hips, but then was grabbed around the head and flung to the floor. He cried for help.

Garbofasse and a dozen more men hobbled down from the Gatehouse roof. All wore crushed helmets and carried bent shields; their faces were gashed and bruised. They were in a poor state to meet seven ravening corpses, and could barely defend themselves as the dead things raised their mauls and mattocks. Navarre was also back on his feet. Like Ranulf, his mail had protected most of his body from the hail's edge, but his face was almost unrecognisable. His sword had snapped mid-blade. Disgustedly, he cast it away, grabbed up a flail and rejoined the fray.

For minutes on end, battle raged across the Barbican. When the cadavers' weapons broke, they tore into their prey with claws and teeth. They rode every counter-blow, though their limbs were hewed, their skulls shattered. One after another, Garbofasse's mercenaries were despatched. One's helmet was struck with such force that his churned brains spurted through its visor. A second was skewered through the midriff with a broken axe handle. A third was beaten to the ground with an iron bar. A fourth was lifted bodily into the air and carried towards the battlements; his spittle-filled shrieks rang aloud as he was flung over. Garbofasse strove at the monsters with a battle-axe in each hand. Ranulf clove one's head cross-wise, slicing through its open mouth with his blade, shearing off the top half of its skull, though it stayed on its feet, foul fluids gargling in its opened oesophagus.

More of Garbofasse's troops limped down from the Gatehouse, only to be met by another iron hail. This was heavier than any thus far. The usual debris was laced with razor-edged flint. Again, the men were slashed and brutalised. Ranulf staggered towards William d'Abbetot's body, belatedly thinking that saving the engineer's life should be a priority – only to see that what remained of him was being pounded like mulch into the rubble. Even those much younger and stronger than d'Abbetot were cut down. Once the hail had finished, only Ranulf, Navarre, Garbofasse and three of his mercenaries remained on their feet; all had been freshly wounded. The only ones unaffected were the corpses. Though torn anew, in some cases reduced to parodies of humanity – grisly effigies of exposed bone and filleted flesh – they came on as before.

"Back to the Gatehouse," Ranulf called.

These Welsh – if they *were* Welsh, and not from Hades itself – could not be slain or hurt. They could march through their own artillery storm, while the English fell under it like wheat to the scythe.

"Back to the G-Gatehouse... *now!*" he stammered. "We can't win this!"

CHAPTER FOURTEEN

In the disorder that followed the retreat onto the Gatehouse it was impossible for coherent orders to be issued. Five maniacal corpses still held sway on the Barbican, but attempts to place a shield-wall at the top of the Gatehouse stair and bar their path were hampered by yet another iron hail, which now swept the Gatehouse roof, driving those remaining to the downward hatches. In the cramped rooms below it was a chaos of blood, straw and smoke. Throats were raw with shouts and gasps. Men were slumped with exhaustion, caked in dirt and gore, their tabards and surcoats in tatters.

At last Earl Corotocus arrived, forcing his way through, with du Guesculin and more of his household men struggling along behind. Father Benan, white-faced and tearful, brought up the rear.

"What is this madness, Corotocus?" Garbofasse roared, shoving men out of his way. "A third of my troops are dead and they've barely struck a blow yet!"

"They've struck plenty of blows," Ranulf interjected. "Mainly against women and children. This may be the price of that victory."

Corotocus couldn't respond. He was too startled by the bloodied, battered state of his lieutenants.

"What devilry have you unleashed on us?" Garbofasse demanded.

"My lord," Father Benan simpered, "my lord, this is too terrible..."

"Earn your corn, priest!" the earl barked. "Confess the dying, help Zacharius succour the wounded."

"Those... those men," du Guesculin stammered, his eyes bulging as he recalled what he'd seen from the Constable's Tower. "Catapulted alive onto the... and to fight and kill. It must be some kind of illusion."

"You dolt!" Garbofasse threw a crimson rag into his face. "Are these wounds an illusion?"

"Navarre?" the earl said, turning to his most trusted henchman.

Navarre was seated on a stool, sweating, breathing hard, his scalp and face horribly cut. He could only shake his head.

The earl swung to Ranulf. "What of you? You were hand-to-hand with them, damn it, what did you see?"

Ranulf looked him straight in the eye. "I saw dead men walking like puppets, but wielding weapons like Viking berserks. I saw mildewed lumps of carrion, some still coated with grave dirt, raging at us like barbarians."

"Damn devilry!" Garbofasse swore again. "Damn blasted devilry!"

The word went around quickly. Men who previously had been too weary or hurt now leapt to their feet. There was shouting, pushing.

"Enough!" the earl thundered. "You peasant scum! *Enough!*"

A deafening silence followed. He peered around at them. Fiery phantoms writhed on their wounded faces, on the arched brick ceiling overhead.

"You maggots!" he said. "The whole army of the world's dead may be out there, and they couldn't break these walls!"

"They won't need to break them," Navarre said, finally standing. "Forgive me for speaking plainly, but as long as they have the scoop-thrower we can't man the Barbican or the Gatehouse roof."

"And as long as they have the mangonels," came another voice, "we can barely man the curtain-wall."

This was Ulbert. Despite the fearsome attacks on his own position, news had reached him that a company had been wiped out on the Barbican. He'd come hotfoot to find his son. Though he flinched at the sight of Ranulf's lacerated face, he was palpably relieved to find him alive. He turned again to Corotocus.

"My lord, I needn't tell you, but with the curtain-wall lost, all they'll need to do is walk around the outside and come in through the front door."

"We must break the southwest bridge as we planned," Garbofasse asserted.

"That's now impossible," Ranulf replied. "The trebuchet's damaged and William d'Abbetot is dead."

"We should withdraw," du Guesculin urged his master. "Move back to the Constable's Tower."

Ranulf gave him a scornful look. "If the scoop-thrower can strike the Gatehouse roof, surely you see that it can strike the Constable's Tower as well?"

"What are our losses on the south wall?" Corotocus asked Ulbert.

"About half our strength. The fire barricade on the berm has prevented their assault force circling the castle, but it won't last forever."

Before anyone else could speak, there was a ghastly shriek and a mercenary tottered forward clutching his belly, from which a spearhead protruded. Behind him, there was another shriek. In the dim-lit press of damaged, sagging bodies, it was difficult to see exactly what was happening, but the rearmost hatch appeared to have been forced open and a figure had dropped down. It was now assailing another of Garbofasse's men with a scramsax. Its third blow clove his skull so brutally that his brain was exposed. It then shambled forward, striking at anyone within range. An instant later it was face to face with Corotocus. The earl's eyes almost popped from their sockets. The demonic thing was naked of clothing, but it had been stripped of most of its flesh as well. Muscle tissue hung in shreds. All it had for a face were torn ruins. Multiple arrows transfixed it.

Never had a nobleman, even as steeped in blood as Earl Corotocus, seen any creature as mutilated as this and still apparently alive. His eyes tracked slowly upward as it raised the weapon with which to sunder his cranium. And then the reverie was broken, and a dozen blades stormed it from all sides, hacking, slashing, reducing it to quivering pulp, chopping it to segments, which continued to squirm and twitch on the floor.

"The hatch!" someone screamed. "The damn bloody hatch!" Swiftly, the open hatchway was blocked with beams and planks.

"More of them will land up there," Navarre shouted. "We've no option – we *have* to go up and repel them."

"And face the iron hail?" Garbofasse scoffed.

"We could form a testudo..."

"It's suicide!"

Navarre looked to the earl for instruction, but the earl was still mesmerised by the gory fragments scattered at his feet.

"My lord," Father Benan whispered into his ear, yanking the shoulder of his cloak. "My lord... this is not... this is not the natural order of things."

Corotocus finally came round. "What are you gibbering about? Didn't I send you to your work?"

Father Benan shook his head. He half smiled, though there was an eerie light in his eyes, a form of shock or craziness. "My lord, don't you see what this means?"

Corotocus pushed him aside, and lurched over to where Captain Carew sat hunched against a pillar. "Carew?"

Carew said nothing at all; he merely offered up his hands, both bound with bloody rags and mangled beyond use.

"My lord," Father Benan said, grabbing the earl's cloak again. "You once endowed me with a generous chantry. To sing psalms for your soul. Every day and every night, you said... to protect you from Hell's vengeance in the afterlife."

Corotocus gazed down at the severed head of the thing that had just attacked him. To his incredulity, what remained of its tongue was still moving in the cavity where its lower jaw had been. He stamped on it with his mailed foot – again and again, hacking at it with his heel, cracking its skull apart, flattening it out so that its eyes popped out and a noisome porridge of rotted brain-matter flowed across the flagstones.

Father Benan was undeterred. "My lord, I *cannot* save you." He gave a fluting laugh even though tears spilled onto his cheeks. "Not with all the psalms or prayers in Christendom."

Corotocus turned and stared at him.

The priest shook his head frantically. "You may endow a hundred orders to try and bribe God for over a hundred centuries, but He will not listen. This abomination is a sign that you are past help. That God has turned his back on you... "

"Silence, you fool!"

"Not just on you but on all those who follow you. These unnatural horrors are the price we pay for your crimes against God and Humanity..."

"You snivelling louse!" Corotocus grabbed him by the habit and threw him to his knees. "You *dare* hide your cowardice behind Holy Orders? Somebody whip him! Whip him 'til there's no skin on his back!"

There was hesitation before anyone obeyed, which was a new experience indeed for the Earl of Clun. They'd all heard the priest's words. They all knew in their heart of hearts that the things they'd done in Wales under the earl's command would never find favour with Jesus Christ. But much less would it find favour to chastise one of His anointed prelates.

"D'you hear me!" the earl roared at them. "Punish this dog! This traitor who invokes God's curse on us!" Still they were reluctant. "You mindless children! Are you blind as well as stupid? The witchcraft is outside! Since when did God ever send devils to do His holy work?"

"Since when did the king of England send devils to do his?" the priest said with another laugh.

The earl kicked at him, sending him sprawling.

"Do you all hear this treason? Is this a fitting comrade, who switches his allegiance the moment the enemy is close?"

"My lord," someone protested. "A holy man..."

"What's holy about him? You heard his weasel words. If the Welsh get in, he'll no doubt hasten to tell them that it wasn't him. That he advised against this mission, which, incidentally, we are carrying out on the orders of our lord, the king." He spat on Benan's cassock. "Do not be fooled by these priestly vestments. This turd has shown his true colours. He's a snake in the grass, who would deceive us all. Now do as I say. Get him out of here, scourge his worthless hide."

"You heard His Excellency!" Navarre shouted.

To see the household champion hurt, and yet still strong and fiercely loyal to his overlord galvanised the rest of them. Two household knights came forward and dragged the weeping priest away.

"Back to the business at hand," Corotocus said. "Shore those other hatches. Make sure they can't be broken again."

As the mesnie bustled, Ranulf wondered if the earl was at last losing his grasp of military realities. He'd wasted time punishing a malefactor, and yet a desperate battle was raging outside. He was content to close off the captured areas of the castle rather than try to recover them. There were exclamations about this from the more experienced knights. They pleaded with the earl that the Barbican, or at least the Gatehouse roof, needed to be cleared of the enemy, as the warriors catapulted up there would now be able to enter the bailey. But the earl replied that no more than a handful would manage it. The dead could have the Gatehouse roof, but so long as its interior was held from them, the bulk of the enemy would be kept outside.

"Does he fully realise what we're facing here?" Ranulf asked his father quietly. "These creatures can't just be cut down with a sword-stroke. I've seen that for myself. In that respect, each one of them is worth any ten of us."

"He can only do what he can do." Ulbert replied.

"What?"

Ulbert rarely showed emotion these days, let alone fear or panic. But even by his normal detached standards, he seemed strangely resigned to meeting whatever abhorrence was hammering on the hatchways above their heads.

"He can't just wave a wand to make this foe go away, Ranulf."

"Someone waved one to make them come here."

"Then perhaps, as soldiers, it is part of our duty to find this person and kill him." Ulbert moved away. "In the meantime we must look to our friends."

The earl was still issuing orders, fully in command again. When Ulbert and Ranulf confronted him, requesting permission to return to the south curtain-wall and organise a retreat for the troops still holding out there, he eyed them thoughtfully. Any anger he still felt at Ranulf was probably tempered by the sight of the young knight's facial wounds, which proved more than words ever could that he'd fought hard in his overlord's name. In addition, there were practical considerations. To withdraw from the curtain-wall now would be to grant the Welsh unfettered access to the berm and thus to the castle's main entrance. But to leave men on the curtain-wall would be certain death for them, not just from the mangonels to their front, but from the corpses in the bailey who could climb the scaffolding and attack them from behind.

"That would be sensible," he eventually said. "I don't want to do it with the southwest bridge intact, but it seems the bridge is beyond our reach. Very well. The curtain-wall is to be abandoned, but only temporarily. When the time is right, I intend to recapture it."

Corotocus gave the two knights leave and they descended quickly to the next level, crossing over a narrow gantry drawbridge, which spanned the castle's entrance passage and joined with the north curtain-wall. Thirty feet below them, the passage was deserted, but it was easy to imagine that soon it would be packed with struggling forms, their ghoulish groans echoing in the high, narrow space. The main entrance gate was recessed into the Gatehouse on the left-hand side of this passage rather than at its far end, which made assault by ram or catapult impossible. Theoretically, such a gate was unbreakable, but Ranulf could already envisage these indestructible monsters swarming all over it until they'd torn it down with their bare hands.

On the north battlements, he leaned against a crenel to get his breath. He pulled back his coif; his hair was sticky with clotting blood. Many of his gashes still wept red tears.

"Are you alright?" Ulbert asked.

"I think my nose is broken."

"No matter. It wasn't much to look at."

Ranulf half smiled. "A pity it couldn't have been your scrawny neck."

"Do you want to wait here and rest?"

"No. There are many hurt worse than me." They set off. As they walked, Ranulf said: "Father, have you ever heard of anything... *anything* like this before?"

Ulbert pondered; his face was graven in stone.

"I once heard about something," he admitted. "It was two centuries ago at least. A rumour brought back from the East. Bohemond's crusader army was in peril. They'd won the battle of Antioch, but the nobles squabbled and refused to cooperate with each other, so smaller parties of knights set out for Jerusalem without them. Soon they were starved and parched. They fought their way across an arid, desolate land, hunted all the way by Saracen horsemen. When they reached civilisation, they were more like animals than men. They destroyed the Moslem city of Ma'arrat, where the more demented among them prepared a cannibal feast. Even those who'd retained their sanity joined them, tortured by the smell of cooked meat. The Saracens were so outraged by this crime that they too broke God's laws. Their wizards summoned a dust storm to envelope the crusader army when it marched again. Many were lost in the confusion. Great numbers were taken prisoner. A year later, these prisoners reappeared at the battle of Ascalon. They were naked and skinless, having been flayed, but despite this they marched against their former allies. The story is that they marched under banners made from their own shredded hides."

"That's a fairy story," Ranulf said. "Surely?"

Ulbert laughed without humour. "In years to come people will refer to this as a fairy story. But that doesn't make it any less a nightmare for those of us living through it."

CHAPTER FIFTEEN

COUNTESS MADALYN SAT rigid on her horse. A long pole with a gleaming steel point was inserted through a pannier beside her saddle. From the top of it, *Y Ddraig Goch*, the dragon of Wales, billowed on a green weave.

It gave her a commanding aura, a queenly air, but those who knew her would say that her posture was just a little too stiff, her gloved hands knotted too tightly on her leather reins. Though her flame-red hair was a famed glory of the Powys valleys, her fleece hood was drawn up tightly. She wore a linen veil, drenched with perfume, across her nose and mouth. She looked neither left nor right, but focussed intently on the gaunt edifice of Grogen Castle.

From this position on the western bluff, it was difficult to see exactly what was happening over there. Palls of brackish smoke still cloaked the side of the fortress facing the river. The wall on that side had been blackened by fire, and massive projectiles were still being hurled across the water at it. With each monstrous impact, stones and bodies flew through the air, though no accurate tally could be made of the English dead. Likewise on the Barbican, which the great scooped throwing-machine located in the wood beyond the crest of the hill behind her had been pounding with showers of broken stone and metal. Consternation had been caused among its defenders, which intensified massively when, in scenes the countess had never thought she'd witness in a thousand lifetimes, human beings had also been flung up there, spinning through the air, turning over and over. In many cases they'd missed the Barbican altogether, falling short into the moat or striking the castle walls. Even those that reached it were surely landing with such force that they'd be broken to pieces. And yet fighting had followed on the Barbican battlements: figures struggling together, the flashing of blades, bodies and body parts dropping over the parapets, prolonged and hideous shrieks.

Of course, even concentrating on these horrible scenes was preferable to watching the mass of dead and decayed flesh shuffling onto the bluff around her. On first arriving here, she'd tried to steel herself, to face the reality of what she was doing. Initially it hadn't been so bad – one stumbling, ragged figure had seemed much like another if you avoided looking at its face. But it wasn't long before she was noticing the various methods by which these pitiful forms had first been sent from this world: the nooses knotted at their throats, the spears that spitted them, the crazily angled torsos where spines had been broken.

In some cases it had hardened her resolve, reminding her in a way words never could of the depredations inflicted on her people. An old man – eyeless, tongueless, waving stumps for hands – made her weep. A young man – naked, a festering cavity where his genitals should be, a beam across his shoulders, his wrists nailed to either end of it, showing that he'd not just been emasculated but crucified as well – made her seethe with outrage. But as one apparition after another tottered past, it became increasingly difficult to focus on the injustice. A naked pregnant woman, her swollen belly slit open and an infant's arm protruding – and twitching – made the countess's gorge rise. A child torn apart by war dogs, and even now in death unintelligibly wailing – as though for a mother that would never answer its cries of pain and fear – made her clamp a hand to her eyes. A few hours later, even more grotesque figures had begun to appear: those who had died *before* this war – the diseased, the crippled, the starved. In some cases they had died months before. She saw stick limbs, worm-eaten ribs, skulls without scalps, faces that were green, faces that were black, faces that were hanging from the bone.

A tide of raddled flesh and filthy, leprous rags now jostled on all sides of her. The stench was unbearable, eye-watering even through her scented veil. She did her best to remain aloof, as Gwyddon and his acolytes were. But she could no longer look at these poor, corrupted husks. If they made contact with her stirrup-clad boots, merely brushing against them, she cringed. Her mount, which had once belonged to an English knight and had seen much battle, had become skittish, revolted by the smell and alarmed by the meaningless, mumbling discord of the dead. Every so often an instruction from Gwyddon – delivered in the hard pagan tongue of ancient times, rather than the melodious voice of her people now – would despatch fresh cohorts downhill towards the bridge. And how relieved Countess Madalyn was to see the backs of these, though always more would emerge from the woods and hills at her rear, and flow into the gaps.

She tried to console herself with thoughts of romantic myths. The histories of the Welsh had always been notable for brutality and malevolence. The fair Rhiannon tricked her fiancé Gwawl into a magic bag, where he was bludgeoned almost to death by her lover Pwyll, only at which point did he finally agree to release her from the engagement. The beautiful Arianrhod, angered that her family had discovered she was pregnant out of wedlock, cursed her own child, Lleu, for the entirety of his life, the ultimate culmination of which was his marriage to the hag Blodeuwedd, who gleefully murdered him. And yet it was no solace really – not *really* – for these were nought but fancies and folklore. *This* was altogether different. These lumbering wrecks, these sad, rotting travesties who once had been resting in God's sweet earth, who in most cases had paid their dues with agonising deaths and yet now had been called to die again and again and again – they were all *too* real.

The worst incident came in the middle of the day.

The largest projectiles so far impacted on the crenels of the castle's south wall and the roars of battle still echoed from the roof of its Barbican. But the countess was weary with it, reeling with the stench of death. In a moment of weakness, she happened to glance to her right. That was all it was – a glance, very fleeting. And yet, inexorably, as though fated, her eyes were drawn to someone she knew. Before she could think, his name broke from her lips.

"Kye!"

Again, fresh cohorts of the dead had been sent downhill to cross the castle bridge and follow the berm path, and her former bodyguard was going with them. Yet, unlike those others around him, Kye seemed to hear her.

He turned slowly – painfully slowly – to look.

Overjoyed, she dismounted and ran forward, oblivious to the carrion shapes that she thrust out of her way. Kye was a typically handsome son of Wales: tall, huge of build, with his great black beard, black bushy hair and piercing blue eyes.

"Kye!" she said again, elated.

She'd seen him struck down, but she must have been mistaken. He'd been struck, yes, but he'd survived. His even features were unmarked by flame or blade, unbitten by worm. He still wore his gleaming mail habergeon and the red leather corselet over the top of it. His eyes seemed to fix on her, their gaze clear and focussed. As she approached, she yanked back her hood and tore off her veil so that he would recognise her.

He extended a hand of friendship. She opened her arms to embrace him.

And then – horror, despair.

For he pushed her aside, and reached instead for the dragon standard in her horse's pannier.

Some soldierly instinct remained in Kye's curdled brain, some vague understanding that, though he was a combatant, he'd come to this place of battle without weapon or insignia. Now he remedied this, drawing the great banner free. Wielding it before him with both hands, he turned around and continued down the hill with his new comrades. As he went he half-stumbled on a boulder and his head fell to one side, lying flat on his shoulder. A crimson chasm yawned in the side of his neck.

Countess Madalyn tottered away, her veil clasped to her face again, now to stem a flood of tears.

Beyond the brow of the bluff, in a small birch wood, stood a gated stockade and within that a pavilion of gold silk decked with the dancing red lions of Powys. Inside this, the rough grass was laid with rugs and carpets, and there was a banquet table on which food and other refreshments were spread. A smaller table bore inkpots, quills and maps of the castle. In a rear compartment, there was a bed with a lighted brazier to one side, and on the other a silver crucifix suspended from a pole.

That evening, when Gwyddon entered, the countess was on her knees in front of this holy symbol, her hands joined in fervent prayer. Tears still streaked her pale cheeks.

"Countess," he said slowly, "might I remind you... the Cauldron of Regeneration, for all that it calls on great and unknown forces, does not signify the conquest of death."

"No, Gwyddon, it doesn't." She was breathing slowly, heavily. Her brow was damp with perspiration, her eyes red with weeping. "It signifies the conquest of *life*, and all that is fine and sweet and good in this world."

"Countess, we can live our fine, sweet lives when the enemy is destroyed. But to do that we need soldiers. And I have provided you with an inexhaustible supply."

"Leave me, Gwyddon." She went back to her prayers, but the druid did not leave. He rubbed at his beard.

"Tell me, ma-am, did your Jesus Christ not rise from the dead to show your people the way?"

"How dare you!" She whirled around. "How dare you mention our Saviour's name in this place! You are a necromancer, sir.

This thing you have made is a pact with Satan, for which I fear I will pay with my immortal soul."

"Even if that were true, isn't it a price worth paying when so many others will be saved?"

She struggled to reply. It was difficult to counter this point even if she'd wanted to.

Ever since the Normans had captured England, progressively more Welsh land had fallen under their sway – either as punitive official policy or through the ruthless intrusion of the marcher lords. When they hadn't been seizing titles and territory, the Anglo-Norman barons had hatched schemes and offered bribes, stirring dissent, playing the Welsh princes against each other. Always, they'd sought new ways to encroach. Until at last, Edward Longshanks – the mightiest of all England's mighty warrior-kings – had proclaimed suzerainty over the entire realm, crushing the Welsh in all-out battle, then invoking English law and English custom. Castles like Grogen had been built to strangle the nation, not protect it. So the time for talking had passed – the most recent atrocities had surely proved this. The only solution was to fight. But fight with what? England was an empire and Wales had nothing.

"The destruction of Earl Corotocus and his murderous henchmen is the only response you can give," Gwyddon said. "It will signal that the sons and daughters of Wales are no longer English chattels, and that to make war on the Cymry is to invite annihilation."

"Annihilation, Gwyddon, is what I see all around me. I beg your pardon if it turns my stomach." She switched her attention back to her crucifix, rejoining her hands in prayer.

Before leaving, Gwyddon said: "I think you need to rest now, my lady. Your distress is quite understandable. War is indeed hell, and this one is no exception. But there is one thing about this war that will mark it out from all the others – it will be short."

CHAPTER SIXTEEN

THE ASSAULT ON the castle was now two-pronged.

A tide of the dead again forged across the southwest bridge and attempted to circle the stronghold via the berm path. At the same time, with the defenders having abandoned the Barbican, the attackers were able to catapult more and more of their soldiers over that blood-soaked northwest rampart. For every ten of these launched, five or six would be crushed by the impact of landing – often to the point where they were unable to stand – so even after several volleys of corpses had been discharged, only a relative handful, maybe twenty in total, were capable of continuing the assault. But this handful proved to be much more than just a thorn in the defending garrison's side.

With the roof hatches to the Gatehouse sealed, the Welsh corpses stumped through the postern and down the Barbican stair into the bailey. Here they met a few wounded stragglers who'd retreated without orders from the south curtain-wall, and tore them to pieces. Advancing past the Constable's Tower, they were deluged by more missiles, but bore through it without loss, as their comrades had done outside, and entered the southwest tower by its ground floor door. The ballista crews were too preoccupied trying to rain destruction onto the hordes of cadavers crossing the southwest bridge to notice. Only when blades or clubs fell on their backs or heads, or fleshless claws wrapped around their necks from behind did they realise the danger. Their gasps and grunts of effort became screams of fear and rage. They fought back with their spanners and mallets and knives, but the snarling dead fell on them with bestial fury.

The ballista rooms turned to abattoirs as their occupants were mauled and clubbed and hacked to death. The interlopers then climbed to those higher levels manned by the royal crossbowmen. Bryon Musard shrieked orders with froth-flecked lips as the dead clambered into view. They were assailed with every type of implement, but, already raddled beyond recognition as human beings, it made no difference to them. Hatchets clove their skulls, crossbows were discharged into their faces from point-blank range – and didn't so much as hamper them. Bryon Musard died as the bolt he'd just let loose was yanked from the throat of his target, and plunged to its feathers into his right eye. Others were strangled with their own bowstrings, or beaten with their own helmets until their heads and faces were black and purple jelly.

On the topmost turret of the tower, the bowmen, having recovered jugs and pots left by the drunken Bretons, had made naptha grenades. They lit these and flung them down through the hatches as the dead tried to ascend. Smoke and flame exploded upward, but still the dead came. Blazing from head to foot, they continued the fight, slashing the screaming crossbowmen with burning claws, embracing them in their flaming arms, falling over the battlements with them.

With the southwest tower and the ballistae lost to the English, the dead now thronged over the southwest bridge unimpeded. The berm was cluttered with rubble and charred bones, but they proceeded along it at speed. The English on the curtain-wall attacked them with whatever they could, but still had no shelter from the mangonels across the river, and now faced a new danger: on top of the southwest tower, the dead took possession of discarded crossbows and began discharging them. At the same time, those dead who had infiltrated the bailey began to scale the scaffolding or file onto the curtain-wall from the door on the southwest tower.

The troops on the south wall, mainly comprising men-at-arms and the earl's indebted knights, were made of doughtier stuff than the crossbowmen, but were unused to a foe like this. When Ulbert and Ranulf arrived there, having circled around the north and east-facing curtain-walls, they found a scene of total disorder. Wounded men staggered towards them along the parapet, stumbling through a wreckage of broken bodies and smashed timber hoardings. Even as Ranulf and Ulbert watched, three more projectiles came hurtling across the river. These were the so-called devil's sachets, each linen sack bursting in mid-air, raining colossal slaughter on the fleeing defenders.

"Move onto the east wall and the north walls," Ranulf shouted as men pushed past him. "Take up new positions. The mangonels can't reach you there.

"It isn't just the mangonels, FitzOsbern!" Walter Margas shouted, pointing behind him. "Look!"

The dead from the southwest tower were now half way along the south wall, shepherding the panicked defenders ahead of them. They were led by a particularly huge and horrible specimen. It was clad only in a ragged, muddy shift, which came down to its knees. Its bearded face was a sickly yellow. Black rings circled its sunken eyes. An odious red-grey gruel flowed from its flattened nose.

One after another, it grabbed any defender it could and flung him howling over the rampart. A longbow shaft slanted down from the southeast tower. It struck the monster squarely in the chest, but had no effect. Gurt Louvain moved to meet it. Ranulf shouted a warning and shoved his way forward, his father following him.

At first things went well for Gurt. He engaged the gigantic brute fearlessly and, with deft strokes of his longsword, cut off one of its hands and clove through its left knee. The monster struggled to retain its balance. Gurt slammed his shield into its head, but it wrestled the shield from his grasp and struck him with its stump. Gurt staggered backward, tripping over a piece of masonry. The thing lurched after him, intent on slamming the shield edge-down onto his body – only to fall victim to its own side's artillery. Two more barrages of rocks came whistling over the crenels. The one-handed brute, and several corpses behind it, were struck full on and thrown down through the scaffolding. A second later, a sack of quicklime followed, exploding in a choking, blinding cloud, which engulfed much of the central wall and many defenders, including Gurt.

"Gurt!" Ranulf shouted, still blundering forward.

Several men caught in the cloud completely lost their bearings. Shrieking as they thumbed at their blistered eyes, they toppled between the crenels or fell through the scaffolding. Others tripped over each other, falling and blocking the walk. Cursing them one by one, Ranulf hauled them upright and pushed them on towards the southeast tower. When the way was clear, he tore a strip from his tabard and bound it over his eyes. Taking a deep breath, he entered the burning fog, working hand over hand along the shattered teeth of the battlements. When he found Gurt, who was lying prone and shuddering, he hauled him backward.

Gurt had been wounded by flying splinters; blood oozed from his cheeks and even through the links of his mail, but he'd reacted swiftly enough to the quicklime to put a hand over his eyes.

"D-dear Lord," he stammered, swaying to his feet. "What do... what do we face here?"

"Go through the southeast tower," Ranulf said, stripping the bandage from his own eyes, but blinking hot, peppery tears. "Find a new post on the east wall."

Gurt nodded dumbly, hobbling away.

"You go too," Ulbert said, appearing from nowhere. "I'll form this rearguard alone."

Ranulf was startled. "Alone?"

"One man on a narrow parapet is as good as ten."

"Let me do it. I'm younger."

"You have much to live for."

"And you haven't?"

"Don't dispute with me, Ranulf."

"So this is finally it, father? This is the honourable fight you've been waiting for? The fight that will kill you?"

Ulbert smiled and shook his head. "This fight will kill us all in due course. Haven't you realised that? Go. The more of us gather here, the easier targets we are for the mangonels."

Ranulf retreated towards the southeast tower. "I'll wait for you on the east wall," he shouted.

"Forget the east wall," Ulbert said over his shoulder. "Forget the north wall as well. With the bailey penetrated, the whole outer curtain's defunct. Get what's left of the men and cross the gantry bridge to the Gatehouse. That may still be defensible."

"Very well, but don't delay. You only need to buy us five minutes."

"I can manage a little longer than that," Ulbert said.

Ranulf peered at his father's back. The rear of Ulbert's handsome red and blue quartered mantel was cleaner than its front – a sure and perhaps disconcerting sign that this was one seigneur who rarely ran from the enemy. As if in confirmation, Ulbert unbuckled his sword-belt and unsheathed his blade.

"Five minutes is all we need," Ranulf called to him. "Your word you won't tarry any longer?"

Ulbert looked back and smiled – and it was a warm smile, the first one Ranulf had seen from his father for a considerable time.

"My word and my pledge, boy."

Ranulf moved on, herding the remaining defenders ahead of him.

"Which, as they were given under duress," Ulbert added to himself, "mean nothing. *Ranulf!*"

Ranulf, about to enter the southeast tower, glanced back one more time.

"Be true to your heart, lad," Ulbert said, staring at him intently. "In the end, when all has come to pass, it'll be the only thing you can trust."

Ranulf swallowed, before nodding and moving on.

Ulbert slammed his visor down, hefted his sword and shield, and advanced alone. The quicklime was settling and, just ahead of him now, the dead emerged through it, their forms shrouded with white. The first one had smashed hips and walked at a crazy tilt. Only its gaping red maw revealed that it was made from flesh and blood. Formerly a rood-worker, it wielded a hand-scythe.

Ulbert charged at it.

"Notre dame!" he roared.

He parried its first blow, and swept its head from its trunk with a single crosscut. It flailed at him with the scythe, but he drove it backward with his shield until it lost its footing and fell through the scaffolding. The next one lunged with a spear. He hewed the shaft, and rammed his blade through its groin – so deeply that he couldn't retrieve it. It went for his throat, but he knocked its hands loose, drew his falchion and stove its skull. It remained standing, so he kicked at it hard, breaking its right knee with his mailed foot; it tottered sideways and again fell through the scaffolding. The third came barehanded, arms spread wide as though to clasp him in a bear-hug. Again he advanced behind his shield, driving it towards the crenels, finally tipping it through the first embrasure. The fourth one, an eyeless, jawless hulk, was equipped with an axe. It smote him on the right shoulder. His mail turned the blade, but the impact was agonising – Ulbert knew immediately that his shoulder was broken. He staggered out of its way, having to drop his shield.

There was a brazier filled with glowing coals to his left. He hurled it at them to delay their advance. The eyeless horror wore a tattered habit, possibly it had once been a monk or friar. It raised the axe over its head, but now the hem of its habit caught flame. Fire licked up its legs and torso, diverting its attention. Ulbert darted forward, plunging the falchion into its chest, grappling with it, lifting it bodily despite the flames, which enveloped him as well and scorched him through his mail, and dropping it over the parapet.

Exhausted and unarmed, he retreated. A quick glance took in the entrance to the southeast tower, thirty yards behind him. It was cramped and chaotic in there – all the south wall defenders had passed through it, but now the archers from the tower's upper levels and roof were flowing down the spiral stair to join the retreat. More time was needed.

Ulbert swung back around, his right arm hanging limp and useless. Lime-slathered corpses loomed towards him. The first, which wore mail but no helmet, had been split from its cranium to the tip of its chin. Both hemispheres of its riven head hung outwards, the eyes several inches apart, the nose entirely divided, only strands of pinkish mucus linking the two halves together. It brandished a spiked club.

Ulbert grabbed an abandoned shield. It was kite-shaped and cumbersome. With his injury it was difficult to manage, and all he could do was raise it as high as possible and try to fend off a series of frenzied blows. Sickening pain spread from his shoulder, filling his aged, tired body, each jolt making it worse. Alongside the club-wielder, a naked woman had appeared with a heavy stone, though she was recognisable as female only by her shrivelled sex organs. In truth she was a thing of sticks, a withered framework to which scarcely a vestige of flesh was attached. With demonic shrieks, she also struck at the shield.

For a brief time her very ghastliness gave Ulbert new heart. These were genuine devils, he realised – denizens of the pit. All his years in the service of self-interested noblemen might now be assuaged. The villages he'd burned, the crops he'd trampled, the livestock he'd stolen, and the many enemies he'd viciously slain who of course were only enemies to Ulbert and Ranulf because the likes of Earl Corotocus had proclaimed them so. And then the Welsh – who they'd hanged and butchered and driven from a land to which their bloodline entitled them more than any number of charters or benefices ever could.

"Nothing I have done in my life is worthy of the title 'knight'," Ulbert grunted as he retreated, the club and stone smashing repeatedly on his shield. "I have failed my wife, my son, my family name and, above all, myself."

His shield flew to splinters. He grabbed up a javelin and hurled it. It buried itself in the chest of the club-wielder, who staggered backward. The fleshless woman came on regardless. Ulbert took her next blow on his forearm, before slamming his mailed fist into her face, crushing her features as if they were carved in turnip flesh. As she swung another blow, he ducked, caught her in the midriff with his injured shoulder and raised her up – though the pain this induced was indescribable. He dropped her through a gap between the crenels, dizzied, almost falling after her. For a second he hung there, gasping. Lifting his visor, he gazed down the burned, blood-streaked wall to the berm, now a forest of arms and heads and raised blades. The howls and shrieks of the damned rose in a hellish dirge.

"I have reneged on my duties to the weak," he cried, "to the poor, to women, to my fellow countrymen, my fellow Christians, and undoubtedly... to God! But all this will be well..."

An arm hooked around his neck, and tried to yank him backward. He jerked himself forward, flipping his assailant over his shoulder. As it fell from sight, he stumbled around. Claws clamped on his throat and attempted to throttle him. They belonged to a gangling thing that was black with rot and clad only in a leather apron soaked with blood. An arrow had pierced it through the back of the head and emerged from its right socket; an eyeball was fixed on the iron barb in a blob of unblinking putrescence.

"All this will be well," Ulbert said again, choking but grabbing the thing's throat in return, and driving its head against the head of its neighbour with such force that both skulls shattered, vile sludge bursting forth. He tore the arrow from its mashed skull, stabbing and hacking as yet more of them surged against him, forcing him backward through the embrasure. He was acutely aware of the abyss behind him, of his strength ebbing, but he stabbed frantically on. "For though I have been worthless in life, perhaps... perhaps with one final deed, I can be worth something in deeeaaa..."

Further words were lost as he plummeted from the parapet, dragging a couple with him by the scruffs of their necks. Six more followed through sheer momentum. For the same reason, Ulbert fell diagonally rather than straight. He didn't hit the berm but the river – though it brought no relief.

Weighted by his mail, he plunged through its green shallows like a spear, and struck the pebbly bottom helmet first. There was a flash in his head, a sound like thunder, and a short but intense spasm of pain in the middle of his back; and then eerie muffled silence, rippling shadows – and nothing.

Nothing at all.

CHAPTER SEVENTEEN

Ranulf was the last of the curtain-wall defenders to reach the northwest corner of the castle, where the gantry drawbridge connected with the Gatehouse. There were one or two behind him, but he waited as they stumbled past. Some were still blinded by smoke or quicklime, others bleeding and limping. All were exhausted, their armour dented, their weapons broken.

Compared to the south wall of course, the battlements of the north wall were undamaged. He stared back along them, maybe two hundred yards, to the tower at the distant northeast corner. The massive structure of the Inner Fort and the Keep prevented him seeing more than that, but there was no sign of Ulbert hobbling in pursuit. Fifty feet below meanwhile, ragged figures had appeared on the north berm, though initially they only came in ones and twos. Every type of mutilation and dismemberment had been wrought on them, but they'd advanced past the east wall without suffering any assault and now would do the same with the north wall, so they were coming on apace. Soon there would be hundreds of them.

He peered again along the north parapet. Still there was no trace of his father. Ranulf was too numb and bone-weary to feel a sense of despair. But the sweat was drying on his aching body, his skin tightening, and inside his chest his heart was slowly sinking. Hope briefly sprang when a tiny shape suddenly emerged from the northeast tower. But another shape appeared behind it, and then another, and another. And he knew that it was *them*.

Mailed feet clumped over the drawbridge behind. A hand touched his shoulder.

"He could still be alive," Gurt said. "Hiding in one of the other towers maybe?"

Ranulf shook his head. "Hiding isn't father's way."

"He's a sensible enough man to know when discretion is the better part of valour."

"Not today, I fear."

They crossed back over the bridge together. Below them, the castle's entry passage was still empty. It was only about twenty feet across, which made it a deep, echoing canyon, though soon, they knew, it would be packed with howling monstrosities. On the other side of the gantry drawbridge, the interior of the Gatehouse was cramped, dark, and stank of smoke, sweat and faeces. The men who'd retreated from the curtain-wall were milling about in confusion. Arguments raged, many of those who'd already sought refuge from the roof insisting that there wasn't room for anyone else. Ranulf glanced behind him again, watching the dead approach along the top of the north wall. Gurt signalled to a man-at-arms to raise the drawbridge. The fellow attacked the wheel with gusto, but found it stiff with disuse.

"Even if he is in one of the other towers," Ranulf told Gurt, "he's as good as dead. In a very short time, these things will infest every inch of this stronghold."

"Except in here!" came a strident voice.

Ranulf turned and saw Odo de Lussac, one of the earl's youngest tenant knights, a freeholder through family ties rather than right of service. He was in a semi-deranged state. His hair was a sodden ginger mop, his lean, pimpled face ash-white. He was grinning, but his eyes were glazed like baubles.

"The Gatehouse is strong," he declared.

Ranulf shook his head. "Its rooftop hatches will only hold for so long."

"We've secured them."

"And when the Welsh bring the earl's mangonels to the western bluff? When they substitute the iron hail with great boulders?"

"The king will come," de Lussac insisted. "They're all saying he's marching from the north. He may only be a couple of days away."

"For all we know, he's already battling hordes of these creatures himself, without the protection of stone walls."

De Lussac's eyes widened with nervous anger. "You're a traitor, FitzOsbern! Navarre is right. You counsel defeatism. You talk as if some unstoppable tide is sweeping the land."

Ranulf tried not to laugh. "Look there!" He pointed through the portal and over the drawbridge. Beyond it, corpses were advancing. "What do you see?"

"I see Welshmen in masquerade!" de Lussac shouted. His tone was shrill, almost hysterical. "I see peasant rabble who have lulled the foolish and the cowardly, such as you, into thinking the ridiculous. I see, I see..."

His words ended in a gargle as a bolt thudded into his open mouth, burying itself in the back of his throat. Gagging, a crimson river pouring from his lips, he stumbled out onto the bridge, from which he plummeted into the entry passage.

"I see one more heriot for the earl's coffers," Ranulf said grimly.

Another bolt flitted past, striking a squire in the back of the skull. There was renewed panic and shouting. White faces, shining with sweat, turned frantically towards the open portal. Ranulf saw that the dead were still ten yards from the end of the north wall, but that three of them were armed with crossbows, which they'd no doubt purloined from the southwest tower. It was incomprehensible – these rotted, mangled carcasses reloading such sophisticated weapons, raising them to their broken shoulders and taking practised aim.

"Hurry up with that bloody bridge!" Gurt shrieked.

"Help me, my lord, please!" The man-at-arms still worked at the wheel, throwing all his weight against it. Beads of perspiration stood on his flustered brow.

Gurt and several others assisted, and slowly, with a grinding of rust, the wheel began to move. But before the bridge could be raised, the first group of dead had stepped onto it. There were four of them in total and beneath their combined weight, the chain-and-pulley system groaned as though set to break. The men on the wheel had to release their grip and the bridge thundered back into place.

"We must clear the bridge!" Gurt yelled.

Ranulf drew his blade and went out there first. Two others followed. One was Ramon la Roux, another of the earl's indebted knights, formerly a landed lord distinctive through the midland shires for his black mantle with its emblazoned white raven. He carried a shield and a battle-axe and wore a tall, cylindrical helm. The other was one of Garbofasse's mercenaries, a huge fellow dressed in studded leather and wielding a massive, two-handed war-hammer. Though twenty feet in length and about six wide, the gantry drawbridge was only one plank thick and flimsy beneath their feet. It shuddered as the dead shuffled across it towards them.

Ranulf spun as he met the first, parrying a blow from its poll-arm and shearing through its left leg, overbalancing it so that it pitched into the abyss. The one la Roux engaged carried an iron-headed club and it smote him on the front of his helm, denting it deeply. He staggered backward, but managed to sink his axe into its left shoulder, cleaving through to the breastbone. It dropped its club and tried to grapple with him. They teetered on the edge until Ranulf struck from behind, severing its spine with a single thrust, twisting his blade around and wrenching it sideways, truncating the horror at the waist. Now the huge mercenary joined the fray, sidling past the knights and knocking the two remaining monsters from the bridge with massive, sweeping blows of his war-hammer.

Soon the bridge was clear, though it would remain so only fleetingly. Wild shouts rang from the Gatehouse, urging them to retreat, to "get back for the love of God!"

Ranulf and la Roux withdrew but, drunk on victory, the mercenary remained and beat his chest, bellowing that he could hold this bridge 'til kingdom come. At which point – with a loud, wet *crack* – he was struck on the back of the head by a cobblestone. He tottered sideways, blood shooting from his nostrils, before falling face-first from the bridge. Ranulf glanced up and behind and saw those dead who'd already taken the Gatehouse roof massing against its eastern battlements. They were ten feet overhead and out of sword-reach, but were now pelting the bridge and its defenders with any missile that came to hand.

"Back inside!" Ranulf shouted, pushing la Roux ahead of him, and having to swat a javelin with his mailed hand, which otherwise would have skewered his neck.

Twenty feet away, more of the dead were reaching the end of the drawbridge, but, as soon as the two knights were back inside, Gurt and his henchmen went at the wheel like things possessed. The bridge rose quickly. One of the dead had placed a foot on it, and subsequently was cast into the gulf. Several more attempted suicidal leaps, hands outstretched, but all missed their mark and followed their comrade to the carrion-strewn flagstones far below. Before the bridge was completely raised, a final crossbow bolt sailed through its narrowing gap and struck la Roux in the left shoulder, punching into his mail. Cursing, he pulled off his broken helm. Normally a gentleman of deportment who favoured short, pointed beards, clean-shaven cheeks and a trim moustache, his face now bristled with unshaved whiskers, and was ingrained with dirt and sweat. Moreover, both his eyes were swollen and his nose flattened and bloodied. The drawbridge aperture closed with a thump and darkness reinvaded the congested space.

Several more torches were lit before it was possible to see who was who. La Roux had slumped to his haunches, clutching his shoulder, from which blood was pulsing. Ranulf knelt to attend him, saying that they had to get him to Doctor Zacharius.

La Roux waved such logic aside. "Damn that!" he said through locked teeth. "Is that it? Is the curtain-wall lost?"

"I think so..."

"And it was a costly sacrifice," came a third voice.

The press of exhausted men cleared to allow Earl Corotocus through. Navarre and du Guesculin stood one to either side of him, each holding a flaming brand.

Corotocus focussed on Ranulf. "They say your father fell?"

"I think that's true, my lord."

"Ranulf led the charge to retake the gantry," someone jabbered. "I saw it myself. His sword was like a thunderbolt."

"I hear this too," Corotocus said with half a smile. "Your father is a sad loss. It will not go without notation in your family's record of service, Ranulf. You may count half your debt to me paid."

Ranulf nodded as he stood up, unable to work out at so fraught a moment whether this was a generous gesture or miserly. Instead, he blurted out something else.

"My lord, we must release the girl!"

Conversation in the crowded room ceased. Corotocus's expression was blank.

"Would you repeat that, Ranulf?"

"Countess Madalyn wishes her daughter returned. I suggest we comply with those wishes."

Corotocus still looked blank. "And if we don't?"

"If we don't, we'll all die in this place. Or worse."

The earl almost looked amused. "Worse?"

The rest of the men listened intently. Flames crackled. From outside came the muffled hubbub of the dead.

"Do these walking corpses serve their new masters willingly?" Ranulf asked, wondering belatedly if it was wise to air this view, but remembering with painful clarity the last words his father had said to him. "I'd suggest 'no'. Are they breaking themselves to pieces on our walls through past allegiance? Again, no. My lord, they've been summoned through sorcery." The earl watched with lidded eyes as Ranulf turned to face the rest of his audience. "We're all in agreement about that. Aren't we? Devilish sorcery. So I ask this: what if the same is done with our own dead?"

The silence intensified as this horrific possibility dawned on the men. Not only might they soon be facing their own slain comrades, but what if they themselves, once cut down, were denied all funeral rites and set to this diabolical work? Wouldn't their very souls be imperilled?

"And to avoid this catastrophe you advocate that we release the hostage?" Corotocus said.

Ranulf nodded.

The earl brooded on this. Still the flames crackled. From beyond the shuttered tower, the howls and groans of the dead seemed to increase. Objects thudded against the hatches.

"You ride well with a lance, Ranulf," Corotocus finally said. "You wield your sword with enviable skill. Yet brinkmanship is not your forte. We have two key bargaining chips here, and you would happily throw one of them away? Does anyone else think that would be wise?"

Several heads were shaken.

"My lord," Ranulf pleaded, "if the girl is so useful a bargaining chip, why not bargain with her now... and save more of our lives?"

"Because of the *second* chip we hold, Ranulf: Grogen Castle itself." The earl faced his men. "The curtain-wall may be lost, but we still have the Constable's Tower and the Inner Fort. Hells, we still have this Gatehouse, which itself can withstand the most ferocious attack!"

"Earl Corotocus!" came a frightened voice from below. "The Welsh are approaching the main entrance."

Corotocus nodded as if pleased. "Come Ranulf. Watch as I send them back to the Hell they've only just escaped."

Ranulf and Gurt followed him down a stair to the second level. From here, they peered through arrow-slits onto the entry passage, which, as Ranulf had predicted, was now crammed with the groaning, jostling dead.

The demented horde beat on the huge, iron-plated gate with limp hands, skeletal claws and every type of blunt or broken weapon, creating a cacophony that grew steadily louder and more frightening. With a single command from the earl, vats were opened on the first level and streams of burning oil vented down. An inferno resulted, the packed dead blazing like human torches – their hair, their flesh, their clothing – yet they pounded on the castle gate with tireless fury. More burning oil was discharged; more of the dead were engulfed. Those at the white-hot heart of the conflagration wilted, sagging to their knees as they were eaten to their bones. Black smoke filled with grease, sparks and vile cinders spiralled into the upper part of the passage.

"Only fire destroys them," Gurt observed.

"And even then it takes an age," Ranulf replied, focussing on one tall, blazing figure, who appeared to have been carrying a banner depicting the Welsh dragon. This banner had now fallen to ashes but the figure was shaking its talon-like fist at the Gatehouse even as flames flared from its empty eyesockets and gaping jaws.

At last, the half-cremated legion had no option but to withdraw. The earl laughed raucously as it left in its wake a mountain of smouldering bones and blackened, quivering carrion. But his laughter faded when it returned half an hour later, carrying heavy chains and hooks.

"Cut them down!" he roared. "Slay them!" Arrows sleeted from the high portals, hitting the scorched figures over and over, but having no effect. "More oil, damn your hides, damn your wretched eyes!"

Yet more fiery cascades were poured from the castle walls, which the dead simply marched through. Again their rent flesh and ragged garb, now besmeared with broiled fat, saw them ignite like living candles. But they were still able to clamber over the charred offal, beat on the gate with hammers and tongs and, thanks to the metal plating having been heated and softened, to secure breaches through which the hooks could be fixed. When they withdrew again, they hauled on the chains in teams, hundreds and hundreds at a time.

"Navarre!" Corotocus bellowed, scuttling down a flight of stairs. "Man the fire-raiser!"

Ranulf and Gurt followed the earl to the first level, which was basically an archery platform overlooking the Gatehouse tunnel.

Below them, Navarre and several others were already alongside the fire-raiser, but now, with a torturous rending of wood and metal, the gate fell. They promptly began working on the huge bellows.

With the gate down, the main mass of the dead came flooding back along the entry passage to attack the portcullis, only to be greeted by clouds of sulphurous flame. With more oil cast from above, it again became a scene from Hell's foundry. But several still made it to the portcullis bars, which they gripped with their bare hands. Further gusts of fire swept through them, peeling away their rotted flesh layer by layer, searing the organs beneath until the vile fluids that filled them bubbled. Again, some collapsed. Others that had made it to the bars were fused there, black and sticky effigies melting onto the glowing ironwork. With the portcullis bolted down and impossible to lift manually, the remaining dead attempted to fix more chains, but now Earl Corotocus descended a ladder and joined the fray.

Calling the fire-raisers to halt, he hurried forward with a sword and mattock. As he hacked at the hooks, a vision of grinning, half-melted lunacy tried to grapple with him through the red-hot bars. He plunged his sword into its chest, only to be spattered with sizzling meat. Other men assisted him. With frenzied blows from axes and hammers, the hooks were broken, the chains severed. The defenders retreated and the fire-raising recommenced – gales of flame, like repeated blasts from a furnace, incinerating even those sturdiest of the dead who still clutched at the bars.

By now the stench and smoke had become intolerable all through the Gatehouse. Men staggered down its tunnel and out through its rear entrance onto the Causeway, coughing, choking, rubbing at streaming eyes. Others vomited or fainted. Ranulf was rigid as a board as he strode out among them. Ignoring everyone else, he headed straight for the Constable's Tower.

"Where are you going?" Gurt called after him.

Ranulf made no reply.

CHAPTER EIGHTEEN

On FIRST ARRIVING at Grogen Castle and imprisoning Gwendolyn of Lyr, Ranulf took charge of two keys to her cell. When Murlock the mercenary replaced him, he only handed over one of them. At the time he hadn't been sure why. Had he genuinely felt such concern for the prisoner that he might want to come back and check on her welfare? Or was it the case that, right from the outset, he'd viewed her as a possible source of advantage to him?

Either way, as he re-ascended through the dripping darkness of the Keep, its mighty walls having silenced the sounds of battle without, he knew that he must tread warily.

On the Keep's seventh floor, its arched passages opened into numerous cobweb-festooned chambers. In one such, the garderobe, he saw Murlock standing with his back turned, grunting as he urinated into the privy chute, a brick shaft some four feet in diameter which fell right down through the innards of the building. Ranulf slipped past and proceeded along the passage, until he reached the door at the far end. He inserted his second key and turned it. Once inside, he closed the door behind him as quietly as he could.

Gwendolyn sat in the same place where he'd left her, only now she'd brought the lantern over. Its tiny flame illuminated little more than a few feet, though it revealed that she'd collected the blankets and gathered the little dry straw she'd been able to find, making a nest for herself. On his entry, she knelt up, trembling, possibly expecting that it would be Murlock. When Ranulf stepped into the light, she relaxed a little – but only for a second. Despite her earlier threats, his stained mantle, the gashes and bruises on his face, and the blood-clots in his tangled hair came as a shock to her.

"Has he treated you well?" Ranulf asked.

His right hand was clamped on the hilt of his sheathed sword. He knew there'd be a wildness about him, a dangerous gleam in his eye. It was difficult to imagine that he could present a picture of normality after the day he'd experienced. She nodded dumbly.

"And how rational a person is your mother?" Ranulf wondered.

Still distracted by the state he was in, the girl was apparently thrown by this question. "How rational is my...? How rational would yours be, having seen her people massac-"

"Does she want to see more of the same?"

Gwendolyn hesitated before replying. His abrupt tone implied that he was no longer the courteous knight conflicted between duty and compassion.

"By the looks of things," she said, "it isn't my mother's people who need fear massacre."

"This madness has to end, Gwendolyn!"

"You say that now..."

"Be flippant all you wish, girl, but as things are no-one will leave this place alive!" Despite his best efforts, Ranulf's voice rose to a hoarse shout. "And you will roast on a spit before Earl Corotocus gives you up!" He paused, breathing hard. Fresh blood trickled from his brow. "So I ask you again: is your mother rational?"

"That depends on what you propose."

"What I propose is to end this slaughter. What I propose is to exchange the lives of many for the life of one."

"One?" she whispered. "And who is this one?"

"Who do you think?"

She clearly didn't believe him. In fact, she scoffed. "Your overlord? But how could that happen?"

"It won't be easy. A chance will have to arise. But I need to know... is it a risk worth my taking?"

"Sir knight, if you are losing this battle, as I suspect..."

"Don't hang your hopes on that. We're far from beaten yet!" He retreated towards the cell door. "We *may* lose it. But the tide of Welsh deaths will be cataclysmic. Never underestimate Earl Corotocus when it comes to killing. If he dies here in Wales, orders may already have been given to unleash genocide on your people. And by then even *I* won't be around to stop it."

"Better destruction than slavery."

"I'm offering you an easier way out."

"No, you're *seeking* a way out."

"That too."

"Why should we help you?"

"You'll be helping yourselves in the process. You'll be helping mankind."

She watched him warily, wondering what kind of web he was weaving. Again she shook her head. "I don't believe you would hand over your lord and master."

"There was much I wouldn't have believed when this morning dawned." He opened the cell door. "As you wish."

"Wait!" she called. "Wait. I don't even know your name." He ignored her and made to step outside. "If it helps, sir knight, my mother is a *very* rational woman."

Ranulf glanced back; their eyes met. He nodded, closing and locking the door. Half way along the passage he encountered Murlock, who peered at him balefully. Ranulf didn't bother to speak. He didn't even look at the big jailer as he brushed past.

CHAPTER NINETEEN

PRINCE LLEWELLYN OF Gwynedd and his nobles arrived that fine autumn morning in 1278, to find the road to Worcester strewn with rose petals and lined with cheering folk.

The October sun beat warmly on the freshly stripped fields to either side. The blue sky was filled with swallows and only the fleeciest hint of cloud. Half a mile ahead of the prince, beyond the thatched roofs of the town, towered the cathedral – an almost magical structure built from chalk-white stone, its arches and statues climbing one above the other, tier on heavenly tier, its lofty pinnacles billowing with gaily-coloured banners. Ranulf, who was only five years old, marvelled at the sight of it.

Such a magnificent edifice could not have been more fitting a venue for an occasion like this, which every adult he knew had assured him was not just joyous, but very, very important for all of them.

As soon as Prince Llewellyn and his party crossed the border from Wenwynwyn and entered the realm of King Edward, the sun had broken through the murky cloud of early morning, and the woods and meadows had come alive with bird-song. A troop of royal knights and heralds, clad handsomely in crimson velvet smocks emblazoned with the prancing golden lions, greeted them at Leominster, and escorted them through villages thronging with happy faced peasants, across brooks choked with lily pads, and past fatted cattle herded on the bright green pastures.

It was truly a good time to be alive in the marcher lands and the central shires of England, for today's great event – after so many years of strife – would at last signal peace with the great principality of Wales. It was no surprise therefore, that everywhere folk came flocking across the fields, cheering. Not just the peasants on the land with their hoes and ploughshares, but all the freemen and guildsmen of the towns as well; the merchants, the millers, the clothiers, the bakers, the butchers, the farriers, the fletchers, the saddlers – people from every level of society, all singing the praises of King Edward, whose wisdom and diplomacy had brought about this treaty, and Prince Llewellyn, whose courage and foresight had made it possible. With such an alliance, the dark and ravaging forces of war, once seemingly without end in this region, would be consigned to history once and for all.

Prince Llewellyn and his men were themselves a merry band. Dark-haired, dark eyed and, in the prince's case, wolfishly handsome. They had come to England displaying all their traditional banners and standards – the Red Dragon, the Lions of Gwynedd – but for once carrying neither spears nor shields, nor wearing mail. Instead, they sported wedding-day raiment, the prince clad in hose and tunic of forest green, a cape of gold thread, and a green hunting cap with a silver plume.

In the heart of Worcester itself, the cathedral concourse was also decked for this grandest occasion, the stone square carpeted with flowers. Flags and pennons streamed from posts and rooftops. Monks and lay-brethren of the cathedral chapter scampered hither and thither to ensure that everything was just as it should be. For it was here where King Edward would require Prince Llewellyn to offer homage and fealty to the English Crown, and officially recognise Edward as his sovereign lord. Only after this solemn moment, would the prince and his betrothed, Eleanor de Montfort, ward and first cousin to the king, exchange their vows and a holy mass be sung.

It would be a significant occasion, Ulbert FitzOsbern had advised his young son. Only when it was completed could the feasting begin, though already preparations were in progress for this. On a broad meadow just outside the town, where many ornate pavilions – each one representing some great household – had been pitched, long trestle tables were being laid with cloth and arrayed with cutlery. Minstrels were tuning their instruments, jongleurs testing their voices. Kegs of wine and barrels of beer and cider had been gathered in abundance. The delicious scents from the open-air kitchens wafted even through Worcester's crooked by-ways – succulent cuts of meat, pork and venison, basting in their own juices, wildfowl and chickens turning on spits, vegetables boiling in salted butter, the sweet aroma of baking bread.

Of course, the greatest moment of all would come when King Edward himself arrived, escorting his cousin by her dainty hand. Ranulf's father would himself walk in this royal procession, though only at the rear, as a loyal tenant of the one of the king's great barons. The rest of the FitzOsbern family, like the families of other lesser dignitaries, would be forced to wait with the eagerly watching crowd, though they were afforded some solace by having places allocated in one of several roped-off stalls with raised seating, which were ranged at the front of the cathedral concourse. The common folk would have to make do as best they could, peeking out between these flimsy, flag-draped structures, or watching from the high windows and steep, shaggy roofs of Worcester's tall, timber buildings.

Ranulf, uncomfortable in his white hose, white satin tunic and long, pointy-toed boots, sat close and snug against the warm thigh of his mother and held her gloved hand throughout, though her grip noticeably tightened when Bishop Godfrey emerged from the cathedral door in vestments of purest gold, with a gold mitre on his brow, and a fanfare of trumpeters announced that the royal entourage was at last approaching.

When they entered the great concourse they came on foot, having walked from the castle, where they had lodged for the night. King Edward, who strode beneath a scarlet canopy carried by four servants in purple hose and scarlet tabards, was perhaps the most resplendent figure the young boy had ever seen: six feet and four inches tall, massive at the shoulder and with a true warrior's bearing. He had a rich, but neatly trimmed beard and a shock of reddish hair, on which his crown was firmly set. His long tunic was of rich murrey velvet, emblazoned all over with lions, his serge cloak decked in a similar pattern. Behind him came the usual gaggle of prelates in their episcopal purple, glittering with their rings and chains of office, and then the greatest of the great magnates, each one in their own traditional heraldic garb.

The bride herself was a slim, child-like figure. She wore a chaste white gown, tight at the hips but full in the skirt, and walked demurely alongside her cousin, one hand in his. A white fur cape hung from her shoulders and a veil of white lace concealed her features, though her coiled flaxen-yellow hair was visible inside its silken caul, studded with gemstones.

Ranulf had heard that she was a great beauty, but that didn't mean much to him. He'd only ever known one beauty in his short life and, as far as he was concerned, she would never be surpassed – and that was his mother. That morning, when they'd risen in their pavilion to prepare for the day, she'd seemed more gorgeous to him than he could ever remember. Bright eyed and red lipped, she wore a lilac dress covered by a green cloak embroidered with woodland flowers, and her glimmering raven hair was coiled beneath a babette and tied under her chin with a linen fillet. Even in the midst of the cheering and clapping, the banging of drums, the tooting of pipes and brazen batteries of trumpets, Ranulf remembered how much he adored his mother. He glanced up at her, expecting, as always, that she would beam down at him with all the love and happiness in the world.

Except that this time it was different.

His mother was frowning.

Her mouth was a tight, grey line. Her cheeks had sunk and were hued an unhealthy shade of blue. Her eyes had collapsed like tarnished stones into cavernous hollows. When she finally smiled, her shrivelled lips peeled back from brown peg-teeth clamped in a skeletal grimace...

Ranulf sat up sharply, his brow damp.

At first he didn't know where he was.

It was dark and cold, rank with the stench of smoke, sweat and burned flesh. Gradually he noted the grunts, groans and coughs and came to sense the many bodies slumped around him, and his awareness of reality returned. He was on the second level of the Gatehouse, huddled under his cloak and lying in a corner between Gurt and Ramon la Roux. It was probably the early hours of the morning, though from somewhere overhead he heard a faint, echoing *boom*.

From midnight onward there'd been a lull in the fighting. The dead had withdrawn from the entry passage, abandoning their attack on the portcullis, which by then was crusted from top to bottom with the twisted charcoal relics of their vanguard. This had afforded the defenders an opportunity to drink some water, cram some bread into their bellies and catch a little sleep.

Another *boom*, deep and hollow, sounded from overhead. Another followed. And another. Suddenly it was relentless, repeating itself over and over again.

Now that the cold had settled into his body and limbs, Ranulf was stiff all over. As he clambered to his feet, his joints ached and creaked. Other men began to stir. With each impact overhead, dust trickled down onto them.

"What is... what is that?" Gurt mumbled.

"Nothing good," Ranulf replied, heading for the stair.

On the third level, he met Hugh du Guesculin, who was carrying a candle and looked ashen-faced.

"They have a battering ram," du Guesculin said in a querulous tone.

Other men were now milling around them in the darkness, muttering and swearing.

Du Guesculin took Ranulf's arm. "Did you hear what I said, FitzOsbern? Those abominations on the north wall – they have a battering ram. They're using it on the gantry door."

"From the north wall?" Ranulf said. "It must be twenty feet across that gap."

"They've cut down a pine and trimmed its trunk. They can easily reach over. Not only that, they've tied ladders together. Improvised their own bridge."

Ranulf moved past him to the door in question. With each impact, it shook violently.

This drawbridge had never been constructed to withstand attack; it had never really been more than an access point between the Gatehouse and the curtain-wall. In due course, probably very soon, it would be smashed – and the dead would push their own bridge over and flow across it. Though many might be tossed to destruction en route, there would always, as they'd repeatedly proved in this siege of sieges, be more of them. At the same time, they would attack the portcullis again. The crew on the fire-raiser would be overwhelmed from within, and the Gatehouse would fall.

At that moment, sluggish with hunger, muddled by fatigue, Ranulf could not conceive of a single strategy to prevent this. And then, with an explosive report, three of the door's central planks fractured inwards.

"Get the earl," he said, jerking to life.

But the earl was already present, standing alongside du Guesculin. It was Earl Corotocus's manner, even in times of extreme crisis, to be grim but never despairing. Yet now, for the first time at Grogen Castle, his mouth twitched, his cheek had paled to a deathly hue.

"Sound the alarum," he said. "Retreat to the Constable's Tower."

CHAPTER TWENTY

WHEN AN ARMY is prepared to lose thousands upon thousands of its men, or indeed, as in this case, is incapable of losing a single man, the word 'impregnable' no longer applies to any redoubt.

The English bore this in mind as they readied the Constable's Tower to receive the next onslaught. In normal times, the Constable's Tower would have felt far more secure than the Gatehouse. Its parapets were thirty feet higher, and in terms of structure it was altogether more massive, its walls infinitely thicker. It had more vents for oil and pitch and more loops from which missiles could be discharged. In addition, it could only really be attacked from one side. To the east and south it faced into the Inner Fort, the courtyard of which was a good eighty feet below. To the west, it faced into the bailey, which was a hundred feet below. Neither of these immense distances could be covered by ladder or climbing rope – at least, Earl Corotocus's men had never heard of such a thing. But from the north, it was a different matter.

The Constable's Tower's main door was on the north side, facing onto the causeway connecting from the Gatehouse. What was more, the door faced onto this directly, so that a ram could be brought to bear if it got close enough. It would not breach the tower easily: the gate was fashioned from English oak, some ten inches thick, and was ribbed with steel. Behind it there lay a passage beneath a murder hole, another portcullis, and beyond that the fire-raiser, which the English had refuelled. But given the nature of the enemy, nobody felt that these measures provided sufficient protection. What was more, the north wall of the Constable's Tower was only sixty feet high and was a far less daunting prospect than the walls to the south, east and west.

The English did what they could. They gathered new stocks of stones, spears, darts and arrows. They brought up new barrels of naptha. They crowded against the missile-portals and along the battlements, particularly on the north side, overlooking the causeway. Several companies had already been positioned in the Constable's Tower when the earl and what remained of the Gatehouse garrison arrived, but from that moment on there'd been no sleep for any of them. Blunted blades were re-sharpened, shields were patched, new fragments of armour donned. Every man – even if he wouldn't admit it – now looked to his own survival as much as to victory for his overlord.

By first light they were waiting, so tense that they no longer saw the weird Breton scarecrows, which littered the rooftops even of these inner ramparts.

The men had already passed the stage where sweat-inducing fear was an issue. Fear comes before battle rather than during it; it tends to dissipate after the first clash of steel, to be replaced by a duller but more practical state-of-mind in which warriors think purely about necessary actions. One such necessity was that everyone in the castle should now be present. The Constable's Tower was the key to the Inner Fort, and they could not afford to let it fall. Hence, the earl had redeployed every man into this one bastion, no longer concerned about a mingling of his companies or any confusion among his junior command.

Those wounded from the assaults on the Barbican and the south wall lay on its ground-level, wrapped in their bedrolls, gasping and shivering, with nothing to anaesthetise their pain as they awaited transportation to the infirmary, assuming such a luxury would ever come. Father Benan, one who would normally tend to them, was among their number, naked and slumped against a pillar. The only item he wore was a large iron crucifix, suspended by a cord at his neck. He was scarcely able to breathe, so weak was he from loss of blood. His entire body – his back, his buttocks, his shoulders, his arms, his legs – were crisscrossed with crimson stripes.

He was only vaguely aware, when a person came and crouched alongside him, that it was Doctor Zacharius, now with a gore-stained canvas apron over his fine clothes and his sleeves pinned back on forearms equally sullied.

As Zacharius looked the priest over, he mopped sweat from his haggard brow, smearing more blood there. With the few orderlies he'd been given now redeployed to defend the Constable's Tower roof, he'd had to cease working on his patients in order to help his assistant bring as many wounded as he could to the infirmary. Between them, they had improvised a bier by tying a cloak between two poll-arms, but it was still a laborious process, especially since neither of them had enjoyed much sleep since arriving here. But Zacharius, for all his faults, was not a doctor purely for the esteem it gave him. He believed in his vocation and would not shy from the dirt and drudgery of it.

"Benan!" he said into the priest's ear. "Benan, can you stand?"

Benan grunted in the negative, still too dazed by pain and exhaustion to form words.

"Benan, can you can stand and make your own way to the infirmary? I have salves that will help with these welts."

"There are... others," Benan muttered. "Others... worse than me..."

"Benan, some of these wounds of yours need sutures. You may bleed to death."

Bizarrely, Benan smiled, though it was still a picture of pain, his face gray and speckled with sweat.

"Our Lord," he stammered. "Our Lord was... scourged for our sins..."

"Benan, listen to me..."

"I am honoured... by this..."

"Yes, very good. Look, our Lord died, or had you forgotten? Do you want to die as well?"

The priest gave a crazy, fluting laugh.

"Henri!" Zacharius called over his shoulder.

The boy threaded his way across the room. He too was weary and sweating and wore a canvas apron blotched with blood.

"Henri, help me!"

Zacharius took Benan by one of his arms and indicated that Henri should take the other, but Benan grimaced and struggled weakly, until at last they let him go.

"No, there are others. See..."

Benan nodded towards a man seated against the near wall. He was one of Garbofasse's mercenaries and he was dull-eyed with pain. His leather hauberk had been removed to reveal the splintered nub of his collar bone tent-poling the flesh to the left of his neck; its white needle tip pierced through the skin. Beyond him, another fellow, who was unidentifiable he was so covered in gore, slumped with his head hung down. His blood-matted scalp was so deeply lacerated that his bare skull was exposed.

"Look to those... those who need you most," Benan said.

Zacharius hesitated, before nodding at Henri, who moved along and began to examine the casualty with the shattered collar bone. Zacharius meanwhile stood and gazed around the ghastly chamber. The sight of a makeshift field hospital was familiar to him. But this had come unexpectedly. Out in the courtyard, the infirmary was already a shambles of blood, filth and stained bandages. The infirmary beds they'd managed to construct were already filled to capacity. Rent and riven figures lay groaning in the passages between them. But in here it was even worse. The men were huddled wall to wall, wallowing in their own blood. Bowels had voided; there was vomit on the walls. The stench was intolerable.

As Henri attempted to move his patient, whose gasps quickly became shrill bleats of agony, onto the bier, the doctor turned back to the priest.

"I thought God's role was to love us?"

"No," Benan said solemnly. "It's our role to love Him. By action as well as word. That's why we all will die in this place."

"I can see why the earl had you flogged."

But Benan was lapsing back into unconsciousness. "I'm glad he did," he murmured. Zacharius moved away, to help Henri with their next patient. "I'm glad he did, good doctor. It's... my only hope."

The morning wore on and no immediate attack came.

The English watched in silence from the roof of the Constable's Tower. Ninety yards away, at the far end of the causeway, the dead stared back from the roof of the Gatehouse. They also stared from the curtain-wall which, now that it had been abandoned, had been inundated by them. They crowded along the top of it, all around the castle perimeter, and yet were eerily still. If the English had felt they were encircled before, they knew it for a fact now. The dead on the curtain-wall were actually within bowshot from the west side of the Constable's Tower, but as the archers had seen how futile their efforts had been before, none sought to waste an arrow now.

"What are they waiting for?" Navarre snapped. "A bloody invitation?"

"I'd guess munitions for the scoop-thrower," Garbofasse replied. "They threw so much rubble at us before, they probably emptied their stocks. They'll have to scour for miles in every direction to find a similar quantity again."

"At which point our problems really begin," Gurt said.

There were mumbles of agreement. Men glanced nervously towards the western bluff. It was clear to all that the Constable's Tower could also be struck by the scoop-thrower. If this happened, the men on its roof would be distracted trying to shield themselves, while the dead would advance along the causeway unimpeded.

This was Ranulf's suspicion, and it appeared to be confirmed shortly before noon, when about fifty of the dead emerged from the Gatehouse in lumbering work-gangs, and commenced laying out planks, beams and bundles of rope. The English watched, their sweat-filled hair prickling. Soon there was a prolonged banging of hammers and a droning of handsaws. Under the guidance of a twisted, diminutive figure, streaked with blood and dirt, yet with a distinctive gleaming pate, the corpses had commenced the construction of a tall framework.

"Is that William d'Abbetot?" someone asked, incredulous.

Earl Corotocus remained tight-lipped, but was clearly seething. Others were less angry and more bewildered, more horrified.

"I don't know which is worse," du Guesculin said. "That they know how to do that, or that one of our own is showing them the way."

They'd all come to dread this moment, when their own dead might be raised to face them, though so much horror had befallen them since Ranulf had first voiced concern about this that to many it was just another routine body-blow. More important to Ranulf was the object the dead were constructing. It was almost certainly a siege-tower.

"After the Gatehouse, they appear to have reasoned that forcing entry through the gate itself is too costly. This time they intend to come over the top," he said.

"You credit them with too much intellect," Navarre jeered. "Most of their brains are running out of their ears. How can they reason anything?"

But as the day wore on, Ranulf's thesis appeared to be correct. Whatever power controlled the Welsh dead, it also thought for them, motivating them like great swarms of ants, as though they were all of a single, collective mind. The work-gangs, who were tirelessly strong, and who operated with the smooth efficiency of skilled carpenters, continued to build the siege-tower, which was soon sturdy and massive, and rose section upon section until it was seventy feet tall. At the same time, other work-gangs descended the western bluff, carrying wheels, which they'd clearly removed from carts and wagons, to make it mobile. Others drove a team of oxen, to add brute muscle to the assault. Still more corpses appeared through the

Gatehouse carrying heavy iron plates between them. These had clearly been detached from the Gatehouse entrance and would now be hung as fire-proof shielding along the tower's front and sides.

"My lord," Ranulf said, pushing his way through to Earl Corotocus. "It only remains for them to restock the scoop-thrower, and we are in very serious trouble."

"I agree," the earl replied, deep in thought. "Do you imagine they'll opt for another night assault?"

"I doubt they'll be ready in time for that. So if we're lucky, no."

"Lucky?" someone exclaimed. "Is it lucky to have to wait another night before we die and are embraced by that legion of hell-spawn?"

It was a serjeant of mercenaries who'd spoken. He'd already suffered badly through the iron hail. Crude, self-applied sutures were all that held his face together, though his left eyeball was pulped and distended from its broken socket; stinking black humor dripped freely down his left cheek.

Ranulf ignored him. "My lord, I have a plan – but it can only be executed in darkness."

Corotocus regarded him with interest. "A raid perhaps?"

Ranulf nodded. "If a small party of us can get out there and disable the scoop-thrower, it will buy us time... at least for a few days, until they bring the mangonels onto the western bluff and assault us with those."

The rest of the men listened in stupefied silence. Someone finally said: "Are you mad? Out there, where only the dead rule? It's certain oblivion!"

"It's our only hope," Ranulf argued.

"And who would comprise this suicide party?" Navarre scoffed. "We'd draw lots, I suppose?"

Ranulf shrugged. "The rest of you may draw lots if you wish. However, I volunteer to go. In fact, I will lead it."

"Do you have a death wish, Ranulf?" the earl wondered. "First onto the Gatehouse drawbridge. Leader of the forlorn hope. Has your father's demise unhinged you?"

"What I have, my lord, is experience. Remember Bayonne?"

Corotocus recalled it well; his mouth crooked into a half-smile. Others recalled the incident at Bayonne too, though not so fondly. Several of the earl's knights preferred not to dwell on it at all, for it had flown in the face of everything chivalrous they had ever been taught. On that occasion they had been the besiegers rather than the besieged.

It was in the early days of the Gascon war and Bayonne Castle on the River Nive had been captured by French forces. Earl Corotocus led the English army that subsequently surrounded it. The following siege was a prolonged, tiresome affair, both sides suffering from hunger and foul weather. On regular occasions Abbot Julius, of the Sainte Martine monastery high in the foothills of the Pyrenees, had come graciously down and been allowed entry to the castle by the English, to sing psalms for the embattled French. However, the earl's spies soon informed him that Abbott Julius was a cousin of Count Girald, who was commanding the French force, and was passing intelligence about the English strength and disposition. Not only that, he was organising a local resistance movement on behalf of the besieged and offering gold to pirates if they would intercept English galleys, bringing much-needed supplies to the nearby port.

In response, Earl Corotocus despatched a small group of handpicked men, Ranulf and his father among them, who disguised themselves as pilgrims en route to Compostela, and trod the dusty mountain road to Sainte Martine on foot. Only after begging water and a bed for the night, and finally being admitted to the monastery, did they throw off their rags and cowls, to reveal mail, swords and daggers. The monastery was sacked and burned, its lay-brothers slain, its monks – including Abbott Julius – taken as captives of war. A short while later, Earl Corotocus brought these prisoners before the walls of Castle Bayonne, and stood them on ox-carts with nooses around their necks. One word from him, he shouted, and the carts would be hauled away and the brethren left dangling. Inside the castle, Abbot Julius's cousin, Count Girald, had had no option but to signal his surrender.

Though it was well known that Earl Corotocus waged war in the most cunning ways, he was widely reviled for this ignoble act. Complaints were made against him to King Edward even from some on the English side – especially from those paragons of courtly virtue, William Latimer and John of Brittany. King Edward replied that conflict was always a hellish affair, but on this occasion particularly so as it was a straight contest between he and Philip IV of France, one anointed monarch versus another. With the stakes so high, he would not be held accountable for the "improvisational skills of his commanders". A short time later, when Pope Celestine excommunicated Earl Corotocus, King Edward sent an embassy to the papal court at Naples to have it lifted.

"What do you propose?" the earl said.

"Can we talk in private?"

The earl nodded. They crossed the roof and descended into a stairwell.

"I don't know how alert these walking dead are," Ranulf said. "But I don't think we can afford to take chances. Only a handful of men must go – five at the most. I don't even think it wise to take our best. It'll be perilous, and how many will return I don't know."

"All the more courageous of you to offer to lead it, Ranulf." The earl regarded him carefully, almost suspiciously.

"You're wondering if I really have lost my mind?"

"You wouldn't be the only man in this garrison who had."

"My lord, we face an enemy the like of which has never been seen. An enemy that can't be killed. An enemy that threatens our very souls, or so we assume. I'd be lying if I said that I think any of us will survive this siege. Could any man think rationally in these circumstances? I don't know. But we can only do – as my father used to say – what we can do."

"Tell me your plan," the earl said.

"There are plenty of storages sheds in the courtyard. At the very least, we have rope, we have paint, we have barrels of pig grease."

"And?"

"I suggest that whoever goes out there wears minimum clothing. I once heard a tale of how a Roman army was overwhelmed by a Germanic tribe. The Germans came through the benighted forest naked and painted black from head to toe. They were invisible until they struck the Roman camp."

The earl looked sceptical. "And this will fool our dead friends?"

"As I say, I don't know how alert they are. Do they think the way we think, can they even see as we do? But we must prepare as if they can. We must also grease ourselves, so that if they grab us we can still get free. It's all about speed, my lord. So much so that I recommend we don't load ourselves with weapons. We must break the scoop-thrower and get back inside the castle as fast as possible."

"And how would you even get out of the castle, let alone get back inside?

"When I was in the Keep before, I noticed the garderobe chute. It must lead down to an underground sewer. I suspect it passes beneath the east bailey and feeds into the moat. We can exit that way."

"An underground sewer?" The earl raised an eyebrow. "It may be a tight squeeze."

"In which case, the pig-grease will come in useful."

Corotocus pursed his lips as he pondered. "Supposing you succeed, how do you expect to get back inside? Climbing the garderobe chute? How high is it?"

"If we hang ropes down, with knots and loops tied in them, all it will need is for you to have a number of men standing by. The moment we're in position, you can pull us up. We won't need to climb."

The earl now smiled. Irregular warfare was always to his liking. "I think I'm in favour of this plan, Ranulf. But who will you take?"

"Volunteers initially. If there aren't enough forthcoming, as Navarre said... we'll draw lots."

"I want Garbofasse to go with you."

Ranulf tried not to show how much this disconcerted him. "You don't trust me, my lord?"

"I trust the men less. If you get beyond this ring of dead flesh, what's to stop those worthless dogs fleeing for their lives? You'll be there, but you'll be alone. With Garbofasse, you can control things better."

Ranulf had no particular dislike for Garbofasse, aside from him being the leader of a gang of murderers. And the mercenary captain could not really be described as the earl's man the way Navarre or du Guesculin could. But he was hardly someone Ranulf could trust. All of a sudden, the extremely difficult task Ranulf had set himself looked nigh on impossible.

CHAPTER TWENTY-ONE

THAT EVENING WAS a pleasant one, redolent of spring. Though cold, the air was clear and fresh. The sky was pebble-blue, but faded to indigo as dusk fell, and to fiery red as the sun finally settled.

At the far end of the causeway, the siege-tower was almost completed and as ominous an object as any man there had seen in all his years of war. The dead still worked in industrious and eerie silence. The only sound was the tapping of hammers as wheels were attached to the great monolith. Its front and sides were shod almost completely with iron plate. Where the iron had run out, the gaps were covered by shields purloined from the English. As the last vestige of sunlight melted into the west, a single ray shot across the land and burnished the object with flame. Several of the dead, clambering back and forth upon it like beetles, also glinted as it caught their pieces of mail.

The English watched tensely, expecting the tower to immediately roll forth along the causeway. But though the teams of oxen had now been brought from the Gatehouse, no attempt was made to yoke them in place. Gradually, the hammering ceased, and as darkness fell the dead withdrew into their fastness. A legion of them still watched from the western bluff and droves more remained on the parapets of the curtain-wall. If other monstrosities were still scouring the Grogen hinterlands for munitions, there was no sign of it. All were stiff and still as the mannequins that had first confronted the English on their arrival here. As night descended, and cloaked them from view, even their mewling and moaning faded. Soon, only the stink of mildewed flesh bespoke their presence.

A querulous voice finally broke the unearthly quiet. It was du Guesculin. "In God's name, why don't they take action? Do the dead need sleep? How can that be?"

"Maybe their masters do," Gurt said. "We don't know if they–"

"Is your friend preparing himself?" Navarre interrupted, his voice edged with resentment.

On first hearing about the proposed raid, Navarre had volunteered, but Earl Corotocus had refused him permission to go, saying that, from this point on, he wanted his best men with him at all times. Navarre was even more embittered when he heard that Captain Garbofasse would also be going.

"So FitzOsbern, that whey-faced whelp, and now that damn mercenary oaf get the chance to win fame, while I, the household champion, remain coddled in this castle!"

Corotocus had snorted in response. "Fame is for fools."

CHAPTER TWENTY-TWO

THERE WAS NO sign of Murlock as Ranulf stole up through the upper levels of the Keep. The big mercenary was most likely taking full advantage of this long, lonely duty by sleeping. As quietly as he could, Ranulf unlocked Gwendolyn's door, slipped inside and closed it again. The prisoner sat bolt-upright as he approached.

"My lady, can you write?" he asked.

"Certainly I can write."

"Then you must write a letter now." He handed her a folded parchment, an inkpot and a quill. "Hurry."

She took the items hesitantly. "I don't understand."

"I'll be leaving the castle just after midnight. There is a target we must destroy. But I will have another purpose. If I can locate your mother, I will plead for a truce."

"A truce?"

"My terms will be simple. If I return you to your mother unharmed, and hand over Earl Corotocus for whatever punishment she deems fit, she must allow the rest of us safe passage back to England. If you can write a letter vouching for my honesty, I will put it directly into her hands."

Gwendolyn hesitated, as though wondering whether this was some kind of trap, but finally nodded and began to scratch out a quick note.

"How many others are involved?" she asked.

"So far only me."

She glanced up, shocked. "How can I sway her, if only one man is to turn?"

"We have to try."

She put down her quill. "This is an impossible cause, and you know it."

"When men are prepared to make sacrifices, nothing is impossible."

"And will your friends sacrifice their loyalty?"

"In exchange for their lives, yes... maybe. For that's the choice they will face in due course."

She still seemed uncertain, but she recommenced writing. "For all your faults, sir knight, you don't strike me as someone who fears death."

"Maybe I don't any more. But there was something my father said to me before he died..." Ranulf shrugged and waved it away.

"What?"

"Suffice to say, something good must be dragged from the jaws of this catastrophe."

"Will your fellow countrymen define the betrayal of an overlord as 'good'?"

Ranulf couldn't conceal his conflicted feelings about this. The knightly code stated that duty to your lord should be the keystone of your life. Duplicity with the man who had clothed you, fed you, trained you, the man in whose service you were bonded was supposedly a grave sin – even if it was to the benefit of others. Judas Iscariot had handed Jesus to the temple guards because he worried that Jesus's preaching might bring Roman retribution on the Jewish race. It could be deemed that such an act was well intentioned, yet Judas had been reviled throughout eternity as the arch-traitor. And still – Ranulf again recalled his father's words: "Be true to your heart, lad. In the end, when all has come to pass, it'll be the only thing you can trust." And what his heart told him now was that Earl Corotocus had gone too far. In Gascony it had been slightly different – that had been a bitter war waged against an enemy who would stop at nothing to wrest control of English sovereign territory. But here against the Welsh, for all their oft-professed hatred of the English, it had gone too far. There had been too much blood, too much cruelty, too much terror. Little wonder the dead themselves were now rising in retaliation. And *that* in itself, of course, made all other considerations pale to insignificance.

"You haven't seen what's gathering outside, my lady," Ranulf finally said. "The customs we live by, the canons we've tricked ourselves into believing... they don't mean anything any more. The world has turned on its head. All that's left is the difference between those things we *know* to be right and those we *know* to be wrong."

She handed him the parchment. "Here's your letter. God speed you with it, for the sake of both our peoples."

He folded it, inserted it into a pouch – and froze. Gwendolyn glanced past him. They'd both heard a scraping sound as of leather or metal on the other side of the door. Ranulf looked around too and saw that the small hatch in the cell door was wide open.

Cursing, he raced across the room and barged out into the passage. Murlock was twenty yards off, walking quickly. When Ranulf started to run, Murlock started to run too.

Ranulf caught up with him at the top of the first flight of steps. Just as he did, the big mercenary swung around, striking with his dagger. Ranulf threw himself to one side and the blade flashed past, jamming point first into the wall and snapping. Then Ranulf was onto him. They tumbled down the steps together, clawing, wrestling. At the bottom, Murlock landed on top and for crucial seconds had the advantage. He pinned Ranulf down, clutching his throat with bear-like paws, head-butting him in the face. Ranulf struggled wildly, but only dislodged Murlock by driving a knee up between his legs. Murlock rolled away, gagging.

Ranulf got groggily to his feet. His nose, already broken once, was now broken again. Hot tears blurred his vision.

Murlock tried to crawl away on all fours. Ranulf lurched after him, grabbed him by the hair, yanked his head back and fumbled for his own dagger. Before he could draw it, the mercenary slammed an elbow back, catching him in the ribs. Ranulf was mail-clad but the impact was agonising and the air whistled from his lungs. He tottered backward. Murlock spun around, this time drawing his scramsax and swiping with it. Ranulf dodged away, the keen but heavy edge missing him by inches, clanging on the brickwork.

Ranulf drew his own sword in time to deflect the second blow, forcing the mercenary to step backward to the edge of the next stairwell. Murlock lunged as hard as he could with his blade. Ranulf again parried and smashed his left fist into Murlock's jaw. It was as hard a punch as he'd ever thrown. Murlock's head spun right as bloody phlegm spat from his mouth; his very neck seemed to shift on its axis. Ranulf kicked him again, this time with a stamping manoeuvre on the side of his right knee. Murlock's leg buckled inwards and he gave a shill, bird-like squawk. With Murlock's guard now down, Ranulf hove at him a final time, slamming the pommel of his sword between his eyes.

The mercenary stiffened and toppled backward like a felled tree, bouncing end-over-end from one step to the next, his limbs splayed. When he finally came to rest at the bottom, he was face-down and motionless. Ranulf scrambled down after him. The blood from the mercenary's nose and mouth was spreading in a wide puddle. There was no hint of life in his apparently broken body.

Ranulf sat back on his haunches, panting.

Of course, even in this drear and filthy place, so much fresh blood would need to be cleared away if suspicion was not to be aroused. Ranulf sheathed his blade and got quickly to work. He dragged the body by its feet into a dungeon and dumped it in the dimmest corner, where he covered it with matted straw. Taking two more handfuls of the stuff, he went back outside and began to mop the floor.

"What if someone misses him?" came a nervous voice.

It was Gwendolyn. In his haste to catch up with the jailer, he hadn't thought to lock her in again.

"Go back to your cell," he said, scrubbing up the gore.

"But he'll be missed."

"The only time he'll be missed is when we retreat to this final refuge and, trust me, if we get to that stage it won't matter anyway."

"But I..."

"Go back to your cell!" he shouted. "I'll lock you in anon."

She scurried back up the steps.

"You may not believe it," he said under his breath. "But that's by far the safest place in this castle at present."

He heard her door grating shut as he continued to scrub the flagstones hard, conscious that time was running out. The hour was getting late and he was soon due to meet the rest of the raiding party in the courtyard.

CHAPTER TWENTY-THREE

THEY MET JUST before midnight in the main courtyard. Ranulf, Garbofasse and four others: a tenant knight, Roger FitzUrz, a household squire, Tancred Tallebois, an archer, Paston, and a mercenary called Red Guthric – a beanpole of a man, with a hatchet face and straggling carrot-red hair, who Garbofasse said was one of his best.

In torch-lit silence, they removed their mail and their leather and their under-garb, until they wore only loincloths and felt shoes. They then rubbed themselves with black soot – heads and hands as well as bodies and limbs and slathered it with pig-grease to hold it in place. The only weapons they armed themselves with were knives and daggers. Corotocus, du Guesculin and several dozen others watched in silence. Doctor Zacharius had come over from the infirmary. A full day having elapsed since the last attack, he had finally managed to get on top of his casualty list, but he was sallow-faced and covered with other men's blood.

"You fellows look like Moors," he said, rubbing his hands on a towel.

There were nervous chuckles.

"They'll smell like Moors too, when they've finished climbing down the garderobe," someone replied, to more chuckles.

"I knew campaigns in Wales were notoriously hard," FitzUrz said. "But I never thought I'd finish up eating shit."

"Enough!" Corotocus said. "All of you listen to me. No matter what your position, for the duration of this mission you are under the command of Captain Garbofasse and Ranulf FitzOsbern, whose errant status is to be of no consequence. Anyone disobeying their orders will answer to me personally on his return."

There were mumbles of acknowledgement.

They moved to set off, but now Zacharius spoke up. "If you can capture an intact specimen, perhaps I can examine it. Even dissect it. It would be an ungodly act, but are these things godly in any way? It might help us to understand how they are as they are."

Ranulf glanced at him. By his expression, the doctor was perfectly serious. Everyone looked to Earl Corotocus, who seemed briefly intrigued by the proposition, though eventually he shook his head.

"This mission is difficult enough already. If it doesn't succeed, we'll be up to our ears in intact specimens."

The doctor shrugged as if it didn't matter. But Ranulf couldn't help wondering about the wisdom of ruling out such a plan. At present, given his own secret agenda, it would be difficult to the point of impossibility to carry such a thing off, but maybe – if his own scheme failed – it was worth bearing in mind for some time in the future.

"You men need to go," the earl said. "We don't know how long these creatures will hold back for."

They took their ropes and tackle and trooped up into the Keep together, ascending from one level to the next without speaking, their thin-clad feet slapping the dank flagstones. Ranulf was fleetingly unnerved, wondering if Murlock's absence would be noticed. But as it transpired, they were all too focussed on their task. Even Garbofasse, Murlock's immediate commanding officer, paid the missing jailer no heed. They at last entered the garderobe and lowered their ropes down the chute.

Almost as one, they looked frightened. Beads of sweat sat on the dark, oily film coating their brows. In the flickering torchlight, the squire, Tallebois, regarded his comrades with eyes that had almost bugged from their sockets. His lips were wet with repeated licking.

"Looks like the entrance to the underworld," FitzUrz muttered, peering down the black shaft.

"From here on no talking unless you're given leave to," Corotocus said. "We know too little about these Welsh dead. Maybe they can hear you, maybe they can't, but it's a chance you mustn't take. Now... God go with you all."

Ranulf wound a rope with a grapple attached around his body, and clambered over the low brick wall rimming the chute. As he did, he wondered at the irony of the earl's last comment. *God go with them?* With the dead rising en masse, ravening for the blood of the living, did Earl Corotocus seriously think the Almighty was anywhere near this place? And after the slaughter the earl had himself wreaked, did he genuinely believe there was the remotest chance the Almighty would look to English welfare during this tragedy?

They made the descent in twos, for the chute was not wide enough to accommodate all at the same time. Ranulf and Garbofasse went first. As FitzUrz had feared, the brick sides were slimy with human waste. If the stench had been bad outside of the castle, down here the men found themselves in a cloying, malodorous fog, which almost suffocated them. They could virtually taste it – not just on the tips of their tongues, but in the backs of their throats.

The climb itself was exhausting – made in complete darkness, with hands and feet rendered slippery by grease. Several times the men almost slid from the ropes. Frequently, they thrashed about in the blackness, bumping into each other, swinging against the walls. When they reached the bottom, the ordure was over a foot deep, though, thanks to the recent cold, neither as soft nor repulsive as it might have been. Ranulf groped around and found the arched entrance to the drain. This was another nerve-wracking moment. If it was too small for a man to fit down, the mission would need to be abandoned. Thankfully, it was about two feet across and a foot and a half in depth, which meant that, though difficult to crawl along, it would not be impossible.

Their next problem was turning around in the narrow space at the bottom of the shaft, but this Ranulf finally managed to do with much twisting and grunting. Pushing his head and shoulders into the drain, with his hands fumbling ahead of him, again finding more brickwork clotted both above and below with human excreta, he felt as though he was burrowing into the stuff, burying himself alive. How far did this drain run for? If he became stuck, would anyone be able to get him out again? Would the earl care enough to try? The only way was to keep going forward. He'd assumed it would slope downward beneath the east bailey and discharge into the moat. That was a mere fifty yards or more, though, now that he was here, his body enclosed by tight, rugged architecture, with progress only possible by worming forward like a slug, even fifty yards seemed like a massive distance.

He wasn't sure how long it was before he smelled fresh air again. He was already wearied to the bone and felt he'd rubbed his naked skin raw. But at last his hands encountered hanging vegetation. The next thing, he was hauling himself out of a vent that felt no larger than a rabbit hole, and falling face down onto steeply sloped rubble. It was still dark, but Ranulf could now sense the night sky overhead, and, compared to the subterranean realm he'd just emerged from, that was something to offer prayers of thanks for.

Glancing up, he saw stars glimmering through a wash of turgid cloud. The floor of the moat was stony and jagged. The vent was rimmed with brick and, as he'd expected, set into the side of the moat. Much soil had crumbled down from above it, and it was half hidden behind hanging weeds. He remained crouched as he waited for the others, glancing up again, scanning the parapets overhead, which at present were devoid of sentinel forms. A grunting and scrabbling noise reached his ears. It was Garbofasse squirming along the drain towards him.

The mercenary captain was larger in bulk than Ranulf, and was having a torrid time. He only made it to the end of the pipe with difficulty. Ranulf had to reach in, take him by wrists, and pull him the rest of the way. Garbofasse had to suppress cries of agony as he was finally released. Even through his covering of soot and grease, the skin on his ribs and hips was scored by the brickwork and bled freely in many places.

"Name of a name," he panted, crouching. "Name of a God damned name, this had better be worth it."

The other four followed over the next few minutes, all emerging in a similarly filthy and dishevelled state. One by one, they crouched, shivering with the cold and now with the wet as well, for in the last few moments a drizzling rain had commenced.

"Where to next?" someone asked.

"We're on the east side of the castle," Ranulf replied. "If we follow this moat around to the west, we'll likely meet those dead who were cast into it from the bridge and weren't able to climb out again. So we need to get out on this side. After that, we circle around to western bluff via the moors to the north."

There were grunts of assent. If anyone disliked the idea of having to circumnavigate the castle out in the open, he didn't voice it. The thought of having to face the dead down here, in the confined space of the moat, was equally, if not even more, horrifying.

Ranulf swung the rope with the grapple, and hurled it. He had to do this several times before it caught on something that could bear their weight. One by one, they scrambled out, finding themselves on open, grassy ground, where each man lay flat to wait for his comrades. By the time they were all together, their eyes had attuned. Ranulf saw a line of trees to the east of them, but to the north a sloping expanse of star-lit moorland. Nothing moved over there, though it was difficult to see clearly beyond fifty yards or so.

"It's a long way to the western bluff," Red Guthric said quietly. "How long until dawn?"

"We have a few hours," Garbofasse replied. "So we'd better not waste them."

They proceeded north in single file, moving stealthily through thorns and knee-deep sedge. All the way, the mammoth outline of the castle stood to their left, but it provided no comfort, for if they should be attacked now there was no easy way back into it. Despite the darkness, they felt badly exposed. Their nerves were taut. The slightest sound – the cry of an owl or nightjar – brought them to a breathless halt.

Only when far to the north of the castle did they turn west, having to thread their way through swathes of sodden bracken, the stubble of which prickled their feet through their felt shoes. Here, on this higher ground, they encountered the first of the dead. A large, heavily-built woman, naked, with flesh mottled by bruising and a chewed-off noose tight around her throat, lay still in the vegetation. Slightly further on, a youth with an arrow through his neck – it passed cleanly from one side to the other – also lay still. The raiders crouched again, waiting and watching for some time, before Ranulf found the courage to approach.

He crept forward quietly and stood surveying the two bodies, neither of which stirred. At length, he summoned the others, and they hastened past.

From this point on, the hillside was strewn with similarly inert forms. Soon, corpses lay so thick that it was like a benighted battlefield. All of them had done this before, of course: walked dolefully among the slain after some catastrophic engagement. All were familiar with the sight of tangled limbs, hewn torsos, faces frozen in death and spattered with gore. On this occasion, though, it was different. For these beings, though visibly rotting in the mist and rain, had been walking around as though alive not two or three hours earlier. Why they were now 'dead again', if it was possible to describe them in such a way, was anybody's guess.

"Maybe it's over?" Tallebois whispered hopefully.

"Quiet!" Garbofasse hissed.

They continued, keeping low, moving as stealthily as they could. But as the great slope of the western bluff hove in from the left, this became increasingly difficult. There was now scarcely any uncluttered ground to walk on. Ranulf found himself edging uphill towards the higher ground, where a cover of trees had appeared. All the way, he fancied the eyes of the dead were upon him. Were they watching his progress? Could they see anything? Did any functions occur in the addled pulp of their brains? Though he didn't say it, he too felt a vague hope that somehow the spell had been broken, and that these dead were indeed dead again. But he doubted it.

Among the trees, the raiders felt they'd be less visible, though to reach that higher point they had to venture even further from the east moat and their so-called place of safety. The west side of the castle made a dark outline in the night. They could just distinguish the rounded section that was the Barbican, and beyond that the upper tier of the Gatehouse. Further south, at the end of the causeway, was the tall, angular shape of the Constable's Tower. A handful of lit torches were visible on its roof. They looked to be an immense distance away, which was not comforting.

Equally discomforting, in its own way, was the wood they'd now entered – not just because there were further corpses scattered between its roots, but because of its dense thickets and skeletal branches, all hung with cauls of mist. If nothing else, however, the party were soon on a level with the top of the bluff, which meant that they couldn't be too far from the artillery machines. Ranulf halted and again dropped to a crouch. The others did the same. They breathed slowly and deeply, listening for any sound that might indicate they'd alerted sentries, but hearing only rain pattering on twigs and the chattering of their own teeth; every man there was now shivering with the cold and damp.

"We don't know exactly where the scoop-thrower is located," Ranulf whispered. "It must be up here on the treed ground, because it was concealed from the battlements. Judging from its angle of shot, it can't be more than a hundred yards or more to the south of us, but the exact position is uncertain."

"We should spread out," Garbofasse said. "Form a skirmish line. Twenty yards between each man. That way we cover more ground."

Ranulf nodded; this would suit *his* plan as well.

"There's still no movement from these... these things," FitzUrz said. Of the horrible shapes lying around them, some were more decomposed than others, several little more than bones wrapped in parchment. But again, in many cases, their heads were turned towards the raiding party, as though watching them carefully.

"The puppets don't sleep, but maybe the puppet masters do," Ranulf said. "It probably only needs one command to be issued and they'll come raging back to life." He mopped his brow. He was sweating so hard that the grease and soot was running off him in streams. "Form the line. We're moving south... slowly. Keep your eyes and your ears open."

With some hardship in the darkness and undergrowth, they spread out into a skirmish line, Ranulf anchoring it at the north end and Garbofasse at the south, and proceeded again along the top of the bluff. The ground became even harder to negotiate; it wasn't just bulging with roots, but it had been churned to quagmires by thousands of trampling feet. In some cases, the bodies of the dead lay in actual piles, as if they'd been heaped together by gravediggers. Subsequently, the skirmish line extended and warped as the men struggled to keep up with each other. But on flatter ground, they came across the first of the heavy weapons. Many were still in their wagons, unpacked. Several onagers and ballistae had been taken out and were partly assembled, though further corpses were strewn around these. More work-gangs, Ranulf realised with a shudder. This army of reanimated clay could be turned just as easily to tireless labour as it could to war, and of course it never asked for pay. The full extent of the power this gifted its controller was quite chilling.

There was still no sign of the scoop-thrower, though ahead of them, they now sighted firelight. They slowed their advance to a crawl.

In a small clearing, a circle of tents had been raised, with snores emanating from inside them. In the middle of the circle, raised on a mound of hot coals was a large cauldron or cooking-pot. It bubbled loudly as it pumped a column of foul-smelling smoke into the night sky. They halted, wondering what this meant, though each one of them was thinking the same thing: the dead don't need shelter against the elements; nor do they need to sleep, nor to eat warm food.

Ranulf felt a sudden urge to draw his blade, though he knew he had to resist. Glancing down the line, he saw the next man along, Robert FitzUrz, watching him intently, one hand on his dagger hilt. Ranulf shook his head. They weren't here to perform assassinations. How did they know who actually controlled these dead? How would they know they had killed the right people? In addition of course, Ranulf had his own scheme to attend to. He shook his head vigorously.

FitzUrz nodded and passed the message along the line. They continued to advance, skirting around the small encampment, but now with their eyes peeled for the massive, distinctive shape of the scoop-thrower. They'd penetrated maybe thirty yards further on, again having to thread between piles of corpses, when Ranulf spotted something else. Twenty yards to his right, half-hidden by trees, there was a stockade with torches burning on the other side of its open gate. Inside, he made out what looked like a gold pavilion covered with red lions. He glanced left again. Only a couple of the other men were visible beyond FitzUrz. He slowed down so that soon they were ahead of him by several yards. Concentrating on what lay in front of them, they didn't notice that he had fallen behind. He now ceased advancing altogether and, as soon as they'd vanished into the mist and rain, turned and hurried towards the stockade.

When he reached it, he saw that it had a single guard – a living one – on its gate. The guard was young but heavily bearded and, wearing a white gown and hooded white cloak, he looked like a priest of the old religion. He had a curved sword at his belt and a circular shield on one arm, but his spear stood beside him. He looked wet and tired, and was yawning into his hand. Clearly, the last thing he was expecting was some form of attack. When Ranulf lobbed a stone, which crackled in the bushes, the guard turned dully towards it, as if he wasn't quite sure that he'd heard anything. He never saw Ranulf steal up behind, wrap an arm around his neck and throttle him into unconsciousness.

Ranulf took the curved sword before proceeding. It surprised him that there'd only been one guard, though he supposed that with a multitude of horrors to be called on from the surrounding woods, even the most nervous camp commander would feel relatively safe here.

Creeping to the pavilion, he saw a flicker of flame within. He held his breath before entering. This would be the biggest risk of all, but the stakes he was playing for were higher than any he'd known in his entire life. Whichever way he looked at it, there seemed to be no other option than this. Sliding the sword into his belt beside his dagger, he drew the tent flap aside and stepped through.

Beyond, in a small pool of candlelight, a woman sat with her back to him at a small table. Her lustrous red hair, which hung unbound to her waist, revealed that she was Countess Madalyn; there could not be two people in the camp with her distinctive looks. At first she didn't notice the intruder. She was writing what looked like a letter. A number of other documents, already scrolled and sealed with wax, lay alongside it.

When she sensed that he was there, she gasped, spun around and jumped to her feet.

Ranulf knew that he must have made a ghastly sight, though he was surely no worse than the monstrosities that had been lumbering around her for the last few days. He put a finger to his lips, hissing at her to be silent.

"Cry out and call your creatures, countess... and you will miss something to your advantage."

"Who are you?" she breathed, wide-eyed.

She was clearly frightened, but she was angry as well – and why not? She was a great noblewoman, as befitted her impressive stature and fierce beauty. And she was now embroiled in a war for the lives and souls of her people. Slowly, her expression softened.

"I... I seem to recognise your voice."

"We spoke the day before yesterday," Ranulf said. "Just before this battle commenced."

"You were the English knight who advised me that further war was futile."

"And I now advise it again."

He stepped forward. She retreated, but halted when he took the crumpled letter from a pouch and offered it to her. She opened it and read it. Her eyes widened with wild hope.

"You recognise your daughter's hand?" he said.

"Of course. Is she safe?"

"For the time being. I can't say what will happen to her if this siege drags on."

Countess Madalyn glanced again at the letter. "This tells me that you harbour feelings against Earl Corotocus and that you aren't alone. How many do you speak for?"

"At present just myself. But our men are weary and many are wounded. When they arrived here, they thought the war was over. Even the hardiest of them are now losing their appetite for it. What's more, whatever black gate you've opened to summon this hellish horde has left them terror-stricken. Few question the earl's authority thus far. But that state of affairs won't last."

She folded the letter and regarded him sternly. "Earl Corotocus did not hang and butcher my people alone. Why should I spare any of his wretches?"

"Because one atrocity fuels another, countess. Victory for you here will only provoke the marcher barons to make more incursions into your land."

"Then they too will die at the hands of my army."

"That possibility won't stop them coming," Ranulf said. "They won't believe mere rumour. With no-one alive to tell them the truth about what happened at Grogen Castle, they'll bring even greater forces. And with King Edward's might and wealth behind them, they'll soon find a way to tame your festering rabble. The war will go on, an endless cycle of brutality and counter-brutality."

"Interesting to finally hear an Englishman speaking so. Of course, the main change is that now it is you who stares defeat in the face."

"Believe what you wish about me, countess, but you have negotiated peace treaties before. I know you seek a better way than endless violence."

She pursed her lips as she pondered this, before finally saying: "And how do *you* respond, Gwyddon?"

Ranulf was startled when a second figure stepped out of the shadows. He looked like a druid or priest of the old faith. He had broad, pale features, with a long, jet-black beard and eyes like lumps of onyx. He walked with a knotted staff, but looked young and strong, and had adorned himself with ornate jewellery.

"Don't be alarmed, English knight," the countess said. "When Wales belongs to the Welsh again, Gwyddon will be my first minister. No counsel of mine shall be closed to him." She turned to her advisor. "You heard?"

"I did, madam." Gwyddon nodded, never taking his eyes off Ranulf. "And I urge you to tread carefully."

She turned back to Ranulf. "Not only will you return my daughter, but you claim that you will either hand Earl Corotocus to me, or punish him yourself?"

Ranulf nodded, more disconcerted than he could explain by the priest's unexpected presence. He'd faced enemies before, but the hostility emanating from this fellow was almost palpable. The inscrutable onyx eyes never left him.

"And how do you propose to do this?" Countess Madalyn asked.

"I'll need to plan accordingly," Ranulf replied. "But I had to come here first. I had to know if you would be receptive to my offer."

"So you claim to come to us with a plan, though in truth you have no plan at all?" Gwyddon said.

"I didn't say that."

The priest turned to his mistress. "If the choice were mine, the answer would be 'no'. Why should we hear terms from an enemy who has already been crushed?"

"Gwyddon... or whatever your name is," Ranulf said. "The army that King Edward is bringing into Wales has not been crushed, and likely is ten times the size of your miserable host."

"You see," Gwyddon retorted. "He is crafty, this Englishman. Even now, he seeks to elicit information about the progress of his reinforcements." He sneered at Ranulf. "We will tell you nothing. Return to Earl Corotocus and prepare yourselves firstly for death, and secondly for everlasting service in my regiment of the damned."

"Countess, this is madness," Ranulf pleaded. "There is no point continuing this fight."

Gwyddon laughed. "The point is that Wales is on the verge of greatness."

"Wales is on the verge of annihilation," Ranulf countered. "It doesn't matter how long it takes King Edward to get here, or whether he saves *us* or not. In fact, the longer it takes him to get here the better, because during all that time your army will be rotting to its bones."

"And all that time we will replenish it," Gwyddon said. "The more who die, the greater our reserves of strength."

"Is this what you want?" Ranulf asked the countess. "Queen Madalyn of Lyr, reigning supreme over a nation of mindless corpses? Or will it be First Minister Gwyddon reigning over them? I'm not quite clear."

Countess Madalyn's lips trembled as she heard him out, but she said nothing. Ranulf pleaded to her again.

"Listen to me, I beg you. If we return to England, we can tell everyone what we saw here. We can tell the king himself. If all you want is Wales for the Welsh, I dare say you've won it already."

"Until such time as Edward Longshanks invokes aid from the pope," Gwyddon interrupted. "'Holy Father', he will say. 'There are demons in Wales. Instead of directing our crusader armies east, we must send them west.'"

"If that's what you think, shaman, you don't know King Edward very well," Ranulf said. "No foreign armies will ever be permitted onto the island of Britain."

"King Edward does not control the island of Britain."

"As I say, you don't know him very well." Ranulf turned back to the countess. "Madam, however invincible this fellow might have convinced you that you are, it is better to be King Edward's friend than his enemy. Your army of monsters has given you an advantage, so I pray you don't waste it. With might on your side as well as right, isn't it better to talk?"

Gwyddon made to respond, his face written with scorn, but Countess Madalyn signalled for silence. She read her daughter's letter again.

"You speak well for a common knight," she finally said. "But you have no authority to make this treaty."

Ranulf nodded, as though pondering this. And whipped the dagger and curved sword from his belt. "These are all the authority I need!"

The countess stepped back. Gwyddon's eyes narrowed.

"If I was as treacherous as you fear," Ranulf said. "Wouldn't I plunge these blades into your two hearts right now? Instead of vowing to plunge them into Earl Corotocus when I return to Grogen?"

"This is true," the countess said. "He has taken quite a risk to come here. It would be easy for him just to kill us."

"He seeks only to save his men, so they may fight another day," Gwyddon argued.

Ranulf laughed. "After their experiences here, I doubt any of 'my men' – as you call them – would ever glance past Offa's Dyke again, let alone enter Wales. We'll leave our weapons, our booty. I promise we'll march home and harm no-one. Think, madam, how that would help your position once King Edward arrives. I can plead with him on your behalf. Tell him how you punished the criminal Corotocus, but spared the rest of us. Could there be a greater gesture of good will?"

She gazed at him intently, as if he was slowly persuading her. She was about to speak when there came a frantic shouting from outside the pavilion. It was in Welsh, but Ranulf knew enough of the border tongue to recognise an intruder alert – apparently the English were in the camp.

"See how he lies and manipulates!" Gwyddon roared. "See how he buys time for his assassins!"

The countess's expression froze with outrage.

"Ignore my offer at your peril," Ranulf said as he backed towards the entrance. "You've thrown your lot in with a pagan sorcerer. Continue on this path, and who knows – when you get to Hell, you may share your dungeon with Corotocus himself."

He turned and dashed outside, where he met another of the young priests at the stockade gate. The priest had a scimitar in his hand, but was too stunned by the sight of the intruder to react. Ranulf slashed his throat and knifed him in the heart.

Beyond the stockade, there was no immediate response from the dead, who still lay motionless in the undergrowth. But several dozen yards to his right, behind a wall of black and twisting trees, flames were blazing into the night. A great mechanical outline, with a huge throwing-arm, was engulfed in fire. There were more wild shouts. Some were gruff, some sounded panicked. A half-naked figure came weaving between the trunks, stumbling over corpses. It was Tallebois, the squire.

Ranulf dashed to intercept him, grabbing his arm and bringing him to a halt. The squire squawked with fright.

"What happened?" Ranulf demanded.

"We found the scoop-thrower. We brought coals from the campfire and piled straw beneath it. Now the whole thing's burning. We cut its torsion springs as well, broke its winch and pulley-bar. They'll never use it again." Tallebois laughed hysterically.

"FitzOsbern, where the devil have you been?" came an angry voice.

Garbofasse lumbered into view, with the others at his heels. He was slick with sweat, his pale flesh shining between streaks of soot and grease.

"I tried to find the countess," Ranulf said. "How ineffective would the Welsh snake be with its head removed as well as its sting?"

"And?"

"She's around here somewhere, but now there's no time."

As he said this, a terrible voice sounded through the trees to their rear. Ranulf recognised it as Gwyddon's. The druid was chanting discordantly, intoning some hideous spell. As one, the corpses strewed between the trees began to stir, to shudder, to twitch.

"Dear God!" Tallebois screamed.

"Back to the castle!" Garbofasse shouted.

"We'll never make it across the moor," Ranulf said, ushering them downhill rather than back along the bluff. "Head for the river."

"The river?"

"Do as I say!"

But on all sides, grotesque figures were rising quickly to their feet. Paston, standing further away from the others, squealed like a calf as an axe clove his skull from behind.

"This way!" Ranulf bellowed, racing downhill.

The others followed, pell-mell. But it was a chaotic flight. They tripped over roots or were clawed at by spectral shapes emerging from the mist on either side. Garbofasse fell heavily, injuring his knee. Ranulf stopped and turned as the others ran ahead.

"Go!" Garbofasse cried, hobbling back to his feet. "Get away!" He was already hemmed in by mewling figures, so he picked up a longsword and swept it at them with both hands. Two went down, sundered at the waist, but a third, fourth and fifth were soon on top of him. "Go!" he shrieked again, wrestling with them as they snapped at him with their foul teeth.

He managed to invert one and drop it on the top of its head. Another, he ran through with the sword, though it still lunged at him. More joined the fray, bearing him to the muddy ground.

"Go!" was the last thing Ranulf heard the mercenary captain say, though it became high-pitched and incoherent as his larynx was bitten through.

Ranulf ran on down the hill, striking on all sides with sword and dagger. The others were already much further ahead. Even Red Guthric, personally bonded to Garbofasse, scrambled down the slope without looking back – until he too fell. A corpse had dropped on him from a tree. It was a naked stick figure, its skin hanging in empty folds, but it had sufficient strength to knock him to his knees, whereupon it clamped its teeth on the nape of his neck. Ranulf galloped alongside and drove his dagger so deeply between its ribs that its blade was wedged there. The spindly monster dropped Red Guthric and rounded on Ranulf. He slammed his curved sword through the middle of its chest, entirely transfixing it, but still it tried to grapple with him. Leaving both his weapons behind, Ranulf stepped away, stumbling on downhill. Red Guthric was back on his feet and came as well, but on wobbling legs. When another form blundered into his path – this one a bloated mass of swollen, purple flesh – and wrapped him in a bear-hug, he was unable to resist. Helpless, barely able to scream, Guthric was raised and broken across the monster's knee like a plank.

Ranulf ran on. FitzUrz and Tallebois were just ahead but, as the moon slipped behind clouds, they found themselves fleeing through complete darkness. When FitzUrz turned his ankle, it snapped like a stick. He howled as he fell. Ranulf swerved towards him, but before he could reach him another dead thing, gargling black filth but armed with a massive club, ghosted around the trunk of the nearest tree. Ranulf veered away as it commenced to land blow after blow on FitzUrz's unprotected skull.

Ranulf and Tallebois were now the only two left. Both were fleeing neck-and-neck when they skidded out from the trees onto the open bluff to the west of the castle. Vast numbers of the dead were already gathered there and now – as one – turned slowly to face them.

Tallebois slid to a halt, his mouth locking open, his eyes bulging. Ranulf grabbed him by the shoulder and pushed him southwards rather than straight down the slope.

"There are too many!" the squire gibbered.

"Towards the river! Fast as you can!"

Ranulf buffeted more corpses out of their way as they ran. Claws slashed at them; he had to duck a mighty stroke from a long-handled Dane-axe. But the slope was at last dropping towards the Tefeidiad, the moonlit surface of which glittered just below them.

The last fifty yards were perhaps the worst.

"Use your strength, your weight... anything you've got!" Ranulf panted, as the dead closed in again.

Tallebois still had his dagger. When a woman, whose severed head hung down her back on a few sinews, reached out and caught him, he smote her hand off at the wrist.

"That's the way!" Ranulf shouted. He himself had managed to pick up a war-hammer. A corpse stumbled towards him and he swung the mighty cudgel, crushing its cranium. Another came towards him and he smashed its forehead – with such force that a soup of liquid brain matter spurted from its eye sockets.

The river was now tantalisingly close. Though a great mob of the dead were descending from behind, only a relative handful – three at the most – were in front.

"We can make it!" Ranulf shouted.

Tallebois was so racked with terror and fatigue that his voice squeaked. "We'll drown!"

"If you can't swim, just stay afloat. The current will carry us past the castle. We might be able to get ashore on its east side!"

"*Might* be able to?"

"Now you see why we aren't wearing mail!"

The final few feet of slope were steep, muddy and strewn with loose stones. They skidded and tripped their way to the bottom, blundering headlong into the final clutch of corpses. Ranulf hit the first one head-on, barrelling into its chest, catapulting it backward into the river. Tallebois wasn't so lucky. The other two caught hold of him, one wrapping its arms around his waist and burying its teeth into his naked left thigh, the other looping a skeletal arm around his neck, trying to throttle him. With gurgling bleats, Tallebois hacked with his dagger, but it had no effect. The would-be throttler bought its leering visage close to his tear-stained face. He slashed it back and forth, mangling it, chopping it away in chunks, exposing the grinning skull beneath, but not slowing its attack in the least. Its pendulous green tongue quivered as it hung from the chasm where its lower jaw had once been. It raked its bony claws across his chest and belly, drawing five crimson trails through the sooty grease.

And then Ranulf took its legs from under it.

He swept in with a two-handed blow so fierce that both the creature's knee joints were shattered, and the lower portions of its limbs sent spinning into the darkness. It fell thrashing to the ground. The other monster ceased its gnawing on Tallebois's thigh and swung around to face Ranulf. Its nose was missing, along with its upper lip, but its ivory teeth were fully intact and coated with blood. Taking possession of the sobbing squire's dagger, it came hard at Ranulf, aiming a blow that would have skewered him through the heart. He dodged it, spun around and brought the hammer full circle, catching the creature at the base of its backbone, breaking it clean through.

"Into the water!" he shouted, grabbing Tallebois, yanking him to his feet and hurling him over the last few feet of ground into the river.

Before Ranulf followed, he turned just once.

The rest of the revenants were only yards away, looking for all the world like some vast assembly of recking remains ploughed from a plague pit, yet tottering down through the darkness towards him. The one whose spine he'd just broken was still on its feet, but now the upper part of its body had folded over until it hung upside down – as though it was made of paper.

Shaking his head at the sheer perversity of what he was witnessing, Ranulf threw the war-hammer into the midst of them, turned and dived into the Tefeidiad.

CHAPTER TWENTY-FOUR

"I saw great heaps of munitions, my lord. Nails, chains, piles of pebbles from the river shore. *Ahhh...*"

Squire Tallebois gasped as Zacharius inserted another suture through his ripped-open thigh, using a needle that looked like a fishhook. Having washed the filth off with buckets of water from the well, both the squire and Ranulf were now warming themselves at a brazier inside the main stable block. Earl Corotocus, Navarre, du Guesculin and several other senior household knights stood around them, listening to their report. Fiery shadows played on their attentive faces as Tallebois spoke.

Ranulf, who had pointedly said nothing so far, climbed tiredly into his mail leggings. He and Tallebois had managed to scramble out of the river on the east side of the castle, but only with great difficulty. Having met no more of the dead there, they'd needed to clamber back down into the moat and squeeze themselves along the drain. Thankfully, the earl's men had pulled them up the garderobe chute, but by this time they'd been completely exhausted and the last thing Ranulf had wanted was a face-to-face interrogation.

"They were restocking the scoop-thrower, as we feared," the squire jabbered, a vague light of madness in his eyes. "By cockcrow tomorrow, I fancy we'd have been facing the iron hail again. All over again! The iron–"

"But you destroyed the blasted machine?" Corotocus asked.

"Absolutely, my lord. It can't be used any more, *ahhh*..." Tallebois gasped again as a particularly gruesome gash was closed with a single tight thread. "But there is something else. They had also piled up colossal blocks of stone, which looked as if they'd been freshly quarried. The sort a mason might use to lay foundations with."

"And?"

The squire shrugged. "The dead don't build, my lord... do they? Captain Garbofasse thought they were projectiles. He said this meant they were bringing the mangonels to the western bluff. That'd they'd be ready either later today or maybe tomorrow."

Du Guesculin sucked in his breath. "My lord, the iron hail would merely sweep the Constable's Tower roof, but from that close range the mangonels will destroy it! We must retreat to the Keep at once."

Corotocus said nothing.

"My lord, do you hear me? We should fill the Keep basement with supplies–"

"We will retreat to the Keep, du Guesculin, as and when the situation demands it," the earl interjected.

"But my lord, great blocks of stone...?"

Ranulf buckled his hauberk in place, feeling even deeper scorn for the household banneret than he usually did. It was a pity du Guesculin hadn't been so frantic in his concerns when the south wall defenders had had to face these missiles.

Earl Corotocus now turned to Ranulf. "What's your opinion of this enterprise? Did it succeed?"

Ranulf shrugged. "I always said the mangonels would be brought against the west wall in due course, my lord."

"And the scoop-thrower? It's completely disabled?"

"I didn't see that. So I can't comment."

The earl's eyebrows arched. "You didn't see it? How can that be?"

"He wasn't with us," Tallebois piped up. "He went to find the countess."

"You... went to find the countess?" Corotocus repeated slowly, his eyes suddenly burning into Ranulf like smoking spear-points.

"To cut the head off the snake," Tallebois added. "That was what he said."

There was an amazed silence in the stable, broken only by the snuffling of horses and popping of coals in the brazier. Corotocus continued to gaze at Ranulf, a gaze the young knight returned boldly as he adjusted his coif. At last, Navarre stepped forward.

"You expect us to believe, FitzOsbern," he said, his voice a low, ultra-dangerous monotone, "that a man like you, a sentimental fool who'd take the code literally even to the point of his own death, would murder Countess Madalyn in her sleep?" Before Ranulf could reply, Navarre had thrown down his gauntlet. "*This* says differently!"

Resignedly, Ranulf collected his sword-belt from a corner, buckled it to his waist, and reached down for the gauntlet.

"Pick that glove up, Ranulf, and you cross swords with me as well," Earl Corotocus said.

"My lord!" Navarre protested.

"We are *all* of us engaged in a trial by battle!" the earl shouted. "Or hadn't you dogs noticed?" He rounded back on Ranulf. "But you, sir, have some questions to answer. You say you went to look for the countess?"

"The only way for us to survive this situation, my lord, is to parley with her," Ranulf tried to explain.

"And you took that duty on yourself?"

"*You* weren't there."

"You insolent..." Navarre snapped, but the earl raised a hand for silence.

"It wasn't my initial plan," Ranulf added. "But it seemed like a sensible idea at the time."

There was another prolonged silence. Earl Corotocus watched Ranulf very carefully. Thus far unscathed by the siege, the earl's smooth, handsome features were pale with anger, his blue eyes blazed – but, as always, he was in full control of his emotions.

"I take it you failed?" the earl finally said.

"Yes," Ranulf admitted, truthfully.

They continued to stare at each other intently, as if both parties were waiting for the other to give something away.

At last, the earl sniffed and said: "You and Tallebois get yourselves some food, and them some sleep. I want you back at your posts by dawn."

As Corotocus walked back towards the Constable's Tower, Navarre hurried across the courtyard to catch up with him.

"My lord, my lord... FitzOsbern is a traitor."

"I know."

"You should have let me kill him."

"And divide the company in two?"

"He won't have that much support."

"He has more than you think," Corotocus said. "He's ended the iron hail. He's the man who held the Gatehouse bridge, remember? He's the one who warned us that we might soon be facing our own dead. Even the household men were listening to that."

"Sire, you are Earl Corotocus of Clun, first baron of the realm. FitzOsbern is nobody. A former wolf-head, a rogue knight who–"

"The men are frightened, Navarre!" Corotocus snapped, stopping in his tracks. For a fleeting second, he too looked vaguely unnerved. "They are also tired. They don't share our desire to show King Edward that the Earldom of Clun can hold the Welsh at bay." He strode on. "Besides, I'm not convinced that in a straight duel you'd be able to kill him."

"He'd be the first one to beat me..."

"There's always a first one, you imbecile."

They mounted the ramp to the Constable's Tower. Ordinarily there'd be guards on its entrance, but now all available men were on the walls. Corotocus and Navarre's iron-shod feet echoed in the tight, switchback stairwell as they ascended to the battlements.

"In that case, arrest him while he's sleeping," Navarre said. "Bring charges, make it legal."

"Much as I'm loathe to admit it, we need his sword. We need everyone's sword." The earl halted again, thinking. "But from now on, Navarre, stay close to him."

"Of course."

"Watch his every move." Corotocus smiled coldly, as though anticipating a treat. "When the time is right, Ranulf FitzOsbern will learn what it means to defy my will."

CHAPTER TWENTY-FIVE

IN THE DARKEST and quietest part of the night, with his assistant sleeping in the wagon, Doctor Zacharius made a solo round of his infirmary, checking bandages and dressings, delivering herbal draughts, either to relieve pain or induce sleep. Most of the casualties were at least comfortable, though the air was filled with coughs, whimpers and soft moans. Once he had finished, Zacharius crossed the courtyard to one of the other outhouses, where a copper bowl filled with water simmered over a brazier. First he washed his hands, using sesame oil and lime powder, and then, one by one, cleansed his surgical implements, towelling each one dry and laying them all out on a fresh linen cloth, which he'd spread on a low table.

"Doctor Zacharius?" someone asked from the doorway.

Zacharius turned. One of the earl's knights stood there – in fact it was the young knight who had survived the mission to destroy the scoop-thrower. Zacharius had seen him many times before and, though he had never had cause to treat him and didn't know his name, he had always thought him a sullen fellow.

"Do you really believe that dismembering one of these creatures will help us understand why they are invulnerable to death?" Ranulf asked.

Zacharius continued with what he was doing. "In truth, they aren't invulnerable to death, are they? From what I hear, these things are already dead."

"You know what I mean," Ranulf said, entering.

He'd finished another late meal in the refectory, as the earl had instructed, but sleep had eluded him for the last hour or so – for two main reasons.

Firstly, though he didn't think he could have done much more than appeal to Countess Madalyn's humanity, which was well known throughout the border country, he wasn't absolutely sure. He hadn't known the priest, Gwyddon, would be present. That had caused an unforeseen problem. Likewise, the Welsh had discovered that the English were in their camp sooner than he'd hoped. None of these things had been under his control. But couldn't he have reacted more appropriately? Perhaps he should have killed Gwyddon. Perhaps he should have taken Countess Madalyn hostage? It would have been difficult, but maybe he could at least have tried. Uncertainty about this was now torturing him.

The second reason was Doctor Zacharius and his comments before they had departed – about returning with a captive specimen. Of course, once the mission had got under way that would have been totally impractical, and Ranulf had quickly forgotten it. But now, with the diplomatic door closed, all sorts of wild thoughts were occurring to him. Had he missed another opportunity to turn the tide in their favour? But what did it actually mean to eviscerate something – even something as hideous as these walking dead – to take it apart piece by piece while it writhed and thrashed, purely to learn how it was composed and controlled? Such knowledge was surely not intended for Man; this was what Ranulf had always been told and had always believed. Such things were best left to God –

and yet, after what he'd seen here, particularly outside in the rain and the mist, a terrible fear was now taking root inside him. At the end of the day, if God came down to Earth enraged and cast celestial fire on his children, would those children not justifiably seek to escape it – even if it enraged God all the more? Willing martyrs were made of very rare stuff indeed; only now was Ranulf realising this.

"I can't answer your question," Zacharius said, still cleaning his tools. "But put it this way, I don't believe in sorcery."

"Even after everything we have seen with our own eyes?" Ranulf asked.

"Oh, it exists... superficially. But when a man performs acts of 'sorcery', what he's really doing is manipulating the laws of nature in ways not yet known to the rest of us."

"And you think you can learn about such laws by opening the flesh of one of these walking dead?"

"The Greek physician, Hippocrates, was convinced that diseases did not afflict mankind as a punishment from the gods, but because the systems of organs that make up our bodies were for some reason malfunctioning. He developed many remedies through his studies of the human body, often after life had expired. He saved innumerable lives and the human race was no worse off for that. The Roman doctor, Galen, produced countless books containing detailed sketches of human anatomy, which enabled his students to treat a variety of previously serious ailments with simple procedures. My proposal was similar, if not exactly the same – a straightforward investigation, the results of which might benefit us all."

Ranulf pondered this.

"Why do you ask?" Zacharius wondered. "Are you planning to go out there again, when the last time only two of you returned alive?"

"The choice would not be mine," Ranulf said.

"In which case don't agonise over it. The reality..." Zacharius shrugged. "The reality is that I am neither skilled nor experienced enough to reach immediate and accurate conclusions. I would need the assistance of other learned doctors. In addition, it would take time, which we clearly will have less of once the fighting recommences. I would also need a better place in which to work. Somewhere light and dry to tabulate my findings, collate my samples..."

"I don't understand any of these things."

"But you evidently *do* understand that this battle will not be won by the usual means. You proved that not two hours ago."

"It wouldn't take a clever man to realise that."

"No, but it would take a brave one to admit it." Zacharius continued cleaning his implements. "What are you called?"

"I am Ranulf FitzOsbern."

"You're one of the earl's indebted knights, are you not?"

"I am."

The doctor smiled to himself.

"Something amuses you?" Ranulf asked.

"It certainly does. You occupy the lowest of the equestrian ranks, yet you speak to Earl Corotocus almost as an equal."

"At some point I'll be punished for that."

"I've no doubt you will. But he tolerates you for the time being because during this crisis he clearly considers that he needs you. And after what I heard you tell him, about your wise attempt to parley with Countess Madalyn, I would make the same decision."

"It was a poor plan. It failed."

"At least it was a plan. And you have *my* commendation for it, FitzOsbern, if no-one else's."

There was brief silence, Ranulf eyeing the gleaming knives, scalpels and forceps arrayed in their orderly rows.

"Why do you clean those things so thoroughly?" he asked.

"Because I will have to perform more surgeries with them."

"Is one man's blood poisonous to another?"

"Maybe. I don't know for certain, but why take the risk?" Zacharius laid down another tool – a screw-handled speculum, which he regularly used to open and clamp deep wounds in order to remove foreign objects buried inside them. "It may also be that even the smallest speck of filth will cause an injury to fester, and lead to blood disorders and death."

"You have a strong instinct for your profession," Ranulf observed.

"As do you."

"All I do is fight. Any man can fight."

"I can't. Not to your standard."

"But almost no-one at all can do what you do."

Zacharius smiled again. "Don't flatter me too much, my friend. We all have our instincts. That stubborn fool Benan's instinct tells him that only God can save us now. He thus refuses to allow me to treat him. He wouldn't even be brought down here to the infirmary, but insisted on making his own way from the Constable's Tower to the chapel, where there is no bed, no warmth – and he had to crawl on his belly most of the distance, because he's lost too much blood to stand. But that's all to the good, he says. He has to win back the Lord's favour, and the only way to do that is by self-imposed penance."

"You criticise him for it?"

"Not really." Zacharius sighed. "Who is to say that I am right and Benan is wrong? If forced to make a judgement, I suppose I'd always rather men solved their problems by shedding their own blood rather than the blood of others."

"And yet you'd have no qualm about cutting one of these creatures open to examine its entrails... even if it is bound with chains and completely harmless?"

"None whatsoever."

"Some might say that God would object."

"Some might also say that if a man were brought to me with a mangled limb, God would object to my removing that limb in order to save the man's life. Do you think He would, FitzOsbern? When in all the great hunting-chases of England, limbs are regularly lopped for the far less edifying reason of punishing poaching, and yet those wielding the axe are almost never struck down or even castigated by holy Church, as far as I can see?"

Ranulf struggled visibly with his doubts.

"Surely this is not a difficult concept for you?" Zacharius said. "You who this very night has defied the conventions of his own martial world, bypassing your overlord to make what you believed was a correct decision? But don't trouble yourself with such seditious thinking, my friend. I understand your reservation. How many sacred cattle can we slaughter before we have nothing left to defend? Perhaps it's better to return to your post on the castle wall and leave me in my hospital, where we can both stick to our allotted tasks, which..." He lowered his voice until it was almost inaudible. "Which, in truth, will yield the world little."

Ranulf moved away from the outhouse, still deep in thought – only to return a few moments later.

"I can't capture one of these creatures for you," he said from the doorway. "It would be impossible, so there is no point in my even offering to try. But I'll remember what you said for the future."

Zacharius nodded, as if that was as much as he could expect.

"And I will try to get you out of here alive," Ranulf added. "If I can."

"I wouldn't take any more risks if I were you, sir knight. Not on my behalf."

Ranulf shook his head. "You haven't been outside. You haven't seen what we're facing – not up close. The walls of this castle will not hold them for long."

"And more's the pity." Zacharius shrugged. "I'll never enjoy a comely lass again."

"That said, it's not unfeasible that one or two of us may escape. You should be among them."

"Battle my way to safety, you mean?" The doctor smiled. "My dear FitzOsbern, didn't I just tell you; I'm a lover, not a fighter."

"Maybe we can smuggle you out?"

"And would you smuggle my patients with me? You'd need to, because I won't abandon them."

Ranulf felt frustrated. "But what you've said here needs to be understood more widely."

"As I say, there are other doctors more learned than I."

"Doctor Zacharius! This thing that's been unleashed... it won't end here."

Zacharius regarded him carefully, before shaking his head. "You think more deeply than is good for you, FitzOsbern. More deeply than is good for any of us." He had now finished cleaning his implements and began to wrap them in separate bundles of clean cloth. "Go back to your post."

"I fear Christendom faces a graver peril now than ever came from the Moslem desert or the Mongol steppe."

"Then why should I want to survive to see it?"

Ranulf had no immediate answer to that, because it was a sentiment he was slowly starting to share. Zacharius would no longer talk with him. In fact, he would no longer even look at him. So at length the young knight did as he was bidden, and returned to his post.

CHAPTER TWENTY-SIX

As DAWN APPROACHED there was, for the first time that year, a feeling that winter at last had flown. Despite the chill, an apricot sky began to arch its way eastwards. Suddenly the trees were rookeries of twittering birds, their bare, twisting branches laden with buds and catkins, their roots resplendent as the first spring flowers poked through the drifts of rotted leaf.

High above Grogen's western bluff, in a circle of gnarled and ancient oaks, there was a wheel-headed cross, cut from granite and carved all over with intricate knotworks, which its coat of green lichen did little to conceal. This was where Gwyddon found Countess Madalyn. She was kneeling in silence before the ancient edifice, a veil over her hair, her joined hands wrapped with prayer beads. Gwyddon regarded her scornfully, before dismounting.

"We are ready to resume the assault, countess. This time I recommend that we press it night and day until the English are broken. Give them no respite at all."

She made no reply.

"Countess Madalyn..."

"I am praying, Gwyddon!" she hissed.

Gwyddon stood back respectfully. The countess's horse was tethered to one of the oaks' lower branches. A few feet above it, a pattern of curious notches scarred the side of the tree trunk, bulging and distorted as though thick layers of bark had overgrown some inscribed image. By the looks of it, it had once been a face. There were similar markings on the other trees.

When Countess Madalyn finally stood and removed her veil, Gwyddon was still waiting for her.

"Were you aware this place was once sacred to an older god?" he said. "You Christians supplanted him. As you did in so many of our other holy groves."

"On the contrary," she replied, looking pale and drawn. "We cleansed this place."

"Its air is certainly sweeter than the air down in the valley."

Countess Madalyn grimaced. "The stench down there is unbearable. I couldn't tolerate it any longer."

"Sadly, it's a price we must pay."

"And what other price must we pay, Gwyddon?" She didn't even look at him as she untied her horse.

"Countess, I understand your concerns, but answer me this: would you have your Welsh countrymen die in droves? Because that is the alternative, I fear. Had we attacked Grogen Castle with an army of the living, ten thousand of us, maybe more, would now lie slain."

The countess didn't mount her beast but stood against it, her head bowed. She appeared weary, almost tearful. Her right hand clutched the bridle so tightly that its tendons showed through her white silk glove.

"I see you don't dispute that fact, at least," he said.

"Gwyddon!" She rounded on him, but more with desperation than anger. "This thing you – *we* – have done is an abhorrence in the eyes of God!"

"In what way, madam? Our soldiers know no terror as they are sent to battle. They feel no pain when they are cut down. For all we know, their spirits are already in God's hands. We are merely making use of their remains."

"And in the long-term, Gwyddon, what do we plan to do with those remains?"

Gwyddon had not been prepared for this question.

"The young English knight was right, was he not?" she said. "This army of ours will simply rot. Soon it will be nought but clacking bones. And what then? We make more, as you threatened? Is that your plan? How *many* more, Gwyddon?"

"These husks are a matter of convenience, countess. When we no longer have need of them, we will dispense with them."

"Will we? And will we then compose our armies of living men – those who *do* feel terror, those who *do* feel pain?" She gave a wintry smile. "I see your concern for human suffering is also a matter of convenience."

"And do you think Earl Corotocus would have any of these qualms?"

"Earl Corotocus is one man, Gwyddon." She became thoughtful. "That young knight said there are strong feelings against him."

"And at the same time, that young knight's accomplices destroyed the very weapon with which we were stripping their battlements of armour. Clearly, that was his real objective."

"He could have killed us both. Would that not have been a more useful objective for him?"

"Even if he spoke the truth, the chances are that he's dead. Only a couple of them, at the most, made it back into the castle."

"Nevertheless..." She climbed into her saddle. "We need to speak with them."

"Earl Corotocus will never negotiate unless it's from a position of strength. And King Edward is exactly the same. This is why ruthless individuals like them will always succeed... and why radical means are needed to stop them."

The countess wheeled her horse around. "We've already stopped them. Earl Corotocus and his army can't wreak any more damage. They are trapped."

"As is your daughter, madam."

The countess paused to think. "Would it serve their purpose to harm her now? They know what their fate will be if they do. My decision is made, Gwyddon. We will maintain the siege, but there will be no further attacks unless the English provoke them. In the meantime, I will send messages to King Edward."

"Who even now is entering Wales from the north."

"All the better." She made to ride away. "Let him see our power first-hand."

"And what if he likes what he sees, and tries to claim it for his own?"

She reined her horse, gazing down at him.

Gwyddon shrugged. "Edward Longshanks is a crafty tactician. He has no truck with honourable warfare. As far as he is concerned, victory is all. When he sees what we have done here, he is more likely to be inspired than frightened."

"What exactly are you saying?"

Gwyddon climbed onto his horse. "I'm saying that if King Edward felt you were pliable, he would certainly sit at the negotiating table, especially with such a prize as the Cauldron of Regeneration to be won."

"You think me a fool, Gwyddon? I would never bargain away the Cauldron. In any case, it would be no use to the English without your arcane knowledge. Unless..." She looked slowly round at him again. "Unless that also is available to be won? Would you share your knowledge, Gwyddon? With the English?"

"Under torture, madam, a man may share anything."

"Ohhh, I see." She regarded him with new understanding. Her wintry smile had returned. "So Wales and the Welsh are also a matter of convenience to you?"

"Wales and the Welsh are my future, madam. As they are yours. Thus, I feel we must destroy the invaders utterly. That is the only kind of message King Edward will understand. We proceed with the assault, yes?"

He posed it as a question, though it was clearly more of a statement. As such, Countess Madalyn made no answer.

"One more thing, madam," Gwyddon said, as he turned his horse around. "If it suits you, you may remain here where the air is fresh and the grass green rather than red. After all, there is no longer any reason for you to witness these terrible events. You made your appearance on the first day, as required. Your part in this affair has been played."

He spurred his horse away, leaving Countess Madalyn alone in the grove of mottled oaks.

CHAPTER TWENTY-SEVEN

WITH THE DAWN came the dead.

Heralded by a dirge of howls and moans, they crammed along the causeway, a hundred abreast, pushing their siege-tower ahead of them, its mighty wheels rumbling on the timbers. The English responded in the only way they knew how, with showers of arrows and stones. But it made no discernible impact. The oxen, to prevent them being wounded or killed by the castle defenders, were being driven beneath the shelter of the siege-tower's ironclad skirts. As the great structure drew steadily closer, it could be seen that assault teams of the dead were already gathered on top of it. Its gantry bridge, perhaps twenty feet in length, was currently raised, held aloft by two leather thongs, either of which a simple blow would have cut. The lip of the bridge was fixed with iron hooks, so that when it fell across the Constable's Tower's stone parapet, it would catch and hold itself in place.

The earl's best fighting men waited for it, armed not just with shields and swords, but with bills, spears and a stockpile of naptha grenades. Earl Corotocus also had an onager brought forward and devil's sachets packed with bricks broken from the rear battlements.

"They must not cross!" Navarre bellowed, as the tower halted in front of them. "Not one of them!"

When the bridge fell, poll-arms were lifted to prevent it making contact, but the first of the dead merely scrambled to the top of it and leapt. At least five plummeted to the foot of the tower, but three landed safely and a savage melee commenced as they laid about them with axes and mattocks. A retaliatory storm of slashing blades soon hacked them to pieces, but not before the poll-men were themselves cut down and the bridge crashed onto the battlements.

"Onager!" Earl Corotocus roared.

His engineers were already in place, and the first devil's sachet loaded into the bucket. But before the lever could be pulled, the dead on the top of the siege-tower let loose a blizzard of arrows and crossbow bolts. Space was immediately cleared, maybe a dozen men, including those on the onager, struck down. Ramon la Roux, already grievously wounded from the fight at the Gatehouse, pivoted around grey-faced, blood oozing between his lips. A missile had pierced his breast to its feathers. He staggered a couple of yards, fell against Ranulf and dropped to the floor.

With gurgling groans, the dead threw down their bows and, bristling with swords, hammers and cleavers, advanced across their gantry. They were mid-way over, when Ranulf threw himself onto the onager's lever. The complex throwing device had been tilted upward on rear support blocks, so that its payload travelled in a straight line, rather than arcing through the air. As such, ten heavy projectiles were now flung clean into the approaching horde. The first few were felled by gut-thumping impacts, their bodies shattered into glistening green and crimson scraps; those behind went toppling over the side. Two projectiles continued through, striking the rear of the siege-tower's upper tier with pulverising force, smashing an entire section of its framework. But fresh cohorts of corpses were now flooding up its timber throat. While men-at-arms hastened to crank the onager back to full tension, Navarre and others lobbed naptha grenades across the bridge. Several struck the dead full-on, engulfing them in flame; others dropped down inside the siege-tower, spilling fire through its joists and beams.

"More naptha!" Walter Margas shrieked, only for a blazing figure to leap down and wrap its arms around him. Ranulf hewed it from its shoulder to its breastbone with a massive stroke of his longsword. But Margas was already horribly seared. He staggered back to his feet, a twisted, drooling wreck, only to be struck in the face by a javelin, which didn't penetrate deeply but laid his cheek open to the glinting bone beneath.

Though entire sections of the siege-tower had now caught fire, the dead continued to clamber up through it and rampage across the bridge. The onager was again sprung. Its deadly cargo was catapulted through the advancing mob. Yet more went spinning from the bridge, but others made it onto the battlements. One of them sent shockwaves through the English by the mere sight of him. He was a giant of a man, naked save for a loincloth, covered in soot and grease, and armed with a spike-headed mace. The flesh across his throat was gruesomely mangled. His face had been bitten over and over, his scalp almost torn from the top of his head, but it was perfectly visible who he was – Captain Garbofasse, late of the earl's mercenary division.

With black gruel vomiting from his mouth, Garbofasse gave a guttural, inhuman roar and, swinging his brutal weapon around, smote the skulls of two of his former hearth-men, dashing their brains out where they stood.

Other corpses lumbered down behind him. One was recognisable as Roger FitzUrz. The other, walking with a bizarrely crooked gait, was Red Guthric.

"Repel!" Earl Corotocus bellowed, advancing to battle himself, his sword and shield hefted.

With a furious clangour, the two forces met, blade clashing on blade, on mail, on helmet and buckler, falchions crushing shoulder-joints, axes biting through foreheads. The squire Tallebois fell at this point, Red Guthric, his former comrade, hurling him shrieking to the ground and striking at him again and again with a scramsax, cleaving him from cranium to chin three times, each breach an inch from the next, so that his head fell apart like a sliced loaf.

"Ladders!" someone cried.

All along the battlements to either side of the siege-tower, crudely constructed ladders were appearing. Ranulf dashed towards the nearest, but a monstrosity had already appeared at the top of it. Ranulf grabbed a spear, and as it tried to climb through the embrasure, transfixed it through its chest, forcing it backward into the abyss. The next one up, he clove between the eyes and across the left hand, severing all its fingers and costing it its grip. It dropped like a stone, knocking off one corpse after another all the way to the bottom. Ranulf was thus able to grab the ladder and push it sideways. It collided with a second ladder, which also collapsed, depositing maybe thirty more of the dead into the wailing mass of their comrades far below.

Earl Corotocus, meanwhile, was engaged in a savage cut-and-thrust with Garbofasse. The earl took blow after blow on his shield, which already was beaten out of shape, but at last made a telling strike of his own, ripping open Garbofasse's unguarded belly so that a mass of glistening, coiling entrails flopped out. Garbofasse seemingly felt nothing. He raised his mace with both hands, only for Navarre, who had despatched his own opponent, to sever his legs from behind, and then hew and hew at him as he lay there, until he was nought but a pile of twitching, dismembered meat.

The interior of the siege-tower was now a raging inferno. The frantic lowing of the oxen trapped beneath it became a shrill squealing as they were burned alive. One or two dead still attempted to scale up through it, but they too were consumed. So great was the heat that the siege-tower's iron skin began to soften and slide loose. With a splintering crash, the gantry bridge, burnt through at the joints, fell onto the causeway.

The ladders still had to be dealt with. Ranulf had knocked down two, but there were maybe ten others. The English went at them hammer and tongs, splitting the skulls and sundering the limbs of those attempting to climb up and, where possible, smashing the upper rungs, so that the ladders fell in two halves. But now there was another threat. In some cases, the dead had started circumnavigating the Constable's Tower, spilling around the Inner Fort via the bailey. What was more, on the curtain-wall their work-teams had erected rope-and-pulley systems and were hauling up scorpions and other bolt-throwers, with which they hurled grappling hooks linked to nets, climbing ropes and more scaling ladders to the top of the Inner Fort walls. At eighty to a hundred feet, these great ramparts would normally be unassailable, but now the English watched agog as the dead hauled themselves up the sheer edifices with comparative ease.

Drenched with sweat and blackened by smoke, Earl Corotocus had to shout to be heard in the midst of this chaos. His efforts were further hampered as flights of arrows swept up from the causeway. While the bulk of the dead now queued in orderly fashion to ascend the ladders, others – those still equipped with bows and crossbows – stood back and launched their missiles. They took particular aim at those English attempting to throw down the ladders. Ranulf, Navarre and others were forced to step back as a stream of shafts rattled through the embrasures. Gurt Louvain was spitted through the palm of his left hand. Cursing, he snapped the shaft and, with clenched teeth, yanked it free. He bound the wound with an old rag, but it had soon turned sodden with gore. Hugh du Guesculin, who had hung back as much as he could during the fray, was struck a glancing blow to the helmet, which made him hang back even further, though he continued to bark at his master's underlings, calling them cowards and curs.

Also shouting like a madman, Earl Corotocus stalked up and down, striking at any corpse that vaulted through onto the battlements and, where possible, sending men to the south side of the tower, where, beyond a narrow gate, the wall-walk of the Inner Fort began. Diverting along this, they were able to cut many of the climbing ropes that had so far been attached. Large numbers of the dead were thus precipitated a huge distance into the south bailey, where they were literally broken into pieces.

But this wasn't the whole of it.

Some of the bolt-throwers had projected their missiles through the arrow-slits on the Inner Fort's south-facing wall. These connected with buildings inside, such as the barrack house in the Inner Fort's southwest corner, and the great hall in the southeast corner. Frantically, small groups of defenders, led by archery captain Davy Gou, hurried indoors. In the barrack house, where most of their bedrolls were spread on piles of hay, several of the dead were already forcing their way through the arrow-slits. It would have been impossible for living men to enter via these horribly narrow apertures, but the dead cared nothing for crushed bones and torn skin. Gou and his men met them in a whirlwind of blades. As throughout the battle, only complete evisceration and dismemberment would account for the intruders, and, long before this was achieved, many an Englishman's throat had been torn, eye plucked, or limbs sheared.

The battle now girdled two thirds of the castle, and raged on in this murderous fashion for the entire day. On top of ramparts now washed with blood and strewn with dead and dying, the English held out as best they could. Whenever one ladder was thrown down, another replaced it. When one marauding band was repulsed, a second would immediately follow. More and more dead archers were gathering on the causeway. Thanks to their capture of the earl's heavy weapons train, they appeared to have limitless ammunition, and with arms and shoulders that no longer tired, with bowstring fingers that no longer bled or blistered, they poured it over the battlements relentlessly.

And all the while cacophonous booms sounded through the structure of the Constable's Tower, for the burnt wreckage of the siege-tower had been hauled away and an iron-headed battering ram brought forth. A band of corpses, maybe thirty strong, slammed it again and again on the central gate. No amount of pelting with rocks, stones and arrows would dissuade them. So immune were they, they didn't even carry shields over their heads.

Down in the courtyard, the infirmary had been swiftly overwhelmed. Zacharius and Henri laboured feverishly in the midst of blood-drenched bodies piled three deep. Having long exhausted their supply of intoxicants, they concentrated on those who required the least painful procedures, moving straight from one man to the next, pumping sweat as they extracted arrow heads and broken shafts, stitched or cauterised gaping wounds, severed shattered limbs with as few clean strokes of the saw as they could manage. The shrieks and gasps rang in their ears.

Experienced as he was, Zacharius was strained almost to breaking point. On previous battlefields, he'd had orderlies to assist him and, if not orderlies, volunteer monks and nuns from nearby communities. Now there wasn't even anyone to hold or tie the struggling patients down. And there was no end to these patients. Beyond the stinking confines of the infirmary, they were scattered like leaves on the cobblestones of the courtyard. More and more were brought down, many in so dreadful a condition that nothing could be done for them.

Ranulf FitzOsbern came shouting and pushing his way in. He was half-carrying and half-dragging one of his comrades, a fellow knight called Ramon la Roux. From one quick glance, Zacharius deduced that la Roux was already dead. An arrow had pierced his chest clean through; he'd already bled so much that his entire tabard was slick with gore – there could scarcely be a drop of the precious fluid left inside him.

"For God's sake!" Zacharius shouted. "I'm not a miracle worker!"

Ranulf shook his head. "There's nothing you can do?"

"Surely you know the answer to that, you damn fool! Haven't you fought enough wars?" Zacharius whipped around to where other maimed soldiers waited to be treated, watching him with harrowed eyes. "Haven't you *all* fought enough wars?"

"He helped me earlier," Ranulf muttered. "I thought I should at least try."

"A nice sentiment. But somewhat misplaced in this pit of Hell!"

Ranulf finally nodded and let the dead weight that was Ramon la Roux slide to the floor.

"Not in here!" Zacharius bellowed. "This is a hospital, not a blasted mortuary!"

Without a word, Ranulf took la Roux by the heels and dragged him outside onto the cobblestones, where he had no option but to leave him among the other piles of dead or dying men.

Briefly, Zacharius followed him out, mopping his hands on a crimson rag. "Dare I ask how the fight is going?"

Ranulf gave this some thought. "No."

"What's that?"

"You asked me a question, did you not? I gave you my answer. 'No'." Ranulf turned and trudged back towards the Constable's Tower. "For the sake of your own sanity, don't dare ask how the fight is going."

It was now late afternoon and just as Ranulf re-ascended to his post, word reached Earl Corotocus's ears that bolt-throwers were assailing the Inner Fort from the east side, a part of the stronghold which, up until now, had not been struck at all.

"We're spread too thinly," he said to Navarre. "We haven't enough men to cover the entire perimeter."

"My lord, if we retreat now the Inner Fort will fall. We'll only have the Keep left."

Corotocus nodded grimly. "Agreed. We must hold at all costs. The king will come. I know he will."

But beyond Grogen Castle, there was no sign of the king. In fact, quite the opposite. For a brief startling moment, Ranulf had a chance to glance out over the Constable's Tower parapet, and found himself focussed on a landscape literally swamped by tides of the dead. For as far as the eye could see, from all directions, their cursed and bedraggled legions were advancing towards the castle. This vision alone might have been enough to send a man mad, but then, if it were possible, something even more frightening happened.

With a collision like a thunderclap, an object impacted in the middle of the tower roof. It was a massive thirty-gallon barrel, which partially exploded and ejected burning naptha in a wide arc, engulfing maybe twenty of the earl's men. It didn't break apart totally, but bounced thirty yards, crashed through a door and hurtled down a spiral stair in which numerous wounded awaiting transport to the infirmary were crouched or lying, immersing and igniting them one by one. A second such missile followed immediately afterwards, this one a colossal earthenware pot. It struck the western battlements, blew apart and spurted liquid flame all along the rampart, swallowing some half a dozen defenders who were cowering there.

Every man still on his feet spun around towards the western bluff, where the three great siege engines, *War Wolf*, *Giant's Fist* and *God's Maul* had finally been assembled. Tremulous prayers seeped from throats already hoarse with shouting and screaming, as a third incendiary came tumbling down across the valley, black smoke trailing through the air behind it.

CHAPTER TWENTY-EIGHT

COUNTESS MADALYN HAD often heard it said that King Edward of England was a tyrant.

Her own people had no time for him, seeing only a despot and conqueror who betrayed his own chivalrous ideals with acts of cruelty and barbarism. But the English had a different view of their ultimate liege-lord. They regarded him as a great war-leader, but also as a font of justice. Any man, it was said, no matter how base, could approach King Edward and beseech him person-to-person. The king had reformed the entire legal system in England in favour of the lower classes. He'd installed a *parlement* at Westminster as a permanent institution. Clearly there were huge contradictions in his character. He was a pious Christian who'd already ridden on crusade once and apparently planned to do so again. He regularly sought diplomatic solutions to international crises; in the 1280s he was known as 'the peace-maker of Europe'. But he notoriously detested the enemies of his countrymen, and when he waged war against them it was a ghastly form of total war, designed to terrorise their populace into subservience.

Could she deal with such a man? Would he even grant her an audience, given what he'd done to Dafydd ap Gruffyd, whose rebellion twelve years ago had been rewarded with a particularly torturous fate; Prince Dafydd's body torn with pincers and hanged until half dead, whereupon it was disembowelled and hacked into quarters?

It was an onerous decision that she faced. But as she stood among the trees on the western bluff and gazed down on Grogen, she became increasingly certain what that decision would be.

The three giant catapults that Gwyddon had captured from the English were now in place on a plateau slightly lower down. Again and again, they lobbed huge, fiery missiles, each one of which trailed across the darkened sky like a comet and impacted on the fortifications with a flash like summer lightning. Night had now fallen fully, which gave the entire business a demonic aspect. The sky was jet-black, but at the same time red as molten steel. Liquid fire raged high on the battlements and streamed down the castle's outer walls. Sulphurous smoke, infernally coloured, belched from its arrow-slit windows. A cloying stench of burning mingled with the more familiar reek of decaying flesh.

Countess Madalyn's dead army seemed numberless as it trudged down the slope like some vast herd of mindless cattle, moaning and mewling as they crossed the southwest bridge and followed the berm path, finally entering the castle through its forced-open Gatehouse. She felt numb as she watched them clamber like ants up ladders and ropes, not just on the Constable's Tower, but all around the walls of the Inner Fort. Even from this distance, the ringing of blade on blade assailed her ears. From so far away, the screams of rage and death sounded like the squeaking of rodents, but there was no end to it. The English were still resisting, as the young knight had threatened they would. But surely they couldn't hold for much longer, and when every one of them was put to the sword, Gwyddon's abomination would be complete. King Edward the crusader would then have no option but to fall upon the Welsh as a nation of devils.

Countess Madalyn felt nothing – neither fear, nor remorse – as she turned and climbed into her saddle. Her bolsters were already filled with food and water. She also had a knapsack containing gold and jewellery as proof of her identity, which she concealed carefully among her saddlebags. Drawing a rough, homespun cowl over her head, she kicked her horse forward.

The hillside tracks would be treacherous in the dark. They were narrow, winding, overhung with low branches. But Countess Madalyn knew her native landscape well.

Her native landscape.

It pained her to think that way.

The Welsh were an indigenous part of these British isles, but they had their own culture and customs, their own beliefs, their own long tradition of self-governance. Why could their neighbours in England not see that? She knew that it wasn't the English themselves, but their rulers. Ever since the first Norman kings had created their powerful military state, they'd sought control over the entire island of Britain. For all their airs and graces, for all their pretensions to honour and courtliness, they were at heart a rapacious breed.

It frustrated her, maddened her.

And yet here she was, seeking to parley with one of those very same Anglo-Norman kings. In fact, it was worse than that – with one of the most fearsome and warlike kings that had ever sat on the Westminster throne.

Egging her horse on, she tried to shake these fears from her mind. This was about national survival, nothing less. Not just the survival of Wales in the flesh, but Wales as a spiritual nation. Gwyddon's way was the druids' way. She didn't despise him purely for that. The druids, she knew, had been stalwart friends to the Welsh in their battles against the Romans, the Saxons, the Danes. Everyday Welsh life was flavoured with pagan traditions, mostly of the more benign sort. But Gwyddon, in his overweening ambition, had unleashed a horror the like of which Christendom had never seen and could never tolerate. Even if he was successful, what kind of world was he trying to create where the dead commanded the living? And what would the view of the Almighty be – He, who had forbidden sorcery in all its forms, on pain of everlasting fire?

She rode on, more determined than ever to make a truce with King Edward. She was now descending a wooded brae, very steep and slippery with dew. The air was exquisitely cold in that way that only the air in March can be. Her horse steamed; her own breath puffed in moon-lit clouds. The avenues between the trees were damp, black corridors. Now that the roar of battle had fallen far behind, she heard nothing. Her horse continued to find its own way, with slow, tentative footfalls. Only when they reached level ground, did it increase its pace a little, but she resisted the urge to canter, unwilling to create unnecessary noise. She felt a growing conviction that she wasn't alone. She glanced over her shoulder, seeing nothing but the night. The woods had now thickened, dense clumps of hawthorn closing around her. With a thunder of heavy wings, a large owl exploded from a bough just over her head. Shocked, the countess reined her horse to a halt.

The owl beat its way off into the darkness. She glanced around again. Still nothing: meshed branches, deep shadows. Overhead, leafless twigs laced back and forth across a gibbous moon.

She urged her mount forward. Somewhere not too far ahead there was a mountain stream. Now that the spring thaw had set in, it might be running deeper than usual, but there was a footbridge that she could cross. On the other side of that, a canyon led through to open hillside, below which lay the Leominster road.

There was a crackle in the undergrowth close by. This time she didn't halt, but rode on determinedly. She fancied an indistinct shape was moving parallel to her, about thirty yards to her right. If she listened hard enough, she imagined she could hear a breaking of twigs, a trampling of leaf mulch. Her passage was so narrow that thorny fingers plucked at her, snagging her clothes, catching her cowl. Her mount snuffled loudly, as though nervous. She now sensed movement to her left as well as to her right. There was even greater crunching and crackling in the hawthorn. She dug in her heels, urging the horse forward. It began to trot, and she was forced to duck repeatedly as branches passed overhead.

"Easy, easy," she cooed to the animal. "We are almost at the stream."

It was a relief when she actually heard the waterway, babbling over its stones and pebbles. She wouldn't exactly be safe on the other side of it, but at least she could break into a gallop and put significant distance between herself and Grogen Castle.

And then something stepped out into the path in front of her. Even given the events of the last few days, it was the most horrible thing she had ever seen.

It had once been a man – that much was clear. But what it could be described as now God only knew. The right side of it was intact if somewhat discoloured, but the entire left side of it – its arm, leg, torso, shoulder, even the left side of its face – had been eaten down to the gleaming bones; either by rats or decay, or both.

Countess Madalyn had to stifle a scream of disbelieving horror.

The thing didn't lurch towards her. It simply stood there between the hawthorns, regarding her with its single lustreless eye. The moonlight glinted through the bars of its partly exposed ribcage. It was making its way to join the rest, she told herself. Of course it was. They had been drawn here from all directions. That was its only purpose; to join the siege. Somehow or other, Gwyddon's necromantic skill had implanted a sole directive in the worm-eaten skulls of these walking, teetering husks to capture Grogen Castle and destroy its defenders. It would not harm *her*.

So thinking, she urged the horse forward again. There was no room around the semi-skeletal horror, so she expected it to shuffle aside and allow her passage. But it didn't. When she was a yard or so in front of it, she again had to halt her animal, which whinnied and tossed its head nervously.

"Out of my way," the countess instructed in Welsh, though her voice was unsteady. "Out of my way! Don't you know who I am? I am your mistress, the very reason you walk on this Earth. You must obey my command."

It made no move to comply, though it tilted what passed for its head upward slightly, to regard her more closely. She had to fight nausea when she saw a black beetle wriggle out of the gaping eye-socket and scurry down the rotted cheekbone.

"You must do as I say! Move aside at once!"

In response, its jaw dropped to its chest; for a bemused moment, the countess half expected it to drop off entirely. Instead, the creature groaned – in utterly inhuman fashion. It was like the sound heavy wood makes when straining under pressure; a deep, reverberating creak. Yet there were fluctuations in it, alterations in tone. With hair-raising incredulity, Countess Madalyn realised that this thing, this cast-off human shell, was actually trying to speak to her. Slowly, chillingly, the half-groan-half-jabber rose to a peak of shrillness that was difficult to listen to.

Abruptly, the sound ceased, and the thing lurched forward with lightning speed, trying to grab at her bridle.

The horse shrieked and reared and, before the countess knew what had happened, she'd been thrown to the ground. The impact was in the middle of her back, and drove the wind from her. But her pain was numbed by her fear. Shielded by the horse, which careered back and forth, attempting to wheel on the tight woodland path, she leapt to her feet, gathered up her skirts and plunged into the undergrowth.

She ran breathless and blind, regardless that her clothes were torn by thorns. She fought through them all, tears and sweat mingling on her cheeks. She'd known all along that this would happen, that these blasphemous monsters would at last round on the Welsh as well; that they would seek to devour *all* God-fearing things, for theirs was a realm of darkness, devilry and decay. Even as these thoughts struck her, she tottered out into a clearing, from the other side of which more abominations were advancing. What appeared to be a young woman was approaching, a child walking on either side of her, holding her by the hand. The woman's head was missing from her shoulders, and the child on the left, a boy, had possession of it, carrying it in front of him by the hair. That head, though crudely hewn from its torso, was again trying to speak – perhaps trying to accuse her, the countess thought with dismay – the eyes rolling in its sockets, its lips opening and closing frenziedly, though all that emerged was glutinous green froth.

Screeching like an animal, the countess veered to the left, thrusting again through the thorny scrub. She ran headlong into a sturdy trunk, but rebounded from it, scarcely feeling the blow that she took across her chest. New alleys opened, but figures of lunacy were advancing along them. From all sides, she heard a grunting and mewling, a tearing and thrashing of twigs. But now she heard something else: water again, babbling over broken stones.

The stream. And now much closer than before.

Her heart thudding in her chest, she broke from the cover of the hawthorn wood, and found herself on a rocky, sloping bank. The stream lay directly in front of her, patinas of moonlight playing on it in liquid patterns. As she'd feared, it was deeper and broader than usual. She glanced to her left. Maybe a hundred yards away, the arched outline of the stone footbridge was visible. But even as she peered that way, crooked figures emerged from the trees to block her path. A hand alighted on her shoulder. A brief glance revealed the skin loose on it like a rotted glove, with bare bone fingertips pointing out at the ends.

The countess hurled herself forward, splashing into the water to her knees, her thighs, her waist. Even its icy chill couldn't shock her. Her booted feet slid on its slimy bottom and tripped over shifting stones, but she forged her way into the middle without looking back, her dresses billowing around her. The knowledge that she was now on foot, which would increase her journey-time ten-fold, and that she'd now be soaking wet on a raw, inclement night, meant nothing to her. All that mattered was to escape, to drive herself headlong from these nightmares made flesh that gibbered behind her.

The current in the middle of the stream tugged at her remorselessly, several times threatening to knock her under. She whimpered and wept as she fought it, at one point submerging almost to her shoulders. She prayed to the Virgin Mary for fear that God himself would no longer listen, beseeching the Holy Mother to have mercy on her and on her poor, mistreated people. When she reached the other bank, she had to crawl up it, exhausted, her hair hanging over her face in a stringy mat. And yet she knew those things would be close behind her – even now she could hear them splashing their way across, so she had to get to her feet and she had to continue running, though which direction to take from here she could no longer think.

"Alas, not everyone has the belly for war," Gwyddon observed dryly.

Countess Madalyn looked up sharply.

He was just to the left of her, perched on his saddle, a tall, hooded form silhouetted on the star-speckled night. More of his brethren were mounted up alongside him. Several others, also on horseback, approached from behind her. Behind them came the ragged shapes of the dead.

"Think you so?" Countess Madalyn said scornfully, panting as she climbed to her feet. "And yet here *you* are, far from the fury of battle."

"Battles in which men must suffer are a thing of the past, countess. At least... where *my* army is concerned."

"*Your* army, I see." She gave a wry smile. "But then your army can be anything you wish, can it not? Welsh, English... whoever will offer you the power you crave."

"So you're a student of politics after all, madam?" She couldn't see Gwyddon's expression in the darkness, but there was an irreverent sneer in his voice. "A pity you lack the vision to make it your advantage."

"And how long will that advantage last, Gwyddon? When my life finally ends, which will be soon enough in the eyes of Heaven, what advantage will I have when I stand before my maker? Surely you can't imagine that even if your gods control the universe, they would stand for this aberration you've created?"

He sighed. "Still you fail to understand. Whichever god rules this universe, madam – and I applaud your new open-mindedness, even if I'm not surprised by it – the Cauldron of Regeneration was his, or her, gift to us."

Gwyddon brought his horse forward a few paces, so that his face came into the moonlight. His eyes looked up as he pulled thoughtfully at his beard. When he spoke again, it was in a tone of veneration.

"I told you once before that the Cauldron was not forged by ogres at the foot of a bottomless lake. That was just a fable. In truth, its origin came when it fell to Earth from the stars, a glowing lump of unknown metal. Fashioned into its present form for functional purposes, its latent powers were only discovered by accident. Does that amount to sorcery, when it came to us from Nature?"

Countess Madalyn gazed at him, confused.

He smiled as he continued.

"Is the authority with which I control my minions the result of devilish magic, or merely a side effect of the wondrous object's proximity to my person? Like so many heads of my order before me – going all the way back to Myrlyn himself – I have grown up alongside the Cauldron. I have studied it, possessed it, absorbed its essence, made myself one with it... until now my mere thoughts will manipulate my monsters. Ahhh, I see you are shocked. Yes countess, it's true. Those pagan words, the very mention of which has good Christians like yourself cringing in fear... they are mere stage-dressing."

"You have deceived my people!" she hissed.

"When the English are finished, Countess Madalyn, your people will barely exist."

"Then you have deceived yourself."

He shrugged. "By denying to myself a truth that none of us can be certain of? Hardly. In any case, in the same way that you lack the belly for battle, I lack the knowledge for alchemy. It's a fact of life, but it doesn't concern me overly. The outcome will still be the same."

"And what will that be, Gwyddon – Armageddon?"

"Possibly, though obviously that wouldn't be ideal." He signalled to his priests, two of whom dismounted and approached her. "I still seek moderating influences in my life, if you're interested."

"I would rather die," she said.

"My dear countess... haven't you noticed? Nobody dies any more."

CHAPTER TWENTY-NINE

LIQUID FLAME FLOODED over the parapets of the Constable's Tower. Flights of arrows continued to rattle across its battlements. The dead came too, droves of them pouring up the scaling ladders.

It was a hell-storm, the like of which Earl Corotocus's most hardened warriors had never experienced.

They engaged their enemy on two sides of the tower, slashing with sword and axe as one torn and mutilated form after another came up between the crenels, struck constantly on visor, shield or buckler, occasionally pierced through the hauberk by feathered shafts, and all the time dancing between pools of fire. English numbers had now been thinned disastrously, so that huge, undefended gaps were created. The dead would find these and then they'd be onto the roof properly, causing wild melees that would spill to every corner.

"Ranulf!" Gurt Louvain shouted. The face beneath his helmet was red and streaming in the searing heat; five arrows were embedded in his shield, a fifth looked as though it had transfixed his left arm, though in truth it had only punctured his mail sleeve. "Ranulf, this is madness! We can't hold them!"

Ranulf had just felled another corpse with such force that it had plummeted to the foot of its ladder, taking a dozen more with it. He peered down the sheer, flame-blackened bricks. In normal times, he'd expect to see a mountain of broken, mangled bodies at the bottom. Now all he saw was a compressed mass of shrieking, moaning heads and fists clamped on weapons. It was a similar tale at the far end of the causeway, though he could see that alleys were being cleared as more siege machines were brought forward: an even larger battering ram, equipped with wheels and a head of spiked steel, and two heavy onagers.

"Mind your heads!" someone shrieked.

Another fire-pot exploded in the middle of the roof. Sheets of flame erupted on all sides. Men were enveloped head to foot and ran blazing and screaming between their comrades, buffeting some aside, igniting others, in many cases falling clean through the battlements to a quicker, easier death.

"Gurt, there's nowhere to run to," Ranulf replied, his voice hoarse from shouting, his throat sore with smoke and thirst.

Another scaling ladder appeared in front of him. A corpse was already at the top of it. It was naked, but an iron collar was fixed around its neck and iron manacles around its wrists, revealing that the first time it had died it had been hanged in chains. It carried one such chain now, with which it lashed madly at the two English knights. Ranulf caught the chain and, with a downward stroke, clove the chain-arm at the shoulder. The monster now had only one hand with which to grip the ladder, and Ranulf's second stroke severed that too. When the corpse fell, it again took those beneath it.

Ranulf grabbed the top of the ladder and pushed it. As he did, another wave of arrows scythed across the battlements. One skimmed over his shoulder. Five yards to his left, a mercenary tottered away, spitting blood and phlegm from where a shaft had punched through his cheek. Ten yards beyond him, a tenant knight died wordlessly, struck in the throat.

"There aren't enough of us left to cover this perimeter!" Gurt bellowed. "And even if Earl Corotocus hasn't realised that, the dead will – they'll flow over us like the sea."

Below, more sets of hastily constructed scaling ladders were being passed hand-over-hand along the causeway. In a matter of minutes, the onagers would be within range. Close to Ranulf's right, more of the dead had gained a foothold. They climbed in through the embrasures and fought like dogs with the two or three defenders who opposed them; axes beat on shields, maces hammered helmets, crushing them out of shape.

Sensing that Ranulf was no longer listening, Gurt grabbed him by the collar and yanked him to attention.

"Ranulf, for the love of God listen! You must speak to the earl. Tell him we have to retreat to the Keep!"

Ranulf nodded and turned, only to be confronted by another pack of snarling dead, working their way along the battlements from the west, hacking down all in their path. Tomas d'Altard scrambled away from them, unable to stand because an arrow was buried in the back of his thigh.

"Ranulf, Gurt... save me!" he wept, only for the curved spike of a pollaxe to be swung down and driven through the nape of his neck with such force that its point appeared in his gagging mouth.

"We retreat when we can!" Ranulf said, mopping the filth from his blade and advancing. "Until that time..."

From thirty yards away, Earl Corotocus watched wearily as Ranulf FitzOsbern and Gurt Louvain engaged the latest band of corpses to have mounted the battlements, their blades twirling. Similar fights were raging all over the rooftop, knights and corpses hacking at each other dementedly as they staggered through a wreckage of smashed shields and burning bodies. To make things worse, catapults on the causeway now joined the fray. Heavy hunks of stone and lead were lobbed over the north-facing wall, slamming onto and through the shields of those few exhausted men who still had the strength to raise them.

"My lord!" du Guesculin shrilled, staggering forward, his face stained black with soot, his shield bristling with snapped-off arrows. "It's only a matter of time before the mangonel crews resort to heavier payloads! The Constable's Tower is lost!"

The earl himself bled from innumerable cuts. His once resplendent tabard was scorched and smouldering at its edges.

"And if we retreat to the Keep, what then?" he roared. "It's our last redoubt."

"My lord, they will never be able to capture the Keep. Its walls are one hundred and fifty feet high. No ladders, ropes or throwing machines can assail those battlements."

"He's right, my lord," Navarre said, approaching. Instead of a sword, he now wielded a mattock, its knobbly head caked with brains and human hair. "All the dead in the world couldn't build a pyramid with their own flesh that would reach such a precipice."

"And how long can we hold out in there?" the earl asked. "Are there supplies enough for us all?"

Navarre and du Guesculin glanced at each other. Only half way through the previous day had the earl given orders that sacks of meal and salt-pork and kegs of well water should be taken from the storehouses in the courtyard and placed in the Keep cellars. Neither could answer this question, because the implication was simply too terrible, so Earl Corotocus answered for them.

"The garrison could not last a week on what we've so far managed to store in there, am I correct?"

Navarre wiped blood and spittle from his disfigured mouth. "You are correct my lord. Either way, the majority of the garrison is doomed."

Corotocus looked to du Guesculin. "How many of us remain in total?"

The banneret could only shake his head, sweat dripping from his disarrayed hair. "I can't perform a proper count here, my lord. Of the Welsh who served you – one or two, at most. Of Garbofasse's scum – thirty or so."

"Archers?" Corotocus asked.

"A mere handful."

"And of mine?"

"From the fiefs, less than half – forty. Less even than that from the household."

Corotocus considered. "Send the household men to the Keep," he eventually said. "No-one else."

Du Guesculin looked shocked. "No-one?"

"My household men are the most loyal."

"Your landed vassals are loyal too, my lord."

"My landed vassals have fat fees I can reclaim and re-issue at a profit."

Unaccustomed as he was to seeking approval from his underlings, the earl risked a glance at Navarre, who gave a curt nod. Even in the midst of this horror, with carcasses piled on all sides, du Guesculin was pale-faced as he turned away.

"And du Guesculin!" the earl said. The banneret looked back. "Be furtive, du Guesculin. On pain of your own death, do not cause a panic."

Though the English managed to retake the Constable's Tower roof for a brief time, by knocking down every set of scaling ladders, more were soon being carried forward. In addition, there was the problem of the battering ram.

The great door at the front of the tower was not recessed. This was to give defenders overhead a clear line of attack. But the dead that came against it with their spike-headed ram withstood the hail of stones and spears, though more necks and shoulders were broken than any battering ram party had ever sustained in the history of warfare.

The great door was solid of course, reinforced with ribs of steel. But they pounded it with their unnatural strength and stamina, and at length the ram's steel tip began to tell, tearing holes which the dead could cram their hands into and rend at the timber like wolves at a carcass. Piece by piece, the door was pulled apart, which led to even more frantic efforts above. With nearly all pre-prepared missiles exhausted, coping stones were worked loose from the battlements and hurled down. They struck their targets many times, but to infinitesimal effect. The dead continued their frenzied and tireless assault, regardless of skulls crushed and limbs shattered. They rent and rent at the creaking, splintering edifice. Only when their fingers and hands were ripped away, their arms reduced to slivers of bone in shreds of pulverised flesh, were they hauled backward so that others could replace them. Gradually of course, as new ladders were raised and more and more of their number regained the parapets, this deluge of destruction slowed to a trickle and at last ceased altogether. And finally the door that King Edward's Savoyard architects had never imagined could be broken *was* broken, wrenched from what remained of its hinges and hurled from the causeway. The decayed legion then funnelled en masse into the passage beyond.

Arrows sleeted into them via the murder holes, more stones were dropped, naptha grenades were flung – none of it to any consequence. At the far end of the passage they met the portcullis, behind which the fire-raiser waited. Gouts of white-hot flame billowed through them. Again, they melted like candles or flared like figures hacked from coal. When they threw themselves onto the grille, which soon glowed red with the heat of a furnace, they fried, their liquefied flesh running down its bars in sizzling rivulets. Only when crossbows were passed forward, and bolts discharged through the portcullis itself, one by one picking off the crew operating the fire-raiser, were they able to proceed. With groans of elemental agony, the overheated metal was bent and twisted out of the way and access was made.

The dead streamed through, howling like the devil's Cwn Annwyn, the hounds which from time immemorial had haunted these drear Welsh moors. Only one man was left on the fire-raiser. He was an arbalester formerly of the royal contingent, though few of his companions remained in any part of the castle that he knew of, and even now he fancied some of those he'd lost might be coming against him – not that this was a prime concern. A crossbow bolt had already struck him in the chin, another in the shoulder. Though his blood splashed copiously on the flagstones, he was conscious enough to scream like a child as their skeletal paws grabbed hold of him. Shriek after shriek burst from his lips, his froth spattering their raddled, rotted faces as they carried him to the pot at the fire-raiser's mouth and immersed him head-first in the bubbling mixture that had cut through their ranks with its demonic breath.

Next, they flowed up towards the galleries serving the murder holes. Defenders met them on the stairs with swords and axes. Slashing blows were exchanged. Struggling figures pitched down the stairwell, locked together. But the dead steadily prevailed. When their weapons broke, they latched onto the English with claws and teeth, ripping mail from flesh, flesh from bone. Others of their host, meanwhile, bypassed the battle on the stairs and herded along the main passage to the inner courtyard. Another portcullis awaited them there. Arrows whistled through it from a handful of defenders on the other side, but, unhindered now by fire, the dead fell upon the great iron trellis and began to lift it with ease.

High overhead on the roof, the melee surged back and forth across a carpet of carnage. Blood ran in rivers. Corpse-fires still burned, spreading hellish, stinking smoke. More and more of the dead ascended from the ladders. Ranulf cut his way through half a dozen of them, only to be confronted by William d'Abbetot armed with a club-hammer. In truth, the aged engineer was so mutilated that he was only recognisable by his garb. His face had been smashed to pulp; his lower jaw hung from strands of sinew. Yet still he shrieked like a banshee as he rushed at Ranulf. Ranulf ducked the sweeping blow and ran d'Abbetot through from behind, but of course to no effect. Even with a severed nervous system, the engineer merely turned and sought to attack him again. Ranulf had to wrestle the club-hammer from him and batter him down with one massive blow after another, until he was nought but crumpled flesh and mangled bone.

At which point, a shocking cry went up.

"My lord!" someone cried. "My lord, Earl Corotocus – *the dead are in the courtyard!*"

Every man still living pivoted round where he stood and stared back across the roof.

"We're breached!" Gurt shouted, floundering towards Ranulf, blood streaming from a fresh gash across his forehead. "Ranulf, we're breached! We have to retreat!"

"Where's the earl?" Ranulf demanded.

Other survivors on the Constable's Tower were wondering the same. Over half the garrison had been here at the start of the battle; those who remained were clumped together at the south side, sheltering behind a wall of battered shields. But now there were only a couple of dozen of them, and even allowing for those killed or wounded, that was inexplicable. It was even more inexplicable that Earl Corotocus, Navarre and Hugh du Guesculin were absent, as were several other of the household knights and squires.

"Has the earl fled?" someone asked, by his screechy tone of voice scarcely able to believe it.

"Retreat to the Keep!" someone shouted hoarsely.

"Wait!" Ranulf retorted. "There must be a hundred wounded in the rooms and passages below."

Gurt shook his head. "Ranulf, if we could carry one each, that wouldn't be anything like enough."

Ranulf knew this to be true, but before he could argue further there were muffled but ghastly wails from beneath their feet. They didn't know it, but the dead from the ground floor had now reached the levels where the wounded lay and were working their way among the helpless, bandaged bundles, pounding them with rocks, stabbing them over and over with every kind of blunted, broken blade.

Gurt grabbed Ranulf's arm. "Ranulf, we have to get away!"

"Mind your heads!" someone squealed.

Everyone craned his neck to look up, and beheld the first of three colossal blocks of stone spinning down through the night towards them.

"Gods!" Ranulf swore. "The mangonels!"

The impacts were shattering. Huge sections of the paved roof imploded, an avalanche of masonry, rubble and splintered timber cascading onto the heaps of wounded and the packs of snarling dead currently ravaging them, burying them all together.

"Now we go!" Ranulf nodded, coughing out lungfuls of foul dust. "Now we unquestionably go!"

CHAPTER THIRTY

THE KEEP WAS Grogen Castle's most impressive and indomitable feature.

A great, square bastion, it stood in the northeast corner of the courtyard, where it towered over every other rampart and strongpoint. Though joined from the north and the east to the Inner Fort wall, it was girded on its west and south faces by a dry moat some ten yards across, about forty feet deep and filled with jumbled rocks. There were only three ways to actually enter the Keep. High up, there were two gantry drawbridges connecting with it, one from the North Hall, which, as the name suggested, was built against the Inner Fort wall on the north side of the courtyard, and one from the baronial State Rooms, a wattle and timber building raised against the Inner Fort wall on the east side of the courtyard. These two drawbridges, of course, could both be lifted at a moment's notice, presenting attackers from those directions with an impossible gap to cover and a terrifying ninety foot drop to the moat's rocky floor. The Keep's main entrance was the lower drawbridge. This larger platform crossed the moat on the Keep's west side, about thirty feet above the courtyard itself. Anyone seeking ingress by this route had first to ascend a freestanding stone stair, very steep, which terminated at a narrow lip, thus preventing any organised battering ram party from finding a level surface on which to wield their weapon against the drawbridge while it was raised.

As with all defensive sections at Grogen, the Keep's upper tiers were strongly battlemented and cut with arrow-slits and vents for burning oil. This gave it a broad range of attack all across the courtyard. An ordinary army infiltrating this most central ward of the castle would in effect be corralled between high structures and subjected to hail after hail of missiles from defenders perched on unreachable parapets.

But of course on this occasion it was no ordinary army, and the defenders would be few in number and wearied to the point of craziness. And down in the courtyard, craziness, in fact downright insanity, appeared to be the order of the day.

Wounded men who had already shrieked so long and hard that their throats were raw and bleeding, shrieked again as Navarre and two of the earl's men-at-arms picked them up one by one and carried them by the feet and armpits back across the Keep's main drawbridge, hurling them down the steps. In some cases these victims struck the treads first with their backs or hips, while in others they plunged into the courtyard head first, either way landing with bone-crushing force. The last one, who was probably the heaviest, the earl's men gave up on half way, and tossed him over the side into the dry moat.

"What in Christ's name do you think you are doing?" Zacharius howled, as he and Henri came staggering across the courtyard, having wrapped up their instruments and grabbed what few valuable medicines they could carry.

On seeing and hearing the masses of the dead gathering on the far side of the courtyard, the doctor had been forced to abandon his infirmary. The weeping and imploring of those wounded he'd had to leave behind was a torture that he knew he would never forget. And yet now he had arrived at the foot of the Keep, only to discover the discarded bodies of those paltry few that, over the previous hour, he and Henri had managed to place in the safety of its interior; they'd been flung back out again like sacks of meal. He launched himself up the steps, at the top of which Navarre stood waiting, hands on hips.

"I repeat!" Zacharius thundered. "What in the name of Christ do you think you are doing?"

Navarre regarded him coolly. "There's a place for you and your boy inside here, doctor. But not for a bunch of wretches who, while unfit to wield a sword, are doubtless fit to eat our victuals and drink our drink."

"Those men were my patients, you troll-faced dog!"

Navarre smiled; with his misaligned features it was a chilling sight. "I have my orders."

"We'll see about that!"

Zacharius tried to push past, but Navarre stopped him with a heavy, mail-clad arm. "Alas, there's no time left."

"There's time at least to have you punished, you murdering brigand!"

"It's a pity that I couldn't find you," Navarre said and, without warning, he grabbed Zacharius by the throat.

So tight was the grip that Zacharius could not even gag. He struggled wildly, but he was effete, a fop, and Navarre was the earl's champion. Helpless, the doctor found himself being frogmarched backward towards the edge of the drawbridge.

"Alas," Navarre said again. "I searched high and low for you, but time ran out."

Though he was now fighting for his life, there was no real way that Zacharius could resist this brutal foe. And he knew it. But even then he was unprepared to be pushed backward from the bridge and suspended in open space, his feet kicking ineffectually.

Navarre's smile became a deranged grin. "Still glad your barren spell will end before mine, doctor?"

And he opened his hands.

Zacharius's scream broke from his constricted throat as he plummeted towards the rocks far below – it lingered horribly, before ending abruptly with the resounding impact of meat striking a slab.

At the foot of the Keep steps, Henri stood aghast.

Navarre peered down at him, before shaking his head glumly. "And without your master, what use are *you*?"

He turned idly and strolled back across the drawbridge.

Henri was so stunned that all he could do was stand there rigidly, oblivious to the dirge of demented cries drawing closer and closer from behind. Even when, with a rumble of timber and clanking of chains, the bridge was slowly raised, the surgeon's assistant was too frozen with shock to move. Thankfully, the first blow that fell on him was the last thing he knew, the single stroke of a falchion cleaving his skull asunder.

Just before they vacated the Constable's Tower, Gurt and Ranulf looked down into the courtyard, but there was too much confusion there and around the foot of the Keep for them to focus on any particular detail. As such, neither of them saw the murder of Doctor Zacharius and his assistant. It was a mesmerising scene, all the same.

The dead were now emerging in droves from the inner gate, which was directly below them, and streaming all over the inner ward, swarming between its rickety structures, including the infirmary, tearing them down, setting fire to their straw-thatched roofs. The few remaining domestics – the servants, grooms and pages – who'd deserted from the defences and been hiding, were hauled wailing into the open alongside the wounded, where they were all set about savagely; being beaten, torn, and dragged across the gore-smeared cobblestones. A party of the dead had ascended the Keep steps, but now stood howling in helpless rage for the main drawbridge had been lifted and stood upright against the facing wall.

With the courtyard so occupied, the only way from the Constable's Tower to the Keep was along the top of the Inner Fort wall. Ranulf, Gurt and the sixteen men remaining dashed along it in single file, having to kick their way through yet more piles of ghastly Breton scarecrows, all the time aware that those dead who'd climbed to the Constable's Tower roof were close behind. At the same time they were struck with arrows from the curtain-wall, which accounted for a couple more of their number. The survivors finally scrambled through a nail-studded door into the upper level of the barrack house. It was lit by torches but rank with the smell of corrupted flesh – for the dead who had clambered through the arrow-slits here and slaughtered many of Davy Gou's small group of defenders were still present. They had now scattered the straw bedding and personal baggage of the earl's troops, searching for additional weapons – large numbers of which they had found.

The two bands were not evenly matched – there were many more of the dead. But of course additional dead were now closing from behind. So the English had no option.

"Butcher them!" Ranulf shouted, leading the charge. "It's the only way!"

CHAPTER THIRTY-ONE

THE CHAPEL WAS almost completely dark when Father Benan's eyes flickered open. The tiny candle he'd placed on the altar step was little more than a blob of melted tallow. Slowly and painfully, he tried to rouse himself from the latest swoon that he'd fallen into.

It had taken all the strength he had left to crawl here from the Constable's Tower. In addition, he hadn't eaten or drunk even a sip of water in as long as he could remember. Little wonder he'd been in and out of a dead faint since his return here. The welts that covered his plump body were stiff and aching. The cassock he'd wrapped himself with had adhered in strips to his clotted blood, and wouldn't be removed easily. Slowly, he sat upright on the step. His breathing was low and ragged. He hung his head. Despite the chill, sweat dripped from his brow. By the sounds of it, the attack on the castle was still raging. Thunderous impacts and wild shrieks sounded faintly through the chapel's thick walls.

Benan struggled to think clearly. If nothing else, he knew that he had to get back to his feet. Zacharius would be working out there practically alone. The dying would need shrift. Regardless that he himself was maimed, regardless of this devil's brew that he was part of, the priest knew that he had a sacred duty here. But good Lord, it was icy cold and it was so dark. His sole candle lit only the immediate area around him – the stone step and a patch of rush-covered floor.

He used the bare stone table to lever his shuddering bulk upright. Mumbling incoherent prayers, he bent down, picked up the stub of candle and, as carefully as he could, applied its glowing wick to two of the other three candles that were in reach. The light this created was dim, flickering, and cast eerie shadows over the rows of pews and the narrow aisles between them.

Benan was still glad that he'd taken such a ferocious beating. Oh, he doubted God would be satisfied with a few strokes of the whip; Benan's role in the earl's many atrocities would incur a far greater penalty on Judgment Day, he was sure. But at least it was comforting that he was no longer part of the earl's inner sanctum; that in fact he had more in common with those countless, helpless wretches the earl had slain and brutalised in his quest for power.

Then Benan thought he heard something close by – a rattling sound, as if someone had opened the chapel's outer door. He gazed down the nave. The inner door was half hidden in shadow, but it stood open. The passage beyond it was in inky darkness. Benan waited, but nobody announced themselves.

Suddenly he felt a chill down his lacerated spine.

He clutched at the crucifix hanging at his throat – as he had done throughout his chastisement. It was still sticky with blood, but he barely noticed. He listened intently, but there was no further sound – only the distant, muffled roar of the fighting, which, now that he thought about it, seemed to be penetrating the chapel from all sides – including above. Hastily, he lit the last candle, though it added precious little light to the chamber. He turned again to face the door and felt into the pocket of his cassock. From it, he brought out a scapular dedicated to the Mother of Carmel, made of soft fabric and fastened to a cord. It bore images of the Blessed Virgin and the Holy Child.

Benan regarded the celestial duo. As always, their expressions were serene, untroubled, full of love. Yet for a desolate second they seemed remote. Benan felt a terrible pang of regret for his misdeeds. How he suddenly yearned for that heavenly couple to be with him now – in spirit if not in body, just to bolster his resolve.

He turned again to the empty chapel.

If it was empty.

Fleetingly, he imagined that somebody was down there in the farthest recess. Another chill crept up his spine. Determined to stay calm, he took the iron crucifix from his throat. That was when he noticed that a streak of reddish, fiery light had speared along the floor of the passage beyond the inner door. He'd been right after all – the outer door *had* been opened.

Benan backed up until the altar table prevented him going any further.

The flames from the candles were guttering and cast cavorting shapes on the walls. He mopped his brow and held the crucifix in front of him. It felt good in his hands; heavy, like a weapon. Slowly, wondering if he dared do what he now planned to – a proven sinner like him – he raised the crucifix aloft.

"Glorious prince of the heavenly army," he called in Latin. "Holy Michael, archangel, defend us in our fight against the rulers of darkness!"

He imagined phantoms in the empty pews, regarding him silently. His breath puffed in frozen clouds.

"Come to the aid of the people whom God created in His own image and likeness, and bought at great price from the tyranny of Satan. Holy Church venerates thee as her protector. To thee God handed the redeemed souls, to lead them into the joys of Heaven. Ask the God of Peace to destroy all diabolical powers, so that our foes may no longer control mankind or desecrate holy mother Church."

From the entry passage, Benan heard what sounded like the scraping of bone fingertips along the brickwork.

Fresh sweat broke on his brow. It was impossible for those things to enter here, he told himself. Not that they'd respect the sanctity of a chapel – he'd known enough so-called Christians whose lack of respect had led to them force entry to such sanctuaries, and there shed innocent blood and defile innocent flesh (Earl Corotocus, for one). But the only entrance to this holy place was from the courtyard. If the enemy had gained access here, Grogen Castle itself had fallen.

Benan's sweat-slick hair prickled; he clutched his crucifix all the harder. A stronghold like this could never fall – not so quickly. But still those scraping claws came closer. By the sounds of it, there were several pairs of them.

"Saint Michael!" Benan cried. "Carry our prayer before the face of Almighty God, so the Lord's mercies may descend upon us. Seize the dragon, the old serpent, who is none other than Satan, and cast him into the abyss. We beseech you!"

In the barrack house, the English went at it like madmen, hacking and rending their way into the phalanx of corpses.

Ranulf ripped one gangrenous apparition from its groin to its gullet and a mass of putrid entrails foamed out, the stench of which alone was almost sufficient to knock him unconscious. Gurt's opponent had once been a woman, now its dead skin was mottled blue in colour and bloated out of all proportion. He smote it again and again with his sword as it raked at his eyes, but still it remained upright. His last blow was a murderous downward thrust through the side of its neck, right into the midst of its torso. The thing simply ruptured, like a bladder filled with bile, spraying filth as it seemed to deflate, odious fluids bursting from every orifice.

Other men were not so successful. A mercenary serjeant called Orlac, a doughty fellow by any standards but denuded of his weapons, strove at the creatures with a broken-off table leg. He struck skull-shattering blows on all sides, but four of them eventually overwhelmed him and bore him to the floor, where snapping teeth tore the arteries from his wrists and the windpipe from his throat.

And now the dead from the rear were entering the fray. Two tenant knights turned to face them. But Ranulf roared at them not to act like loons.

"Go forward!" he thundered, clearing himself a path with sweeps of his sword. "Never mind what's behind us!"

Gurt and the others followed, buffeting their way through the narrow gap. And then they were running again, grunting for breath, their mail clinking, their heavy feet thumping on the floorboards. Somewhere ahead, a wide timber staircase swept up to the great hall. As they ascended, they passed numerous embrasures, which gave through to the fire-lit courtyard. Quick, fearful glances showed that it was now totally filled up with the dead, who howled in eerie unison as they tossed the mutilated remains of their victims between them.

When they reached the top of the stair, the doors to the Great Hall stood in front of them. They were partly open. Without hesitation, Ranulf barged through.

"In the name of Jesus Christ, our Lord and God," Benan cried, throwing his voice to the vaulted ceiling. "We undertake in full confidence this battle against the enemy."

Darkness now filled the chapel like swamp water; things writhed and oozed in its murky depths. An appalling odour seeped through it. From all the surrounding chambers came a thunderous cacophony of destruction.

The priest's forehead ran with sweat. "Let... G-god arise," he stammered, his throat dry. "Let His enemies be scattered. Let those who hate Him flee before Him..."

Slowly, his words tailed off.

His fearful eyes had focussed on a spectral figure, which had just come in from the entry passage and now glided across the bottom end of the church. Benan could not believe what he was seeing. It was a bishop – dressed in Easter vestments: the glorious white and gold tabard glittering, the jewel-encrusted mitre worn at an irreverently jaunty angle. The figure was moving swiftly, but with humility, its hands crossed on its breast. Benan had to look again, his eyes straining in the dimness. The figure's feet hardly seemed to be moving. For a fantastical moment, the priest wondered if some radiant soul had risen to help him. Then he saw it stop by the baptismal font, bend down – and begin to drink.

In great, sickening slurps.

Tears of terror dripped down Benan's cheeks.

"Oh Lord... save us," he whispered.

The Great Hall was a grim reminder of what Grogen Castle could have been in happier, more peaceful times.

In due course, if the land had settled and Earl Corotocus had come to feel at home in the stronghold, this vast banqueting chamber would have been transformed: a fire would roar in its immense open hearth, the floor would be strewn with fresh rushes, the tapestries and battle standards, now fouled and defaced by the Welsh, would be replaced. The mouldering food and broken crockery that strewed the table-tops after that rabble of Bretons had roistered here would be swept aside and a feast fit for a king laid out. A scent of roasted fowl and venison would fill the air. Wine and ale would flow. There'd be singing and celebration, a harmonious lilting of pipes and lutes.

But at present, lit dolefully by the first rays of dawn, the place was a desecrated shell filled with wreck and ruin – and with the dead.

Perhaps thirty corpses were present, having come in through the casements or ascended via the hall's second staircase. Against such odds, no sane man would have progressed even a single step, except that none of Ranulf's band had any choice. An even greater number of corpses were clamouring at their rear.

"Straight through them!" Ranulf bellowed.

But it was an impossible situation. The dead didn't just meet them with swords, axes and knives, but they flung javelins and spears from the minstrel's gallery. Three Englishmen went down before they'd even engaged the foe. Ranulf ducked one missile, leapt onto a banquet table and ran down its full length, vaulting the blows aimed at his legs, striking to the left and right with his sword. Gurt tried to take the same route, but was grappled with by a pack of them. With desperate efforts, he flung his attackers off, picked up a bench and, holding it horizontal, drove them backward. As they fell, he trampled over them, and the men coming up behind chopped at them. But those English at the rear were pressed together in the confusion until too cramped to move, and then hewn mercilessly from behind.

"Ranulf!" Gurt screamed.

Ranulf had reached the far end of the hall. Another passage lay ahead of him. The way, it seemed, was clear through to the baronial State Rooms. But he turned back. Gurt was still using the bench to protect himself, but it was being hacked to splinters. He tried to duck behind it, only for a blow from a mattock to tear the helmet clean from his head.

Ranulf went back into the fray. A corpse hove in from his left. It wore only a loincloth and its body was gashed and slashed all over. A blow from a war-hammer had smashed its rotted face. Its nose was crushed and shreds of black tongue hung through a mesh of mangled teeth. For a weapon it wielded a burnt log, which it had lifted from the hearth.

Ranulf fended off two blows and severed its weapon hand at the wrist. It responded by grabbing his throat with its other hand. He slammed his mail-clad knee into its groin, but to no effect. He beat its skull with the pommel of his sword. The skull broke open. Another foul fetor engulfed Ranulf, making him choke – the exposed brain was like a lump of mouldered cabbage. Still the thing tried to throttle him. Only when Gurt appeared, and, with a single blow, shore its arm at the elbow, was Ranulf released. A second blow took its legs from under it and it fell to the floor, a twitching, limbless half-man.

"You were supposed to be helping *me!*" Gurt shouted.

"Next time remind me not to bother!" Ranulf retorted, only to cry in pain as a set of broken teeth clamped on his left ankle.

"God's bread!" he roared, striking down five times at his persistent assailant, the fifth impact so heavy that his blade cut through meat and bones to the flagstones beneath, and promptly snapped in half.

"Jesus," Ranulf groaned.

The weapon that had seen him through countless battles was now less than a foot long and squared off where it should have been pointed.

"Never mind that," Gurt said. "We have to flee."

The rest of the Great Hall was like a butcher's yard. All the other English had fallen, though the dead still ravaged at their bodies, beating their heads with stones and logs, wrenching their limbs from their sockets, hacking them with every type of blade. Gurt and Ranulf might themselves have been overrun, had someone else not suddenly become the centre of the dead horde's attention.

Though Ranulf had barely noticed Morgaynt Carew during the later fighting, mainly because his broken hands and scattered wits had left him incapable of wielding weapons properly, the semi-demented captain of the Welsh malcontents had run with them from the Constable's Tower. But now, at last, his dead countrymen had their claws on him. Incredibly, Carew still lived despite having been impaled on a spear, which had been thrust into his body via his anus and up through his bowels and innards, until re-emerging from his gagging mouth. His eyes rolled from side to side as they raised him upright, planted him on the open hearth and began piling timber from the broken benches around him.

Even with every other atrocity Ranulf and Gurt had witnessed, this was an astonishing sight. And yet Ranulf was no longer surprised. It seemed to him that, as the battle had progressed, the dead had become more and more like the living – as if whatever demonic force possessed them had grown used to its new mantle. Their grunts and mewls had turned increasingly to screams of fury. They had been organised from the start, but whereas initially they'd lumbered like puppets, soon they'd become faster and more dexterous. Worse still, as this grisly spectacle proved, they were showing increasing levels of vindictiveness. No longer were they mindless vegetables acting on pure instinct. Now, as though sensing all together that in Morgaynt Carew they had a *real* enemy, they gathered around the hearth in a mob, howling in monstrous glee, waving their weapons on high as a firebrand was produced and flame touched the kindling.

Did this reflect the nature of the force controlling them, Ranulf wondered, or in the putrid sludge of their brains, did threads of the worst kind of human emotions still linger?

"Ranulf!" Gurt screamed into his ear. "Come on, while they're distracted!"

Ranulf nodded.

They turned and headed into the next passage. But the dead weren't distracted for long. Even as the two knights ran, a group of corpses broke off in pursuit. Those few that had been poorly armed before were well armed now, having taken possession of swords, flails and maces from their English victims. They twisted and staggered as they came, travelling on limbs that were smashed or pierced, or on stumps from which the feet had been shorn, but they showed frightful speed. Their torn faces, crusted with the mingled blood of their victims and their own clotted mucus, were contorted by the madness of the damned.

Father Benan could feel their eyes on him as they advanced like shades through the darkened chapel. The storm in the other rooms had reached a terrifying crescendo, but he continued determinedly with the rite, his body drenched and shaking.

"Behold the cross of the Lord!" he cried, holding up the iron crucifix. "Flee, bands of enemies!"

Still they came, horrible manifestations of the night, the stench of carrion pouring off them in waves so thick the very air swam with it. One by one, they smashed the pews, ripping them up from the stone floor and casting them aside.

The priest held his ground on the altar.

"The Lion of Judah, the stem of David has triumphed!" he shouted, but his voice was lost in the tumult. "God the Father, in the name of Jesus Christ thine son, may thy mercy be upon us all." He had to duck as a something was flung at him. It missed his face by inches. But he had the fleeting fancy that it was somebody's torn off hand.

"We drive thee out, unclean spirits, whoever thou art!" His throat was raw with shouting. "Every devilish tribe, in the name of God and by the power of Our Lord Jesus, be thou uprooted and driven from those fashioned in the likeness of God and redeemed by the precious blood of the divine Lamb."

He made a hurried sign of the cross. But no scream of tortured souls greeted this powerful symbol, no reek of burning flesh. The thing in the bishop's vestments was at their forefront; now that it was close, its once ornate robes looked filthy and had been shredded as though by an eagle's talons. Benan tried to focus on this fiend in particular. Had it really once been a bishop of the Christian church? Had the dark magic that had invoked this army of the dead seeped down into some cathedral crypt, where sacred bones lay in tranquil repose? As it stepped up onto the altar, he moved forward to meet it, hoping to recognise its face and maybe reason with it. But all he saw, when they were almost nose-to-nose, were the startled features of Otto, the earl's portly cook. They had been torn from the Brabancon's head in one piece, and draped bloodily over this abomination's own desiccated visage.

Benan backed away, fighting to suppress a scream.

"Dare no more, malicious serpent, to persecute God's children! May the Almighty God command thee!"

He made another sign of the cross, but now they were filing up onto the altar from his right and his left. One of them, more bones and filth than actual flesh, had bobbed hair, wore a scarlet fustian gown and a fashionable beret with a rolled brim, indicating that high ranks of layity had also joined the unholy legion.

"May God the Father, God the Son and God the Holy Spirit dispose of thee, foul demons!"

With each incantation, he made signs of the cross, but still they advanced. He scrambled around the altar table and limped to a smaller table at the back. Here sat a leather satchel containing his most precious belongings. From inside it, he took a lidded chalice. As he opened it, he continued to pray.

"May Christ take thee in His hands!" He opened the chalice, thumbing out three blessed wafers, and turned back to the invaders. "He built the Church on firm foundations and promised the gates of the Underworld would never prevail against her."

He broke the wafers into fragments and scattered them around him in a semi-circle.

"Thou art commanded by the sign of the holy cross!" He thrust his crucifix at them. "And by the mysteries of the Christian faith. Thou art commanded by the sublime virgin mother of God, Mary, who from her conception has trodden on your crown."

Again, he made the sign of the cross and, momentarily, their advance seemed to falter – but only for fleeting seconds. If such a thing was possible, the expressions on their decayed faces seemed to have changed, from inhuman anger to something like curiosity.

"Thou art commanded by the apostles! Thou art commanded by the blood of the martyrs!"

One by one, they circled around the altar table.

For the first time in his life, despite all that he'd turned a blind eye to in the service of Earl Corotocus, Benan felt his faith begin to ebb. Never had he imagined he would face an enemy like this, though perhaps, in private, he might have said that he could manage it – that with the fist of the Almighty clenched above him he could stand off the hounds of hell. But still they approached.

"We exorcise thee, cursed dragon!" He lifted the cross as high as he could. "And all these, thine apostate followers! By the living God, by the true God, by the holy God!"

Their hands clawed as they reached for him.

"Flee, Satan!" he screamed. "Thou inventor and master of every deception, thou enemy of Mankind!"

As one, they halted.

Benan gazed, blinking, from one to the other. Though they crowded around him, only affording a few feet of safety, an absurd hope suddenly rose in his breast.

Had the ancient rite succeeded? It would have amazed him if it had. Though Benan had scorned Earl Corotocus for his excesses, he'd feared from the outset that his long record of collaboration with the nobleman had damaged him in the eyes of Heaven. He had simply *known* that God would not send his angels down to assist. That Christ would *not* appear by his side, armed with a flaming sword.

And yet the devils' advance had apparently ceased.

Benan glanced down. The fragments of sacred wafer lay in a distinct line between him and them – like a barrier. Not one of them had set foot across it. His heart rate increased; he felt the beginnings of hope.

"We command thee! We command thee..." Benan's voice rose triumphantly, only for his words to tail off again.

For with slow, malicious pleasure, the thing in the Episcopal vestments shook its head from side to side and with a single, deliberate step, crossed over the holy fragments. The others copied it and, raising their claws, took hold of the shrieking priest from all sides.

Benan dropped to his knees. His eyes were screwed shut as multiple dead fingers groped through his hair and over his tear-sodden face. His heart throbbed in his chest, but, with a core of steel that even he didn't know he possessed, he proceeded with the exorcism.

"Make way for Christ, in whom thou couldst find none of thy works! Bow beneath the mighty hand of God..."

He dared to look up at them again. It seemed that every demonic face in creation was peering down at him. Crushed, pulped, rotted, scabrous masks of what they'd once been, and now possessed by some force of evil no man could understand, exuding it like a fog of death.

"Tremble and flee at the invocation of the holy name of Jesus, before which all Hell will shake. At the name of Jesus, to which all powers on Earth and in Heaven are subject, which the cherubim and seraphim unceasingly praise, saying 'holy, holy, holy is the Lord God of Hosts."

Fascinated, they ran their hands over his plump, naked flesh. They found his many welts.

"Our help is in the name of the Lord," Benan croaked. "The name of the Lord! God of Heaven, God of Earth, God of angels, God of apostles and martyrs..."

His voice rose to a castrato screech as, one by one, they dug their bony claws into his wounds.

"...who has the power to give life after death because there is no other god than Thee."

And then they ripped, tearing the wounded tissue from his body like fabric from a seamstress's dummy. His keening howl might have shattered the eardrums of anyone human.

"For thou... thou art the creator of all things visible and invisible," he sobbed. "To whose reign there shall be no end. We humbly prostrate ourselves before Thy glorious majesty... deliver us..."

He screeched again as more meat was rent from his bones.

"... deliver us from the infernal host..."

He batted at them with the iron crucifix, until the bishop-thing snatched it from his grasp.

"Hear us, Father. Hear us..."

But his words ended and all that came from his mouth were scarlet bubbles. The white-hot fire that engulfed him was fading, but he had no strength to stand, and they had to hoist him to his feet. His vision was darkening. The end was coming, he knew. Though it hadn't quite come yet, and he was still compos mentis enough to feel wonder that the bishop-thing was now offering the crucifix to his lips.

How strange, Benan reflected, that after everything they'd subjected him to, they were giving him a chance to make good his martyrdom. He leaned forward to kiss the holy symbol, as so many saints had done in the past while bound to racks or nailed to crosses – but the object was withdrawn before he could make contact.

To his pain-fuddled bewilderment, it was lifted up above his eye-line, where he lost track of it altogether, until he felt its cold iron base placed on top of his cranium, in the very middle of his tonsure. Other dead hands now clamped Benan's head to keep it steady. His confusion lingered a little longer, but a whimper of understanding broke from his blood-slathered lips as the bishop-thing began to press the crucifix downward with crushing force, driving it inch by agonising inch through his skin, his bone, and finally into his brain.

The last thing that Father Benan realised, before his world winked out of existence, was that, if nothing else, when he too walked with the dead, the sign of his faith would be planted in the top of his skull.

CHAPTER THIRTY-TWO

LIKE THE GREAT Hall, the State Rooms, which would normally form private apartments for the castellan of Grogen Castle and his family, had been ransacked; their exquisite furnishings were smashed or stolen, their tapestries and wall-hangings torn down. Welsh profanities had been written in excrement on the whitewashed walls.

The casements here, while not exactly arrow-slits, were still tall and narrow, set in deep embrasures, and had been covered with sheets of tinted horn, though many of these had been shattered, for grapples had been shot through them.

"Which way?" Gurt said, as he and Ranulf entered the first room, breathless.

Ranulf knew that these State Rooms were located in the southeast corner of the inner court and, indeed, casements looking down into the bailey stood in front of them as well as to the right. This meant that, to reach the Keep, they had to head through the arched portal on their left. Before they did, they closed and bolted the door behind them, but almost immediately there were smashing impacts on the other side. Gleaming axe-heads appeared through the shuddering wood.

"That way," Ranulf said, pushing Gurt towards the arch.

"What are you doing?"

"I'll try to slow them down."

Gurt nodded and hurried out of sight. Ranulf turned back to the door, against which a storm of axes and hammers was now raging. Amid the shattered furniture, he found a wrought iron candelabra, the central stem of which was a tall, spear-thick shaft tapered at its tip to a needle-point. He rammed it against the door, wedging its base under the central transverse plank and planting its tip between two floorboards. This braced the door well, though more axe-heads burst into view. Now they were being twisted, worked from side to side in the gaps they had made, cracking the wood, forcing the planks apart. Ranulf backed away. The inside of his mail was awash with sweat. He suddenly felt intolerably tired; every cut, bruise and sprain ached. He turned to follow Gurt – only for something to catch hold of his bitten ankle. Glancing down, he saw an arm extended from beneath an overturned divan.

Another of the dead things now dragged itself into view – or rather, it dragged its upper half into view. It had been severed at the waist, and not by a clean blow either. A jumble of ropy innards slithered behind it, drawing a slug-like trail of crimson slime. Ranulf tried to yank his foot free, but the thing had a firm grip and now sank fingernails encrusted with grave-dirt into the injured joint. Ranulf yelped. Instinctively, he drew his sword and prepared to slash through the offending limb, only to remember that his sword was now a third of its normal length. He cursed.

The monster reached with its left hand and took hold of his sword-belt, by which it hoisted itself to waist height. It was climbing up his body, bringing its face ever closer to Ranulf's – though so caked with mud and blood was that face that only its gaping maw was visible; a maw in which the tongue was alive with maggots, in which only brown shards remained of its teeth.

Ranulf stabbed frantically down at it.

The squared-off sword was still sharp enough to rip repeatedly through flesh and bone, to plough what remained of that countenance to vile jelly. With its left hand, the monster tried to grab his sword arm, but this weakened its purchase on his belt, and he was able to fling it to the floor. Before it could right itself and come after him again – he had a crazy mental image of it running crab-like, balanced solely on its hands – he snatched the candelabra, and thrust it down into the horror's chest, driving the point through its heart, and, with a grinding squeal of wood, transfixing it to the floorboards, where it commenced to thrash and bellow like a maddened bull.

No longer braced, the door shuddered and split even more violently, but the bolt seemed to be holding – at least for the moment.

"*Ranuuulf!*" Gurt's distant voice halloed from beyond the archway. "Where in God's name are you?"

"I'm coming!" Ranulf replied, tottering after him.

He entered a lengthy gallery, which, half way along, turned from stone to timber and thatch and opened on its left hand side, where it overlooked the courtyard. At its far end, he could see the gantry drawbridge connecting with the portal in the Keep's south-facing wall. A figure had just emerged from that portal, walking backward onto the drawbridge. Its grimy green livery revealed it to be Gurt. He was arguing with someone.

"Just wait!" Gurt shouted. "Damn your eyes!"

Ranulf was perhaps twenty yards away when he realised what was happening. The drawbridge, which of course spanned a ninety-foot drop into the Keep's dry moat, was rising slightly. It seemed that somebody inside the Keep was determined to close it. Gurt had clearly argued for it be kept open for Ranulf, but had now had been forced to add his weight to the bridge.

"You damn slave!" Gurt shouted in through the Keep entrance. "Less than a minute is all I ask!" The drawbridge had risen half a foot. Gurt, struggling to maintain his balance, drew his sword and pointed it into the darkness. "I swear, I'll take this out of your hide!"

"I'm coming!" Ranulf cried hoarsely.

Gurt glanced along the gallery and his bloodied face split into a relieved grin.

"He's coming now," he said loudly.

Ranulf reasoned that one of the earl's men-at-arms would be inside there, working the drawbridge wheel. But the fellow who now stepped from the darkness behind Gurt, unnoticed by him, was no man-at-arms – it was Navarre. And he had drawn his trusty dagger. Without a word, he raised it over his head and drove it down hard, ramming it between Gurt's shoulder blades.

Ranulf slid to a stunned and breathless halt.

Gurt had gone rigid; his expression of relief had rapidly transformed to one of bemusement. He half-smiled and tried to speak – though no words came out. With a weak gesture towards Ranulf, he tottered slightly, his knees buckling. But it took a shove from Navarre to help him on his way, pitching him head first into the gulf.

"Guuurt!" Ranulf screamed, as his friend dropped from view.

Navarre glanced uninterestedly across the drawbridge towards Ranulf, before turning and walking casually back into the darkness of the Keep.

"Raise the bridge," he told someone.

Five seconds later, Ranulf arrived at the end of the timber gallery, but the bridge had already been drawn up out of his reach, marooning him there. With a heavy *clunk*, it came to rest against the facing wall – a good ten yards away.

Ranulf teetered on the terrifying brink. Far below, the tiny shape of Gurt lay still in the foot of the dry moat. Even from this distance, a crimson stain could be seen creeping out around his splayed green cloak. Ranulf might have gone cold at the thought that this shattered fragment was all that remained of the closest comrade he'd had during the fight for Grogen Castle. He might have gone colder still at the thought that, with all the other indebted knights slaughtered – in fact with all of those not bound in Earl Corotocus's personal *mesnie* dead, including his father – he didn't have a friend left in the world. But he was already cold, deeply cold. Not just clammy with sweat, but chilled to the marrow by the nightmares he'd witnessed and partaken in.

He was so numbed that it was tempting to simply remain here and await the inevitable. There was nowhere else to go anyway. Every ten yards along this timber gallery, a stout post connected with its roof, so it would not be difficult to climb up there. But the roof was of thatched straw, which could easily be penetrated by spears or eaten by flames, and beyond that there was nothing. The only solution it seemed was to kneel and offer contrition for his sins, praying that the end might come quickly.

But Ranulf did none of these things.

Instead, he turned and walked back along the gallery towards the State Rooms. He now understood what had motivated his father during his final years: that the antidote to a wasted life could only be a worthwhile death; that the price of living without honour could only be to die covered with it.

Yet Ranulf did not intend to die.

Not yet.

As he'd fought through the barrack house and the Great Hall, it had occurred to him several times that his demise was nigh and that perhaps he should welcome it as a just desert rather than fear it. But now he consciously and determinedly sought to avoid it – because there was something very important that he had to do first.

He entered the room where the legless monstrosity was pinned to the floor. It remained fixed down, but on seeing him became wildly animated, struggling, grunting, tearing handfuls of flesh from its own torso as it sort to dig the implement out. Meanwhile, the door connecting with the Great Hall had almost been battered through. One hinge had come loose, and great chunks of woodwork were missing. The parchment-faced figures beyond gave shrieks of glee when they saw that Ranulf had returned.

Ranulf ignored them. He righted the fallen divan – a luxurious piece of Italian furniture, with a carved wooden base and thick fleece for upholstery – and shoved it across the floor until it was beneath the first casement through which a grapple and a rope protruded. Climbing up, he was able to reach the grapple and pull it down. It would be typical of his luck, he thought, if another dead Welshman was on the end of it and now came through the aperture screaming and raving. But that did not happen. The rope was limp and he was able to reel in forty or fifty yards of it, before drawing his broken sword and chopping it through.

He coiled it over his arm as he headed back to the Keep gallery, though now, with a deafening crash, the door behind him fell and the dead surged through. Ranulf broke into a run, shedding his mail piece by piece as he did – first his coif, then his hauberk, then his leggings. Each time it was difficult, the straps and buckles caked with blood, vomit, excrement; all the glutinous residue of death. He was half way along the gallery, into the timbered section, when he cast off the last piece. His felt and woollen under-garb was so sodden with sweat and urine – he'd lost count of the number of times he'd voided his bladder during the last two days, having had no time to find a quiet corner – that it clung to him like a second skin, but at least it was light, enabling him to run much faster. However, undressing en route had slowed him down, and a quick glance over his shoulder showed that his enemies were as close as ten yards behind, their dirge of shrieks and moans deadening his ears. Knowing that he had one chance only, he unloaded the rope, took hold of the grapple – three iron hooks welded together – and flung it up towards the top of the gantry drawbridge, which was about a foot lower than the lintel of the portal beyond it.

The grapple caught and held.

Ranulf didn't bother looking round. The dead were right at his back – their stench engulfed him, their claws were reaching for him. With no time to rig a harness, he wound the rope around his hands and threw himself into open space. Their howls of rage turned to groans of despair as he swung down across the gulf.

The Keep wall rushed towards him. He'd intended to extend his legs and flatten his feet, to brace himself for impact, but the rope spiralled and he struck the sheer bricks with heavy force, his left hip and the left side of his ribs taking the full brunt.

Seconds passed as he hung there between Heaven and Earth, his vision blurred with tears and sweat, his wrists burning as they supported the entire weight of his body. Finally he was able to focus again; he peered upward. The flat cliff-face of the wall rose inexorably to a sky now tinged pink by dawn sunlight. The rope from which he hung was a taut sinew, which creaked and twisted. He glanced towards the lip of the gallery. The dead clustered there, watching him, even though some of them lacked eyes and some even lacked faces. So great was their press, that one or two fell, hurtling down. Several, he saw, had axes, spears and knives – all potential missiles. How long before they, or whatever controlled them, realised they could still reach him? How long before his strength gave out regardless?

Young as he was, Ranulf's military experience was already sufficient to guide him through extreme pain and exhaustion. The usual trick was simply to pretend that it wasn't happening, to imagine that your agony was just like any other sensation, something minor and tolerable, until you actually fooled your own brain. This always took an immense feat of concentration, though it was easier to do it when you were lying on a battlefield nursing a wound than when you were hanging by weakening arms over a ninety-foot chasm.

Grunting with effort, he turned himself around and planted his feet against the wall. With his mail leggings gone, he only wore light felt shoes. Their soles lacked grip, but he had no choice. The climb that faced him was thirty feet at least and he couldn't manage that by the strength of his arms alone. His injured ankle felt as if hot coals were being crushed into it as he began the long upward walk, step by unsteady step. His shoulders seemed as though they were being wrenched from his torso, as he pulled himself along the rope. The palms of his hands were scored, blistered, already slippery with blood.

He wasn't long on the bricks. Soon his feet were on the timbers of the drawbridge, but that was no consolation. On this smoother surface, he began to slide and lose his purchase. Wind whistled around the side of the Keep, tugging at him, freezing his sweat. But he pushed on, refusing to think of the perilous drop at his back. He wasn't sure how far he had to go when the first axe buried itself in the wood alongside him. This gave him renewed impetus. A spear stuck to the left, and he climbed all the harder.

Now he was focussed on the grapple at the top of the rope, which was suddenly in sight. But the last ten feet were the worst. More missiles were flung, only missing him narrowly. His pain had become torturous – not just in his wracked limbs, but in his chest, where his heart thundered until fit to break, where his lungs wheezed as they dragged in so much air that he thought they would burst.

Ranulf knew he couldn't have gone much further when he finally clawed his fingers over the bridge's upper rim. His back muscles tightened like bowstrings as he hoisted his body up that last foot or so. Sweat poured into his eyes; his limbs were numbed by the strain, which didn't diminish even when he made it onto the top. For a moment he lay lengthwise, gazing back across the gulf. The dead were still watching from the timber gallery. Another of them threw something – a maul, which spun right at him, and might have shattered his skull had it not impacted on the brickwork above his head.

Slowly, shaking as though with fever, feeling hollow and bloodless throughout his body, Ranulf slid beneath the lintel and lowered himself into the Keep by his hands. He hung there briefly – it was still a significant distance to drop, ten feet or more - but finally he let go. He landed on the paved floor with foot-stinging force, dropping to his haunches and rolling.

When he sat up, still gasping for breath, he was in a stone passage lit by torches, which led to a stairway at its far end. There was a recess just to his left, which, as he'd suspected, contained a wheel-and-pulley system. The crank-handle had now been removed and a steel peg knocked into place, to lock the mechanism. Another room adjoined this, possibly a guardroom.

As Ranulf got to his feet, a figure in a studded leather jerkin emerged, carrying in one hand a scabbarded sword and in the other a large mallet. The figure, Haco, a surly, black-bearded type who served as one of the earl's men-at-arms, stopped dead when he saw Ranulf. He was so surprised that his mouth dropped open.

"Closing our doors a little prematurely, weren't we?" Ranulf said.

Haco threw the sword down, and took a wild swipe with his mallet. Ranulf ducked it, and looped an arm around Haco's neck, quickly walking him backward. Haco gargled for breath, lost his footing and fell. As he did, Ranulf slammed the back of his skull against the paving stones as hard as he could. Haco was left dazed, allowing Ranulf to snatch the mallet from his twitching hand, and apply two swift and fatal blows to his forehead.

Stripping the jerkin from the body, Ranulf donned it himself, cast the mallet aside and picked up the sword. It was a broadsword, heavier than Ranulf's longsword if several inches shorter. It was a less sophisticated weapon, but it would be easy enough to wield. Instead of a sword-belt, its scabbard was attached to a harness, and designed to be carried on the back. Ranulf fastened it into place, adjusted it slightly so that its cross-hilt was in reach over his left shoulder, and moved along the corridor into the depths of the Keep.

He was still fatigued beyond belief, still riddled with pain. But the new task he had set himself would not wait.

CHAPTER THIRTY-THREE

"Navarre!" Ranulf shouted, reaching the bottom of the penultimate stairway.

He was almost at the top of the Keep. He'd seen no major evidence of occupation on any of the levels he'd ascended through, which indicated how few men the earl had left. Since Haco, he'd encountered nobody at all – until now. Navarre, who was part way up the stair, turned in surprise. But that surprise didn't last. He grinned and descended again, loosening his sword in its sheath. He had removed his hauberk, but had retained his mail leggings, which were fastened over his homespun shirt with leather straps, so he was nearly as ill-attired for combat as Ranulf.

"FitzOsbern," Navarre said, sounding pleased. "I was hoping you'd get through."

"Damn shame *you* have, when so many decent men haven't."

"They all fell in a good cause."

"They fell because you and our dog of an overlord led them

to certain death. And in Gurt Louvain's case, because you murdered him."

Navarre pulled on his gauntlets. "Ah yes, Louvain. Well, I'm afraid he was being awkward."

Ranulf drew the sword from the scabbard on his back. "Then allow me to be the same."

Navarre grinned again. With his bisected face and mangled mouth, it was a picture of demonic evil.

"I'm so glad you said that, FitzOsbern." With a rasp of metal, he too drew his sword, swishing it back and forth in front of him. "Our overlord forbade this once, seeing some possible advantage in keeping you alive. But the time is past for uncertainties of that sort. Doubtless, he also wanted Doctor Zacharius to live, but, when the moment of truth came... well, these free-thinkers are an expensive luxury, are they not?"

"Zacharius? You killed... ?"

"Again, all in a good cause."

Stupefaction seeped through Ranulf like a slow poison. He could barely comprehend what he'd just heard.

"You cretinous oaf!" he roared. "Do you realise what you've done?"

"I know what I'm about to do. I'm about to rid Earl Corotocus of his last dedicated enemy. Compared to you and your nest of traitors, FitzOsbern, those creatures out there will be child's play."

"Navarre, even Corotocus doesn't deserve a madman like you!"

Navarre laughed. "Enough talking, FitzOsbern. On guard!"

They circled each other like cats, each man watching the other intently. It did not go unnoticed by Navarre that Ranulf was breathing heavily from his exertions below, and that he carried himself stiffly. This of course offered an advantage that a champion of Navarre's experience could not resist exploiting.

With a wild laugh, he struck first, jabbing his sword-point at Ranulf's face, though this was a feint. Typically sly, he'd also produced his dagger in his left hand, and this he now thrust at Ranulf's midriff. However, Ranulf saw this, and smashed the sword aside, before striking the dagger from Navarre's hand with a blow so fierce that it sent the weapon spinning into the shadows. Navarre snatched his hand back, scowling. Even tired, it seemed that FitzOsbern's main strengths, namely his supreme hand-eye co-ordination and the blistering speed of his ripostes, had not deserted him.

Navarre, who relied more on sheer power, stepped backward, but only to regain his balance in order to strike again, this time with a two-handed stroke from overhead. Ranulf fended it off with a mighty *clang*, but the impact dealt his shoulders a jolt that he felt all the way down his body. He realised that his limited energy was flagging already. If he were to survive this contest, he would have to end it quickly.

"You were never going to last through these border wars, FitzOsbern," Navarre scoffed. He struck again, but again Ranulf parried him. "A man with a conscience is a man who is fundamentally weak."

"And *you'll* last?" Ranulf grunted through gritted teeth, striking back swiftly. "You think there's any way out of this spider-hole your master has led you into?"

Navarre didn't immediately reply. Again, the speed of Ranulf's counter-blows had taken him by surprise. His teeth too were now gritted, his facial groove so red and enflamed that it looked set to crack open.

"Loyalty to one's lord is all," he snarled. "Betrayal of that creed merits ignominious death!"

Their blades clashed furiously as the fight spilled along the passage, sweat spraying from their brows, sparks flashing in the dimness. But Ranulf's growing exhaustion was giving his opponent the upper hand. Blow after heavy blow rained down on him. It was all he could do to fend them off, never mind retaliate. At last he was backed against a row of iron bars. Sensing victory, Navarre stepped forward with a demented grimace, and lunged hard at Ranulf's chest – only for Ranulf, with his last ounce of stamina, to step nimbly aside. Navarre's sword-arm passed through the bars and wedged there – just briefly, but long enough for Ranulf to turn and slash down hard, severing the limb at its shoulder.

Navarre didn't have time to scream.

The second stroke took his legs from under him, shearing them at the knees. The third was a downward thrust, delivered as he lay on his back, piercing him clean through the middle of his grotesque face, finally splitting it apart into the two separate hemispheres that for so long it had desired to be.

The sudden silence in that dark passage was ear pummelling. The echoing clangour of blade on blade dissipated quickly in the Keep's far reaches.

Ranulf sank to his knees, gasping, leaning on his upright sword. So tired was he that he thought he would pass out. Sweat dripped from his chin, blood trickled from his numerous cuts, all reopened through sheer effort. Many moments passed before he was able to shift away and fall onto his side. More time passed as he lay there, the painful beating in his chest subsiding with torturous slowness. At length, he looked up and took in his surroundings. From somewhere overhead, he could hear a booming and derisive voice. He knew this could only mean one thing.

Earl Corotocus had entered negotiations.

Gazing down from the top of the Keep at Grogen Castle was like gazing from some colossal escarpment. From this dizzying height, the surrounding mountains were more like foothills. The broad flow of the river, sparkling so magnificently in the rising sun, resembled a garden stream. The rest of the castle's ramparts were so far below they looked like an artist's miniature.

But Earl Corotocus felt neither superior nor confident as he stood on this lofty perch. He didn't even feel as if he occupied a strong position. The entire rest of the fortress –its bailey, its walks, its battlements and towers – were crammed with cohorts of deranged, howling cadavers. They were packed so tightly in the courtyard that scarcely an inch of ground was visible. The same was true of the encircling landscape, at least to the north of the Tefeidiad. The western bluff was hidden beneath a tide of human flotsam. On the sweeping northern moor a host was gathered so immense that it seemed without limit. Even if it hadn't struck Corotocus before, it struck him now that an army of the dead was the largest army that could ever be assembled – for on the Anglo-welsh border, in Wales, and in much of England as well, there was no end to those unjustly slain or deprived to the point where death came too early. Even King Edward, with all the arms he could muster, would have difficulty hewing his way through so vast a multitude.

For this reason, if none other, the earl had now decided – somewhat belatedly, he supposed, though he would never admit it to his retainers – to parley. Ninety yards to his west, on what remained of the Constable's Tower roof, stood several recognisable figures: the statuesque form of Countess Madalyn, with her flowing red hair and imperious aura, and the hooded figures of her priestly acolytes. As these self-appointed leaders stared back at him, possibly realising the stalemate they had at last come to, their monstrous followers fell eerily silent.

"I repeat, Countess Madalyn," Earl Corotocus boomed. "Your forces will never enter this last bastion. They will dash themselves to pieces on its walls, or decompose until they are bones and slurry before the slightest breach is incurred."

Corotocus knew they'd understand this. Time was the one thing an army of the dead lacked. The earl's men, who had only been able to stock enough supplies for a couple of weeks at the most, would eventually die famished or parched. But the besiegers would rot. It seemed an even bet which would be the quicker process.

"You cannot storm us!" The earl's confidence grew as he continued to bellow down to them. "My mighty mangonels will make no impact on these impregnable walls, even if you could manoeuvre them into a suitable position. As you can see, the only possible ingress is via the west or south drawbridges. Maybe you think you can batter these down and create bridges of your own, as you did at the Gatehouse? But I defy you to try, countess. In both cases, the buildings closest to these bridges, the baronial State Rooms and the North Hall, are made from timber and wattle, and have thatched roofs. That was a deliberate ploy by the designers of this castle. I need only have flaming arrows shot down upon them and those structures will burn to ashes. Part of your army will be consumed. The rest will remain as they are now, helpless even to get close to us."

The earl looked around at his men. They were huddled behind him, maybe thirty in total. They were a craven looking bunch: wounded, filthy, red-eyed with fear and exhaustion. Knights were indistinguishable from men-at-arms. Even so, they regarded him with awe. They had come into this place knowing it was their last refuge, believing it would only delay the certainty of death. But now their master's words gave them hope. Could it be that he was speaking truthfully? Had he again plucked them from the jaws of disaster?

He turned back to shout again. "Your only option, Countess Madalyn, is to withdraw. Return your army to the soil from whence it came and await the king's judgement, which I assure you will be fair."

He was surprised when the voice that called back was not Countess Madalyn's, but that of a man. It was deep and melodious, with a Welsh accent and a strong note of authority.

"Earl Corotocus, Countess Madalyn no longer deems you a worthy negotiator. All of your former promises proved to be false."

"Who speaks?" the earl shouted.

"You must produce a different spokesman."

"Who speaks, I say?"

"I am Gwyddon, Countess Madalyn's senior counsellor. You no longer have a part to play here, Earl Corotocus. Until you produce someone whose word we can trust, you and your men remain under sentence of death."

"You insolent dog!"

"Which sentence to be carried out at the first opportunity."

The earl rounded on his men, scarlet-faced. "Bring her forward!"

Gwendolyn of Lyr, her head held proudly, was brought out from the bedraggled ranks and led to the parapet, where the earl ordered her to stand in one of the embrasures. She was pushed so close to its brink that her toes curled around it. Once there, he had her hands twisted behind her back and bound to an iron ring set into the stonework. Of course, this small safety measure could not be seen by the figures on the Constable's Tower. All they saw was a girlish figure, naked save for a red and blue harlequin cloak, standing on the edge of extinction.

Again, Corotocus shouted across the courtyard. "You think I won't cast this child down, countess? Surely you know me better than that?"

"Mother!" Gwendolyn called in her native language, certain that none of her captors would understand her. "Do not listen to them. They will not risk it. They have just secured..."

Corotocus himself leapt up alongside her and thrust the tip of his dagger under her chin. "Silence, you little harridan!" His Welsh was imperfect but adequate. "Hold that tongue, or I'll slit it down the middle and leave you with two!"

Gwendolyn clamped her mouth shut, but blinked fiercely, determined to eradicate any tears caused by the gusting wind. She was determined the English would not think her afraid. The earl gazed back to the Constable's Tower, but saw no obvious consternation. Countess Madalyn was close to the battlements, watching intently, but the priest who had spoken – the one called Gwyddon – was conferring with his henchmen, almost casually. Finally there were nods of agreement from the priests, and they wrestled forward two figures of their own, placing them in embrasures as well. By these prisoners' livery – a surcoat of blue and white chevrons and a crimson tabard bearing three golden lions – they were Walter Margas and Davy Gou.

Corotocus and his men were startled to see that any of their comrades had been taken alive, though both prisoners were streaked with char and ordure. They stood boldly, their chins upraised, but shivered with pain and fear. If Corotocus had been close enough, he'd have seen Margas's cheek hanging in a bloody flap, exposing his clenched molars.

"An awkward situation," du Guesculin said quietly.

Corotocus gave him a withering look, before turning to his other men. Two of his household archers were still in possession of their longbows and had quivers containing a few arrows each. He signalled them.

"Make sure your aim is good," he said.

At one time, such a cryptic order would have left them bewildered. But under these circumstances, there seemed no question about what was being demanded of them. Both bowmen stepped forward, knocked arrows and let fly. They had had much target practice over the last few days. Perhaps this explained why both shafts hit cleanly, one striking Margas in the middle of his chest, penetrating to his heart, the other catching Gou in the throat, sinking to its feathers.

The two corpses crashed from the parapet, turning over and over as they plummeted into the courtyard.

There was no word of complaint from Corotocus's men, all of them having moved unconsciously into that dark, soulless realm where the loss of any life is a price worth paying if it might save your own.

"Have you any more for me, countess?" Corotocus laughed. "I have plenty of arrows."

"Such is the reward for blind loyalty," came a weary voice.

Corotocus spun around. Gwendolyn looked too, surprised to hear a familiar tone.

Ranulf trudged forward from the door connecting with the lower levels. His face was haggard, damp with seat. His clothing and the blade of his drawn broadsword were both spattered crimson. Corotocus in particular looked stunned. He glanced past Ranulf through the doorway behind, at which Ranulf chuckled.

"Don't waste your time looking for Navarre, my lord. He's already in Hell. Which is where you'll soon be."

"Archers!" du Guesculin shouted.

The two bowmen stepped forward, fresh arrows knocked to their strings.

"So this is the great marcher baron!" Ranulf scoffed. "Who, even when his world has come to an end, sends other men to fight for him."

"You betrayed us, Ranulf!" Corotocus growled, pointing a shaking finger.

"That's not how I see it."

"You would have delivered us all to those things."

"No!" Ranulf said, pointing back. "I would have delivered *you*!" He turned to the rest of the company. "Would any man here object to that, if it meant that you would be saved? Are the bonds of fealty so tight that, on this man's orders, you would strike blow after blow against the innocent and then take his punishment for him?"

There was no response.

There were still one or two honourable knights among this wretched band – men who had held vigils, gone on quests, ridden in the tournaments wearing the colours of fine ladies. But all were now grizzled, begrimed, stained over and over with their own gore and the gore of others. They were more like sewer rats than men. Reduced to this forlorn state, perhaps it was no surprise that none seemed willing to side with him. The only safety they knew, and it was a slim one at that, lay with their overlord.

"If you fall defending this stronghold," Ranulf asked them, "what do you think will happen to Earl Corotocus when the king arrives? He may be punished for stirring up a hornet's nest the like of which the world has never seen. But what will that punishment involve? The confiscation of estates? A money fine? *You* meanwhile will be dead! Everyone you ever served with will be dead! Or worse – enslaved for eternity by satanic magic, forbidden entry to God's kingdom."

"You speak treason" someone cried, fear making him angry. "Not just against the earl, but against the king."

There were mumbles of agreement. Others too began to shout and hurl abuse. Ranulf hung his head tiredly. He didn't suppose he could blame them. Most here owed everything they had to Earl Corotocus. They knew no other life.

"He is indeed a traitor," du Guesculin said, venturing forward now that he could see there was no fight left in this rebel. "But he sins not just against the king. He's allied himself to these demons... to Lucifer himself."

Ranulf shook his head with contempt. "You're a liar, du Guesculin. You're the worst liar of all, because you've seen what this madman's cruelty and tyranny has brought, and still you side with him."

"For crimes against God there can be no forgiveness," du Guesculin retorted. "Archers..."

"Wait!" Corotocus shouted. After initially seeming afraid, albeit very fleetingly, he'd now re-assumed his air of lordly confidence. When he spoke again, it was in an even, almost affable tone. "I don't necessarily share that view, du Guesculin. That certain evils cannot be forgiven. God does not share it either."

"My lord, I..." du Guesculin protested.

"Silence!"

Corotocus eyed Ranulf as he walked around him. Ranulf still had his broadsword and could have cut his overlord down at a whim. At this proximity, even two flying arrows couldn't have prevented it. But as always – and Ranulf cursed himself for this – he felt it important to know what Earl Corotocus was about to say next.

"Did you really slay Navarre?" the earl asked. He sounded impressed.

"It was the easiest but worthiest accomplishment of my life," Ranulf replied.

"Hmmm. I understand your feelings. He was a difficult fellow. He always felt challenged by you, of course. At least it's been settled in the honourable way."

"You're out of your mind, la Hors."

"Possibly, Ranulf, possibly."

"You should kill me now, my lord, because when I'm able to I will surely kill you."

"Let's not be too hasty. There's a method even to my madness." The earl put a thumb to his chin as he pondered. "Seeing as you've accounted for Navarre, I'm afraid it now falls to you to complete his final task."

"I don't take orders from you any more."

Corotocus sighed. "I see. Well, answer me this... do you wish what remains of our company to die? Do you wish them torn apart on these ramparts, or trapped in this place until they're forced to feed on each other? Is your hatred of me so irrational

that you would sacrifice what's left of your comrades to so
ghoulish a fate?"

Ranulf glanced at the rest of the men. Their expressions had
changed, the hostility of a few moments ago replaced by an
intense, childlike fear.

"There may be one or two worth saving," he said.

Corotocus laughed. "And it won't be difficult for a warrior
like you to do it." He moved back to the battlements, looking
down towards the Constable's Tower, where Gwyddon and the
other druids were still in debate. "As you can see, Ranulf, we've
reached an impasse. But I have a plan to break it, one that will
save all our lives. Unfortunately, when we leave here... someone
will have to stay behind to keep charge of this hostage. Navarre
didn't know it, but he was due to be volunteered."

"The generosity with which you reward your servants knows
no end," Ranulf said.

"Serving me is its own reward. Or so I'm told. But let's assume
that *you* volunteer for this task. It won't be as onerous for you
as it would have been for Navarre, you having already made an
alliance with these creatures, or at least with their mistress."

"That didn't go quite as I planned," Ranulf admitted.

Corotocus gave him a frank stare. "The alternative is that I
push this girl over the edge right now, because she'd be no use
to us any more."

Ranulf said nothing. There was nothing he *could* say. Yet again
the earl's wiles had backed him into a corner. Pleased, the earl
leaned over the battlements and again bellowed to the group on
the Constable's Tower.

"You can cease that pointless gabble!"

The druids turned and regarded him.

"There is nothing for you to discuss!" Corotocus shouted. "The
situation is perfectly simple. If you try to enter this Keep, the
girl will be thrown to her death. If you refuse my men and I
permission to leave safely, she will starve with the rest of us. And
if you ever again presume to bypass my authority to negotiate
with my underlings, she will die under a flensing knife."

They made no reply.

"Am I clear?"

Still they made no reply. Gwendolyn shot the earl a scornful look. Corotocus noticed this, and for a second Ranulf thought that he was going to drive his dagger into her back. But again the earl kept control of himself. In truth, Corotocus, though he could sense his men watching, witnessing this continued disrespect, knew that he was not in as strong a bargaining position as they might believe. He could not keep the Welsh girl standing on this parapet forever. Brave as she doubtless was, she was half-naked, shivering and weak from lack of sustenance. If she collapsed in full view of her mother, even though safely tied, it could have a disastrous effect.

"My terms are these, countess!" he called down. "They are non-negotiable, but under the circumstances I think they are generous. My retainers and I are leaving Grogen Castle. You will have your creatures clear a path for us. That path will remain clear until we are far from this place. In the meantime, your child will remain here on the brink of oblivion. If any attempt is made to interfere with us, she will be pushed to her death. If any attempt is made to halt our retreat along the river – and be assured, from this vantage point we can see as far as the English border – she will be pushed to her death. However, once we have departed safely, the man I leave behind will stand down and you may retrieve your child unharmed."

"I have to give you credit, my lord," Ranulf said. "When it comes to saving your own arse, you're quite the genius."

"I meant what I said, Ranulf," the earl replied. "About liking men who tell me the truth. If you survive this, there's still a place for you at my court."

"I doubt your court will be around for very much longer. Even if you get away from here, what's to stop this horde sweeping over the border after you?"

"The bachelry of England. What else?"

Ranulf shook his head. "I'm not sure even the bachelry of England will be enough."

"Earl Corotocus!" a voice echoed up from the Constable's Tower. It was Gwyddon again. "By the good grace of Countess

Madalyn of Lyr, you and your men may leave Grogen Castle. She gives her word that you will not be molested so long as her daughter is safe."

Corotocus treated his men to a satisfied smile. A few managed to return it.

"Then we have our truce." he called back. "But first I have one more demand."

"Speak."

"Our horses. We will not walk from here like yeomen farmers. We will ride out as we rode in, knights."

There was a pause, and then: "That is acceptable."

The earl nodded, turned to his men and pulled his gauntlets on. "Ready yourselves. Take only your weapons. No supplies – those will only weigh us down. Once we're away from here, we can gallop to the border."

There was a slow bustle as it gradually dawned on the men that their ordeal might be coming to an end. A few stood dazed, not totally believing it.

"Move yourselves!" the earl shouted, his voice a whip-crack. "This window of opportunity may be brief."

Ranulf walked to the battlements. Despite the deal that had just been struck, he was surprised to see a long, meandering alleyway clearing through the mob filling the courtyard. It led from the base of the Keep to the ramp entering the Constable's Tower. Beyond that, he could see a similar space being made along the causeway. With a whinnying and clopping of hooves, horses, made skittish by the stench of their lumbering grooms, were brought from the stable blocks and led to the bottom of the steps at the Keep entrance.

"How can you agree to this?" Gwendolyn hissed at Ranulf, her eyes filled with emerald fire.

"It doesn't please you?" He was surprised. "This way, everyone gets what they want."

"Except justice."

"How much justice are you looking for? Most of those men who came here and violated your people are dead."

"And the one who commanded it? What will happen to him?"

Ranulf shook his head, peering over the parapet again. "I'm more concerned about what will happen to me. How much control does your mother have over these creatures?"

Gwendolyn glanced down as well. Only now did she really seem to focus on the army that had come to liberate her; she found it impossible not to cringe at some of the things she saw.

"There's a good chance," Ranulf said, "that once the earl is gone and the Keep thrown open, their vanguard will ascend to this roof before your mother does. Will they listen to orders from you? I find that doubtful."

Gwendolyn shrugged. "You've played your part in this tragedy, sir knight. What will happen to you will happen."

"Well that's encouraging..."

"What in the name of Heaven do you expect?"

"I want Corotocus punished too," he whispered. "It's because of him that my father died and my friend was murdered. If I survive this thing, I would like to be the one who follows him to England and exacts vengeance."

"And I should give you the means?" She snorted with derision. "You think that because you are slightly more enlightened than most English knights, that means I like you? Even for the small part you've played in the disaster that has destroyed my country, I loathe and detest you."

"You little ingrate!"

She turned pointedly away from him.

"Ranulf!" Corotocus said, returning. He'd now donned a full basinet helm with an open visor, and wore a fresh cloak and tabard over his mail. His longsword hung at his left hip and a two-headed battle-axe at his right. "I trust you aren't thinking of abandoning your post while we're in the process of leaving this place?"

"That's something you'll find out for yourself when you try to leave," Ranulf said.

"Very clever," Corotocus sneered. "But I know you, boy. And I know your conscience. If you let this girl loose or even neglect to guard her so that she gets loose of her own accord, there'll be nothing to stop her calling across the castle that she's safe. If we aren't away from here by then, these monstrosities will fall on us like mad beasts."

"My lord, why don't you just leave while your household thinks you're wonderful? Because when you get back to England, they'll begin to realise the depth of your defeat, and then you'll be regarded somewhat differently."

Corotocus chuckled. "Don't make the mistake of thinking this is over, Ranulf." He turned to Gwendolyn. "Nor you, you Welsh harlot! This affair isn't over."

Gwendolyn didn't deign to look at him.

"Your people have won the battle," he said, "but not the war. We'll be back, and there'll be the devil to pay. Now mind what I say, Ranulf. Neglect your duty here and these hell-hounds could fall on us when we're most vulnerable."

"Why tar everyone with your own brush, my lord? Countess Madalyn gave you her word as a noblewoman that you would have safe passage."

"No... Ranulf." Corotocus shook his head pensively. "No. That Welsh wizard gave me his word. I don't know what that means exactly, but it disconcerts me a little."

Corotocus moved away, descending the stair. Du Guesculin and the rest of the household filed quickly after him.

Puzzling over that final comment, Ranulf looked across the courtyard to the roof of the Constable's Tower, where Countess Madalyn stood as she had before against the battlements. She had not moved since he had first arrived here. Neither, as far as he had seen, had she joined the debates of her underlings, though that did not necessarily mean that she hadn't issued quiet commands to them, as she undoubtedly would in normal times. However, for some intangible reason, Ranulf now felt a creeping chill in his bones. Why was she so still? Why had she not led the negotiations herself? It was not Countess Madalyn's way, he was sure, to leave something so important to somebody else. But neither, he thought with a shiver, was it Gwyddon's way.

CHAPTER THIRTY-FOUR

EARL COROTOCUS UNDERSTOOD the importance of appearance.

The new cloak and tabard he'd donned were thus far unsullied. The black and crimson of his household devices glittered in the dimness of the Keep's interior. He brushed as much grime, dust and blood as he could from his battle-scarred mail. He'd even fluffed the crimson plume projecting from the crest of his helm. When he reached the Keep's lowest level, he strolled fearlessly along the stone passage to its main entrance, his spurs clinking on the flagged floor, one gloved hand clamped on the hilt of his sword. The men – those living, who now cowered nervously behind him, and those dead, who waited outside in silent expectation – had to know without being told that Corotocus was of a superior caste. It was essential he cut a striking figure, so they'd realise immediately that, by his very nature, this was a man untroubled by the events of recent days, a man who took torment and destruction in his stride because it was part of his born duty to do so.

As well as appearance, Earl Corotocus also understood the importance of propaganda.

"The battle is now over and, because of me, you fellows have survived," he said, turning to his household in front of the main portal.

Their faces were milk-pale in the gloom.

"This time yesterday, you were staring annihilation in the face. But now I have bought your futures back for you. Remember that when you are far from this place. Each one of you here owes me more than he could ever repay in a thousand lifetimes."

"They'll gladly devote the remainder of this lifetime attempting it," du Guesculin replied.

Corotocus eyed them sternly, as if daring anyone to disagree. He straightened the edges of his cloak and turned back around. "Lower the drawbridge."

With an echoing rattle of chains, the timber gate was lowered. Daylight flooded in, making them all blink. The reek of death followed, thick as swamp mist; the men choked and gagged. Up until now they had not come face to face with so concentrated a mass of their enemy.

Earl Corotocus's face, however, showed neither disgust nor revulsion. He walked boldly over the bridge, his hollow footfalls resounding across the otherwise silent castle, until he had reached the top of the steps, at which point he halted and gazed down.

The dead gazed back, rank after close-packed rank. Straight away, there were those among them he recognised. Craon Culai, with his body so crushed that only his face was distinguishable; Odo de Lussac, burned almost to a crisp, a crossbow bolt projecting from his charred mouth; Ramon la Roux, an arrow still embedded in his heart. Even Father Benan was present; he seemed to have dressed himself in hanging rags, thick with blood and mucus, until the earl realised that these were actually remnants of his own flesh. Most bizarrely, the priest's iron crucifix protruded from the top of his skull, where it appeared to have been hammered into place. Others were indistinguishable even as human, horrible remnants of men and women who had died by axe, sword, spear or noose, or whose torn and forgotten husks had lain mouldering in the ground for weeks, feasted on by worms and maggots. Every sickly colour in the spectrum was represented: blue faces, white faces, green faces, black faces, yellow faces, purple faces. There were faces without skin, skulls without hair. Were it summer, the earl imagined this ghastly host would be engulfed in swarming flies. No doubt countless such vermin were already hatching from the clusters of eggs lodged in their pulped flesh and yawning sockets.

Despite this, he walked casually down the steps, to where a troop of thirty or so horses was waiting. By good fortune, the nearest was his own black stallion, Incitatus, a powerful battle-steed bred and trained to smash through lines of infantry, though the challenge this time would be to keep the tempestuous brute in a relaxed state. To Corotocus's surprise, the dead had even saddled it for him, correctly. In fact, they'd saddled all of the horses. He glanced towards the stables, and there saw Osric, his former groom, a reaping hook buried in the side of his neck, standing by the open door – as if in death he'd automatically re-assumed the role he'd played in life. Just to be sure, the earl checked that his saddle was secure and that his animal's bit was in place before climbing into his stirrups.

Others of his company were now descending after him, but they were stiff with terror, clinging together like children. Almost invariably, they scurried frantically down the last few steps, grabbing the first mount they could, and vaulting onto its back.

The passage across the courtyard was still open, but looked narrower than it had from above. It would not be easy traversing it with an army of standing corpses ranked to either side. Corotocus peered to the top of the Constable's Tower. The rigid shape of Countess Madalyn gazed down at him, her priests alongside her. There was no conversation between them now. Their attention was fixed unswervingly on the departing English.

"Hurry," the earl said to his men, the last few of whom were traipsing down the steps.

Wheeling Incitatus around, the earl set off first, walking the animal at a steady pace. The passage was so narrow that, at most, they could travel only two abreast. Du Guesculin hastened forward to be alongside his master. Aside from the clopping of hooves and timorous snuffling of brutes, there was no sound at all, which, now that they were so close to their foe, was not surprising – for there was clearly no more life in these beings than there was in strips of hanging leather or piled-up cords of wood. They were inanimate, soulless; genuinely nothing more than mummified carcasses cut from gibbets or ploughed up from burial pits. Except that, as the English passed, their heads slowly turned, tracking each departing horseman one by one.

"My lord, will we face this gauntlet of the damned all the way to England?" du Guesculin said, in a whisper made hoarse by fear.

Earl Corotocus didn't respond. For all his bravado, his mouth was too dry to form words; his back was so straight that it hurt. When he tried to release his hand from the hilt of his sword he found that he couldn't. The fingers had locked in place.

"My lord, I said..."

"I heard you the first time!"

"Will we?"

"Who am I, God? What more to you want of me? I've gained you a free passport, haven't I?"

"A passport to what?" du Guesculin wondered.

CHAPTER THIRTY-FIVE

"At least untie me," Gwendolyn protested. "There's no blood left in my fingers."

Ranulf, the only other person left on the Keep roof, peered down the wall to where Corotocus and his company were now snaking slowly and warily across the courtyard. He glanced towards her, distracted.

"If I do, you must stay in sight," he said. "Your mother needs to know you are safe."

"You really are a good little English soldier, aren't you?"

He bristled at that. "Now you mention it, yes! Just because I sympathise with your position, don't make the mistake of thinking I'd serve every Englishman I know to your vengeance."

"Cut me loose, please."

Reluctantly, he sawed through her hempen bonds with his sword. She stepped back from the embrasure, and leaned tiredly on the left crenel, rubbing at the wheals on her wrists.

She still wore only the red and blue cloak they had given her on the first day. The wind set it rippling on her lithe form.

"You must be frozen," he said.

"You finally notice now?"

"Wait here." He turned and, several yards away, spotted the black and red tabard that Earl Corotocus had discarded when he'd changed. It was torn in places and stained with grime, but it was made from heavy wool and at least it could be worn as a proper piece of clothing.

He handed it to her. "If you can bring yourself to wear these household colours, you should find this more comfortable and a little less revealing. Put the cloak back on over the top and you'll be warm enough."

She took the item from him, now looking thoughtful. "You're not too bad a fellow, sir knight. I've decided that I *will* speak up for you."

He shrugged. "Assuming anyone will listen."

She made to remove her current garb, but then saw that he was watching her.

"If you'd avert your eyes please?"

Ranulf was surprised. "You plan to change here and now? Getting undressed in front of your mother's army is probably not the best idea."

"To offend someone's eyes, they need to have eyes in the first place, do they not?"

Ranulf shrugged again, and turned his back. He peeked over the battlements. The earl and his men were half way across the courtyard, the earl riding tall in the saddle. Ahead of them, the ramp leading up to the Constable's Tower door had also cleared. Far above that, Countess Madalyn and her priests watched, unmoving. Behind him, Ranulf could hear a rustling of cloth.

"I fear Earl Corotocus means what he says," he said. "He'll seek restitution of some sort."

"And we Welsh won't?" Gwendolyn replied.

"Revenge and counter-revenge are a recipe for disaster, my lady. They've made life on these marches intolerable for too long already."

"I agree. So we should end it now, no?"

He smiled. "If only that were possible."

"Wasn't it you who told me that, with sacrifice, anything is possible?"

There was a slight inflection in her voice as she said this, a sudden decisiveness, which made him spin around. As he did, Gwendolyn screamed long and loud. Ranulf was stunned by what he saw.

She had donned the earl's tabard, as he'd suggested, but instead of putting the blue and red cloak over the top of it, she had wrapped this around one of the Breton mannequins – and had now flung that mannequin over the battlements. She continued to scream as it fell, at the same time making sure to step well back from the parapet.

Earl Corotocus thought his eyes were deceiving him.

Even though the object seemed to fall unnaturally slowly, its blue and red cloak billowing like sail cloth, there was no doubt what it was. Its legs were splayed, its arms spread-eagled. The ear-piercing scream lingered on the rancid air, only to be silenced when the object vanished into the dry moat. At first Corotocus was numbed to near immobility. When he finally glanced up again, the unmistakeable shape of Ranulf FitzOsbern was hunched over the Keep battlements.

In that astonishing moment, the world came to a standstill for the Earl of Clun and his remaining household. Each one of them was fixed to his saddle, each one swallowed air the way a parched man swallows water.

Corotocus looked back along his procession of followers. To a man their faces were stark white, beaded with sweat, their eyes bugging. If any were conversing he couldn't hear them thanks to the thunderous roar of his own blood in his ears.

As a wail of anguished rage sounded overhead from the roof of the Constable's Tower, the earl banged his visor shut and, putting his spurs to his horse's sides, urged the beast into a furious gallop. The ramp and open portcullis were only twenty yards ahead of him and he was sure that he could make it through. As he did, he glanced over his shoulder. Du Guesculin was close behind, his face shining wet as he spurred his own steed mercilessly. But now corpses were stirring to demonic life, surging in from both sides, trying to close the passage – against which odds, the rest of the men were too far behind to even have a hope. In ones and twos, they were encircled, their horses whinnying hysterically, lashing out with their hooves, smashing the faces and skulls of their assailants but, as always, to no avail. One by one, the riders were pulled screaming from their saddles and hurled to the floor, whereupon axes, spades, clubs, maces, flails and falchions rained on them in a blur of blood, brains and exploding bone fragments.

Corotocus made it as far as the Constable's Tower ramp before a party of the dead blocked his route. Framed in the V-shaped viewing slot of his visor, this group actually resembled soldiers. They wore steel-studded jerkins and iron caps and had pikes, which they tried to lower to form a hedge.

"Incitatus, the field!" he bellowed, his voice sounding brazen from the confines of his helm.

This was a battle cry his steed was familiar with from many occasions in the past. Before the pikes could be arrayed, it had crashed clean through, scattering the figures like skittles. One tried to grab the bridle, but, with a single blow of his axe, Corotocus severed its arm at the shoulder. Another snatched the horse's tail, only to be dragged along behind, Incitatus's flying hooves kicking it continually in the face, reducing it to mulch. Still the thing clung on, and finally, as it had been trained, the animal pivoted around and trampled the hapless passenger into a carpet of shredded flesh and bone. Again, Corotocus focussed on du Guesculin, who was close behind but was having trouble making further progress. The dead were hampering him from all sides. His horse reared in terror rather than ploughing forward, which attracted more and more of them to him.

Pleased, Corotocus spun his animal round again and charged up the ramp, through the arched entrance to the Constable's Tower and along its main passage, where the clashing of his hooves echoed like hammers on anvils. All the way, he fought fiercely with those corpses attempting to hinder him. Gripping Incitatus with his knees, he wielded his axe in his left hand and his sword in his right. None of his dead foes were mounted, of course, which gave him a huge advantage, though again and again they stood in his path and had to be barged out of the way.

Frantic cries for help drew his attention back to the rear, where, incredibly, du Guesculin had also made it into the building. Corpses were still running alongside the banneret, trying to pull him down. One fell beneath his horse's legs, tripping it. The animal skidded on its knees over the cobblestones, shrieking as hair and skin was flayed from its joints. As it righted itself, du Guesculin cried again for his master's assistance, laying desperately about him on all sides, fighting as hard as he'd ever fought. But those dead in the passage who had unsuccessfully attempted to waylay the first rider now switched their attention to the second.

This was the opportunity Corotocus needed, he realised. Spurring his mount, he galloped on towards the open portcullis at the far end. Another corpse stepped into his path – a near-giant bristling with arrows, who the earl was sure he'd personally had lashed to a tree and shot to death at a village not far from here. The giant was swinging a mighty poll-arm around its head, but, with pure knightly skill, the earl wove around the ponderous figure, burying his sword in its cranium as he passed. Now he had only his battle-axe, but this was all he needed. As he approached the portcullis, he glanced into the right-hand alcove where its main mechanism was contained. A wedge had been hammered into the central wheel. The earl flung his axe at it as he hurtled by – and struck clean. The wedge was dislodged and, as he rode beneath the portcullis, its great iron structure, still bent and twisted from the dead army's attack on it, began rumbling downward. Its impact on the cobbled floor reverberated through the entire tower, halting du Guesculin only a few yards short of freedom.

Corotocus glanced around one last time as he galloped along the causeway. Behind the iron grille, he caught a final glimpse of his lieutenant's despairing face.

"My gift to you!" Corotocus said under his breath. "Go and feed on *him*! He'll make a meal for all of you!"

Du Guesculin chopped wildly at the sea of decay that ebbed around him. The portcullis was so warped at its base that he might have been able to slide his body beneath it. But that would have meant having to dismount.

A claw now took hold of his cloak. He cut the tie, shrugging the garment loose, and, with no other choice, drove his animal back into the bowels of the building, still hacking them down, stomping over those that fell, breaking their limbs and torsos, grinding them into the stones, but having to stand in the stirrups to avoid taking blows himself, and now – suddenly – stopping and gaping with horror. For a veritable flood of black and twisted forms was pouring down the passage towards him, their howls a dirge from the lowest level of damnation.

All-consuming terror had now cost du Guesculin his sense of place and direction, so, when he veered his animal to the right through a very narrow doorway, he had no idea that this was the foot of a spiral stair leading to the roof. Of course, when he discovered the truth, there was no turning back.

It was a perilous ascent for a four-footed beast, rising steeply, turning, turning, turning. Around each corner there was another shambling horror to block his path. He knocked each one aside, or smote it down, their blood and brains splattering up the granite walls as his blade bit through them. But always they were back on their feet quickly, and he heard their echoing ululation as they hastened in pursuit. And then, when du Guesculin thought that things could not get worse, he entered that upper region of the Constable's Tower where destruction had been wrought by the mangonels.

Suddenly he was in open rooms crammed with piles of rubble and burned, blistered body parts. Dust clouds still hung here, obscuring almost everything. Crushed, crab-like shapes clambered or slithered towards him over the mounds of masonry. One of these was still able to stand on two feet and grabbed his bridle. Du Guesculin peered down at Gilbert, his own squire, though he only realised this when he saw the grimy red hose and tunic. The boy's face had melted like cheese and hung from his naked skull in loops and tendrils.

The now deranged horse tried to retreat, but its footing slipped, and suddenly it was sliding backward as the scorched floorboards gave way beneath it. Du Guesculin just had time to leap from the saddle as his mount disappeared, screaming, into the dusty spaces below. Twenty feet down, with a shattering *crack*, its spine struck a stone buttress, which sent it spinning, lifeless, into a void of darkness that was filled with the shrieks of the dead.

Du Guesculin, himself teetering on the edge of the hole, turned on his heel just in time to see the apparition that had once been Gilbert lurching at him, hands outstretched. He drove his sword into its breast, but this did not hold the thing back. Gasping, he spun around and stumbled away, tripping and landing on his knees with such force that one kneecap was split to the cartilage. Choking at the pain, he lumbered on. Another stairway appeared through the gloom, this one leading to the open sky.

Du Guesculin sobbed his way up it. At the top, he found himself on the roof, huge sections of which had imploded from the impact of the mangonel missiles. Beyond the first of these crevasses, Countess Madalyn's druids were ranged in a row: pitiless men – bearded and stern beneath their hoods, their onyx eyes fixed on him intently. On his side, stood the countess herself.

Blubbering spittle, gibbering for mercy, du Guesculin tottered towards her.

"Countess, I beg you, I beg you..."

He dropped to his knees despite the agony this caused him, clasped his hands together and gazed up at her, though his vision was blurred with tears.

"I am Hugh du Guesculin, banneret of Clun, Lord of Oswestry and Whitchurch. I am not without influence. And unlike Earl Corotocus, I can be trusted. Ma-am, listen, please, I beg you. I know King Edward. I can parley for you. I can end this war so that Wales remains with the Welsh, with you as their queen. I can do all this. I beg you, ma-am, listen to me please."

She reached down with both hands and cupped his face, almost gently. He blinked, not understanding what this meant. Slowly, her features swam into focus. They were as handsome and noble as he remembered. But they were also pale and rigid as wax. Beneath her aristocratic chin, a crimson line ran from one ear to the other. When she exerted the necessary strength to drag him to his feet and hoist him into the air, that line yawned open, exposing her sliced windpipe. With eyes of lustreless glass, she strode to the battlements. Du Guesculin's scream was a prolonged, keening whistle as, with one hand at his throat and the other at his crotch, she raised him high over her head.

He continued to scream even when she'd flung him over the parapet, the scream lingering as he plummeted – down, down, down, head first, legs kicking manically, until landing with horrific force on the courtyard floor, where he smashed apart like a beetle under a boot.

From the roof of the Keep, Ranulf watched aghast as these events unfolded. But if it shocked him to the core to see what remained of the earl's household torn to pieces in the courtyard, it was an even greater shock to see what happened to Hugh du Guesculin.

Ranulf turned stiffly to face Gwendolyn. She regarded him boldly, her smudged but beautiful face written with triumph.

"No doubt you're enraged?" she said. "Well, now perhaps you understand how I feel. Justice had to be done."

He stalked towards her.

She didn't flinch. "Now that the guilty ones have been punished, this is where it can end."

"Indeed?"

"Indeed," she said. "You'll thank me for it in due course."

Ranulf didn't say anything else, just hit her – not hard enough to kill her, though he was sorely tempted, but sufficiently to knock her unconscious. She toppled through the embrasure, but he caught her by the tabard and pulled her back to him. In the process, he glanced again into the courtyard, where all the earl's men were now dead, their mangled remains being flung back and forth between the howling cadavers. Other corpses, of course, in fact cohorts of them, were already flowing across the Keep drawbridge.

Ranulf didn't wait to see more. Throwing Gwendolyn over his shoulder, he hurried to the top of the stair.

CHAPTER THIRTY-SIX

EARL COROTOCUS DID not witness the death of Hugh du Guesculin. He never looked back once as he galloped hard along the causeway.

More of the dead were crossing it towards him. But he veered around them. He was no longer armed, but that was of no concern. All that mattered was flight. As the Gatehouse loomed towards him, he was struck by the alarming thought that they might now have closed the portcullis at its front entrance. This goaded him to spur his animal until its flanks bled.

Nobody else obstructed him as he charged in through the arched entrance and up the Gatehouse's central passage. To his relief the portcullis was still raised, though a fresh phalanx of corpses was coming in beneath it. Leaning low, cloak billowing, the earl snapped his reins with fury. Incitatus struck the dead like a streak of black lightning, scattering them on all sides. Corotocus hurtled out of the Gatehouse and into the entry passage. More of the dead streamed along it. He crashed through them one after another, though the main danger here was the charred human fat that seemed to smear every surface. His horse skidded dangerously on it, before righting itself at the end of the passage and bolting eastward along the berm path.

Corotocus might now have been outside the castle, but he was still far from safety. Hemmed against its ramparts by the moat, he knew he had to circumnavigate two thirds of the entire stronghold before he would reach the river, at which point perhaps the most desperate gamble of all awaited him – crossing to the other side in full mail.

The decayed horde was gathered en masse beyond the moat. Their demonic lament rose to a crescendo when they beheld him, but aside from throwing spears, rocks and other improvised missiles, they could not reach him. Small groups were still drifting along the berm in his direction, still seeking to enter the castle. But as long as they remained in these restricted numbers, he knew he was a match for them.

"Incitatus, the field!" Corotocus bellowed.

The mount was now galloping at full speed. Blood streamed from its flanks, not just where the earl had spurred it, but where the dead had clawed at it. Foam flew from its bit; its eyes burned like rubies, as if it somehow knew that these clusters of stick-figures cavorting towards it were responsible for its pain. It clearly relished the collision as, one by one, it bounced them out of its way.

Corotocus yelled with laughter. Occasional missiles hit him, but his mail or helmet deflected them. He rounded the castle's northeast corner, to find more of the dead approaching from the southeast. If such a thing were possible, they seemed surprised to be confronted by the fugitive. Again, he crashed through them, delighted as they were chopped apart beneath his hooves or smashed against the castle's skirted wall. At one point he encountered a dead woman carrying a dead child. Though pale of skin, they were barely marked by the grave. The clothes they wore – the woman's dress, her linen veil and wimple, the wooden clogs on her feet, the baby in its swaddling – they were all spotlessly clean. Fleetingly, they might have been alive, but, even if they had been, the earl would have ridden them down just the same. The woman was catapulted into the moat, losing the child as she fell. They both landed skulls first on the rocks below, their arms and legs spread-eagled. The earl rode on. Directly ahead lay his salvation, but also his deadliest obstacle. The Tefeidiad.

In normal times, to leave Grogen Castle, one would turn at its southeast corner, and follow the berm all the way to the southwest bridge. But beyond that lay the western bluff, from which the vast majority of Countess Madalyn's army were still pouring across. So only the Tefeidiad provided a possible escape.

As they reached the southeast corner, Corotocus reined his beast to a halt, its hooves ploughing furrows in the dirt. He loosened the strap beneath his chin, and threw his helmet off, shaking out his sweat-soaked hair. Then he unlaced his cloak.

The river glided past ten feet below. It was about sixty yards across to the far side. Only small numbers of the dead were visible over there, compared to the titanic horde on the other sides of the castle. But Cotorocus knew the river was too deep at this point for Incitatus to simply wade across. He had no doubt that his horse could swim such a short distance, but could it swim it with an armoured rider on its back? It was a chance Corotocus was prepared to take, because there was no time to remove his mail carapace as well.

He urged his animal to the edge. Breathing hard, lathered with sweat, the spirited beast might have been game for almost anything at that moment – but jumping into a broad, fast moving river? Snorting with alarm, it held back.

"Yaa!" Corotocus shouted, jamming his spurs into his mount's sides.

He could sense more of the dead approaching, both from the right and from his rear. He risked a glance. The dispersed groups that he'd thundered through with such ease had got back to their feet and turned in pursuit of him. Even greater numbers were headed towards him from the direction of the bridge.

"Yaa!" he cried again, goading his steed.

The first of the dead were only a few yards away, reaching out with their fleshless claws, when Incitatus's growing fear overcame its instincts. With a wild neighing, it leapt from the bank. Corotocus clung on as best he could. He knew that his extra weight would be a stern test for the beast, but, encumbered with mail, he couldn't afford to be dislodged.

Initially they both plunged beneath the surface, the icy, brown water closing over their heads. But then they broke back into the air again and, with a truly colossal effort, the horse began to kick its way forward. Corotocus hung onto the reins as the river flowed heavily against him. He tried to float his body as much as possible, but in his mail he wasn't buoyant. They were only a quarter of the way across when the poor animal started to sink, the water rising up its neck and up the earl's body.

"You damn coward, Incitatus!" the earl snarled. "Don't you dare fail me now! Not when we're almost home."

Of course, they weren't really 'almost home'.

Increasing numbers of the dead were appearing through the trees on the south shore. As they'd shown throughout the siege, these rotting cadavers appeared to be connected via some kind of inexplicable 'hive' consciousness. Several times during the siege, it had been remarked on by different men that they moved en masse and attacked together "like ants". In similar fashion, they'd now apparently become aware that the earl was escaping and were scrambling to intercept him. But in reality they were still few and far between on the far bank. Once he was ashore, he was sure he could get through them. From there it was only a day's ride to the English border and through woods and open countryside. No more blind alleys, no more embattled ramparts. Incitatus would make it for him, but, if the proud beast's heart burst asunder in the process, it was a price worth paying.

As if sensing the faith its master was putting in it, the horse renewed its efforts to reach the other side. They were now half way across, the icy flood breaking over their heads, the terrible undertow tugging at them. They'd already drifted maybe fifty yards. Without needing to look, the earl could sense Grogen Castle falling away to his rear.

But the rocks on the south shore were much closer. The trees loomed larger; he could see the spaces between them and the tangled undergrowth.

Then there was a crunching of shingle and the earl's heart leapt again. Incitatus had found the riverbed. The Tefeidiad was getting shallower. Suddenly, the charger was moving with greater strength and purpose. Corotocus alighted himself properly on its back. He tried to sit upright, though the water still came as high as his waist. He punched at the air with triumph – just as something being carried on the current collided with him.

It was below the surface, and at first he thought it was a fallen log or branch. Then he realised the truth. It was a body, so covered with weed and river-mud that it was only vaguely distinguishable as human. Not that it was human in any true sense.

With one hand, it grabbed at the earl's bridle.

With the other, it grabbed at the earl.

Corotocus shouted, but now he had no blade to fight it off with. An even deeper fear went through him when he realised that his assailant was wearing chain-mail and coloured livery – it was one of his own knights.

"Desist, you dog!" he cried. "You traitorous..."

Bracing its feet against the horse's flank, and with a single mighty heave, the dead retainer hauled its former master from the saddle.

Incitatus, weary but at last unburdened, continued on its way, wobbling ashore on foal-like legs, before trotting away to the east, dripping and shivering, unmolested by the ranks of corpses gathering there. A few yards away, Corotocus floundered, even though he was only now in three or four feet of water. His attacker had got to its feet and clamped one hand on his throat. Though hampered by his mail, the earl struggled back gamely. He hadn't come all this way to be thwarted at the final post. He struck his assailant over and over. They wrestled together, went beneath the surface again, broke back into the open air. The earl felt his strength ebbing while his assailant seemed tireless – but it was only when they came nose to nose that Corotocus of Clun suddenly realised the full peril of his predicament.

He froze with fear and disbelief as he stared into his opponent's face. Though smashed and wounded, though bloated from its immersion in the icy depths, and despite the brown river water gurgling from its gaping mouth, that face was horribly familiar.

"Ulbert!" Corotocus choked. "Ulbert, don't you recognise me, your lord and master?"

What had once been Ulbert FitzOsbern clearly *did* recognise Corotocus. For the grotesquely distended lips, which had once spoken only words of wisdom to the nobleman, now curved into a most fiendish grin.

Corotocus shrieked madly, insanely, as his former vassal tightened its one-handed grip on his throat, and, planting its other hand on top of his head, plunged him back beneath the water. And this time held him there.

CHAPTER THIRTY-SEVEN

WHEN GWENDOLYN OPENED her eyes, her jaw ached abominably. At first she was disoriented, her vision blurred. She tasted blood and realised that she was wringing wet all over.

Confused, she sat up on a bed of damp vegetation. As she hung her dizzy head, it gradually occurred to her that the suffocating stench of death had dissipated. Instead, there was a fresh woodland fragrance. In fact, it was more than fresh. A soft rain was falling.

"The rain?" someone said, as though reading her befuddled thoughts. "Damn it... the rain!"

"What?" Gwendolyn glanced around. "Where am I?"

Her vision swam into focus. There were trees on all sides, many lush with catkins. She was sitting among young ferns, springy and bright green. Ranulf stood a few yards away. He held out cupped hands with which to catch the rainfall. When they were full, he sniffed at them gingerly.

"The rain," he said again. "I think it's in the rain!" He turned to look at her, so dumbfounded that her wakening had made no impact on him. "Have you smelled it?"

Gwendolyn shook her head. "The only thing I can smell, is..."

Her nostrils wrinkled as she detected a slight fetor. But it didn't take long to trace it to her tabard, which was streaked with a foul, sticky residue of human waste. It smeared her face as well. Good Lord, it was even in her hair. Now that she looked at Ranulf closely, she saw that it coated him as well, not that he seemed concerned.

"Where are we?" she demanded.

"A Welsh forest, Lady Gwendolyn." He regarded her sternly, as if finally realising that she'd come round. "The sort of place your druid friends would feel very at home. Do *you* not feel at home with them?"

"The castle, I..."

"The castle is that way." He pointed into the woods behind them. "About two miles, I'd say. I'd have got further, but I've been fighting continually for the last few days, I've barely eaten and even your sylph-like form became heavy after a time. You see, even the most gallant of us knights have our limits."

"You still haven't released me?" she said, incredulous.

"You broke the truce. What do you expect?"

"Are you mad?" She jumped to her feet, though it briefly made her dizzy again. "It was over, it was all over."

"On the contrary. It's only just beginning."

"You poor English fool. My people will keep coming after me."

"It could be you flatter yourself, my lady."

"You think they did all this for nothing?"

Ranulf shrugged. "If all they want is you, go to them. I'm not stopping you. You're not my prisoner."

She looked bewildered. "Then why am I here?"

He tore up a handful of ferns and commenced scrubbing the slime from his clothing. "Believe it or not, I brought you here with me for your own protection."

"What are you talking about?"

"If you hadn't been so busy plotting the death of Earl Corotocus and his household, you might have seen what was really happening back there."

"I'll lie for you," she said, backing towards the trees. "I'll tell them I fled the castle on my own. I'll pretend you are among the dead. It's the best I can do for you."

"Go ahead."

"They may want to know how I escaped."

"Through the garderobe sewer." He threw the filthied ferns away and grabbed up some more. "We used it before to launch a raid. The ropes were still in place. It was not difficult."

She nodded, but was unnerved by his oddly matter-of-fact attitude. "You should return to the English border quickly. It's the only hope you have."

"It's more hope than you have, if you're heading where I think you're heading."

"You're quite wrong about this." She tried to make her voice more confident than she suddenly felt. "I've seen what they are. I know it's hideous, an aberration. But I am Gwendolyn of Lyr. They will not harm me."

"Really? You don't sound too sure."

"My mother commands them."

Ranulf laughed, but it was a wry laugh, lacking humour. "Your mother is merely their figurehead. She can easily be replaced... and sooner rather than later she will need to be." He eyed her carefully. "*You* would suffice in that role as well, I suppose, until such time as you too needed replacing."

"This attempted trickery is unbecoming to a knight, even an English one."

"If you wish to go, go. I'm past caring." He turned and strode off eastward. "Fare you well."

Frustrated and frightened, Gwendolyn hurried through the trees after him.

"You can't expect me to go to England with you?" she said, having to trot just to stay level with him.

"I don't ask you to. The likelihood is that you wouldn't be safe there either. Not for long. None of us will."

"You just resent that the Welsh have found a way to fight back."

"The Welsh!" he hissed, suddenly rounding on her. "The Welsh no longer exist! Did you or did you not see that?"

Despite everything, she was taken aback by his ferocity. His eyes blazed; spittle seethed at his lips. It was as though some intense emotion that he'd been bottling up inside had suddenly burst free.

"T-that's... that's not true," she stammered. "My mother..."

"You mother has *joined* them!"

There was a long, dull silence, during which Gwendolyn's look of slow-dawning horror gave Ranulf no pleasure whatsoever.

"Probably against her will," he said, "though I doubt that's any consolation to you."

"What do you mean she's joined them?"

He strode on. "What do you think I mean?"

She ran after him again. "You're lying!"

"Go back and find out for yourself."

"Are you telling me my mother is dead?"

"I'm sorry to have delivered it so brutally."

"Sir knight, stop if you please! I command it, stop and talk to me!"

Reluctantly, he halted and swung around to face her.

"I asked..." She stumbled over the words, her lovely green eyes brimming with tears. "Did... did you actually *see* this?"

Ranulf didn't need to speak. His harrowed expression said it all. Gwendolyn wept for a moment, though, perhaps remembering her noble lineage, she managed to get hold of herself again with remarkable speed.

"What... what am I to do?" she finally asked.

"What are any of us to do?"

Tears ran freely down her cheeks again, but she shook her head defiantly. "I must still go to my people."

"Then come with me." He pointed towards England. "Like it or not, your people lie this way now."

A few days ago, she'd have endured unimaginable torture rather than admit such a thing. But since then she'd seen for herself the ghoul-like creatures that had brought death to the English interlopers. Though it was from on high, she'd witnessed the ferocity with which they'd beat and strangled and torn their enemies. She'd heard their inhuman groans, their demented screams. Above all, of course, she'd smelled them – the maggot-riddled carrion that passed for their flesh. Did she really wish to ride at the head of so hellish a horde? It was highly unlikely – nay, it was impossible to imagine – that her mother would be willing to do so, for all her rage and anguish at the crimes committed by the English.

When Ranulf walked on, Gwendolyn walked behind him. She had to struggle to control her sobs, which now bespoke pain and bewilderment as much as grief.

"And try not to cry too loudly," he said over his shoulder. "We don't know who's listening."

She glanced at the trees to either side; the only sound from them was the pattering of rain. And yet there were many dark places there.

"Are we not away from danger yet?" she asked.

"This rain is falling everywhere."

"Everywhere?"

"Near enough everywhere. Can you imagine what that means?"

Gwendolyn stopped in her tracks, and looked behind her. The springtime woods were a riot of green bud and pink blossom. Overhead, blue sky broke through fleecy cloud. Mellow warmth had settled on a landscape which only a few days ago had glittered with ice and frost. Somewhere in the woods, the voice of a cuckoo was heard. The season was in full bloom. There was an air of rebirth. And yet – he had said 'everywhere'.

This tainted rain was falling *everywhere*.

Chilled to her marrow, Gwendolyn of Lyr again ran to catch up with Ranulf FitzOsbern. She hardly dared think how many graveyards lay between here and safety. Or where safety, if such a thing existed, might actually be found in this new, nightmarish world.

EPILOGUE

DEAD BODIES WOULD no longer be a feature of battlefields, Gwyddon reflected as he strolled through the precincts of Grogen Castle, while his army departed north.

Oh, the great stronghold was still a grim sight, its ramparts broken, many of its towers and inner buildings burned to blackened frameworks, its walls and walkways splashed with blood, strewn with arrows, spears, swords, smashed shields, severed limbs. There was scarcely a corner of it where evidence of horrific violence was not on full display. Though he was now completely alone here, if he stood still and listened, he fancied he could hear the harsh song of blade on blade, blade on shield, blade on mail, the cries of anger and pain, the thunder of collapsing masonry as catapulted missiles wrought cataclysmic destruction. The air was still rank. Dust, smoke and soot still hung in ghostly palls.

And yet there were no dead bodies anywhere.

Those slaughtered English who had not been caught in the morning's rain, those who lay inside perhaps or under parapets, had in due course been treated with the cauldron brew. Then they too had risen to their feet and marched north. It was now late afternoon, and apparently King Edward had reached Conway. But for all that he routinely sewed those lands he planned to conquer with spies and informers, he would not fully understand the nature of the enemy that was moving to meet him. Most likely he would not even believe the stories he was being told.

Gwyddon would not be part of this next clash, of course; nor would any of his priesthood. They had withdrawn to their sanctuary under the mountain, and shortly he would be joining them. He anticipated with some confidence that King Edward would be defeated. The king reportedly had fifty thousand men, but the army marching to halt him had already swollen to many times that number, and, as Earl Corotocus had discovered, it was invulnerable to most, if not all, earthly weapons.

The absence of Earl Corotocus from the English slain was a minor irritant to Gwyddon. Those killed in the courtyard had eventually been laid out in a row, so that he could examine them before they were recalled. Though many had been mutilated beyond recognition, Gwyddon had eventually concluded that the earl was not present. His helmet and cloak had later been discovered next to the Tefeidiad, but not his flesh. In itself this was not massively important. One man alone, even one man who could call on substantial powers if he returned to England, would be no great threat. Most likely the earl had died in the river anyway, and his carcass had been washed away. Gwyddon would have liked to know for sure, but it was no disaster that he didn't.

He walked up into the Keep, his footsteps echoing through the dank passages and empty rooms. He entered the garderobe and peered down the black shaft, in which hempen ropes still hung. It was possible that the man who had led his men out into the courtyard had not been Corotocus, and that the real earl had escaped this way. A few others among the English almost certainly had. Most probably, they had taken Lady Gwendoyln with them, for she too had been missing when the final body-count was made. Again, this was no great disaster. Ideally,

Gwyddon would have kept the heiress of Lyr alive for as long as possible. She would have become the new symbol of this uprising; the excuse for the insurrection. Around her otherwise completely insignificant person, they could have rallied in vengeance for the 'murder' of Countess Madalyn. But such concepts as justification and lawfulness were fast becoming unnecessary. As it was, Countess Madalyn made a more than adequate stage-prop. She still rode at the head of the army. In a few weeks' time, when her ligaments were so rotten and her bones so brittle that she couldn't climb onto a horse much less ride one, Gwyddon would have to think of something else. But that was a problem for the future, not the present.

Overall, he was very satisfied with the way the siege had progressed. Even those one or two English who had survived could now be of use. They would return home and spread the word that Grogen, King Edward's mightiest bastion, had fallen within a matter of days, and that Earl Corotocus of Clun, his fiercest dog of war, had been vanquished. The fear and confusion this would cause would be worth more than threats delivered in the Welsh tongue ever could.

And then of course there was the bliss of victory. Even here, in the foulest chamber in the foulest building of the entire castle, Gwyddon was imbued with it, almost light-headed. How could he not feel triumphant; how could he not feel his own glory wrapped around him like a silken cloak? The first blow in the war to end all wars had been struck – and what a blow it was. The enemy was reeling with it. Of course, it was important not to be totally overcome with one's own importance. There was much to do yet if he was to realise his dreams of conquest. But there was no denying that this had been a more successful start to his campaign than he had ever imagined possible.

He turned to leave the garderobe, and was confronted by a shadowy figure standing in its doorway. Gwyddon stepped forward, curious.

It was one of the English. A large, burly fellow, wearing a steel-studded leather hauberk, covered in fragments of straw. His face was black with clotted blood from a brutally smashed nose, his hair and beard thickly matted by it. He was solid on his feet, but very still. He regarded Gwyddon with dull, ox-like eyes.

"Go north," Gwyddon told him. "Join your comrades. The great battle goes on."

The creature responded by hitting him under the sternum.

At first Gwyddon was merely shocked. He thought the creature had struck him with a clenched fist. But then a slow, agonising chill began to ebb through his lower body. He looked downward, and saw the hilt of a dagger jutting from his midriff. He tried to grab hold of it, but there was no longer strength in his arms. He glanced up at his assailant, his mouth dropping open. This creature was indeed English, but not one of their dead.

His vision fading, Gwyddon sank to his knees. Try as he may, he couldn't give voice to the anger he suddenly felt at his own folly. The Englishman now crouched in front of him, took hold of the dagger and yanked it loose.

The druid grunted; his onyx eyes rolled white. But that didn't concern Murlock the mercenary, for whom other men's deaths had been the currency of life since childhood. Pulling the druid's beard aside, he inserted the dagger into the Adam's apple beneath and sliced it neatly from one side to the other. The crimson gout that throbbed forth lasted only a couple of seconds, before the body slumped heavily to the floor. But only when Murlock was sure the druid was dead did he strip the moon-crescent pendant from his throat, the gem-encrusted rings from his fingers and the silver dragon-head pin from his robe.

Murlock examined each item one after another, cleaning the gore from them with his own beard. He smiled, pleased. He'd been deeply unconscious for a considerable time, but his instincts had not deserted him. When he'd first come round beneath that pile of rancid straw, his first aim had been to get even with Ranulf FitzOsbern, but time had clearly overtaken that ambition. Whatever had happened here, the earl's army had been crushed, and the Welsh themselves had now departed. It was not the ideal outcome, especially with those who owed him wages slain. But the upside was that there was nothing to stop him going home.

He wrapped the valuables in a leather pouch and stuffed it under his belt. Before leaving, he flung the druid's body down the garderobe chute, where most likely it would never be found, though first he searched it thoroughly just to ensure there was nothing else of worth that he'd missed.

He chuckled.

It might have been a distasteful habit of his, but whichever war he was fighting in, whether he was on the winning side or the losing side, Murlock had always believed in making his service pay.

Paul Finch is a former cop and journalist, now turned full time writer. He first cut his literary teeth penning episodes of the British TV crime drama, *The Bill*, and has written extensively in the field of children's animation. However, he is probably best known for his work in horror.

To date, he's had ten books and nearly 300 stories and novellas published on both sides of the Atlantic. His first collection, *Aftershocks*, won the British Fantasy Award in 2002, while he won the award again in 2007 for his novella, *Kid*. Later in 2007, he won the International Horror Guild Award for his mid-length story, *The Old North Road*. Most recently, he has written two *Doctor Who* audio dramas for Big Finish and is now busy writing a third. His no-holds-barred cop novel, *The Nice Guys' Club*, will be published later this year.

Paul lives in Wigan, Lancashire, with his wife Cathy and his children, Eleanor and Harry.

TOMES OF THE DEAD

Now read the Prologue from the next exciting book
in the *Tomes of the Dead* collection:

The
VIKING
DEAD

Toby Venables

UK ISBN: 978-1-907519-68-0
US ISBN: 978-907519-69-7

£7.99/$9.99/$12.99(CAN)

Coming April 2011

WWW.ABADDONBOOKS.COM

PROLOGUE

S<small>KALLA SAT, HIS</small> hands resting on the pommel of his sword, his chin resting on his hands, staring at the pile of bodies.

The still-warm corpses steamed in the cool air of the clearing. Behind him, his black-clad men, done cleaning their weapons, stood in silence, waiting – for what, they knew not. Some, perhaps, suspected. But only Skalla knew for certain.

To his right, he heard feet shifting nervously among the damp leaves. That would be Gamli. Skalla had had his eye on him for some time, aware that he had started to lose faith in their masters. More than once he had questioned their orders. It took a brave man to do that. Or a stupid one. Skalla knew Gamli was no fool – but he also knew the man's boldness hid deeper fears. Fears that could spread, infecting the others, contaminating them with doubt. That, he could not allow. It threatened everything they had built here.

He ran his fingers through the black bristles on his chin, then up to the scar that passed through his left eye. It ran from his

forehead down across his cheek, and had left the eye sightless –
a milk-white, dead parody of its darker twin. He pushed at the
edge of his helm, relieving the pressure on his forehead for a
moment. The scar tissue itched badly today. It always did after
combat – the result of the heat and sweat. Not that what had just
passed could truthfully be termed 'combat'.

There had been six in all. Perhaps seven. He couldn't remember.
They were the ones who had been locked up the longest, those
meant to be forgotten. The ones who ran, who broke down, who
refused to work, who fought back. The biggest heroes and the
biggest cowards. All the same, now. They had also been kept
separate all this time – well away from the various wonders and
horrors that had been unfolding. That, Skalla suspected, was one
of the real reasons for this little outing to the woods. True, his
masters had no further desire to waste food on these lost causes.
But they were also wise enough not to waste an opportunity.
They would make some use of them, even in death.

And so, they had marched them to this lonely spot, shackled
and at spear point, and forced them to cut logs for firewood.
They had performed the tasks well, considering their chequered
histories – some, almost with gratitude. Perhaps, thought Skalla,
it simply felt good to have a purpose again. He had not told them
they were gathering wood for their own funeral pyre.

The killing had been quick. Regrettably, the kills were not
as clean as he'd hoped. There were struggles, cries, prolonged
agonies, repeated blows. From the start it had not been the most
straightforward task. No damage to the head or neck – that's
what their masters had specified. The order had bemused Skalla's
men, and in the heat of the slaughter – one could hardly dignify
the killing of these unarmed, underfed wretches with the term
'battle' – he could not be sure how closely they had adhered to
it. At least one had taken a glancing sword blow across the top
of the head – protruding from the heap, Skalla could see his
hairy, blood-matted scalp, flapped open like the lid of a chest,
the yellow-white bone of the skull grinning through the gore.
But it didn't matter now. It was done. It would matter again soon,
though. Then they would see.

"We're done here," said a voice behind Skalla. It was Gamli. He had stepped closer to where Skalla was sitting. Clearly he was impatient to leave. Perhaps he understood more than Skalla had realised.

"We wait," said Skalla, in a monotone.

"For what?"

"Until we are sure."

"Sure?" Gamli's voice was edgy. As always, he tried to cover it with a kind of swagger. "What is there to be sure of?"

"That they're dead."

Gamli laughed emptily, his throat tight. "Why not burn them now and have done with it?"

"Are you questioning me, Gamli?" Skalla's eyes remained fixed on the corpses.

A kind of panic entered Gamli's eyes. "Not you. I would never... But the masters... There are... doubts about them." He looked around as he said this, as if expecting support from his fellows. None came.

Skalla did not move. "I pledged my sword to them," he said, "and you swore an oath of allegiance to me. You do not question one without also questioning the other."

Gamli stood motionless, robbed of speech.

"Step back into line," said Skalla.

Before he could do so, a sound came from the heap, and an arm flopped out of the tangle. The men's hands jumped to their weapons. The arm hung there, motionless – quite dead. Olvir – one of the three crossbowmen – broke the silence with a nervous laugh. "For a moment, I thought..." He was interrupted by a low groan from the centre of the heap. Skalla stood slowly, hands still upon his sword, and flexed his shoulders. It was part of his ritual before combat.

"Gas. From the bodies," said another of the men, nervously. "They can do that." Olvir began to draw and load his crossbow. The others followed suit.

From deep within the pile came a weird, semi-human grunt, and the whole tangle suddenly shifted. As one, the men drew swords and raised crossbows. The uppermost body – a skinny man, whose abdomen was split open, and whose right arm had been all but severed – slithered from the top of the heap. The hand that had loosed itself from the pile twitched, its fingers beginning to straighten.

"It's beginning..." said Skalla. The first hollow moan repeated itself – to be joined by two more in a kind of desolate, mindless chorus. As they watched in horror, dead limbs moved, arms flailed and grasped, lifeless eyes flicked open.

"This can't be happening." said Gamli. From the heap, one of the men – a solid, muscular fellow who had taken two crossbow bolts through the chest, one of which had pinned his right hand to his sternum – staggered unsteadily to his feet. For a moment he seemed to sniff the air, then turned and lurched towards them.

Skalla spat on his palms and raised his sword. "Aim for the heads," he said, and swung his blade with all his strength at the dead man's neck. It sliced clean through, knocking the attacker off his feet and sending his head bowling into the bushes. Already two more were on their feet – the skinny man, his right arm hanging by a sinew, his glistening guts dangling between his legs, and the scalped man, his hair flapping absurdly to one side like a piece of bearskin, who Skalla could now see had been killed by a heavy sword blow to the left side of his chest, the upper and lower parts sliding past each other gruesomely with each lurching step. A crossbow bolt hit the skinny man in the shoulder, spinning him round. "In the head!" called Skalla. As the skinny man resumed his steady progress a second bolt thudded into his eye, knocking him flat. A third flew uselessly past the scalped man's ear. His arms reached out, grasping at Skalla, as another three grotesque figures rose stiffly behind him.

The rest of Skalla's men, momentarily mesmerised by the scene unfolding before them, now threw themselves into the fight. Gamli stepped forward first, grasping the scalped man's outstretched arm and hurling him to the floor. Drawing a cavalry axe from his belt, he flipped it around and, with one blow, drove its long spike through the exposed skull. As his other men hacked mercilessly at two of the remaining ghouls, Skalla advanced to finish off the third – a once fat man with folds of saggy skin beneath his ragged, filthy tunic. Skalla recognised the stab wounds in his chest – wounds that he himself had delivered with his knife. The fat man's left arm – bloody and slashed where he had attempted to defend himself from Skalla's blade – waved before him, his right, bloodier still, hanging crippled and useless by his side. Skalla raised his sword steadily, waiting for the right moment. The man's hand, formed into a claw, swayed and snatched at Skalla, his jaws opening and closing like those of an idiot child, dribbling bloody drool down his chest. But as Skalla began to swing, something pulled him off balance. He stumbled and fell, his foot caught. When he looked down, he understood. The seventh prisoner – his spinal cord severed, his legs useless – had dragged himself along the forest floor, and now, bearing his teeth, Skalla's ankle gripped in both hands, was biting on his leather boot. Skalla recoiled in disgust, kicking at the ghoul's slavering, gap-toothed mouth, but the tenacious grip held, and over him now loomed the fat man, moaning and clawing at his face. Too close for an effective blow, Skalla abandoned his sword and scrabbled for his knife but, before he had time to draw it, another sword blade was driven hard into the fat man's mouth, sending him choking and tottering backwards, his teeth grinding horribly against its metal edge. It was Gamli's sword. Skalla regained his feet, took up his own sword once more and brought it down with a crashing blow, cleaving the skull of the crawling man in two. He gave a nod of acknowledgement to Gamli, and scraped the man's brains off his boot with the point of his blade.

It was over. And his men, thankfully, had escaped unscathed.

"So it's true," said Gamli, surveying the carnage that surrounded them. "Our worst fear has come true."

Skalla ignored him, wiping clean and sheathing his sword as he hunted around for the head of the first of the undead men. He would take that back to his masters.

"I'm sorry," said Gamli, bowing his head. Skalla turned to face him. "I will not question you again."

"No," said Skalla. "You will not." And without blinking he stabbed Gamli in the side of the throat with his knife, severing both carotid arteries, before pulling the blade forward through his windpipe. Gamli collapsed in an eruption of blood, his last cry turned to a choked gurgle of air bubbling and frothing from his neck.

As he pumped crimson onto the forest floor, a contorted expression of disbelief frozen upon his face, Skalla looked upon him for the last time. "I did not kill you before only because I needed your sword," he said matter-of-factly, and stepped over the body. The other men drew back perceptibly as he approached. He scanned their faces one at a time, then sheathed his knife.

"Burn them," said Skalla, the still-living Gamli convulsing behind him. "All of them."

The
VIKING
DEAD

Toby Venables

Coming April 2011

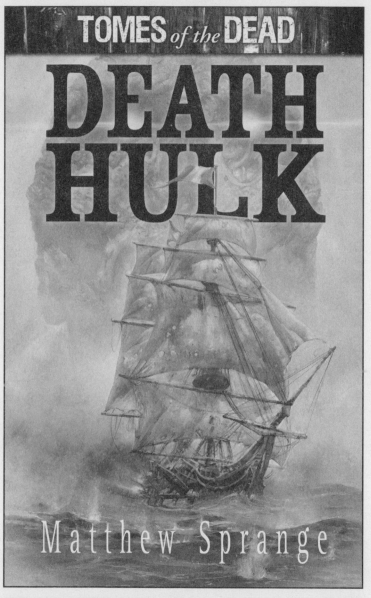

TOMES *of the* DEAD

DEATH HULK

Matthew Sprange

ISBN: 978-1-905437-03-0
UK £.6.99   US $7.99

Abaddon
Books

TOMES *of the* DEAD

THE WORDS OF THEIR ROARING

Matthew Smith

ISBN: 978-1-905437-13-9
UK £.6.99   US $7.99

Abaddon
Books

TOMES *of the* DEAD

THE DEVIL'S PLAGUE

Mark Beynon

ISBN: 978-1-905437-41-2
UK £.6.99   US $7.99

Abaddon
Books

ISBN: 978-1-905437-72-6
UK £.6.99   US $7.99

Abaddon
Books

TOMES of the DEAD

ANNO MORTIS

Rebecca Levene

ISBN: 978-1-905437-85-6
UK £.6.99   US $7.99

Abaddon
Books

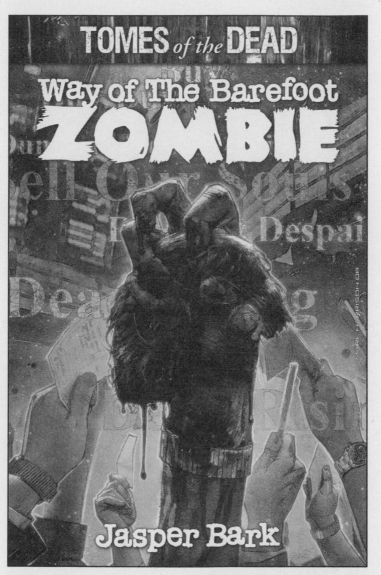

Visit www.abaddonbooks.com for information on our titles,
interviews, news and exclusive content.

 ISBN: 978-1-906735-06-7
UK £.6.99   US $7.99

Abaddon
Books

Follow us on twitter: www.twitter.com/abaddonbooks

TOMES of the DEAD

TIDE OF SOULS

SIMON BESTWICK

Visit www.abaddonbooks.com for information on our titles,
interviews, news and exclusive content.

ISBN: 978-1-906735-14-2

UK £.6.99   US $7.99

Abaddon
Books

Follow us on twitter: www.twitter.com/abaddonbooks

TOMES *of the* DEAD

Hungry Hearts

GARY McMAHON

Visit www.abaddonbooks.com for information on our titles,
interviews, news and exclusive content.

 ISBN: 978-1-906735-26-5
UK £.6.99   US $7.99 Abaddon
Books

Follow us on twitter: www.twitter.com/abaddonbooks

TOMES *of the* DEAD

EMPIRE OF
SALT

WESTON OCHSE

Visit www.abaddonbooks.com for information on our titles,
interviews, news and exclusive content.

 ISBN: 978-1-906735-32-6
UK £.6.99   US $7.99

 Abaddon
Books

Follow us on twitter: www.twitter.com/abaddonbooks